THE CREATOR

By L. M. Peralta

THE ELEMENTALS TRILOGY

The Elementals
The Council
The Creator

THE ARCADIAN STEEL SEQUENCE

The Wings of Heaven and Hell
The Seven Archangels of Heaven
The Seven Princes of Hell

United Trace

THE CREATOR

BOOK THREE OF THE ELEMENTALS

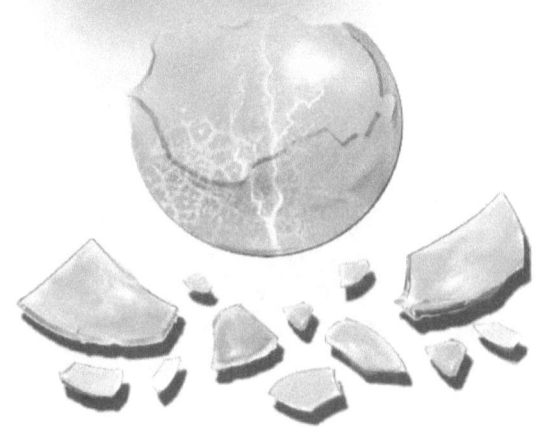

L. M. PERALTA

First Paperback Edition: July 2016

Summary: Sara has learned Bolton is alive and wants to start her life with him, but first she must battle the creature she discovered in the depths of Omega Ray.

ISBN: 978-0-9888448-4-1

For Marie Peralta,
Whose pride and love for me and what I do is something that can't be
measured and is much cherished.

Thanks, Mawmaw!

Beneath the broken promises, links lie,

Forgotten connections revealed, revived;
Lost strings are taken up again to tie,
And the dreams that had faded come back alive.

The far off past and the present combined
Will make the wayward future seem so clear;
And elements once lost will be refined
But sadly bring new enemies to fear.

Darkness controlled shall spread before night falls,
And many will flee the threatening fight;
Yet some will stay to challenge the black walls
Because deep inside angry pall is light.

The gifts he gave shall be suppressed
For all doubt to be put to rest.

MIRMINA

Prologue: The Wayward Son

If He should kill us for our Sins, it would be the Lies that we drown in.

TALON looked down at his burnt hands and touched the deep, burning rip in his soot covered face. He sat on the steps outside Element under the night sky. The thick smoke drifted across the sea. The darkness covered the stars.

The heavy door to Element opened, and a small woman came out wrapped in a heavy shawl against the cold. Her petite form cast no shadow in the dark, and her feet made no sound as she descended the stairs, but Talon could sense her presence. The honey-suckle smell of her perfume wafted through the air. She sat next to Talon whose eyes were still fixed on his blackened hands.

"I saw you from the window," Brina said. "Why don't you come inside?"

Talon was silent.

Brina could not see the smoke against the dark sky. She could not see where the blackness obscured the stars.

She watched him as he looked down at his hands. Her

eyes were glassy. "You think all you have are those two hands."

Her mind drifted to the past when their only worry was finding time to see each other between trainings. Talon would steal kisses from her in the hallways, and they would laugh like children. He was not much younger then, but it seemed that in the past few years, he had aged a great deal.

One day, he came home to Element with that burn on his face, but he wouldn't tell her how he got it. She cleaned his wound in silence and dressed it with aloe leaves. He left before the wound could heal. Brina didn't know where he had been. He came to see her once in that time, but barely spoke and wouldn't answer questions. He was there and not there at the same time. He wasn't the man she had once known.

"I did this," Talon said.

"What? What happened?"

"I'm the reason he came here." Talon's eyes burned and watered as if he was still fighting through the smoke.

"Hephaestus." The name fell from Brina's lips. He had haunted Talon's dreams. Brina would lie awake and listen to Talon's tortured voice call out that name in his sleep.

"I said this time would be the last." Talon gazed beyond to the starless sky. "But there is one more thing I must do before the guilt destroys me. I have to leave."

"But, why?" Brina's eyes were tired.

"Trust me. I have my reasons."

Green ivy crept up the stone steps. The pressure behind Brina's eyes built, but she fought back the tears. They would be no help to her anyway. Her tears would not change Talon's mind. They hadn't before.

Talon tried to meet her eyes. "I have something I wanted to give you when I returned. I wanted it to be special. I'm afraid it's too late now, but I wanted you to have it."

He reached into the pocket of his tattered pants and brought something out, concealing it in his clenched hand. He took Brina's hand, placed it in her palm, and folded her fingers over it.

Talon stood from the stone steps. Brina hastened to stand beside him. His body towered over hers.

He hurried down the steps of Element and was soon consumed by the darkness.

Brina, absorbed in Talon's hasty farewell, gazed after him in the distance as he disappeared. Once he was gone, she looked down at her clenched fist and opened it. A golden ring rested in her palm.

THE cold wind blasted the mountainside from across the sea. The water in the distance was iced over so ships could not travel through. Tips of ice jetted from the ocean.

The world was gray, a cold gray that chills.

The howls echoed through the frigid night as an unnatural creature stalked the valley where Eli's stone castle huddled. The creature's thick, matted fur was wet with the monster's drool, which dripped from its sharp teeth like melting ice.

Talon leaned against the crumbling stone walls of Omega Ray. He wore a cloak as black as the sky to conceal himself in the darkness. His eyes pierced the night, and his eyeballs shined off the flickering light of the torches. The guards would not notice the specks of light among the white flurries of snow and ash.

Eli's palace sat in the center of the ruins, and Talon stood two buildings away and breathed heavily. He couldn't control it. His hot breath preceded him through the darkness like a spirit leading him into the black wilderness.

Guards circled the stone castle. Fero, a young man, not quite out of apprenticeship, was among them. He was learning what it takes to be a sentinel and mercenary of Hephaestus. Talon had been the young man's trainer, and he had trained him well.

He remembered when he came to Element still a young boy, clinging to his mother and scared of being confined in the walls around him. He had come from Lumina, the city across the sea. His mother owned a shop on the outskirts of the city.

He had comforted Fero when the message arrived that thieves had broken into his mother's shop, robbed and beat her, and left her for dead. Her death had brought Fero to his knees and when he rose, he swore he would never be a victim again.

Talon cringed to see him among his brother's army.

Though the castle was heavily guarded, Talon knew Hephaestus would not allow the boy to live in the same quarters as he did, not even his own nephew. He had a hate for what Bolton was. He would be tucked away, out of sight.

Talon peered into every window he passed, gazing upon the sleeper inside, and risking that one of them could open their eyes at any moment and see him staring back. Some of the windows had wooden shutters that barred his view. He was getting closer to the cliff when he came upon what he was searching for. The window was unobstructed. The shutters were swung open.

Sheltered in bed, with the blanket up to his chin, was his nephew. He was a small boy, seven years of age. He was a miniature of his father. His blond hair was long and growing over his eyes, which were squeezed shut.

Talon climbed through the window, his black cloak

sweeping the dust from the window sill. He walked over to the boy's bedside.

The young boy turned in his sleep, tortured by a bad dream, but Talon dared not wake him for fear he would cry out. His voice would echo into the night, alerting the guards.

He lifted the boy from his place of slumber. He could see the burns across the boy's shoulder as the oversized night-gown crept down his arm.

The boy stirred, but did not wake.

Talon placed one foot out the window and planted it on the ground. He brought the boy out through the window still cradled in his arms. Talon ducked his head and climbed out. His back pressed against the wall, he looked around.

Talon crept along the ruined stone wall and took ad-vantage of his brother's weaknesses.

He stopped to rest against the cold winds of Regret Mountain, took off his cloak, and wrapped Bolton in it. He lay the small boy on the ground and turned to gaze upon the distance he would have to cross. He could see beyond the snow to the grassy plain of Jetty Verte and the Crystal Forest. The blackness of D'arkadia obscured all else from view.

Bolton rustled in his sleep. In his dreams, he could feel the cold wind against his cheek. He awoke to find himself in the expanse of white snow. He looked up at Talon, still staring into the distance. The boy sat up.

"Who are you?" Bolton asked.

"I'm your uncle." Talon's eyes didn't stray.

"You're not my uncle. My uncle's there." The young boy pointed in the wrong direction, not knowing from where he had come.

"I'm Talon," he said instead.

Talon understood why Eli had no fear of the boy's escape.

He would have died out here in the cold, wandering aimlessly.

Bolton stared at him, at the long burn mark on his face. His small eyes narrowed. "Are you taking me back home?"

"That is not your home," Talon said.

"Not that place. I mean where my mom lives."

Talon's eyes met the boy's. He had hoped he would not see the pain there, that it wouldn't make him cry. Talon didn't know how to comfort a child.

"Bolton." Talon reached out to put his arm around the boy's shoulders, but Bolton flinched away. Talon withdrew his hand, sorry he had frightened him. He had thought that touch would somehow make the devastating news easier to hear. "Your mother's dead."

At the words, Bolton shot up from the snow and backed away from Talon. "Liar!" he screamed. His small feet dug into the snow, wetting the hem of his nightgown.

Talon feared Bolton would catch his death out in the cold and everything he had done for Ana would be for nothing. He had to save her son.

"Wait." Talon took a step towards him. As he did, Bolton shocked his outstretched hand with Lightning.

Talon cursed. He stopped, shaking the pain from his palm. "I see you take after your father."

"My dad ran. He should've helped Mom. I hate him."

Talon could see the anger boiling behind the young boy's eyes. He had never seen something so immense occupy such a small space.

"Calm down," Talon said.

"Stop lying to me!" Bolton shouted.

"Your parents are dead," Talon said as gently as he could.

The boy settled in the snow and looked down at his ankles but not really seeing them. He wiped away the hot tears.

"Where are you taking me?"

"To a new home," Talon said. "That's what your mother would have wanted."

Bolton rose from the snow. He had given up his tears. He slowly started to believe Talon.

But Talon had lied to him.

His father was alive.

1

LONG WAY HOME

They could not die, and life had become a burden. We decorated Them with gifts of jewels, colorful garments, and the Best of our Crop which They would not Eat. And Yet still we gave it to Them. They were our gods.

THE sky brightened as Sara and Bolton approached Jetty Verte. The darkness loomed above the snowy peaks of Regret Mountain like a bad storm just beginning. They did not look back despite the feeling of something lurking behind them. The cold wind blasted their backs and pushed them further from the dark city.

Sara stared at the man beside her. He was like a ghost, not quite real.

Bolton's eyes met hers. "What is it?"

"I'm not convinced. I might be dreaming, or I might be dead."

"You're neither. I'm here right and so are you." He put his hand on her shoulder.

Sara felt the warmth of it spread through her. He could not be a ghost.

"Do you think Farah and Rodan will still be in Tosia when we get there?" Bolton asked as they walked across the plain. Their feet met the softer ground.

"I don't know. I wasn't myself when we were there. I'm not sure if they know where we are. If they did, they would come as soon as they could."

Miles away, the inn was a blotch of gray against the green.

"It's strange," Bolton said. "I've only been awake for a short time, and everything's so different. You're different."

"I hope that's not a bad thing."

Bolton shook his head. "No. It's not that. It's just . . . I have a lot of catching up to do."

Sara stopped, but did not look at him.

Bolton halted. "Sara?"

"I have something to tell you," she whispered.

He stepped closer to her.

Sara looked up into his eyes. "Your father is here."

"Here?"

Sara nodded. "In Mirmina. He came here from the Insula."

Bolton backed away from her. His head was in his hands. After several moments, he looked up. "Where is he now?"

"I don't know. But there's more. You have a brother."

"A brother?"

Sara nodded. "Your father's son. He raised him when your mother and you were gone. I'm sorry. I know it's a lot, but I had to tell you."

Bolton rubbed his temples with the palms of his hands.

He sighed. His father was here. The thought of seeing him made Bolton feel weak. He remembered the day Talon told him his father was alive. Bolton had resigned himself to the fact that his father was dead, and there was some relief in that. The man had abandoned him to an evil tyrant to save his own life. He had let his mother die. "I don't want to see him."

"I understand." Sara diverted her eyes from him, and sadness marred her voice. "I thought you should know."

Bolton took a step closer to her and put his arms around her. "I'm glad you told me. That's not something I would have liked to be surprised about. In that cloud in Lumina. I thought I saw my father, but I thought it must have been a dream. That made it easier. But maybe it was really him."

He backed away from their embrace to look at her.

Sara nodded. "He didn't tell us who he was. Not at first. When I found out, I was angry with him. I remembered what you told me, and I was so angry with him."

TIRED and hungry, Sara and Bolton walked until the sun was high in the sky. They made it to the inn across the plain. The door remained open, swinging in the breeze. The years of weathered travelers shuffling through its door had left the dirt pathway beaten and worn. The dust, unsettled by the breeze, drifted in the air right outside the inn.

Sara ran her hand through the grass where she sat. The blades wafted in the warm breeze.

Bolton yawned so hard his eyes watered.

"There's no food for miles, and it'll be days before we reach Tosia," Bolton said.

"We have to push through," Sara said.

"You sound like Spire."

Sara smiled. "Well, she rubbed off on me."

"How is she doing?" Bolton asked. "I didn't see her back in Tosia."

"Spire is having a baby."

"Wow." Bolton shook his head.

Sara hoped Spire and Decca were okay, that the Council had not found out about their connection to Sara, that they weren't using them to get to her.

Clouds covered the sun as afternoon faded to evening. The wispy shields of white darkened the sky, and the land became gray.

Sara looked off into the distance as if she could see beyond the snowy mountain and into the valley of Omega Ray.

"What is it?" Bolton leaned in closer to her.

"That man," Sara started. She could still feel the cold in her bones. "The one with the mark on his face. I've seen him before." She remembered how he left that cryptic message and disappeared into the darkness like he was made of the very mist that had settled at the bottom of the gorge. *You let him out!*

And Sara knew she had let out pure darkness from the depths. She had felt it crawling inside her body like a disease, clawing at her soul.

Bolton tried to meet her eyes, but they were fixed on the mountain. She was in a trance.

"Where have you seen him before?" he asked.

Sara shook her head.

"You don't know?"

"It's not that . . . I've seen him in dreams."

"What dreams?"

"I saw him lift the sphere from its pedestal in D'arkadia and break it in half, and I saw him with that creature beneath the dungeons. They knew each other."

Bolton felt a chill ride up his spine. "That man wasn't human." His body looked like the grave had claimed him long ago. Yet, his voice was clear as glass.

"I don't know what he is," Sara whispered as if someone would hear them. "But that sphere has lay broken for so long no one remembers it. That man couldn't still be alive."

"What do you think he wanted?" Bolton asked.

"I think he wanted that creature to remain locked away. And I let it out."

Bolton rested his hand on top of hers.

Sara looked away from the mountain and into his eyes. "You're back," she said. "I've been walking around for three years thinking you were dead."

Bolton lifted her hand and kissed the back of it. "I would have come as soon as I awakened. I had a fever when I left that gorge. I wasn't thinking straight."

"I thought it would be me," she said.

"What would be you?"

"That I would be dead," she said. "I never envisioned a future beyond that battle. And then you were gone. At the banding ceremony in Lumina, I couldn't be happy. I didn't know how to be happy because I shouldn't have been. Part of me was disappointed that I hadn't died."

"You shouldn't say that," he said.

"But it's true. I was tired. I had resigned myself to death the day Rodan and I escaped Fortress Tower. It was the same feeling I got yesterday before I saw you, only more intense. That it would be better to sleep and not wake. That it would be easier."

"That was the darkness. That wasn't you," Bolton said.

Sara looked down into her lap. "Once Hephaestus was gone, things were supposed to get easier. If I was meant to live, I've already done enough."

"Sometimes we don't get to decide what happens to us," he said. "It just happens."

Sara lifted her head.

The pink scar running down Bolton's face reminded her of Talon. Talon was scarred, and he ran. He left Brina behind. Bolton had returned, thoughts of escaping the world had never entered his mind. She marveled at how two men could go through the same thing and make very different choices.

She was angry at herself for not daring to go back for Talon's blade. It should be in Element where he could be remembered.

"It'll be dark soon," Bolton said. "Do you want to sleep in there?" Behind him was the abandoned inn.

Sara shook her head. She recalled the blood-stained bed and the feeling of something watching her in the dark. "Let's sleep under the stars. It's warmer here. The dust will choke us in there."

THAT night, they slept outside the gate surrounding the inn. The white paint had started to peel from years of abandonment. The nails rusted, and the rust spread, creating a muddy red in the space around each nail.

Bolton slept with his back against the wooden gate. Sara's head was against his leg. Her eyes darted beneath the lids like someone zigzagging to escape a pursuer.

In her mind, she was running, trying to escape an invisible hunter. She could feel the darkness closing in around her like fading dusk, the sun sinking below the horizon, giving way to a moonless, starless sky.

Soon, Sara could not see where she was running nor

could she feel the ground beneath her feet. She ran in boundless space, without existence and without end. It stretched out beyond her imagination and continued to expand into nothing.

Sara woke from her dream as if her body was expelling a disease dangerous to it. Her arms lifted her up.

Bolton was still asleep against the gate, his breathing steady and unhindered. Sara imagined that very few things could wake him from such a slumber. He had experienced a restless sleep for three years. In that sleep, he had used up all his dreams.

Sara looked up.

The moon was clear in a sky filled with stars. Their glow lit the ground to a dull, dark green. In the distance, the crystals of the forest glowed to remind her of their journey.

She was not in the boundless space, and she was grateful. She tried to settle back to sleep, but it would not come to her. Her mind feared another dream.

Folding her arms across her chest, Sara walked toward the cliff overlooking the sea. Her feet padded the grassy ground. She was careful to step over the deep crevasses that wrinkled the plain and looked like narrow, dried up streams from above.

Once she stood at the edge of the cliff, her eyes gazed out at the dark water.

Further out toward Omega Ray, a thin sheet of ice covered the water. The ice thinned until the water was unobstructed.

The roots of the trees lining the cliff stuck out of its side. Some grew down to the sea where rocks lined the hard, sandy coast, making a fall treacherous.

She couldn't see the lands further out in the distance, sheltered by the great expanse. She didn't know what lie beyond this world with its bounds and limits, but there was more, more than her eyes could see.

Wind carried from across the sea and met Sara on the cliff. Farah would be worried for her. She wished she could tell her she was okay.

She remembered how Rodan sat with her in her daze, trying to comfort her, begging for a response. The pain and worry in his eyes stayed with her.

Did they find Veil? Was he dead?

The thought saddened Sara. She had seen kindness in him, but he was led by the wrong hands. The torment and torture of years had turned his soul dark. Still, it was not up to her to mend it.

The creature Sara met in the darkness had a strong connection with the energy seeping from Veil in the cloud. There was that same feeling of despair, only stronger and more profound.

Sara looked behind her.

There was nothing there in the dark.

At her back, the wind urged her away from the sea.

Bolton had returned, and all she could think of was the torrent of trouble that had arisen in those few weeks she had journeyed with Farah.

A journey that began to ease the mundane existence Sara's life had become had evolved into a quest much more multifarious than Sara had wanted to take.

Three years ago, she stepped out into the wilderness to fight a battle she didn't need to fight. Bolton told her she didn't need to martyr herself. Yet, she still did. Now, she was given the same choice.

But this time would be different.

Looking at Bolton's sleeping form against the wooden gate with the breeze on her back encouraging her toward him, Sara vowed that her involvement in this greater trial would end. This wasn't her fight any longer, and she wasn't going to step forward and make it so.

She would tell Farah this when she and Bolton found her.

And she knew what Farah would say.

It was too late.

Morica Council was looking for her. If Veil was alive, she was still his wife. If he was dead, so was she. The Council would not let her walk away. Their pride, like something with teeth, would want to destroy her.

She had already martyred herself.

2

ONWARD

We bowed at Their feet, and Built Their Sparkling Temples across Mirmina. People began to Pray there. Not Everyone was Blessed with Their Gifts, but Everyone wanted to be.

THE crystals glowed in the moonlight like beacons among the trees. The grassy plain winded through the wooden columns until it disappeared among the bushes and brambles.

Sara and Bolton followed it through the trees. Their footsteps left soft imprints on the ground. Their bodies were lethargic.

Sara stumbled against a tree. Her feet slipped among the roots.

Adrenaline in his veins, Bolton caught her around the

waist before she slumped to the ground. But he could not prevent the fall. Bolton was too weak to maintain his balance as he grasped Sara. They collapsed.

After the initial shock, they laughed at their own distress.

Sara rose to her feet. She offered her hand to Bolton, who took it. She grinned until the shuttering in her stomach reminded her she was hungry.

They became dizzy and disoriented as they walked through the trees. Neither said a word for hours as they mustered all the energy they had left to remain on their feet. The path in front of them was becoming blurred and unfamiliar.

"Sara, look!" Bolton spotted wild berries among the bushes. He ran to them with all his effort.

Sara followed.

They knelt, wrenched the berries from among the leaves, and packed them into their mouths, barely chewing before they swallowed. Soon their eating slowed, and they were content. Their stomachs were no longer making mournful and desperate sounds. They settled on the ground and reveled in their fullness.

As night fell, laughter drifted through the forest.

Sara rested on a flat head crystal beside the bush decorated with wild berries. Bolton sat with one hand resting on his knee and drank water from his canteen, freshly refilled at the lake. He had been in the middle of a story.

"So, then Rodan's so mad, he just clocks me in the jaw."

"He hit you?" she asked.

"Yeah, the man looks civilized now, but he was a barbarian when we were growing up."

Sara smirked.

"So," Bolton said, "I tell him, 'Look, she wouldn't have even noticed you if I hadn't said something.' I can't blame the guy though. I probably would have been a little embarrassed too if my best friend had to ask a girl out for me. Hey, but I was a kid, I was just trying to help." Bolton smiled. "Nothing ever came of it though. His fault, not mine."

Sara laughed. "He didn't want you fighting his battles."

"I wasn't fighting the battle. I was just handing him the sword."

Their laughter sang through the trees until it faded into the distance.

Bolton's eyes fixated on a cluster of trees nearby. In the clearing beyond these trees, he had warned her about the ambush. He had told her he was a liar. But Rodan had been a rock. He saved her. Bolton never had.

"Bolton?"

Bolton walked over to her and sat. "There's been something I've been meaning to ask you."

Sara looked into his eyes. "Anything."

"In the past two years, has there been anyone else?" he asked. "I know what happened with Veil . . ."

"No, there hasn't been anyone else."

Their eyes locked, and Sara became very aware of her breathing. It was unsteady, and ragged. She pondered at every new detail of his face. The way the scar settled jagged against the soft skin of his cheek, creating a shallow, white valley. The way the light from the glowing crystals made his skin glow.

While she was captivated, Bolton's lips met hers.

It took a moment for her to get her bearings, but soon her arms were around his neck.

Bolton pulled away. "I kept this for you." Bolton handed her a folded piece of paper from his pocket. "I found it at the bottom of the cliff before I crawled out."

Sara unfolded it. It was a drawing of her mother. Sara gazed at it. The charcoal had muddied the picture in some places, but Sara's intent was still clear. It was more than just her mother's image that gave the picture significance. It was also the memories of those times when everything was so new and fascinating, and when everything she did felt right beyond any doubt.

"I don't draw anymore," she said.

"Why not?"

Sara looked down at the picture as she spoke. "There always seemed to be more important things to do."

Although the thick foliage blocked the light from the burning sun, the crystals at the foot of every tree glowed with such brilliance that no lantern was needed to see through the forest. Smaller crystals sparkled like fireflies along the branches touching the sky.

Bolton and Sara needed to move. They gathered as many berries as they could, stuffing them in their pockets for the road. Bolton suggested they get an early start and walk all day and night across D'arkadia without rest. Sara agreed, not knowing if the Beast would re-emerge as the other Protectors had across Mirmina.

The Dark Sphere had felt heavy in her hand as she pulled it from the depths of the Aether. The Beast's duty had been to protect something that, in Sara's experience, could only cause pain. She wondered how dark the heart of the Beast must be. She felt a portion of that darkness in the cave when she felt the Beast's sadness like a thick fog from which she could not escape.

She had felt for the Protectors, but she had not given much thought about the entrapment they felt, the overwhelming need to guard the spheres. Not until she saw through a

Protector's eyes did she realize their limited freedom. It wasn't happiness nor was it sadness. It was duty.

She had felt trapped by duty once, a duty to hide, to stay alive, not just to protect herself, but to protect a future beyond herself. But she had one thing that the Protectors did not have. Choice.

Still, there was one anomaly. Could Thermal feel the pull of the element, the weight of the Wind Sphere beckoning his protection?

Spire had explained that the sphere no longer called to Thermal, but after feeling that pull herself, Sara wondered if Spire had been wrong.

Sara and Bolton continued through the trees. Bolton led the way, and Sara watched his back as she followed.

When, if ever, would she lose that surreal feeling when she was around him?

When he fell from the cliff, her heart sank as if she had missed a step at the top of a tall staircase. And after the fall, when the realization that he was gone finally hit, it had felt like an amputation. Now, though he was here with her, Sara didn't feel a sense of completeness. Instead, she felt like a living limb had been replaced by a wooden one, a façade.

She shook the thought from her head, angry with herself for thinking it.

Ahead of them was D'arkadia. As they walked through the trees onto the plain, their eyes met a duller light.

The darkness across the plain had eased, and the sun's light was no longer blocked by the gloom. The hard and uneven ground was visible, and grasses, aided by the sun's light, peeked out from the cracks.

There was an abandoned shop and light posts that had been damaged by the Beast long ago. The people of Breeze had erected them in the hopes of taking advantage of the land. But the land would have never been right until the Beast's mind was right.

The Beast had been led by a broken sphere, still resting on its pedestal. It had cracked the Beast's brain like glass. The pull of the sphere weakened so the Beast could roam across the plain. It believed everyone who passed through to be a threat.

The energy of the sphere seeped out like pus from a festering wound, polluting the sky with darkness. For hundreds of years it remained like that until Sara pulled the sphere from its pedestal. Now, the sun could beat down on the earth, warming it.

Soon, the ground would become soft from the rain and grasses would grow again.

With the increased visibility, Sara could now see that a river ran through the land to the east. It trailed down in tiny tributaries right before the edge of the forest.

Bolton touched the post of one of the lights.

"Farah told me that the people of Breeze built these."

The light posts went miles into the sky.

Sara looked up at the immense structure.

Bolton followed her eyes. "Impressive."

"She would be looking for me," Sara said. "She never gives up."

"I just hope she and Rodan didn't go too far in their search," Bolton said.

"I hope they didn't go to Lumina . . . or Vella City." Sara shook her head.

"They won't get themselves caught. And even if they do," Bolton said, "there's one thing I know about Farah: she doesn't stay caught for long. When we left Element, that wasn't Farah's first time beyond the walls. Her father dragged her back half a dozen times."

"I just hope she's rational about all this," Sara said.

"When have you ever known Farah to be rational?" Bolton asked.

"I don't want them getting themselves into trouble because of me," Sara said. "The Council is looking for me, and that means they're looking for them too. If the Council finds them, they'll do anything to discover where I'm hiding. Not to mention the spheres. Rai took them from Vella City."

"They're smart," Bolton said. "They're not going to get themselves—"

Bolton grabbed Sara's wrist.

"Shh," he said in a harsh whisper as he guided her around the back of the shop.

"What is it?" Sara whispered.

"Someone's out there."

Sara peered from around the corner of the shop.

In the distance, a man was walking over the plain. His hair was a light, red-blond, and he had a large sack on his back.

"That's Tacitum," she said.

Bolton's hand was on Sara's shoulder. "Who?"

"I met him in Lumina. He's Solace's brother."

"Solace, the innkeeper?"

Sara nodded. "He was working for Atrus in Wyvek. I wonder what he's doing here."

Sara emerged from behind the shop.

"Wait!" Bolton said.

But she made her way across the barren earth to Tacitum who was wiping the sweat from his brow.

Bolton sighed and followed her.

Tacitum looked up as Sara approached.

"Do you remember me?" she asked.

Tacitum thought for a moment. He pointed his finger at Sara. "You were the one in Lumina, the one who asked me about the Sphere Protector."

Sara nodded. "What are you doing out here? Did you ever get in touch with your brother?"

Tacitum shook his head. "He doesn't understand that I'm an artist. I'm not a businessman. I can't run a shop like he does. But I need work. Now that Boss left and the factory went to ruin, I'm not making any money. I can't sell my work in the streets of Lumina."

Bolton approached them, interrupting Tacitum's explanation.

"This is Bolton," Sara said. "He's traveling with me."

Tacitum shook Bolton's hand and forgot his story.

"Can I see some of your work?" Bolton asked.

Tacitum's eyes grew wide. "Of course."

He shrugged off his bag and retrieved a rolled-up painting. He unrolled the painting and held the top edge between the finger and thumb of his right hand and the bottom with his left.

The painting depicted the deep depths of a cave and from it, tiny pulses of energy swept across the ground like worms.

"Where did you see this?" Sara asked.

"Not see," Tacitum said. "I dreamed it."

He rolled up the painting and placed it back in his bag. He stood and put the bag back onto his back.

"What takes you to D'arkadia?" Bolton asked.

Tacitum blinked twice. "A messenger came to Wyvek. He said Boss was in Vella City awaiting us. That he had a new factory there. The *Lacwanx* are on their way as well, as fast as their short legs can carry them. I need the money so I'm willing to make the journey."

Bolton scratched his head. "You're talking about Atrus, right?"

Tacitum shook his head and shrugged.

"Boss is Atrus," Sara said.

"Well, that can't be," Bolton said. "Atrus is not on good terms with the Council. We failed to defeat Veil, so the Council would not be looking to cut him a deal. He's hiding with Vassal and Pentagon. There's no way he's in Vella City."

"I don't understand," Tacitum said.

"You shouldn't go to Vella City," Sara said. "I don't know why, but they're tricking you into thinking Atrus is there."

"Why would they want to trick me? I am but a simple painter. Or trick any of us for that matter? The only work we can do is build flying ships for Atrus."

"That's it," Bolton said. "They want you to build their chariots since they don't have Atrus anymore."

"Then I'll be on my way," Tacitum said.

"What? Don't you understand?" Sara asked.

"If they will pay me for the same work I was doing for Atrus," Tacitum said, "I will do it."

"Morica's dangerous," Sara said.

Tacitum clenched the strap of his bag. "Not more dangerous than dying."

3

NIGHTFALL

As a child, I did not Fear the Night, but The Darkness that He brings, that I Fear.

AS they got closer to Tosia, night fell, and the Chariot was nowhere in sight. Even in the darkness, they would not have missed the large structure. The plain was so flat, they would have seen the outline on the horizon before light left the sky. But there was nothing.

Right before dawn, they made it to the entrance of Tosia. Tosia was still abandoned. The earth was blackened. The branches of the great tree were dying. There was a large hole in the ceiling overhead, sending the sky into the town. The shop doors were closed, and the streets were empty. Their friends had long gone.

"Where would they go?" Bolton asked.

Sara shook her head.

"We should rest and see if we can find some food," Bolton said.

Sara nodded. Her arms were folded, and she had a nervous look in her eyes.

"What's wrong?" he asked.

"I hoped they would be here. That's all."

"They're fine. I'm sure Thatch is the only one who can fly that giant contraption out of here. They're probably looking for us."

"Well, that," she said, "and I haven't had the best memories here."

"It'll be okay," Bolton said. "I'm here. We won't stay long. We can sleep outside."

Sara nodded.

Bolton took her hand and led her to the shop at the corner.

He tried the door, but it was locked. With his hand on the handle, he shouldered the door and busted it open. The wood splintered and rested like matchsticks on the ground.

The shelves were stocked with jars of preserved food.

Bolton took a basket from the counter and loaded it with jars. Glass chimed against glass as he placed the jars in the basket.

Sara stood by the door, her mind so full of thoughts that it had not quite caught up. But just as her hand touched a basket, she heard shouting.

Bolton placed the basket on the ground and walked over to the door. He peered outside to the town center near the Domum Fidei.

Morica guards had gathered outside. They brandished their black batons. At their sides were guns. The head guard shouted orders to the others.

"They're looking for Veil," Sara whispered over Bolton's shoulder.

The head guard retrieved a key from his pocket and placed it into the lock. He opened the door to the Domum Fidei, and the guards entered, their guns ready.

Bolton moved away from the door. He tapped Sara's shoulder and motioned for her to come back into the shop where he retrieved the basket full of jars.

Sara took hers and pulled jars from the shelves and placed them into her basket until it was full.

Once their baskets were heavy with glass jars, Bolton and Sara made their way to the rotted door that served as the entrance. It was open, and outside was the chariot that Atrus commandeered.

The hatch door was ajar. Several engine parts had been disassembled and taken away.

"It looks like Thatch took some of the parts," Sara said. "It won't fly."

"It looks like he took the turrets," Bolton said.

A thunderous sound, the sound of bullets loosing from guns hammered in their ears, followed by desperate screams.

"Come on." Bolton took Sara's arm.

They ran through the trees, deep into the woods outside Tosia.

Once he was satisfied they had made it far enough, Bolton stopped running, and Sara followed his lead. They gasped for breath, mostly from fear.

The screams of those men had sent a chill down Bolton's spine, a cold he could not shake. He sat unsteadily on the grassy earth.

Sara settled down next to him on the uneven ground.

Some of her jars had broken from being jostled against the rest. The juices of the pickled figs leaked out inside the basket.

"We forgot to fill our canteens," she said.

Bolton spotted a small pool of water close to a tree nearby. He snaked over to it and knelt, dipping his palms into the water. He brought his water filled palms to his lips and drank.

Sara opened a jar of pickled figs and ate them with her fingers. The dark juices stained her fingertips a deep purple.

In moments, the hunger of days was satisfied.

Sara looked down into the jars, forlorn. "Do you think they killed him?" Sara asked.

Bolton leaned against the tree. "Who?"

"Veil."

Bolton shook his head. "We couldn't do it. I doubt a couple dozen Morica guards could handle him."

Part of Sara was relieved Veil did not die that way.

"We can't stay here," Bolton said.

"We need to sleep." Sara let the water wash her stained fingers.

"Not here."

"Then where?"

Bolton listened.

The sound of screaming had long ceased.

"We'll make it to the Lake," he said. "Once we have a boat, we'll take shifts."

"We'll never get across that way. We'll need the both of us to row."

"We either do that or risk our safety out here . . . with a Dark Elemental."

Sara nodded. She picked up the basket of pickled figs and started walking to the Lake.

Bolton got up from against the tree, picked up his basket,

and jogged to catch up with her. "You're angry with me?"

Sara shook her head. "No, you're right."

"But you're still angry with me."

"But you're right," she said.

Sara continued walking.

"Can we please talk about this?" he asked.

"About what?"

"You're treating me like a stranger. In fact, this whole journey has been like that, like you're uncomfortable with me. What's going on?"

Sara stopped walking, but she didn't turn to face him.

She stood in silence.

Bolton wordlessly urged her to explain. He was on the edge waiting for her answer.

"You were dead." Tears welled up in her eyes.

Bolton turned her around by the shoulder. He saw her tears.

"You were dead," she said, "and everybody left. It was only me in Element by myself. I was like Brina, waiting for Talon, only I knew you would never return."

Bolton embraced her, and Sara leaned her head on his shoulder.

"Now," she said, "I don't know how to be with you. Only moments before you died, I thought you had betrayed me. I never expected you to return. And you come back, and you expect me to pick up where we left off."

"No." Bolton shook his head.

"It might not have been three years for you, but it was three years for me, three years of knowing you were dead." Her words came out choked and hesitant until her breathing slowed and her shoulders stopped shaking.

"I'm sorry," Sara said. "The past few days, I haven't

known what to feel, and I'm hating myself for it. I used to dream you would come back, and in those dreams, it felt right. It was easy for me to be with you."

Bolton pulled back and looked into her eyes. "I can't imagine what you're feeling right now, but I do know one thing—I want to help you get to know me again. Will you give me that chance at the very least?"

Sara nodded.

Bolton smiled. "Come on. It will be easier to catch up when we get to a safe place."

They walked through the trees to the Lake de Somnia, careful to stay a distance from the cleared path.

A boat was docked on the Lake. Sara and Bolton stepped down into it and placed their baskets in the bed of the vessel.

Sara took the oars.

"What are you doing?" he asked.

"I'll row first."

"No, I'll do it."

"So you can row the entire way without waking me?" she asked.

"Of course not, I'll be useless to you tired. I just can't sleep yet."

Sara handed him the oars and settled down in the bed of the boat. The gentle rocking of the boat on the water lulled her into a deep sleep.

SARA was in a darkened room, but she could make out the faces of Lucerna and Tacitum. They stood against the wall and stared into the nothingness behind her. Their faces were blank. They were statues, unbreathing.

She thought she could see where the room ended, but further back than she had imagined the wall to be, seven figures emerged.

Not able to make out their faces, Sara squinted against the darkness. Still, she could not see who they were, but their footsteps were strong and able.

One walked foremost in front of the others.

As they walked further into the brighter dimness, his face revealed itself to her.

Sara's eyes fought against the darkness so fiercely that the strain was making them hurt.

But then, the patchy skin became apparent as did the smell of rotting flesh.

And a voice croaked from the decaying mass. "My children."

SARA shot up in the bed of the boat.

The water rocked beneath the hull.

The oars lay abandoned by her side. The ship had been tied to a pillar of the missing dock, which had been shaken from its foundations.

It was only her in the boat.

Sara looked around frantically.

Where was Bolton?

Had she dreamed it all? Him? Their journey?

Then who rowed her here? Who tied the boat?

"Bolton!" she called.

Shaking, she emerged from the boat and stepped onto the shore.

"Bolton?"

Bolton appeared from around the bend.

"Where were you?" she asked.

He walked over to where she stood on the shore. "I took a walk to Wyvek temple to stake out the place, make sure there weren't any Morica guards sneaking about over there."

"You lied to me," she said.

"What do you mean?"

"Why didn't you wake me?"

"I couldn't. You were sleeping like the dead. I tried to wake you on the way over, but it was no use. I was fine letting you sleep anyway because I couldn't. It looked like you might have been having a nightmare though. You cried in your sleep. What was that dream?"

"I don't remember," Sara lied.

"Well, Wyvek looks abandoned. The doors to the temple are blocked with metal contraptions, and all the buildings in town are still boarded up."

Sara hadn't expected any less. She knew Atrus was on the run, and the people of Wyvek had left long before.

She marveled at her dream. *What was Lucerna doing there? And Tacitum. Who were those people in the darkness?*

She remembered Tacitum's painting. It had scared her. That his dreams were so like her own. *But he had seen the Sphere Protector, so it was not a coincidence that he would have seen the glowing worms, but how would he have known about the cave?*

Sara reasoned that he was only in her dream because she met him in D'arkadia and saw his painting.

The dream left her confused and shaken.

Mostly, she recalled the feeling of being connected. She felt the energy from their bodies as they moved forward.

"You need sleep," Sara said. "You should rest here. I'll stay up."

Sara settled on the soft ground near the Lake, and Bolton rested his head in her lap. She tried to find comfort in that.

He fell asleep quickly and easily.

4

AWAY

People go into the Dark Palace, and They do not come out. They have been Chosen for Something Greater and Beyond Our Understanding. Still, I do not wish to be Chosen.

RODAN looked out the window as the Chariot made its way to Caleena. He sighed. "We should be looking for Sara and Bolton."

For hours, they had searched Tosia for them. They had looked everywhere save the locked shops and houses. They called their names through the woods all the way to the Lake.

Stannum's metal fingers clicked as silence draped the room.

Rai was at the wheel. She was in a dark mood. Vassal had decided that he, Pentagon, and Atrus would board with them. It was too high profile to continue to sail through the skies in a Morica vessel. So, Thatch stockpiled some of the parts for repairs, and Vassal and his companions took flight aboard the Chariot. Rai was not pleased by this compromise.

Lucerna remained in a deep sleep, so deep, she didn't stir. Efforts to wake her were fruitless. They all feared that if Lucerna did wake, she would be in the same hopeless trance as Sara.

Farah was petting and cooing to Orka like she was a baby. Despite Sara and Bolton's absence, she couldn't help but be glad to have her companion back. Orka nestled her head into Farah's hair. The little bird relished the attention.

"We searched all of Tosia," Thatch said. "I don't know what happened to them, but it had been hours. If we would have stayed any longer, Morica would have come."

"But we should continue searching," Rodan said. His hopes were higher than his logic.

"Where?" Rai asked with a sharp edge to her voice. "Where are we going to look for them? There's only one way that Sara could have gone."

Everyone aboard the Chariot knew what Rai meant: The Cliff of Broken Promise.

"She didn't jump," Rodan said.

"You saw how she was." Rai masked her despair with anger.

"Don't say that," Farah said.

"That wouldn't explain what happened to Bolton," Rodan said.

"Yes, it would," Rai said.

"You're saying they both jumped?"

"Stop it!" Thatch said. "Wherever they are, we'll find them or they'll find us. Right now, we must keep moving. Morica has a bounty on our heads. The best thing to do is to get to Caleena where we can pick up more supplies, and then leave the mainland. Maybe go to Breeze."

"Breeze?" Farah said. "That's the last place I want to go."

"But it's the safest. Shift's there now."

Farah folded her arms.

Orka chirped.

Despite Farah's theatrics, she wanted to see her brother. She just did not want to admit it. It upset her that Shift did not stay with Thatch to look for her. His pride had won him over like it had in the past.

Rai flew under the clouds. Caleena was below them. She landed at the docks. There were usually so many ships at the docks, coming and going, the Chariot would not have otherwise been able to land there, but the ships were gone. No workers piled crates along the wharf ends.

The air held a sense of stillness.

It was quiet. No gossip littered the walkways. There were no guards.

Farah and Rodan donned the hooded cloaks they had taken from Tosia and exited the Chariot. Walking up the wharf ends, there was not a single villager to be seen. The huts and shops were deserted.

Farah walked into a shop and stuffed her canvas sack with food. She pulled down breads, moldy cheese, and jars of preserved fruits.

"What are you doing?" Rodan asked.

"Taking. This place is obviously abandoned. This food will perish if we don't eat it. Plus, finders keepers and all that." Farah hastened to fill her bag with as much food as possible.

Orka landed on the counter and picked at a loaf of bread.

"You don't have to rush. Everyone's gone. It's not like we'll be caught." He placed items into his sack as well, moving slower than Farah.

"Spire and Decca live here. I'm worried about them," Farah said. "We have to fill our bags and get back to the Chariot. I think it would be best to move on to Elementa. Whatever happened here, Spire would have survived. She may have gone there. The sooner we get out of here, the sooner we can start looking for them."

"But what if she was on the first ship to Lumina."

"That would be unfortunate for us. I don't think I could convince Thatch to go to Lumina. Being on Morica's radar, Lumina would be one of the worst places we could go aside from marching up to the Council palace in Vella City. But Spire would go to Elementa. I know it."

After their bags were filled, Rodan and Farah climbed back into the Chariot and ran to the control room.

"Thatch," Farah said. She waited until her breathing slowed. "Yep, the place is definitely abandoned. No sign of anyone. I think Spire and Decca might have made it to Elementa. We should go there."

"I don't know if that's a good idea," Thatch said. "Morica's presence is strong in Elementa."

"We have to make sure Spire and Decca are safe," Farah said. "Please, Thatch, we have to do this."

Thatch sighed. He looked at Rai and nodded.

The Chariot sailed toward Elementa.

FARAH sat at Lucerna's bedside.

She had not stirred.

"How is she doing?" Rodan approached them and took a seat next to Farah.

"Nothing yet. I've never seen someone sleep without tossing at least a little. Her chest isn't even rising and falling."

Rodan held his metal buckler to her lips. Warm breath fogged the clear surface. "She's breathing."

"What can we do for her?" Farah asked.

"Here, all we can do is wait. When we get to Elementa, we can call for a doctor, but I don't know how much help it will be. She's exhausted her energy. Her element is strong."

"I still don't understand where it came from. At Element, we learned of all the elements that ever existed, even the lost ones. This wasn't one of them. What do we even call it?"

"Light," Rodan said.

"Do you think she's the only one?"

Rodan nodded. "The sphere has no pedestal. Without one, the sphere's energy cannot flow through the earth to endow others with its gift."

"But what about Lucerna?"

"I don't understand it," Rodan said. "We learned that the sphere's energy is derived from the souls of the Keepers, who the Creator gathered for such purpose. Beyond that . . . I don't know."

"Lucerna found a book," Farah said. "In it was the history of the people of Dustpath. It spoke of the Keepers and the Creator, but it's not the story we were told. In it, the Creator did terrible things to his people."

"The Builders?"

Farah nodded.

"The book could have been a forgery," Rodan said.

"I don't know. It seemed legit."

Rodan looked out the windows of the loft.

Elementa was visible in the distance.

"Growing up," Farah said, "I always wondered why the Creator would make the spheres in the first place. No book or trainer could ever answer that for me."

"I think the answer lies with the Protectors. They are the oldest beings in all Mirmina. They have been around since the Builders erected the sanctums."

Farah laughed. "Well, it's not like you can ask a Protector a question. If you got close enough, you wouldn't get an answer. You'd get attacked."

Rodan looked at Lucerna. "I wonder what she can see in the darkness."

FARAH sat with Orka at the bar by the windows. She petted the little, green bird and talked to it in an intelligent voice.

She spent many moments gazing out the windows. In the distance, the sea stretched out beyond Elementa. She marveled at it and realized that never had anyone journeyed out across it, at least not anyone she knew. People simply sailed from one city in Mirmina to the next without ever going beyond to the south.

Thatch had detected energy further out, but he said it was an anomaly.

Farah wondered how true that was.

After all, the Insula was out at sea. She wondered how many other lands were out there as well.

As a child, the older apprentices at Element used to scare her with tales of the Dark Lands, the lands beyond Mirmina, but those were only stories.

The Dark Lands harbored all matter of unmannered savages who did not know civilization. They had large mammoths to transport them across the plains, and the large feet of the mammoths thundered and shook the ground.

They did not have buildings or government. Instead, they lived in tribes, dressed in skins and roamed about the land like animals with no system of letters, symbols, or numbers from which to communicate.

Mirmina was once like the Dark Lands, but once the sphere sanctums were created, people took advantage of their gifts. This helped them to master their lands. Because the Dark Lands did not share a landmass with the lands of Mirmina, its people did not derive the same benefits.

As she got older, Farah had not bothered with such tales. It was only now that she had traveled the lands of Mirmina that she started to wonder about the Dark Lands and the people who might inhabit them.

Surely, it could not be just Mirmina and the ocean. There must be lands beyond the horizon.

Orka chirped, pulling Farah out of her revelry.

The Chariot shook, and Farah leapt from her chair.

Orka flapped her wings through the air above Farah before landing back on her shoulder.

Farah watched from the windows as the Chariot was jolted from left to right and back again in an erratic dance. Wind battered the Chariot as Rai tried to land. The Chariot shuttered in the fierce gales.

What is that?

On unsteady feet, Farah made her way to the lift to bring her down to the control room. Once the doors opened, she used the wall for support as she stepped into the room. She held onto the rail to keep her balance.

Rodan stood next to Stannum and braced himself by holding onto the chair bolted into the floor. Thatch was in his seat next to the blue screen, and Rai was at the steering wheel.

"What's going on?" Farah asked.

Orka chirped.

The wind roared outside.

"It has to be a Wind Elemental." Rai muscled the wheel

to maintain control of the Chariot.

"The energy is impressive," Thatch said. "If Thermal was still connected to the sphere, I would venture to guess it was him."

"It would have to be a very powerful Elemental for all this," Rodan said.

"I might need a second pair of arms," Rai warned as she began to lose control of the Chariot.

The Wind tossed it sideward through the air. It was dangerously close to plummeting to the ground.

Orka flew to the seat Rodan held onto. She struggled to keep her balance as the Chariot sailed uncontrolled through the air.

Farah rushed over, letting go of the rail to get to Rai. She lost her balance and fell onto the steel floor with a hard thump.

"Farah, you okay?" Rodan yelled.

Farah nodded. She stood with great effort. She stumbled to the steering wheel and reached over Rai to help her steady the wheel against the Wind.

Together, they righted the wheel.

The Chariot sailed through the tremulous atmosphere aided by every ounce of effort Farah and Rai could put into steering it.

"This has to be more than one Wind Elemental. It could be an attack," Rodan said. "Maybe we shouldn't land."

"We have to find Spire," Farah said. "We have to make sure she's safe."

"You're not even sure she's here," Rai said.

"I know Spire will be here," Farah said, "and she might be able to help us find Sara. She knows her better than anyone."

Farah put all her concentration into steering the Chariot. "I wish Thermal was here." Farah was surprised that the words escaped her lips. She had never gotten along with the great bird Thermal, but she knew she needed him. He had disappeared after being released by Thatch when they rescued Sara from Vella City. Thermal was wounded when he left. Farah wasn't sure that he made it. The thought made her uneasy.

5

THE STRONGEST

*The Gifts come in Varying Strengths. I have seen a Child with more
Power than a Man.*

VASSAL, Pentagon, and Atrus stood in the hallway outside the roof of the Chariot. The three were newly
rested.

Farah had fought to keep Atrus from boarding the vessel.
She told Thatch that Atrus had stolen his blueprints from
Breeze and was modifying chariots for Morica, but Thatch,
knowing they might need the help of an extra mechanic, con-
ceded to allowing Atrus aboard.

Pentagon did away with his councilor uniform. He
donned the clothes Shift left on board when he took General
Riee's place as leader of Breeze.

Vassal leaned against one wall with his head down. He

was aware Rai did not appreciate his presence aboard the Chariot. She had been vocal about it before they left Tosia and called him a traitor not to be trusted. Knowing he needed to get aboard, he took the blows. He could not fight Morica alone, and Mordecai wanted his head. They had failed to kill Veil, but if they had succeeded, he now doubted that Mordecai would have let them live.

The Chariot shuttered, knocking the three worn-out villains to their knees.

Atrus braced himself against the wall as the Chariot lurched to one side then the other. "What's going on out there?"

"The ship is under attack." Vassal unsheathed his sword and made for the elevator to the control room.

Atrus and Pentagon followed.

Rai, with Farah's help, landed on the hill outside town. The atmosphere of Elementa had changed. The wind cut through the streets. Morica flags ripped through the air. It was a cloudless storm.

It had been like that for days. The merchants in the marketplace could not stop the wind from ripping down their stands, so they peddled on the streets and sold their wares from outside their homes.

"This is definitely a Wind Elemental, and a very strong one." Farah's hand sheltered Orka from the biting gusts.

As they walked through town, the wind tearing through their hair, Rai kept looking back at Vassal walking a few paces behind them with Pentagon and Atrus. She eyed him, her hand resting on the handle of her sword.

Thatch had stayed behind to watch Lucerna. She had not awakened from her slumber. The rapid movement of her eyes under her lids told Thatch she was dreaming, but there was nothing anyone aboard could do for her.

Farah led the way with Rodan beside her. She was anxious to get to Element. Spire would be there.

She concentrated on the Wind, trying to calm it, but it was too powerful. Sensing that it was unnatural, she wondered at the strength of the Elemental who was calling these gusts. Never had she known of an Elemental this strong. The command of the winds was unmatched and masterful.

It had to be an army.

With effort, they made it to the steps of Element. Rodan knocked on the heavy oaken door. No one answered.

Farah stepped up and banged on the door. "Hello?"

"Something's wrong," Rai said.

"Rodan, stand back." Farah grabbed his arm, and Rodan moved away from the door.

Farah sent a gust of Wind that ripped the door off its hinges. The door clamored into the entrance, hitting the back wall.

They followed Farah into Element.

It was quiet except for the Wind sifting through the doorway. Their feet tapped on the marble floor as they crossed the entrance hall.

Farah peered into the rooms as they went down the hallway. They were abandoned. "I don't think anyone's here."

"Maybe the Council finally managed to shut it down." Vassal said.

Farah opened the door to the training field and looked across the expanse. Beyond the field was the groundskeeper's cabin. Light emitted from the windows. Farah ran out across the field. The wind made her clothing cling to one side of her body and her hair whip her face. Orka sneezed as Farah's blonde hair accosted the tiny nostrils above her beak.

The others followed Farah as she approached the cabin. Her fist hammered the door.

Decca answered the door, losing it against the Wind. The door hit the side of the cabin hard, splintering the wood. "Farah! What are you doing here?" he yelled against the roar of the Wind.

Farah's company caught up to her.

The Wind stopped blowing, and the roaring in their ears ceased. All was quiet. The grass stopped stirring and the long arms of the willow tree terminated their frantic dance.

"Spire must have calmed her down at last." Decca sighed.

"Who?" Farah asked.

"The baby."

"Spire had her baby?"

Decca nodded. "It's a girl. We named her Canace. Come in. They're in the bedroom."

They entered the small cabin.

"A baby did all this?" Rai walked through the door into the small room.

On the sofa, Sev read Decca's ruined book. Several of the pages were torn and ripped out and the binding had been destroyed.

Sev still wore the uniform of a Morica guard, but he was not one of them.

"What's the Blue Jay doing here?" Farah eyed Sev.

"The Protector in Caleena went rogue," Decca said. "He helped me get Spire out of there."

Sev looked up as the guests entered. "Looks like we'll have to expand into the main building."

"Tough luck," Rai said. "Farah tore off the door."

"Unfortunate that."

"I want to see the baby!" Farah exclaimed with so much

vigor it was as if she used all the energy in her body to make the request.

"This way," Decca said.

Farah and Rodan followed. Rai turned and faced Vassal as he, Pentagon, and Atrus joined them.

"You stay here with the Blue Jay," Rai said. She watched Farah and Rodan as Decca led them into the next room. She turned back to Vassal and folded her arms across her chest.

"We don't need a babysitter," Atrus said.

Pentagon took a seat next to Sev on the sofa.

"You're a Councilor," Sev said. "You'll need to hide the bleached hair if you're trying to disguise yourself. Just because you're not wearing your robes doesn't mean you won't be recognized."

"What are you still doing here, Guard?" Vassal asked with reproach.

"It's Sev." Sev extended his hand. Vassal made no move to reciprocate the gesture. Even if Vassal had wanted to, he would have not been able to extend his right hand to Sev. It was wooden.

"We aren't too trusting of Morica now-a-days." Atrus's gun was visible in his holster at his waist.

"I can understand that," Sev said.

Rai settled into the corner with her arms folded. She watched the band of men with narrowed eyes.

"I've never seen a woman give a man such a death stare," Sev said.

Vassal walked to the window. "Then you've never wronged a woman."

SPIRE sat up in bed. Her back relaxed against the headboard

cushioned with piles of pillows. The baby, calm after the cyclone, rested in her arms. She nestled the side of her face into the nook between Spire's chest and arm.

When Farah and Rodan entered, Spire's eyes lit up. She almost rose from the bed, but stopped for fear the infant would wake.

Decca stood by Spire's bedside.

"She's beautiful," Farah whispered.

"I would let you hold her," Spire said, "but I'm so glad she finally decided to go to sleep. The Wind was battering against the windows. Decca was afraid she'd break the panes."

"That was all her?" Farah asked.

Spire nodded.

Farah and Rodan looked down at the baby, no more than seven pounds and no bigger than a loaf of bread and yet so powerful.

Spire strained her neck to peer around them. "Where's Sara?"

"We lost her in Tosia," Rodan said.

"Lost her? How?" Spire asked.

"Have you heard the news from Lumina?" Rodan asked.

"About the dark cloud?"

Rodan nodded. "We were in it. It was an Elemental . . . a Dark Elemental. It touched Sara, and her mood changed. She wouldn't speak. She showed no expression. We went to Tosia to chase the Dark Elemental, but we lost him. That's when Sara wandered away from the Chariot."

"This was in Tosia?" Spire asked. "Do you know where she might have gone?"

Farah shook her head. "We scoured the place and couldn't find her. All we can do now is keep an eye out."

The baby in Spire's arms stirred, moving its plump little hand against her face. The tiny fingers uncurled and reached upward. Spire rocked her. "You have to find her. Morica will be looking for her after what happened in Vella City."

"You know about that?" Farah asked.

"All of Mirmina knows," Spire said. "Mordecai is blaming it on all of you. All of us."

"We'll find her," Rodan said.

"That puffed pigeon, Mordecai, needs to stop blaming us for the problems he causes," Farah said.

"What else is he saying?" Rodan asked.

"That you are responsible for the missing spheres and the rogue Protectors," Spire said. "And he won't stop at that. There are already warrants out for your arrest. You must stay outside the cities and away from all eyes save the ones you trust."

Spire cooed at the child in her arms.

"Well, the plan is to go to Breeze," Rodan said.

Farah folded her arms.

Orka whistled.

"Breeze, hey," Decca put in. "That would probably be the best place."

"For all of us," Farah said.

Spire looked up.

"I thought you were against the whole idea," Rodan said. "Now you're suggesting we all go."

Farah nodded. "That's right. Spire and Decca too. There are no Protectors in the Windy Desert, and the people could help Canace control her element. At the very least a city of Wind Elementals could help her to calm it. Dad would love it because Canace would be powering his windmills."

Everyone was pensive for a moment.

"That might not be such a bad idea." Spire looked down at her child.

Decca put the palm of his hand on the baby's small head. "When do we leave?"

"When was the last time you saw the Fire Sphere Protector?" Rodan asked.

"Three days ago, in Caleena," Spire said.

"We have to move fast," Rodan said. "The Protector might make its way over to Elementa. We could stock the Chariot with supplies and be on the move by tomorrow."

"Spire just had her baby," Decca reminded them.

"I'll be fine," Spire said, "and they're right. Canace is safer in Breeze than she is here." She turned to Rodan and Farah. "Tell the others we'll leave by tomorrow evening. Decca, you and Sev should go to the markets to get supplies. It's too dangerous for you all to be seen in town."

Decca nodded. "Come on, you'll need somewhere to sleep for the night, and there are plenty of empty rooms in Element."

Rodan and Farah walked with Decca into the sitting room where Rai, like a statue continued to watch Sev and the worn-out villains with reproach.

Sev turned around on the sofa when Decca walked in. "Any news?"

"We're leaving for Breeze tomorrow."

"All of us?"

Decca nodded. "I'll show you all to your rooms for the night. I have the keys."

Atrus shook his head. "I can't go back to the Windy Desert."

"You're either with us or you're not," Farah snapped. "We'd all be more than happy to leave you."

She walked past Atrus and out the door to the training field.

"Are there any other women you've scorned?" Sev grinned.

Vassal walked out the door without saying a word. Rai's eyes were glued to him as she followed him out. Rodan, Pentagon, and Atrus followed with Decca. He closed the door behind them.

Sev looked over the sofa at the closed door. The wood trembled, and the boards that made the door shook with a gentle rattle of the hinges.

The Wind had started up again.

6

THE ABANDONER

Some have left. Even those with Gifts have left. My Fear will not Over-whelm My Desire to remain Close to My gods.

SARA and Bolton passed Wyvek temple now abandoned and bloody where the pulsating worms had eaten the flesh of the living. The Rebel Resistance came to bury the dead, but the walls and floors were still stained with blood.

Bolton remembered when they carried Sara's body outside the Lightning temple, and he thought, "This is the end of it . . . I'm no longer needed." He thought he could walk away then, that they would bury her, and he would be done with Hephaestus.

So many times, he had expected her death, and so many times, he was comforted by it. Now, he could not imagine her gone. How would he survive?

And yet she had lived through his death. She had survived it.

"We should go to the Rebel Resistance," Sara said.

"What about Solace's Inn?"

"It's too close to Lumina. Morica will be looking for us. It's too dangerous."

Bolton knew they had to stay in hiding, but he did not trust the Resistance fighters. He remembered, three years ago, when they kidnapped Sara like it was yesterday. His blood had not yet had time to cool.

Still, Sara was right. He had tasted the Council's wrath, and they would be no match for it alone.

Bolton nodded.

He walked with Sara to Resistance Headquarters. The entrance was disguised as a large boulder that loomed overhead. There was a brass chain that when pulled, pushed the boulder back, revealing the hidden training place among the rocks.

A soldier guarded the entrance. He wore a tattered uniform, and held a spear. Although he possessed a weapon of steel, this didn't mean he wasn't an Elemental. Vassal made sure each of his fighters were trained to wield a blade.

Sara approached the guard.

"Stop, right there," the guard warned, his lance pointing in Sara's direction.

Bolton stepped in front of her, but Sara stepped to the side and spoke to the man.

"Sir, my friend and I know Commander Vassal. We have been to your hidden training grounds before. We are friends of Rodan and his father, Jin."

The guard kept the spear pointed at them, but his piercing glare softened and went from quizzical to kind.

He lowered his spear. "You are Lady Sara, the Water Elemental," the man said in realization.

Sara nodded.

"Commander Jin has been waiting for your return, but he thought his son would be in your company. I hope there's no bad news."

"No," Sara said. "We were separated that's all. Rodan is smart. He'll be fine." She gulped.

There was sadness in her eyes, and Bolton took note of that sadness.

Rodan had been there for her when Bolton was not. He wondered how many times they had sat up at night talking about the past or maybe the future.

The young guard pulled the chain, allowing the large rock to shift aside. The rock moved with a groan as its gritty face rubbed against the surface of the sub-rock.

Sara and Bolton passed through and walked along the rocky path to the barren training field. The field was full of tents. Fighters were marching and training with their weapons of steel in the hot sun. The light gleamed off the blades, scattering white highlights on the red ground.

In the center of it all was Jin. He shared the same broad jawline as his son. His dark hair had grayed in places, and his squarest forehead sat above dark, narrowed eyes.

Jin gave out commands. He led Vassal's army in his absence. Jin had not wanted this job. He wasn't a leader. He had looked up to heroes all his life and now he was expected to be one.

He had traded his silver armband for a bronze one and donned his new title as Commander Jin. His son was so like him.

Jin's eyes were sharp, and he saw Sara and Bolton's approach from yards away.

As they got closer, Sara recognized Jin. When they had closed the gap between them, Jin asked, "Where is Rodan?"

"I got separated from him," Sara said, "but he was off the meli by the time we arrived in Lumina. Bolton and I have been traveling ever since, looking for our friends, but I'm afraid it's too dangerous for us to be on the road for long."

Jin nodded. "Morica guards are everywhere now. On the roads, in towns, and cities."

Jin looked at Bolton. "Your name's Bolton?"

"Yes, I'm a friend of Rodan's."

"A good friend. He used to talk about you. Thought you were dead."

"Not dead," Bolton said. "Just out for a while."

"Well," Jin said, "you should stay. There are a couple extra tents. Dinner is in a few minutes, and we all eat around those long tables. You're welcomed to take your places once you've settled in. If you want to wash up, there's a lake some ways back. It's hidden by wild brush, but it's there."

Sara nodded.

Bolton looked around at the Resistance fighters. He was not happy they would be staying. When Sara told him Rodan had joined the Resistance, Bolton was astounded. Rodan had talked about his father and vowed never to join them. He blamed them for his father's absence. Bolton could not imagine Rodan now sitting among them.

Jin had a fighter escort Sara and Bolton to their two separate tents nestled farthest from the training fields.

Sara touched Bolton's arm. "What's wrong?"

"I didn't say anything."

"I can see that look in your eyes," she said.

"I don't trust them."

"I can understand that," she said. "With the Resistance siding with Morica, but this is a new faction. They call themselves the Rebel Resistance. They're against Morica."

"That guard had a weapon pointed at you," Bolton said.

"He didn't know me. They must be that way to stay protected here. The more people they let in, the more risk they run of Morica finding out where they are."

"Well," he said, "that doesn't help me sleep at night."

WOODEN plates and platters rested on the long dinner tables. Each platter was filled with barley cakes, boiled radishes spiced with coriander, chickpeas, cooked pheasant, and hard cheese. Wooden pitchers filled with honey mead decorated the tables, and the aroma perforated the air.

The tables were set outside in the large aisles between the two armies of tents.

Beyond the rocky plain, the land stretched to the horizon. Trees and tall shrubs grew in the distance.

The fighters took their seats, Sara and Bolton among them. With only berries in their pockets, their journey did not offer them much in the way of food. The feast before them was much appreciated, but it soon turned bitter.

Across the table, several seats away, Bolton's eyes met the eyes of his father. He sat among the soldiers. His blond hair, lighter than Bolton's was tied back. His eyes, blue and regrettable, turned down to the table when they met the piercing eyes of his son.

Benn had traded his beaded robes for the tattered suit of a Rebel Resistance fighter. He would have loved to marvel at how much his son looked like him, but he could feel the anger like something alive crawling down the end of the table, its crooked elbows bent and its jaws opened wide to reveal the bloody throat and sharp tongue.

Bolton rose from the table. His father was poison to him.

Sara got up from her place and followed Bolton as he stalked away among the tents. She grabbed his arm, and he turned to face her.

"I'm sorry," Bolton said. "I can't look him in the eye. Not now. I've only just gotten used to the fact that he is here in Mirmina. Now knowing he is sitting at the very same table . . . it just . . . it makes my blood boil," he said with a snare.

"But we have to stay."

"I can't stand him!" Bolton said in a harsh whisper, then softer, "That man has been the nightmare I've dreamed since I was a four-year-old kid being ripped from my mother's arms. And you know what? That was my very first clear memory, abandoning me and my mother like the coward he is. And now the Resistance is giving him sanctuary."

Bolton paced, his head in his hands.

"I understand." Sara tried to comfort him. Her eyes affixed to the rocky floor.

Bolton regretted his anger, not because it was living inside him, but because he showed it to her.

He lifted her chin and kissed her.

They lingered there until the air invaded the space between them.

"We can go," Sara said.

"Go where? You're right. We can't go to Lumina. That would be too risky. You heard what Jin said. Morica runs Mirmina now. There's nowhere else to go." He sighed, his eyes to the ground. "I'll have to get over him. We're going to be here for a while. I can't risk your safety because my father's a coward. That would make me just like him, unwilling to face my demons."

Sara took his hands in hers. "I'm with you."

He smiled, her glistening eyes drawing his mind away from everything that was his father.

He was back at the lake in the Crystal Forest, his arms around her as she called Water from the ground, encasing them inside the watery walls.

Sara and Bolton walked back to the table and took their places. The food was going around, and they were ravenous. Minds bigger than their stomachs they filled their plates until morsels tumbled over the sides.

AFTER dinner, the moon was high in the sky. The Resistance fighters shuffled back to their tents for the night, tired after the long day of training and because their stomachs were stuffed with warm food.

Sara and Bolton rose from the table as well, helping to carry what was left of the food to the storage tent. The Resistance fighters on duty thanked them, and ambled off to their respective tents.

The weary couple walked to their tents on the far side of the field. They strolled hand and hand, delighting in the fullness of their bellies, and marveling in the comfort the night would bring as they slept in their warm tents. But their revelry was interrupted.

Benn was walking in the opposite direction and stopped when he saw his son.

Bolton was face to face with his father, not knowing what to say or do.

Sara tried to shoulder the burden.

She took Bolton by the arm. He could feel her urgency. "Let's go."

But Bolton didn't move. He planted his feet and glared at the man in front of him. His very presence was an insult. "What are you doing here, old man?"

"The Rebel Resistance is giving me sanctuary." His voice was deep yet tentative. It sent a chill down Bolton's back how much it sounded like his own.

He was the replica of his father reborn. Bolton hated it.

"If you have to be here," Bolton said. "I don't want you to talk to me. I don't want you to look at me or try to meet with me on the field. Just stay away."

Sara clung to his arm.

Benn's eyes glistened, but his mouth formed a hard, thin line. "Your mother asked me to leave. I could see the fear in her eyes. I didn't—"

Bolton shrugged away from Sara. He grabbed his father's head in his hands, pressing his palms into the sides of his face. "Don't you do that!"

He forced Benn backwards.

Benn put his hands on his son's shoulders, trying to wrench himself free, but Bolton held on tight, forcing Benn back still more.

Benn lost his balance and fell hard upon his back.

Bolton fell with him, his hands wrapping around Benn's throat.

The pressure of his hands around his father's neck distracted him from all else. He could not feel Sara's hands on his back. He could not hear her voice shouting, "Stop!"

Benn's face turned red. His hands struggled in vain to loosen his son's grip.

Bolton raised his fist into the air, ready to strike Benn.

Lightning struck the ground close to Benn's face. Its force did not come from Bolton, but from his father. He could have struck him if he wanted to.

"Stop this!" Jin's voice rang out.

A Resistance fighter grabbed Bolton's arm and pulled him up.

Bolton's head was hot. He did not resist. It was not until then that he noticed the eyes of the Resistance fighters upon them. They had gathered in a circle around him and Benn.

He looked down at Benn, red-faced and gasping for breath.

"Stop making excuses," Bolton shouted. "Just say it. You left my mother because you're a coward." Bolton was so angry that tears surged down his cheeks.

Sara's eyes were wide as she looked at Benn, still sprawled on the ground.

The old man was weak and wanted forgiveness.

Bolton did not want it to be this way. He had wanted to meet the evil man who abandoned him and his mother. He thought he would seem like Hephaestus to him, powerful and in need of being stopped, that killing him would be a blessing on all Mirmina. But instead he found an old man and a true coward. And somehow that made it harder. Benn was not worth his anger.

Bolton shook his head and tore through the crowd.

7

MALACHI

I place My hands on the Ground, and the Crops Grow. They need no Water, no Tending, Only My hands.

THE dawn crept in like a dying thing. The light crawled over the horizon and touched the rocky walls that bordered the Resistance Headquarters. Just beyond that was a troop of travelers. They wore hooded cloaks, the hems skirting the ground, gathering dust. Their heads were down as they walked as if the rising sun would burn them. The shade of the great tree where they once lived had left many of them with milky white skin, unused to the heat of Dustpath's desert air.

They had traveled on little food or water from their home after the darkness had attacked it. A few faces and hands remained blackened by the permanent soot. They had tried washing it away in the waters of Wyvek, but the dark stuff had affixed itself to their being.

After many days of hiding out in Wyvek, finding that the city had been abandoned, they could not remain there any longer. There was no sustenance there, and the water was brackish.

They had seen the lightning over the horizon, and they knew it did not come from any natural source. That is how they came to the hidden door of the Rebel Resistance. The hooded folk flocked to the entrance and overwhelmed the gatekeeper.

Malachi lifted his hooded head. "Please, we know you are Elementals. We require safe harbor until the danger to our home has passed."

Malachi's blue eyes, like crystals peered down at the gate-keeper. Age wrinkled his face, and his white hair and beard contrasted with his dark brows only peppered with white hairs. Folds of skin gathered under his eyes and created soft pillows of flesh.

The gatekeeper gazed upon the multitude of people at the entrance and was unaware that hundreds of others waited beyond the rocks. "A few miles ahead of here is Lumina. I'm sure you and your people can find decent lodging there," Fer said, knowing full well that Lumina's inns were full and that people slept in the streets.

Malachi shook his head. "My people need food, water, and rest. We can't bear another day's journey. Please, we have sparklings, and we are farmers by nature. We can tend to your fields and harvest food to earn our stay."

"I'm sorry. You'll have to move on."

Malachi stepped forward, and the others, heads still bowed followed him.

Fer gripped his spear, but Malachi did not flinch nor did he back away. He gazed at the gatekeeper as if puzzled by his reaction.

Keeping his spear pointed toward Malachi, Fer took a javelin from against the rocky wall behind him and threw it over the entrance.

The wooden javelin clamored in the distance, and feet marched toward the entrance. Arrows, ready to loose, pointed at the travelers. Jin stepped forward from atop the rocky wall and peered down at their guests. Sara and Bolton watched the commotion as the fighters raised their arrows at the newcomers.

Malachi alone looked up to greet him. "We mean no harm, but I can't suffer my people to die out here."

"We'll send food," Jin shouted from above. He could see the hundreds in his flock, waiting beyond the rocks. "But I'm afraid your people can't stay here. We don't have the room."

"We have no place to stay. Our home was attacked. We need lodging as well as food."

Cree leaned toward his Commander and whispered into his ear.

"Dustpath is in ruins," Jin said, "but some of the buildings still stand and can provide shade and limited comfort until you can move on. We'll give you enough food to last a couple of days if you ration it, but that's all I can afford you. If you need escorts, my soldiers can lead you to Dustpath."

"I thank you for your kindness," Malachi said, defeated. He backed away, and Fer relaxed his weapon.

"We should go," Sara said. "They may know something about Farah and the others."

"The people of Tosia were long gone by the time we got there," Bolton said. "They might not know anything."

"It doesn't hurt to try."

Jin and a few of his men escorted Malachi and his followers through Dustpath. On their backs, they carried large sacks of food. Far to the west, the dust had uncovered the ruins. They set the sacks down.

The barren land stretched out for miles. Malachi did not look pleased. No ordinary farming could make this land fertile again.

"You are Earth Elementals," Jin said.

"We do not use our elements. It is against nature," Malachi said.

Jin knelt and concentrated. From the earth sprouted a fig tree. It grew twice its size in less than a minute and bore ripe fruits as if it had been growing all winter. Jin rose. "That's all I can do, but your people number into the hundreds. Just think of how much food you could grow here. You can craft wells for water and irrigate the land."

Malachi thought about Jin's proposal as his people dragged their feet in the heat. "We don't use our elements."

The two groups parted.

"Wait!" Sara fought her way to Malachi. "We want to talk to you."

THE people of Tosia took refuge in the ruined buildings of Dustpath. They cooked lizards over a fire. The food the Resistance had provided was being rationed out to supplement the lizard-meat.

Malachi sat with Sara and Bolton inside one of the ruined buildings.

"What is it that you have to tell me?" Malachi asked.

"We were separated from our friends," Sara said, "and there aren't many people we can ask. They were last seen in

Tosia."

"No one walks through Tosia anymore."

"They were looking for someone," she said. "They're flying in a large chariot in the sky."

"The shadow?" Malachi asked.

"What?"

"There was a shadow. My people looked up, and they saw something that should have been a bird, but it couldn't be. It flew through the sky without wings."

"In what direction was it going?"

"South towards the city of Lumina."

Sara saw a woman pull the meat from a lizard and feed it to the baby cradled in her arms.

"Are your people used to eating meat?" Sara asked.

"No," Malachi said. "We are used to eating from the earth and the Great Tree, but here we have no choice."

"But you do have a choice," Bolton said.

"The path you lead," Malachi said. "Although I agree with you, I can't ask my people to do that. It is abhorrent to them."

"It would be to save your people," Sara said. "They'll die out here in the desert without food, and Lumina is overfull. I doubt the markets can stay stocked. You are Earth Elementals. You can supply enough food to feed all of Mirmina."

"That is not our place."

"It is exactly your place," Sara said. "It is what you were meant to do. This place used to be the home of your ancestors. Nature didn't send the winds and the rain and the heat to destroy your crops. That was something unnatural. It was the same darkness that attacked Tosia."

"How would you know that?"

"Your people had a history that was forgotten, and I can

prove it to you once I find my friends."

Malachi listened to her words with eager ears. They sounded genuine. He looked at his people.

For days, they had suffered on the road from Tosia, and for days, they had thirsted and hungered in the streets of Wy-vek. Many had left Tosia without money or clothing, their valuables dripping with black soot. They were sick and dying. Something needed to change.

THE sun retired from the sky, and the desert winds, unhin-dered by vegetation, chilled the weary travelers.

Children burrowed their heads into the arms of their par-ents, and those without parents burrowed their heads into the sand.

Malachi looked over his people. He was unable to sleep.

He had the power to save them in his hands. The vines grew above his palms into the air. His father had taught him to hide it, but he couldn't stop.

Since he was a boy, he couldn't suppress his element like the others. His father had told him it was important he be like everyone else. "They have beliefs, son. Beliefs that scare them."

Malachi did not hold those same beliefs, but he respected his people. He only voiced their principles because his people needed that security. It would be difficult to turn them away from it. There were others like him who could not suppress their elements.

After days of struggle and starvation, Malachi could not patronize his people with their beliefs any longer. He had to think of what was best for them and that was their survival. *What would their beliefs matter if they did not live to pass them on?*

As the vines grew, they sprouted tiny, red grapes. Malachi

marveled at them. He set the vines on the ground. The roots dug into the sand and pierced the dark earth beneath.

THE sun warmed the sands. Between two ruined buildings, the grape vines grew, trailing the ground like the veins of the earth.

A young boy and his friends approached the vines. The boy plucked a grape and held it into the air. The children marveled at it and kept their eyes glued to the raised grape against the sun.

Like a victory run, the young boy, grape pinched between his finger and thumb, hand extended to the sky, ran back to where the others settled.

Malachi sat among his people, his legs folded. His eyes were pensive.

The young boy ran up to him.

Malachi looked up.

The boy tossed the grape into his lap.

Malachi took the grape between his finger and thumb and turned it in the light. "Do you know how this came to grow in the desert?"

The young boy shook his head.

"This power," Malachi said, "is in all of us."

He stood and threw the grape into the sand. The people scrambled to get it.

"We have journeyed long, away from our home. One more day without food, without water, and we will die. The Resistance gave us sustenance, but it will only last so long. If we are to survive, we must find the strength within ourselves."

Malachi sat back down in the sand.

Someone had eaten the grape.

All was silent until voices rose to a roar and deafened the

whistling of the wind through the ruins.

Someone from the group stepped away.

He stood in the center and faced Malachi. He looked around, seeing the people bicker and doubt. Kneeling, he placed his hands on the ground.

This did not escape the attention of Malachi. He had known the man well. His name was Dorsey, and he had dabbled in his element, like Malachi, unable to keep it suppressed. Now, he stood before him, a beacon among the doubters.

Energy ran through the ground as Dorsey placed his hands deep into the sands. Roots came up over his palms and up his arms.

The people stopped their chatter and fell into silence.

Dorsey stood and backed away. He controlled the branches as they rose into the sky. Leaves and fruits grew from the limbs of the small tree until the fruits matured to ripeness. The plums darkened until they were almost black.

Dorsey approached the tree and plucked one of the fruits. He tossed it into the crowd, and the people gasped.

An elderly man caught it. The man looked at the plum and turned it in his hands.

Children peered over the man's shoulder as he marveled at the fruit.

His mouth became wider than his eyes, and he bit into the fruit.

The people stared as the dark juices ran down his arm and stained the sleeve of his hooded cloak. They rushed to the tree and pulled the fruits from the branches until the tree was bare. They ate the fruits to the pits, which fell to the sands.

The juices stained their sleeves and purpled their palms. But the tree could not feed them all.

Malachi looked over the crowd, at the people washed

over with violet juices and the others licking their lips at the fresh smell of plums.

Dorsey, exhausted, knelt in front of the tree.

Malachi rose and clapped him on the shoulder. "This," Malachi shouted, "is our legacy." From his feet, a suffusion of green swept across the sand.

Some of the people tried to back away from the invading greenery, but it washed over them as rapidly as water rushing from a dam. Others knelt, trying to summon their elements. Some were successful. Others had suppressed their elements for so long, they had forgotten them.

Trees, vegetation, and fruits rose from the earth in a great rush. The barren, sandy plain turned green. Vines crept up the ruins and along the ground.

The travelers became exhausted and rested among the fresh grasses.

Malachi looked over his people and smiled.

8

THE GROWING LAND

*Our Children will not Question their Powers. They will not know a
Time without Them.*

SARA awoke to the sound of marching.

The Resistance fighters trained on the field, far from
Sara's tent, but the barren earth offered no buffer for the
sound.

The rocky earth could grow no crops. The Resistance
would send fighters, dressed in common clothes to purchase
food from Lumina, but Lumina's markets were running out
of stocks.

Ships no longer came in from Caleena to re-stock their
wares. By mid-morning, the marketplace in Lumina was
empty of all stores. People, too afraid to venture to other parts,
were going hungry in the streets of the city.

Sara lifted the folds of the tent and blinked against the sun. She looked over to Bolton's tent and wondered if he still slept.

A Resistance fighter walked down the row of tents. He handed Sara a loaf of bread. "You can get water from the lake."

The lake was miles from her tent.

Every other morning, they sat at the long tables for a breakfast of wild rice and dried fruit with honey mead, but this morning was different.

Jin was unused to leadership. Knowing Lumina's supplies were low, he should have rationed the food, but he had failed in that necessary wisdom. He had given the bulk of their supply to the wandering people of Tosia.

Sara did not see the fighter leave any bread at Bolton's tent. She wondered where he was.

She walked to the lake to get water to quench her thirst and wash her face.

Behind the rows of tents was a rip in the land. Over the edge was a cavernous vault, the bottom of which was hidden in darkness. A rocky path led over the rip and to the other side of the rocky plain. Water washed onto the rocks below. The spray was warm.

It was now mid-morning, and the fighters had started their combat training. The clash of blunt steel echoed in the distance.

The land was more uneven on the other side of the rip. In the expanse was greenery, oddly placed among the barren rock.

Through the trees, Sara could see the lake, greenish blue with short grasses growing from its shores. The lake was small and hidden by the trees. Behind it was a tall rock wall. The tops of the trees prevented Sara from seeing where the wall ended against the sky.

She walked to the edge of the lake and knelt by the water.

Across from her, on the other side of the lake, Benn was perched at the shore. Water dripped from his light-yellow beard.

Sara didn't acknowledge him.

The water was cool in her hands and smooth through her fingers. She cupped her hands and, leaning over the lake, brought the water to her face.

The water washed over her. She felt its pull inside her. Alive and pushing against the dam. It dripped from her fingertips.

When she opened her eyes, a shadow draped her in darkness.

She looked up.

Benn stood over her.

She backed away from him. "What do you want?"

Benn knelt. "I want you to talk to my son. I need him to hear me out."

Sara shook her head. "Why should I help you? There's nothing you could say to him."

Besides what Bolton had told her about him, this man had tricked her into letting him aboard the Chariot. He had lied to the son he raised in pursuit of the one he abandoned. Sara could not imagine what he thought he could gain from a talk with Bolton.

Benn sighed. His head was bent low. After a moment, he walked away, discouraged by her silence.

Sara was relieved he had gone.

She stared into the water. It did not move. She sat at the

lake for hours staring at it, willing it to splash, swirl, do something.

She closed her eyes. She could feel the weight of the water. She could sense its nature. It was part of her.

Bolton tore through the trees, breaking Sara's concentration. "You have to see this!"

If she had not heard his voice ring out, Sara would have thought, at a glance, that Benn had returned.

HOLDING Sara's hand, Bolton led her to the entrance of Resistance Headquarters.

Atop the boulder, they fell to the ground.

Forty travelers from Tosia stood at the entrance with sacks of food. Some carried woven baskets of fruits and vegetables. Children held up carrots and sticks of celery.

Malachi was at the head of the group. "As a thank you for saving my people."

A thick root grew from the ground and over the edge of the boulder. Jin descended upon it until his feet touched the rocky ground at the entrance.

He stood in front of Malachi.

"You were right," Malachi said. "My people need to harness their potential." He looked up at Sara who stood at the edge of the cliff with Bolton by her side. "We've been suffering for too long."

Jin patted Malachi on the back and nodded to the guard who in turn pulled the rope, releasing the stone wall. The boulder moved against the rocks below until the path was clear, and the people of Tosia moved through, carrying with them the sacks and baskets of food.

JIN sat with Malachi in the large tent. They sipped on the

juice of the oranges Malachi and his people had brought.

The tent used to be Vassal's. Awaiting his leader's return, Jin had left the tent as it was when Vassal had left. Above the bed was a dagger, its tip stained with blood. In the corner of the room was a table with four chairs.

Malachi lifted his cup and took a long, slow gulp. He placed the cup back down with a thump.

Jin leaned forward in his chair. "Your people can stay as long as you like. The land here is rocky and barren, but you may be able to make it grow again."

Malachi shook his head. "These are not all my people. We will make the travel back to Dustpath. We have built our home there now."

"That's good." Jin took a sip of the juice.

"We only require one thing. We need protection." Malachi's eyes widened as he gave Jin a knowing look.

"You need manpower?" Jin asked.

"We are a placid people, but I understand now that that is not wise. I can't ask my people to fight. They are not warriors. But for the price of food, I was hoping we could reach an agreement."

"You'll supply us with food if I supply you with fighters?"

"Not many. We aren't going to war. We only need men to patrol our borders, to make sure no one attacks us."

"You'll bring enough food to feed my army."

"We have enough food to feed both my people and yours, if not all Mirmina," Malachi said. "We need only men to help us to secure our land."

"I think that could be arranged."

Jin and Malachi shook hands.

SARA and Bolton helped the people of Tosia and the Resistance fighters as they stored the sacks and baskets of food.

The people were weary from carrying the food to the Resistance. Malachi had only taken those who were weak in their element or had not yet mastered it. The others bore the burden of using the energy of their elements to keep the land fertile in Dustpath.

A young boy played with his friends after the work was done. They let their hoods fall from their heads and threw an apple back and forth to one another.

The apple flew to the young boy. It hit him in the chest and fell to the ground. The boy's hands were pinned to his sides. He stood as if in a trance. His eyes were large and fixed on the ground.

Roots ripped through the rocky earth, traveled around the boy's legs, and enveloped his torso. They tightened around him.

The boy screamed.

Bolton rushed over to him. "Calm down."

The boy shook his head.

"Listen. Close your eyes."

The boy looked at the wide eyes of the people who had gathered around, his own people, unable to help him. Gasps rang through the crowd.

The roots squeezed the boy's waist.

"Don't look at them. Close your eyes, and listen to my voice," Bolton instructed. "Can you do that?"

The boy nodded, took a deep breath, and closed his eyes.

"That's good. Now, listen to my voice. Block out everything else."

He nodded.

"Okay," Bolton said. "Now, I want you to imagine the

roots drawing away from you. I want you to feel the energy curling back inside you."

The boy's eyes screwed shut.

"You can do it."

The roots loosened their grip on the boy.

The boy looked around. Relief rang on his face.

Once the boy was free, Bolton raised up his hand. The boy high-fived him and grinned.

Sara looked on as Bolton comforted the child.

Benn was watching too.

She did not know what the old man was thinking, but he had an urgency in his eyes. Sara did not like to see it there.

As the boy concentrated, the roots recoiled into the earth. The rocky ground remained upturned where the roots had busted through. Rich, red soil lie beneath.

Exhausted, the boy sat on the ground where he stood.

Bolton patted him on the back. "It used to happen to me when I was a kid. You'll learn to control it."

Malachi watched from the entrance of the tent. He walked over to Bolton as he stood from the ground. "My people could use a teacher. Many of them do not yet know how to use their elements. We could use your help."

Sara waited for Bolton's answer. She could see Benn out of the corner of her eye. Benn's urgency was so apparent, it seemed as if an invisible rope was pulling him in.

Bolton did not like the company of the Resistance fighters. He would find any excuse to leave. "Sure. I guess I know a few things that might help."

Sara followed Benn's eyes to the young boy.

He was playing again as if nothing had happened. He was happy.

Sara could not help but recall Benn's relationship with

Balin, how he helped him handle his element. She wondered if Bolton remembered more about his father than he admitted.

Bolton and Malachi shook hands.

Part of Sara was angry. In all the time that they had been safe in Resistance Headquarters, Bolton made no effort to help her with her element. He was the first person to help her call Water. Yet now, it was like he had forgotten.

Still, she had never taken the time to tell him about it.

At times, she felt that it was her burden to bear, that she had no right to ask.

But then again, Bolton never asked, never offered. She wondered if he cared now, or if time had changed things.

It was harder to talk to him.

"What's wrong?" Bolton stood in front of her.

The people of Dustpath, led by their leader, walked back to the entrance.

"It's nothing," Sara said.

9

THE WIND MADE CHILD

Our Fear is that One day, Children will take Their Gifts for Granted. And that They will Anger the gods with Their Lack of Appreciation.

THE wind hissed under the door as the baby turned in Spire's arms. Spire was at a loss. She wanted to believe her touch could sooth the child like magic, but Canace continued to cry despite Spire's efforts. In truth, the baby cried when she wanted to cry, and when she cried the Winds raged all day until she fell asleep.

Spire was exhausted trying to calm the child.

Gusts battered against the windows so at any moment the glass panes might give way and come crashing across the worn, wooden floors.

"Shh . . ." Spire hushed the child, but to no avail.

Decca had crossed the training field to help Rodan and

Farah find rooms for themselves and their friends. The task would prove not too difficult as the trainers and apprentices had abandoned Element when Morica Council started to make repeated visits. Element had become deserted except for the few souls who stayed in the upper rooms of Element and kept to themselves.

Years ago, when Spire was a young girl, Element was thriving. Apprentices flooded in, and the trainers numbered into the hundreds. She still remembered the feeling of smallness when she arrived, barely five years old, clenching her father's warm, calloused hand.

She looked up at his weathered face with wide, scared eyes as a woman, only two feet taller than her escorted them around Element and showed them the field and the room where Spire would sleep.

But Spire hadn't wanted her father to leave her in this place. She wanted to return to their farm outside the city. She wanted to help her father tend the garden and look after the goats. She didn't want to be here among strangers.

Her father had insisted. This was the place for her, among her own where she could learn to control her element and not be ruled by it.

He had no way of raising an Elemental child. His mother could call Wind, but he was no Elemental nor had his deceased wife been able to manipulate the elements. She had died the day Spire was born.

So, a year before Spire and her father were escorted through the halls of Element, he knew this would be her destiny.

They were in the heat among the grassy plain spread out before her father's land. The dry heat favored not even a gentle breeze.

As her father rested among the grasses, Spire ran, sweeping her hand through the tall blades of grass. The Wind picked up with hasty quickness, cooling the sweat on her father's neck.

He looked up at his young daughter. Her eyes were closed, and the gusts swept in a whirlwind around her. He walked up to her and put his hands on her shoulders.

Spire's eyes popped open, and the Wind stopped, leaving the grasses swaying.

The look of concern on her father's face was something that, as a child, Spire could not quite understand.

As the breezes lighted her fingertips, she could feel the energy welling up inside her.

As the months went by, her energy only strengthened until she would wake in the night, the energy too great to bear. It would burst from her like the contents of a bag overfilled. The Wind would rush around, shattering her small window and racking her bed against the wall.

Her father would rush in to sooth her, but the Wind would not calm until the energy left her body, and she fell asleep.

That was when her father decided Element was the only place for her.

Spire watched as a tall man with dark hair passed her. He had a weapon of steel at his side, not like the blades her father used to chop wood on the farm, but a longer, thinner blade forged in the unnatural Fire.

She stared as the man disappeared around the corner.

The small woman smiled above her and opened a door in the long hallway. The room had a large window and a bed in the center with chairs for visitors.

Spire's tears came and, in an instance, she felt her father's warm embrace, yet she could not see him through the tears blurring her vision.

In Element, Spire grew to control her power, and one day she was called to her father's bedside. He was dying.

No longer the young girl that she once was, she sat beside him. She held his worn hand, now growing cold. That was the day she told him she would leave with Decca to retrieve the Water Sphere, that it might be the way to stop Hephaestus.

Her father looked up at her with weathered eyes. His once dark hair was grayed and thinning. His wrinkled hand reached up to caress her cheek.

"You're special," he had told her. "You can do so much for this world, but that doesn't mean you have to martyr yourself to it."

She tried to teach Sara the same thing. She looked down at her child, and the Wind battered at the windows. She worried for her future.

FARAH and her company had settled in that night. She and Rodan visited Spire and the baby the next day.

Spire feared the unnatural Winds would send Morica their way, and she would not only be endangering the life of her friends, but also the life of her newborn child.

She could not stand the thought.

Decca and Sev had gone to the marketplace to get food to stock the Chariot for their trip to Breeze.

Spire's body was numb from lying in bed.

"To breathe fresh air," Spire said.

Rodan went to the window and placed his hands on the hinges.

"No," Spire said. "Something could fly in and hurt the baby."

Branches torn from trees by the Wind had hit the window and threatened to break the glass. Decca had closed the shutters, leaving the small bedroom dark.

"Do you want me to get you a book from the library?" Farah asked.

Spire shook her head. "I need to go outside, stretch my legs."

"Here, I'll take her," Farah said.

Spire was tentative.

"If she gets cranky, I can give her right back."

Spire sat up in bed, cradling Canace in her arms.

She rose from the mattress and placed the baby in Farah's arms. Farah nestled the child close to her chest. She cooed at the baby and made exaggerated faces. Orka leaned over Farah's shoulder to get a better look at the child.

Canace laughed and reached up for Farah's face. The Winds calmed, and the low-hanging branches of the tree at the lake only skirted the water.

Spire breathed a sigh. "How are you doing that?"

"I don't know. Intuition, I guess."

Spire frowned.

"Oh, no, I didn't mean . . ." Farah said. "Spire, you're a great mom."

"It's okay." Spire placed her palm on the baby's crown and kissed her forehead.

She walked outside the cottage and blinked in the light of the sun. Dew wet the grass. She wrapped her white robes around her so that her body could not be chilled by the cool morning breeze. A few wisps of her dark hair played across her face.

Spire closed her eyes

Winds ripped through the forest toward Caleena as she

screamed inside herself. Once the energy was released, the stress of the past and the impending days eased itself into a small corner of her mind.

She sighed.

She looked out over the forest as the trees settled after the Wind. Black smoke rose into the air. In a flash, the trees in the distance were ablaze.

"Oh, no," Spire breathed the words. Her slippers padded against the soft field to the door of the cabin. She wrenched the door open and tore through the living room to the bedroom. "We have to go, now!"

Farah was still cradling Canace.

Spire took her from her arms.

"What's wrong?" Rodan asked.

"Grab your bags and canteens. We have to get out of here."

"Wait, what's happening?" Farah asked.

"The Protector is coming."

Farah and Rodan ran to their rooms and grabbed their bags and canteens.

Farah banged on Rai's door. "Rai!" She slapped the door with her opened palm. "Hey!"

Rai opened the door, her sword in her right hand. "What?"

"The Protector."

That was all Rai needed. She rushed to her bedside to grab her bag, and she was out the door.

Rodan ran through the halls and shouted a warning to all who remained. "The Protector is coming."

Hearing Rodan's warning, Atrus and Pentagon stepped outside their rooms and looked at each other from across the hallway.

Vassal stood in the hall. "What's taking you fools so long? They'll leave us here to fend for ourselves. I don't want to take on another Protector, do you?"

Atrus and Pentagon got their things and joined Vassal in the hallway.

The three worn-out villains kept up with the others in the entrance hall. They were on their way out with the trickle of occupants that had remained in Element. Their feet thundered down the steps.

"We have to find Decca." Spire cradled Canace against her chest. She had wrapped the child in white linen.

The baby cried, and the Wind picked up to a roar.

"We will," Farah shouted over the Wind.

From the steps, they ran into town. Spire kept her head low against the Wind. People came out of their shops and houses.

"The Protector is coming!"

Feet thundered through the streets. People panicked, throwing their belongings out of second-story windows to meet them on the streets.

"Decca!" Spire shouted, clenching her crying baby in her arms.

Thatch ran into Rodan who headed the group.

He stopped.

"Morica . . . chariots . . . on the horizon," Thatch gasped. He had run all the way from the hill.

"We have a bigger problem." Rodan patted him on the shoulder, encouraging him to turn and run back. "The Protector is coming from Caleena."

Thatch could not ask questions for lack of breath. He just ran, slower now after he had exerted himself. He fell back behind Rodan.

"Morica and a Protector?" Atrus shook his head. "What a day."

At the word that Morica was on its way, Vassal placed his hand over the hilt of his sword.

As they ran through the market, Spire wondered where Decca had gone. Everyone was running now. She thought Decca might be among the crowd.

The Winds were rough, and they fought against them to get to the hill. The townspeople ran to the ships docked on the beach. Feet dug into the sands, and legs burned.

The smoke coming from the forest thickened until the skies were almost black. The tops of the trees were ablaze, and the fire was spreading.

Spire looked back. The trees swayed to give way to something big. The noise of the crowd, the shouts, the hammering of feet, became dull in her ears. Tears filled her eyes. "Decca!"

But in the crowd, she could not see his face nor the flash of his bright hair.

The crowd split away from them as the townspeople ran to the northwest shore. They exited the town gates and neared the hill.

10

KIN

I need to Memorialize this Time, so that the Story of Their Coming will be Remembered.

"THIS is the time before the storm, when the world was building upon the energy of the past in droplets like rain. And the young and the old alike dressed in skins, hunted and gathered their food across the plain, having no home.

"It was a time when the sun, and the moon, and the stars spoke," said the storyteller, his audience a small group of children. Adults stood by to listen before passing on.

"In this time, the world was just beginning, and the people then didn't look like we do now. They were born like animals with sharper teeth and abler hands. They had no religion, nor politics, only life and death."

The storyteller wore a tattered garment dyed deep red. The torn robe had been dyed long ago, but the dye was so rich, it had stained his light brown arms, and when he lifted them to gesture as he told his story, the sleeves rolled back, revealing the burgundy pigment of his skin.

His beard was black and oiled. His dress and appearance was so outlandish that new-comers to the market thought he was a traveler as well. But he had been a fixture in Elementa for years and had maintained a tan and dyed beard to achieve a more eccentric look.

As he told his story, his eyes were wide. He was possessed in the telling: his arms flying out madly and his teeth shining in the sun.

The sky was clear, and the marketplace bustled with people carrying gossip with them like a well-worn coat. The streets were more crowded after the attack on Caleena. While others fled to Lumina, a vast many more took to Elementa.

The displaced people flocked to the inns and hostiles of the town, and others, unable to afford lodging, congested the alleyways and the narrow streets of the city.

The large farms and fields bordering the town provided enough food for all who remained, and unlike in Lumina, the marketplace was as stocked as it had ever been.

Decca and Sev moved through the marketplace and picked up food and supplies for the trip to Breeze. They filled their bags with cheeses, bread, barley, mushrooms, and dried fruits. Decca shouldered his bag once it was full.

Decca missed his home in Caleena. Of his mother, he remembered one thing that he had separated from all his warm and despairing memories of her. She told him when he was a child, after his father died and before his brother left, that what she was about to tell him would help him all the days of his life.

"Don't live life like you're always running toward something," he heard her say. "Find someone who loves you, and be something that you can understand."

He imagined that as she said these words, she was not only saying them to him, but to his father.

Decca had lived by her words. He tried not to lust for money or glory.

But he had made mistakes. Once he thought that he should be better, that he should make a difference. In that, he nearly lost everything, his freedom, and the woman he loved.

From then on, he had not made the mistake of living any other way than simply living.

He was no hero to anyone but his family, and he preferred it that way.

Carrying five canteens each, strapped onto their bags, he and Sev walked to the communal well outside the town.

Exhausted, Sev put down his bag as soon as they made it to the well. He breathed in quick, shallow breaths.

Decca, who was used to such work, was breathing evenly and effortlessly, needing no time to rest. With the rope pulley, he lowered the water bucket down into the well. Once the bucket was submerged in water, he pulled it back up.

He took a canteen from the side of his bag and dipped it into the water of the bucket. Once the canteen was full, he capped it and moved on to the next.

Sev, still gasping for breath, sat on the stone ledge surrounding the water. He reached a hand up to signal to Decca. "Hey . . . you can take a minute."

Decca looked down at Sev. He wanted to get the canteens filled and get back to his family. "I don't need one."

"I know, I know . . . but just sit down, will you?"

Decca sat beside his less able companion.

He noticed when they were fighting the guards back in Caleena that Sev had speed, but he lacked strength.

Decca was the opposite. What he lacked in swiftness, he made up for in brute force. His muscles never tired, but his large stature and build made him slow.

"You're a good man," Sev said. "You love your family, and you're a good friend." Sev blinked against the sun.

"Where are you going with this?" Decca was grateful that Sev had helped them get out of Caleena, and he had grown to trust him, but he did not like the strange way Sev stared at him. After all the barking Sev did, telling him to get back to work, he wondered why the man praised him now.

"I wanted to tell you a story."

Decca was quiet. He did not understand why Sev was trying to flatter him or tell him stories. He just wanted to get back to Spire. The longer they stayed in Elementa, the more he worried about Morica guards and Sphere Protectors. This was no time for stories.

But Sev did not seem to be of the same opinion. "It's about a man who left his family to join the Resistance," he said. "His father had died, and he left his mother to raise his little brother, barely twelve years old. He told his mother he was leaving because of duty, because he had to follow in his father's footsteps, but truthfully, he left because he couldn't deal with it anymore. He couldn't be the man of the house.

"So, he shrugged off his responsibility and joined the Resistance. Years later, and growing more regretful each day, the man returned to his home to find his mother and brother gone. He discovered that his mother had died, and his brother was in the wind."

Decca leaned forward, eagerness in his eyes. It was as if

Sev was holding up two identical paintings and asking him to find the discrepancy.

"He stayed with the Resistance for many more years, never raising a family, not feeling worthy of one, scorning many lovers and refusing to settle down.

"Then the Council rose, and he joined, eager to prove that he was worth something . . . but he found no more purpose in that than he did in joining the Resistance.

"He needed to find his little brother to make things right between them.

"He heard that a man by his brother's name was living in Caleena. So, he asked to be stationed there so that he could find this man."

Decca rose from his seat. He turned to face Sev and towered over him, blocking the sun. His mind raced with all the reasons for the coincidence, but there was only one.

"I took the name Sev when I joined the Resistance. I wanted to forget about my past. My true name is Shilo."

Decca knew that name. It was his father's name. It was his brother's name, the brother who left him and his mother among the thieves and beggars of Lumina.

Shilo stood from his seat on the ledge, but Decca's shadow still engulfed him. "I wanted to see what kind of man you had become. I wanted to make sure that I hadn't ruined you."

Decca was still shocked. "You weren't around to ruin me," he breathed.

He looked at the man like he was a puzzle that he had struggled over for days. Decca had often dreamed in his childhood of his father's return, of his brother's return, and it always filled a place inside him. But this was nothing like his dreams. Instead, he felt a gulf that he had long forgotten widening until the emptiness itself left him callused and confused.

"Where did they bury our mother?"

The question took him aback. "Our mother." For years, it had been "his mother," his dead mother who was the only one who loved him. After she died, there was no "our," "we" only "I," "me." And, however unfulfilling, Decca had taken it as a simple fact of life.

"They didn't bury her," Decca said. "We couldn't afford the burial so they burned her and spread her ashes out to the sea."

He said this without feeling. His eyes did not become glassy nor did his voice tremble. It was not as if he could have saved her. He had cried hard for weeks over her, and all his feelings could not make her breathe again.

After his mother had died, Decca, still a child, went to live in Elementa as the groundskeeper's assistant. When he was older, the groundskeeper died. Decca found the old man in his bed, stiff and unmoving. Only fourteen at the time, Decca buried him without telling anyone. Like Decca, the man had no family.

Decca would become the next groundskeeper except no one would bury him. They would burn him and spread his ashes like they did his mother.

But then, he saw Spire.

He spotted her training on the field in Element. Her dark hair was long and contrasted against her white skin. She was just starting to master her element.

He loved her even then in those childlike moments where he would watch her from across the field without her knowing.

As he grew older, he began to dream of his own family,

one that he would grow and nurture.

It was hard for him to be angry with Shilo. He thought he had died long ago like his father. He was more shocked than angry. The thought of seeing his brother again had never crossed his mind. Now, his mind was alive with thoughts of reconcile. Would his dead father rise out of the ground to meet him?

He could only think of one thing to do.

Decca extended his hand. "I'm glad you came back."

Shilo who had been bracing himself for the fall, stared at Decca's hand.

"Are you going to take it?"

Shilo extended his hand tentatively, and then with more confidence, shook his brother's hand which engulfed his.

"Now let's get these canteens filled," Decca said.

They filled the remaining canteens in silence. Decca could feel the weight of the air around them, and he knew Shilo could too. Once the last canteen was filled, they headed for the Chariot, the silence weighing them down like a wet blanket.

Outside the town walls, they had not heard the roar of the crowd or seen the smoke rising above the trees.

They approached the large structure on the hill at the coast of town.

The Chariot had gone through a few modifications. Thatch had added mounted machine guns atop the roof and loaded them with bullets from Atrus's stockpile.

He had learned everything he needed to know about guns in books from the old world. Since the day Morica chariots unloaded bullets onto them, Thatch had poured over the books and studied every detail until he could understand the mechanics.

Decca and Shilo stood atop the hill. Smoke climbed from the trees and fire burned the tops like a red carpet, but another problem arose.

Morica chariots sailed above the sea and headed for the town.

The people below ran like ants through the town streets, and the wind kicked up as if it was trying to help the people forward.

Upon taking in the disaster, Decca took not a moment more to think. He dropped his bag and the canteens and ran for the town gate.

Shilo followed in close pursuit, keeping pace with his brother as he hulled his bulky mass toward the town entrance.

People flooded out of the gates like water from a broken dam. Among them, Spire clinched her baby to her breast. She looked around, not seeing Decca beyond the green hills.

Farah beckoned her to run, and they ran toward the Chariot.

Her face was the first Decca saw as they came over the rolling hill. Her white nightgown was bright in the sun and whipped in the wind as the baby against her chest cried.

At that moment, all those dire thoughts that came rushing into his head despite his desire to stop them were replaced by hopeful ones.

Decca ran up to them and hugged the child and its mother. Both wept with relief.

It was short-lived as the chariots grew closer, and the smoke grew blacker.

They ran for the Chariot and into the engine room.

Once they were all inside, Thatch slammed his fist against the button beside the hatch door. The large, metal ramp lifted from the ground and sealed itself to the frame.

Decca had his arms around his wife as if he could protect her and his child from all that was bad in the world.

Decca did not understand.

After every mistake he made in pride, he was punished. But now, he had lived the simple life that his mother had wanted. Yet, he had made no mistake, and his family was now in danger. He had made himself a mere insignificant presence in a world much larger, and now it was as if he was called to stand and speak. It had been so long, he did not know how.

He looked down at his child, nestled in his wife's arms.

She could never have a simple life, which meant neither could her father.

His mother had wanted him to live a life that he could understand. Now, cradling his wife and child in his arms, knowing that, for them, he would have to rise to something greater, there was nothing more understandable than that.

11

A MAN

They were Our First Teachers and I, one of Their First Students.

BOLTON'S skin was tanner now that he was traveling daily in the hot sun on Dustpath Road.

The people of Tosia were once again the people of Dustpath. They occupied the buildings that still stood like beacons in the sand. However, vegetation replaced much of the sand.

Malachi cautioned his people against allowing the plant life and vegetables to spread to the road. He feared travelers would see and invade upon their land. Instead, Malachi's people nestled among a circle of ruins near a dried up well.

Malachi's city was green among the gray.

Still, maintaining the greenery without the power of Elementals proved difficult. It had not rained on Dustpath in many years. The grounds were as dry as the roads and un-suited for sustainable vegetation.

But, with so many new Elementals with plenty of built up energy, the people of Dustpath thrived.

Malachi had wanted a well, but even with all their ener-gies combined, the most powerful among them could not move the earth deep enough to find water.

Without a source of water, they drank the juices of the fruits.

The soft grass felt strange against Bolton's feet after walk-ing on the firm sand. Every day, it took him a few hours before he adjusted to the atmosphere.

He could breathe easily, which made it harder to go back to Resistance Headquarters. But there was another reason he liked spending his days in Dusthpath: his father.

The old man had been stalking around watching him ever since he arrived. He could feel Benn's eyes on him everywhere he went.

Yet, he never dared follow him to Dustpath.

Sara didn't journey with him either.

They had sat together and talked. They met at dinner, but Bolton could still feel her distance like a gulf between them. He didn't know why it was there. He couldn't talk to her about it. He was afraid of her reasons.

As he took the long walks to Malachi's village, he often thought about what he could do to make it right, but he wasn't sure what he had done in the first place.

He had died.

That might be the crux of the issue. Sara had said so.

But he couldn't help that he had been gone. He couldn't turn back time and make different choices.

He had come back to life. Wasn't that enough?

THEY sat at the dinner table, stretched long across the plain.

Bolton reached for Sara's idle hand, but seeing his gesture out of the corner of her eye, she moved her hand onto her lap.

The Resistance fighters talked and laughed around them, but Sara and Bolton ate in silence.

Bolton felt that if he said anything it would only make it worse.

Once dinner was finished, Sara rose from the bench and took her plate. She reached for his, and Bolton grabbed her wrist.

"We need to talk," he whispered.

"Not now."

"At the lake."

The lake would be cleared. The fighters always washed up before dinner.

Sara nodded, taking his plate.

They walked to the lake together, both silent.

Bolton wanted to talk to her, but he had no idea what to say. He had wanted the walk to help him think of something before they made it to the lake, but he found himself struggling to find words for the journey instead of the destination.

He found none.

He resigned to ask her what was wrong, knowing that he thought he might be able to comfort her in the right way. He pushed back the leaves and allowed her to pass.

Sara sat by the coast.

Bolton settled down beside her. He watched her searching eyes as they looked across the water. Bolton handed her the paper and charcoal clenched in his hand. "I thought you should start up again."

Sara looked down at the items in her hands. "Thank

you."

"Since I've been back, all I wanted to do was to find you," Bolton said. The words fell out of him. *This isn't the way I wanted this to go. But it's too late.*

Sara looked up at him.

"And I kept getting caught up in things," he said. "Every obstacle that could present itself did, and I was left wondering if I would ever find you."

Bolton placed his hand over hers.

His head was down, looking at their hands intertwined. "When I found you out there in Omega Ray. In my head, I was saying *finally*. Now, everything is going to be okay because I found her. But I didn't for once think that you would have moved on, that you would have stopped thinking of me because you had three years of waiting, I'm sorry, not waiting, of thinking I was dead. And just after you accepted that, I was back. You were telling me back in Tosia that you don't know how to act around me, well, I don't know how to act around you either. I woke up, and I was only missing you for a few weeks, compared to the years you've had without me, and I'm still nervous as hell that I don't know you anymore. And the more I think of it, the worse it gets."

Sara listened to him until he started repeating himself and shaking his head. She placed her hand against his cheek.

"I don't want us to be strangers anymore," she said.

He hoped that her response would make him feel like things were mended, that they could continue where they left off, but Sara's answer made him feel like she anticipated more mending ahead of them.

Sara stared out into the water, and Bolton watched her gaze.

"It's your element, isn't it?" he asked. "It hasn't come

back."

Sara shook her head.

"You should come with me . . . when I help the children on Dustpath."

"I think I'd like that."

BOLTON woke with the morning. He exited his tent, shortly after Sara emerged from hers. It was like they were on the same plain again. He felt more connected to her.

After eating breakfast, they walked down Dustpath Road together.

Sara smiled at him.

Bolton could feel the warmth not only on his skin, but throughout his body.

He and Sara had journeyed many times together down this road.

Sara helped the children of Dustpath. Though she did not have her element, she remembered what Spire had taught her and carried those lessons on to them.

Bolton could tell the experience made her feel fulfilled.

She was happier.

In exchange for the lessons, Malachi offered Bolton and Sara the kindest hospitality, making sure they were well-fed and comfortable.

The people of Dustpath created living dwellings from the overhanging trees and vines. Soon the ruined buildings were blocked by trees, shrubbery, and vegetation.

There were fields of fruits and vegetables. The people harvested and carried them in large, woven baskets.

Jin had sent Resistance fighters to live among them and guard the land and the people. They had abandoned their tattered clothing for the robes of Tosia.

But the people stopped donning the hoods, and instead let them fall down their backs. Some lifted them to their heads, but not out of ceremony but to shield against the glaring sun when they were in the fields.

Large trees shaded the dedicated living areas.

The greenery was visible from the road.

FOR weeks, Bolton had been training a new apprentice, Shashi. Shashi's element matured not long ago, and instead of using the usual methods to repress it, her mother wanted Shashi to embrace her element as the others had so that she could be a benefit to the people.

Shashi was a reserved child, a product of her upbringing and her surroundings. She was also a quick and eager learner.

Malachi usually came to greet Sara and Bolton and ask if there was anything that they needed, but this time he had a request. "You are the Water Elemental?"

Sara nodded.

"Can you sense water beneath the ground?" Malachi asked.

Sara closed her eyes. She felt the pull of the water deep beneath the earth. It was alive and connected to her despite her lack of control over it.

She nodded with her eyes still closed. "But I can do nothing to bring it to the surface."

"That's alright," Malachi said. "Knowing it is there makes the enterprise less hopeless."

"You have another plan to retrieve it?" Bolton asked.

Malachi nodded.

"We will slowly use our elements to move the earth."

"That might take a long time," Sara said. "The waters rest deep in the ground. There is much pressure against the pull. They could be beneath many layers of rock."

"I appreciate your concern," Malachi said, "but my people do not have the energy to move the earth too rapidly. We must work together and do with what we have."

BOLTON knelt in the grass to talk to Shashi. She was beginning to get control over her element. Instead of suffusing a field with flowers and exhausting her energy, she was now able to control the growth, focusing on one or a few flowers at a time. Soon, she would be able to help her mother in the vegetable garden.

Before Bolton had taken her as an apprentice, Shashi would wake with thick vines and flowers covering her small cot and pinning her down to it. She would awaken panicked and call for her mother. She would have bouts of energy where her element would take over, and she would pass out from the effort.

Bolton had taught her how to be calm in the chaos. Only then would she be able to control her element.

As a young boy, Bolton's element had come to him suddenly. He was not with his mother or father, he was alone in a room in Omega Ray, and he was crying.

Lightning erupted in the distance beyond the cliff. There were no rain clouds in the gloomy night just the dark skies hanging over the city like mourning garb. The more he cried, the more the skies filled with Lightning until it reached a level beyond his control. His throat was raw, and he missed his mother. But his tears were also for his father. He had abandoned him.

He hadn't seen Benn approach. Nor had he heard his footsteps across the soft grass.

"I need to talk to you."

Bolton looked up.

His heart sank. His father had invaded his sanctuary. He glared into the man's crystal blue eyes until he saw his own reflection.

"I'll be right back," he said to his young apprentice.

Shashi nodded.

Benn followed him down the field.

Sara was across the field with three apprentices. She looked up and caught Bolton's eyes.

Bolton mouthed, "I'll be okay," as he walked away with Benn. This assurance did not seem to comfort her. She kept her eyes glued on Bolton.

Bolton and Benn stopped in the far field, out of hearing of the others.

"What do you want?" Bolton asked.

"You're a good trainer."

"I know that you didn't come all the way to Dustpath to say that."

"It's your brother," Benn said.

"What about him?"

"I left him on the island."

Bolton sighed and shook his head.

"He's very strong," Benn said, "but lacks direction. He needs someone who can help him control his element. I've seen how you are with these children. You can help him."

"And why can't *you* help him?" Bolton asked in a harsh whisper. "He's your responsibility."

"I know, but I can't face Abby."

"Abby?"

"His mother."

Bolton crossed his arms over his chest and looked at the ground.

"But you could go," Benn said. "Meet your brother. Help him."

Bolton stared at his father. He felt his hate like something hot inside him. "You're a coward."

"Don't be like me then."

12

THE PROMISE

*They wanted Us to Follow Them like Children. When we are Born,
Mothers and Fathers are like gods to us. As we Grow, we Must follow
Their Laws or Suffer the Consequences. But once we are Grown, we
start to Question Their Teachings and Their Laws.*

BOLTON walked with Sara back to Resistance Headquarters. He kept looking back to see if Benn was following them.

"Are you okay?" Sara touched his shoulder.

"Yeah."

"What happened back there . . . with your father?"

"It's nothing. The old man just doesn't know when to
quit."

Sara reached for his hand.

Bolton took hers, and they walked hand in hand until they

reached Resistance Headquarters.

Fighters moved back and forth across the field. Some walked to their tents. Others headed to the lake to wash up before dinner.

Jin approached Sara and Bolton.

"How are Malachi and his people?"

"They're stronger," Bolton said.

"Let Malachi know, if there is anything we can do for them, we are at their service."

Bolton nodded.

At dinner, Bolton pushed his food around on his plate. Frustrated he put down his fork and left the table.

Sara followed him.

"What is it?" she asked once she caught up with him. "You don't have to keep it bottled up."

Bolton stopped. He sighed and shook his head. "It's my father. Look, I just . . . I just need some time to think."

"Okay," Sara said.

"I'm sorry. I have a decision I have to make first."

"I can help you."

Bolton shook his head. "Go. Eat. After dinner, I'll tell you more."

Sara nodded and walked back to the table.

Bolton watched her go before making his way across the plain.

The nerve of his father to ask him to shoulder his responsibilities.

For years, under the watch of his uncle, Bolton had wondered if his father still loved him, if he thought about him and his mother, if he wondered if he was alright. But Benn had started a new family and forgot about them.

Now, he was running from his new family just as he ran

from Bolton and his mother.

Bolton did not want to go back for his father, to keep his promises. But he imagined his brother, still a kid, wondering where his father had gone.

Bolton remembered all those nights, lying awake, remembering his father, smiling, lifting him, his feet scraping the sand, sending grains into the air. The smell of the sea, the warmth.

For Balin, his father gave him a name and walked away.

Bolton felt sorry for Balin.

Benn had left him too.

BOLTON kept walking until the sun was low in the sky.

He walked over the dark shadows of the trees to the lake's edge and waded in the water. Across from the lake was a stony wall. He swam to it. The stone's surface was uneven, a series of jutting ledges offered the prospect of climbing.

Bolton's hands and feet found those ledges, and he climbed. The effort of the task helped him to exhaust his energy, to fight against his element.

He felt like a rag doll bursting at the seams.

He grunted as he climbed. His boots were heavy with water. Once one foot left the ledge, it found its way to another ledge until Bolton was at the top.

He was breathing heavily by the time his hand found the top of the rock. Pulling himself up, he turned over with his back to the ground, his legs dangling off the edge.

He lay there for a time, looking up at the stars, the vast darkness with pinpoints of light.

A bolt of Lightning zapped the ground close to his face. He could feel the heat of the Lightning after it had gone. He sent another bolt of Lightning far out across the plain. It hit the sandy ground near a tree.

Bolton turned over and got onto his knees.

The sand and dirt from the climb and the ground beneath him stained his shirt and pants. The rocky climb had worn the bottoms of his boots.

The plain before him stretched out to the sea. It was barren except for the few small trees that dotted the ground. The plain was made of hard sand and dirt.

Bolton stood.

Lightning struck again and again in rapid succession.

Bolton balled his hands into fists and looked up as the sky seemed to open for the impending bolts. They struck the ground with such speed that, in a blink of an eye, they would be missed.

But the zipping sound and the smell of heat could not escape his ears and nose.

Bolton loved the sound. It was like rapidly ripping paper.

The bolts lit up the sky and came in a steady harmony.

One of the trees suffered victim to the lashing bolts. Its trunk was split down the middle, its leaves were fried by the fire.

The smell of burnt wood stung his nose.

Bolton collapsed into a sitting position on the ground, a look of defeat in his eyes.

He ripped off his boot and emptied it on the sand. The glistenings fell out onto the hard ground. He counted the golden coins. He counted them again.

Sighing, he gathered them up and put them back into the boot.

He laughed until his laughter turned to tears.

He walked to where the tree was still burning, its leaves like paper curling in the sand. He knelt beside it, worn and dejected. He stayed there until his breathing calmed and his eyes dried.

Tracing his finger in the sand, he made a small circle. He traced and traced until Lightning sparked from his fingertip.

It seared the sand.

He stopped.

He gazed at where the sand was scorched and he felt the heat.

With effort, he pressed the finger of his right hand together and claw-like dug his hand into the hard sand until the surface broke.

There was dirt under his fingernails as he used both hands to dig through the sand until he found it, a small glass ring.

He lifted it up to see it by the light of the fire. The glass was tarnished, and slightly brown. With the ring in his pocket, Bolton walked back to the edge of the rock overlooking the lake.

The dark waters gleamed in the stars as they became unsettled by the leaves falling from the trees.

Bolton dove down into the water, wetting his clothes which had only moments before became dry again. The moon was now high in the sky and surrounded by the stars, like sentinels. Bolton floated on his back, his view of the sky obstructed by the overhanging trees.

The water washed away the dirt and sand from his hands and clothes. For hours, he floated on the warm water until his eyes started to droop.

He made his way to the coast and sat among the rocks at the water's edge. His head was in his hands. An hour passed before he stood and walked through the trees to the wide plain before Resistance Headquarters.

His boots made swampy, slushing sounds as he walked

across the plain. By the time he reached his tent, the sun's light peeked over the horizon.

He looked over at Sara's tent.

He thought about whispering her name against the rough fabric, but he didn't want to wake her.

He blinked against the sun as he lifted the flap to his tent. His body sank onto the worn cot, and his eyes closed and he fell asleep.

LIGHT gleamed in from the entrance of his tent. Bolton heard the Resistance fighters marching. Jin's voice bellowed across the plain.

Bolton blinked the sleep from his eyes.

His body hurt, every muscle was sore and his energy was drained.

He had missed breakfast and lunch.

Light flooded in, and Bolton turned his face into the pillow. When the light left the tent, Bolton turned back.

Sara carried a basin of water. "You're awake." She placed the water at his bedside. "Are you okay?"

Bolton nodded.

"You scared me last night when you didn't come back." She took a rag from the basin and wrung the water out. "Here."

She wiped his face with the rag. She placed the rag back into the basin and wrung it out again.

"I'm sorry," he said as she washed his face.

"I just don't know what could have upset you so badly. I saw that look in your father's eyes. He wanted to ask you something."

"He did ask me for something," Bolton said.

"What was it?"

"A favor . . . a promise he should have kept.

Sara waited.

The answer would not satisfy her. "I have to go."

"Where? Why?" The words tumbled out of her lips like an instinct, on edge and feral.

"He wants me to protect my brother."

Sara looked at the ground.

"To control his element," she whispered.

She met his eyes. "I'm going with you."

"You can't."

"I don't under—"

"I don't have enough glistenings to pay the ferryman for the both of us."

"Then we'll get more."

"Sara, you can't."

He could tell that frustration and confusion dawned inside her.

Sara shook her head.

He took her hands. "Listen to me. I'm coming back. Don't I always come back?"

She laughed behind the tears.

"Yeah. That's what I'm good at." He smirked.

She wiped her tears. "I know you would come back to me. I just don't want you to go." She looked down. "But you have to."

Bolton nodded and kissed her forehead.

Sara's eyes met his.

He cradled her face in his hands.

Their lips touched.

He leaned into the kiss despite the sore muscles in his arms and back. For a moment, he forgot the pain and the regret.

He pulled away from her.

Sara's eyes were still closed, but she opened them once she felt the space between them.

Bolton locked his eyes with hers. His fingers intertwined with hers. "Do you still love me like you did three years ago?" he whispered.

Sara's eyes never left his. "For the past three years, I've been angry, confused, but I never stopped loving you."

Bolton held her hands tight. Then he reached into his pocket. "I have something to ask you, then . . . before I go." He revealed to her what he'd taken from his pocket—the glass ring forged from Lightning.

The air was tight as Sara hung on his words.

"Will you marry me?"

13

THE GARDEN

Why would They put Something so Tempting in Our Path and then ask us to Resist?

THE large tree's roots spread over the earth. Its branches hung low, and strings of white flowers descended from the branches to the ground.

The live oak looked as if it had been growing for years, but it had only taken root a few days before. The people of Dustpath had nurtured its growth, in remembrance of the great tree of Tosia, which could be seen in the distance, blackened and dying. But soon the branches of the living tree would grow to block the view of the dying one.

A garden grew around the tree with green hedges bordering the flowers. The flowers were white, pink, and blue violet. Some trailed along the ground up to the roots.

Moonlight glowed on the tree. Foxes and rabbits of the desert inhabited the green space. It was a safe enclosure, an earthly paradise.

Sara and Bolton faced each other. They held each other's hands.

Greenery and flowers softened the ground, alive beneath their feet.

With all that was beautiful before them, for a moment Sara forgot Bolton was leaving. Her fears of his departure were released. The garden was all there was.

Malachi stood under the tree.

No one else knew they had come to meet in the forest.

Malachi stepped forward. "Are you ready?"

Bolton nodded.

Malachi placed one hand on their intertwined ones. He closed his eyes. "Now you will feel no cold, because you will provide warmth to each other. You will suffer no storm, because you will shelter each other. No longer will you feel the ache of a broken heart, because you will comfort each other."

Malachi removed his hand from theirs.

Bolton took the ring from his pocket and placed it on Sara's finger. The glass gleamed in the starlight.

Malachi closed his eyes and placed his hands together in front of him. "When we are born, we each have a separate path. These two paths have now been joined and there is but one path before you. Walk with each other on that path."

Bolton and Sara joined in a kiss.

Once the ceremony ended, Malachi shook Bolton's hand. He handed him a bottle, dark with rich liquid. "A gift."

Bolton tilted the bottle. The dark wine slushed around inside. "Thank you."

"You will be missed," Malachi said, "but you have helped

my people greatly. This gift is not enough thanks."

Sara's hand was in Bolton's.

"It's more than enough," Bolton said.

Malachi patted him on the shoulder. "Enjoy married life, the both of you." He walked back to his dwelling among his people.

Bolton smiled at Sara and kissed her. "We should be getting back. It's dark."

Sara nodded, her eyes dewy.

They walked hand in hand back to Rebel Resistance Headquarters.

Fer was waiting for them.

Bolton nodded as they approached, and Fer pulled the handle, causing the rock to scrape across the gritty surface, allowing them enough room to pass through.

They walked together back to their tents.

They stood in front of the two tents.

Sara looked up at Bolton. "Stay with me in my tent tonight?" She smiled.

They laughed.

As she joined him, she remembered the garden and all the life that was there.

SARA awoke in Bolton's tent the next morning.

The light from the sun entered through the slit in the tent's entrance. The line of light ran through the middle, separating them on either side.

Sara stared up at the fabric that made up the ceiling. She was happy for a moment. Then she remembered he was leaving.

Bolton leaned over and faced her. "Good morning." He half yawned the words.

Sara smiled at him. "Good morning."

"Do you want to get up, get moving?"

Sara shook her head violently. The earlier the day started, the earlier he would start his journey to the Insula.

"Okay." He laughed at her exaggerated gesture.

He lifted the raindrop gemstone from her chest. It was secured on a golden cord around her neck. He marveled at how it changed color when it hit the light.

"Anything?"

Sara shook her head.

"You can still sense the water. It'll come back."

"Even if it does," Sara said, "I've lived so long without it, I don't think I could control it anymore."

"That man in Omega Ray, you said you knew him?"

"Yeah. Why?"

"You said you saw him in your dreams?" he asked.

"Why are you asking me this?"

"Shashi . . . she has dreams . . . nightmares . . . about a cave and a man without skin on his face. While I was helping her with her element, she told me about these dreams, and I've been meaning to tell you, but I could never find a good time. For the longest time, I wasn't worried about them, until a few days ago, when I connected them to what you tried to tell me after we saw that man. Why would you be having the same dreams?"

Sara shook her head. "I don't know."

There was fear behind her words.

"It could just be a coincidence." Bolton tossed it aside. "It's probably nothing. I shouldn't have worried you with it. It just got to me for a moment. I didn't want to leave without saying something."

There was that word: leave.

Sara didn't want him to leave. She understood that he had to help Balin, that his conscience and hers would not let him do anything different, but she wanted him to stay. If he left, the dream might end, and she would find herself kneeling alone on the steps of Hephaestus's stone palace or by herself, in Brina's reading chair, having dozed off after reading one of Brina's many books of poetry.

Sara kissed him hard until her lips ached.

After a moment, he gently pulled away from the kiss. "I'm coming back," he promised her. Bolton kissed her hand and eased out of bed.

"So soon?" she asked.

"You must be hungry?"

"I want us to take our time," she said.

"We will," said Bolton.

Sara and Bolton emerged from the tent hand in hand. It was mid-morning, and the sun crept toward its highest point in the sky. They sat down to a cold breakfast of fruit and barley porridge.

They were the only ones there until Jin sat across the table from them. "I hear you are leaving."

Bolton nodded, his mouth full. He swallowed. "I'll be gone for a few weeks. I'm going to the place where I grew up."

Sara listened to the promise of a few weeks. She doubted Bolton would get to the island and back in that time.

"You are traveling by foot?" Jin asked.

"By boat."

"Crossing the sea has become more dangerous now that Morica has those flying vessels."

"They won't find this ship," Bolton said. "It doesn't sail in their channels."

"Alright then." Jin stood. "Safe travels. You can take anything you might need from our store room, food, supplies."

He patted Bolton on the shoulder. "It was good to have you as our guest."

Sara hated the way Jin said good-bye like Bolton was not coming back.

Bolton helped her to gather the dishes and bring them to the washroom. She helped him fill two bags of food and strap on two canteens of water for the journey.

They brought the bags to his tent.

Benn was waiting for them outside. He looked like he had not slept. Dark circles brooded beneath his eyes. "You decided to fulfill my request."

"It's not for you, old man," Bolton said. "It's for the son you left on that island, wondering where his father is and why he left him."

"I've made mistakes."

"Mistakes?" Bolton said with a snare. He turned his back on his father.

"You're doing the right thing. I wish I could do the same."

Bolton turned back around.

Sara could read the anger on his face.

"You want to do the right thing? Then *you* go back." Bolton reached into his pocket and threw the golden coins at Benn.

Some hit his chest. They scattered on the ground around him.

Bolton took Sara's hand and tore through the tent's entrance.

"Don't let him get to you," Sara whispered.

Bolton took a deep breath. "He asked me to help my brother, and he throws it in my face."

"You're not doing it for him."

Bolton's breathing slowed.

Rustling sounded at the tent entrance. Benn stepped in.

Sara wrapped her hand around Bolton's arm.

Tight-lipped, Bolton glared at him as he walked to the small table at the entrance. Benn placed the golden coins on the table. "I can't." He left the tent with his head down.

BOLTON shouldered his bags. He and Sara had walked to the lake to fill the canteens.

As Sara helped him with the bags, she noted their weight. She knew by the end of the journey the bags would grow lighter. She hoped he had enough supplies. She worked in silence, making sure the bags were secure.

She had helped him pack extra clothes for the journey: the tattered uniform of a Resistance fighter. She doubted he would wear it.

Once he was laden with supplies, Bolton kissed Sara. He put his hands on her shoulders. There were no more words between them.

Bolton smiled. His silent assurance, promising his return.

Sara smiled back weakly. She walked with Bolton to the entrance of Resistance Headquarters.

Fer pulled the handle, opening the massive rock door.

Sara watched on the ledge as Bolton emerged on the other side.

For weeks, the Rebel Resistance had sheltered them among the rocks. It was a secluded, safe place, like the garden.

Bolton looked up to the ledge before he left. Sara was waiting there for him. He waved to her. It was a solemn wave.

She waved back.

He left the garden.

14

FROST

The People bang at the Gates because They want to see Their Gods.
The Power is Consuming Them.

TACITUM traveled over the tiled marble path to Vella City. The Council Palace loomed in the distance, close to the cliff. Its marble exterior was cold and intimidating.

Tacitum rubbed his hands together.

Why is it so cold?

For a month now, he had been battling a chill he could not shake, and it was only worsening with each day.

He crossed his arms over his chest, keeping his frigid fingertips close to his armpits.

He glanced behind him to make sure that his paintings were still in his bag. He hoped the journey had not ruined the canvases.

Maybe in Vella City the people would find his work impressive, and he would not have to work for Boss or the Council or anyone but himself.

He thought of living in that marble palace while painting away on a new easel built just for him.

Maybe in Vella City they appreciate art.

Tacitum tried to make his sleeves stretch to his fingertips, but the tattered material frayed when he pulled it.

He walked through the city, noting that the streets were deserted.

Who was here to buy his paintings?

Perhaps he was doomed to haul heavy sheet metal for the rest of his days.

He was approaching Fortress Tower when he was stopped by Morica guards.

"What brings you here?"

"I'm here to see Boss," Tacitum squeaked.

The guards nodded to each other. One took Tacitum's arm, drawing his hand from under his armpit. "This way."

The guard led him to the marble palace. The other guard walked behind him.

Tacitum shivered, not just from the cold, but because his nerves were on end.

The guards opened the heavy marble doors. The doors opened with a low echo within the cavernous building.

The room they entered had a twenty-foot ceiling. The walls and the flooring were made of marble as was the spiral staircase.

The room not only felt cold, it looked cold.

Tacitum tried to put his hands back under his armpits, but the guard seized his left arm. He settled for placing his right hand under his left armpit, letting the guard have his other arm.

A man dressed in violet robes descended the staircase. His old form drooped in his clothes. His back was hunched, and his face was melting so that his eyes looked like tiny slits within pools of drooping flesh.

"Is this one of the workers from Wyvek?"

"Yes, High Councilor Mordecai."

"With whom is Boss working?" he asked Tacitum.

"I don't know what you mean?" Tacitum's voice cracked. "Where's Boss?"

"Bring him upstairs," Mordecai said.

The guard led him to the staircase.

Tacitum stared wide-eyed at Mordecai as they passed him on the steps. He saw the dark pupils of his eyes beneath the folds of skin.

The guards brought him up to the top floor of the palace.

Tacitum was tired from walking. His muscles ached, and his legs were heavy, like his feet were made of lead.

He kept his hand pinned under his arm.

The guard held his arm so tightly, he would have a bruise in the morning. The guard tightened his grip as Tacitum dragged his feet.

Tacitum tried to increase his speed so the guard might loosen his hold, but his leaden feet would not let him move any faster.

With every landing they approached, Tacitum's eyes grew wide, hoping they would stop on that floor, but they dragged him to the very top.

Once on the top floor they led him down the wide, marble encased hallway. Heavy wooden doors lined both sides of the hall.

The guard opened a door, and they escorted Tacitum inside.

The room was windowless and bare except for a tall wooden chair that sat in the center of the room. It had leather straps at the arms and legs.

Tacitum reacted. Adrenaline pumped through his body, and he turned to run, but the guard held him back. The pressure on his arm increased, and he cried out.

Eventually, his energy ran out and his arms hung limp at his sides.

Finally, the guard released his arm.

Tacitum rubbed it with his right hand, trying to massage away the pain.

He felt his bag being pulled from his shoulders.

"Hey!"

But the guards continued to remove his bag. Bag in hand, the guards walked back to the door.

"That's my bag," Tacitum weakly pronounced.

The guards ignored him and closed the door after they left the room.

The door shut with a bang.

Tacitum tried the handle, but it would not budge.

"Hey!" He banged on the door. "Where's Boss?"

He banged again, weaker.

He put his ear against the thick, wooden door. He could not hear anything outside. Exhausted, he collapsed on the floor, his back sliding against the door. He hoped they were careful with his paintings.

THE sun rose and fell. Tacitum could not see it in the windowless room, but he could sense time passing.

He had no food or water.

His stomach rumbled, and his lips were cracked and dry.

He was huddled in the space where he slept.

The floor was cold marble, and the chill that was assaulting his body had increased.

Now, he was visibly shaking and wishing that they had left his bag so that he could eat and use a few blank canvases for warmth.

He daydreamed of cozy fires and warm soups.

Suddenly, light from the hallway flooded the room.

Tacitum blinked against the intruding brightness.

A dark figure stood in the doorway. He was tall and thin, but Tacitum could not make out his face because it was shrouded in darkness.

The light glowed around him.

He closed the door, flooding the room back into obscurity.

Hours ago, Tacitum's eyes had adjusted to the darkness, but now with the assault of light, he could no longer see.

He felt long, bony fingers around his arm, lifting him from the ground effortlessly. He was being dragged across the room. He was forced into the chair in the center of the room. The leather straps were tied tight across his wrists and ankles.

Tacitum struggled, but his efforts were weak and slow.

"What do you want?" He expected his voice to come out in a shout but instead it was soft and cracked in the middle of the question.

His lips hurt when he opened his mouth as if the moisture had been sucked out of them, and he felt the cold, dry air escape from his throat.

He felt fingers on his temples.

Then suddenly, a shock invaded his body.

A flash of electric light glowed in the space between him

and his assailant.

He saw his face for a second before leaning his head back and screaming in pain.

The pain stopped.

Tacitum leaned his head forward, breathing heavy from the exertion. "I don't know what you want."

He felt fingers on his temple again and the surge of electricity.

It grew bright, and Tacitum saw his face.

His features were weathered and stern. He had a prominent brow and high cheek bones. His long nose met a grey moustache, trailing down to a dark gray beard. The contrast of dark and light made the area around his eyes appear sunken. His skin was yellowed.

The pain stopped.

He could feel the man's uncaring eyes upon him.

Tacitum struggled to think of anything to save himself. He recalled what the High Councilor had asked him on the stairs.

Who is Boss working with?

The Rebel Resistance.

But Boss had warned them never to speak of the Rebel Resistance or their Headquarters to outsiders.

He did not care about that now.

The cold fingertips touched his temples.

"The Rebel Resistance," he screamed with all his strength.

The fingertips left his head.

"Their Boss's suppliers. We store sheet metal and scraps there. Behind the big rock along Dustpath."

He felt the cold fingers touch his forehead and the electric energy itching.

"Wait. I know you. I've seen you in my dreams with the glowing worms."

Fulgur removed his fingers from Tacitum's head.

"You were with that man, the one without skin on his face."

Ice had crystalized along the arms of the wooden chair.

The door opened with a squeal.

Light flooded the room as Fulgur exited, closing the door behind him.

"Wait!" Tacitum yelled, still secured to the chair. "I know you!"

He struggled in his binds.

"Untie me! Please!"

TACITUM slept, his head leaning over the side of the chair. The ice had melted and left a pool of water on the floor.

Light intruded, causing him to awaken.

His mouth cracked open to take a deep breath.

He could see the outline of the guards' bodies against the light.

A guard placed a sack in the room.

Two guards walked up to him and started undoing the straps around his wrists and ankles. Once he was free, they made their way back to the door.

"Wait!" he screamed, getting up from the chair and stumbling across the floor. "I'm hungry."

A guard kicked the sack across the room to him. Then they left and shut the door behind them.

The darkness once again consumed Tacitum.

He scrambled to find the sack on the ground.

He felt the rough canvas fabric, and he tore it open, feeling around for what was inside. His hands found what felt like fruit. Maybe an apple.

It hurt his cracked lips as he opened his mouth to eat the apple. The acidic juices stung, but still he ravenously ate until he was sucking the core.

His hands searched the ground franticly for more.

He found a canteen. Tearing off the stopper, he chugged the water down his throat. It dripped off his chin and down his neck.

He wiped his mouth on his sleeve.

His fingertips lighted upon something hard.

It was bread.

His mouth tore at it and swallowed it in whole chunks until it was gone.

His hands once again searched for more. He spread his arms out across the floor, turning around and searching the expanse behind him.

He felt something wet at the base of the chair. He smelled his fingertips to try to distinguish what it was, but it had no smell.

He pressed his face to the floor and slurped up what he could of the liquid.

He searched the entire room again before crying out.

There was no more.

He cried and beat his hands against the marble walls.

"Let me out!"

Frost formed on his fingertips.

15

FATHER

The Builders have Not lost their Purpose now that the Temples have been Built, for there will Always be a Need for the Temples to be Maintained.

MORDECAI could not hear the screams from his room on the uppermost floor of the palace. From the narrow window, the moonlight crept into his room like a desperate man across a desert.

He was at his desk, writing a letter to the councilor in Lumina. They needed more guards in Elementa. There was news that Element had been abandoned.

No one had seen Veil since the incident in Lumina.

Mordecai cringed.

Veil was a loose end that he had to tie up.

He thought he could keep him stable, functional, but the

man had been broken since he was a boy.

Mordecai was never a broken man.

He had known, since Elementals had murdered his parents, that he wanted them all dead.

Veil's breakdown could not have come at a worse time.

Mordecai was so close to making the Elementals bow. He had dreams of herding and imprisoning them. Separating them until they died out.

His wrinkled, veiny hand clenched into a fist.

He had no pictures to remember his parents by. Their features were erased from his mind.

When he was left on the streets after they were murdered, every night he tried to imagine their faces, but all he could see were the faces of their murderers. Hate grew inside him.

Now, he remembered the faces of the murderers better than the faces of his own parents.

Everyone saw his father as a beggar for all the years he knew him.

A filthy beggar.

Many nights he went to sleep hungry, but he loved his father.

When he woke him with his crying, his father would sit by him and tell him stories about how they were going to be the rich ones one day. He told him, the poor were only poor because they were getting ready for their new lives.

You must suffer for greatness.

And he did suffer.

He watched his mother get her neck strangled by a tree root and his father get burned alive by unnatural flames.

His mother died in seconds.

His father breathed with shallow breaths.

Young Mordecai scrambled to his side, holding his waxy

hand in his. The skin on his face was so melted, he was unrecognizable. Mordecai feared that that was the face he would remember.

He whispered in Mordecai's ear, "Hold on for greatness."

Mordecai felt his hot breath in his ear, and then he could hear nothing. The rapid rise and fall of his chest had ceased, and his father stared up at the sky stone-eyed.

He watched his father die in the streets.

People passed but no one tore him away from him. No one came to comfort him. People stared, but no one helped.

After a few days, flies started to buzz around the bodies, and the smell of decaying flesh pervaded the air.

Men came for the bodies.

Mordecai cried when they lifted his father from the ground. He held onto his hand for dear life, but the flesh pulled away from the bones.

Mordecai was left alone, holding a piece of decaying flesh. All that was left of his father.

He put the flesh in a jar and kept it in his pocket.

Mordecai touched the small jar on his desk.

The flesh had turned black and ashy.

"I held on, father."

Mordecai moved his arm across the table as he wrote.

His penknife fell.

Two knocks sounded at the door.

"Not him," Mordecai breathed the words.

He cringed at the thought of Fulgur standing there, his bald head furrowed and stern, his old body and unnatural voice.

He had let the snake slither into his bed.

Mordecai rose from his desk with effort. His old bones cracked.

He reached for the doorknob, and there stood, emotionless, the long form of Fulgur.

Fulgur entered without invite and stood, unmoving.

"What is it?"

"The man you sent from Wyvek," Fulgur said, "he has revealed your enemy to you."

Mordecai recoiled at the youthful voice coming from so old a vessel.

"Where?" Mordecai asked.

"On Dustpath Road among the rocks. I imagine if you fly your contraptions over there, you will find them."

"He's dead," Mordecai said.

"No."

Mordecai was angry. "I told you what to do when you were done."

Fulgur's bony hand wrapped around Mordecai's neck. Without passion, he said, "Mind yourself old man. I am not your servant."

He released Mordecai.

Mordecai leaned over, gasping for air. "What will you do with him?" he asked between gasps.

"Keep him in the room. Nourish him. Keep him alive."

"What can he do for you?" Mordecai asked.

"It is not for me."

Mordecai knew that Fulgur would continue to work him around so he put an end to his questioning.

"I must go," Fulgur said. "My father has returned."

Mordecai marveled at Fulgur's old form. *How old was his father?*

"I am not sure if I will return. Your games have become dull." Fulgur's yellow eyes glared, unblinking in the darkness.

Mordecai opened the door.

Without swiftness, Fulgur left the room, gliding out like a ghost.

Mordecai watched him turn the corner. Then he closed the door with a sigh.

The Elemental, or whatever he was, had been helpful, but Mordecai was glad he was gone. Fulgur had a way of creeping around corners and showing up uninvited.

Mordecai picked up the penknife and sat back down at his desk.

He read over his letter until he was satisfied.

Then he crept into bed.

THE sun was behind the clouds. The hazy light glanced off the marble palace. The sea beyond the cliff stretched into nothingness.

The guards were changing shifts outside the palace, their blue uniforms were bright and clean. A belt wrapped around their waists where their weapons were secured.

Mordecai arose before the sun. He watched the guards exchange from his window. He drummed his fingers on his desk and wondered what he would do now that he found the Rebel Resistance.

Was their leader there?

He needed Vassal dead. The man was a bug in his ear. But he could settle for compromising his army.

He should not have sent Atrus with him. He needed more flying chariots.

He put his father's ashes in the pocket of his long robe and left the room.

Walking down the hall, he came upon the room where Tacitum was being held.

Ice had formed around the door.

"Elemental," he whispered with disdain.

He touched the doorknob. It was cold.

Did Fulgur expect him to keep the Elemental alive?

Mordecai shook his aged head and continued to the stairs. He descended slowly, his long robes sweeping the steps. He met Jove on the stairway.

"High Councilor," they greeted each other.

"You have been busy, High Councilor Mordecai?"

"I need maps," Mordecai said.

"Maps? What for?"

"I've found the Rebel Resistance."

Jove stopped on the steps and stared at Mordecai. "And you plan to attack them?"

Mordecai stared back and did not say a word.

"High Councilor Surnom would not like this."

"Surnom is soft," Mordecai said. "We're not going to rise to power with little factions chipping away at our armies."

"I'll go to my library. I'll get you the maps by tonight."

Mordecai nodded.

"Will you be dining with us?" Jove asked.

"I wouldn't miss it."

THE High Councilors sat around the large table in the marble palace. They were waited on by the lesser councilors, their hair bleached white.

Only one seat was vacant.

The table was filled with roasted pheasant, chick peas, cheeses, wines, and seasoned greens.

The High Councilors had partaken of the wine. Surnom, Romulus and Caduceus were drinking to excess. Jove and Mordecai sipped their wine.

Jove watched Mordecai from the end of the table.

"To a long life," Surnom toasted.

"You've already lived one." Romulus laughed.

Mordecai laughed behind his wine glass.

"So, Caduceus," Romulus said, "how does one extract water from the waterfall?"

Caduceus laughed, spraying his wine across the table. "Why do you need to know?"

"I want to see how much longer our friend Surnom has."

They all laughed.

"You hear that, Gareth, you better prepare yourself. We're already planning your predecessor's funeral."

He winked at the middle-aged man standing behind Surnom.

Gareth smirked, but he dared not laugh.

After the banter died down, Romulus stood. "Well, I guess it's that time, my friends. The night is calling my name softly in her sweet whisper." He took one final gulp of wine and left the table.

Caduceus slinked out of his seat as well and stumbled up the stairs to his bedroom.

Surnom had fallen asleep at the table. His loud snores echoed through the cavernous dining room.

Jove's eyes were fixed on Mordecai.

Mordecai pointed to the door, his glass still in hand.

Jove nodded.

He followed Jove as he walked up the stairs to his library. Jove opened the heavy oaken doors. Behind the doors were rows of shelves with books and rolls of paper.

Jove led Mordecai to the long desk at the back of the room. He unrolled the roll of paper on the desk.

"This is my most detailed map of Mirmina. This is the

Dustpath region." He tapped the area of the map with his finger. "Rocks border a barren plain on all sides. If the Rebel Resistance is hiding among the rocks, the most likely place for them to set up camp is here."

Mordecai nodded. "Can you make a copy of this portion of the map by morning?"

"Yes," Jove said.

Mordecai walked to his bedroom on the top floor of the marble palace. He removed his father's ashes from his pocket and set the glass jar on his desk.

16

RETURNED

*I have Never seen the Creator up close. But even from a Distance, I
Know that He is in an Eternal State of Dying.*

THE walls and ground of Dawn's home where living
roots used to grow were now black and dying. The
leaves were curling in on themselves and falling to
ashes on the floor.

Dawn salvaged some of the herbs before they died. She
used them to make tea for her father and brothers.

Dawn's hands shook as she placed the cup of tea in the
fleshless hands.

Fleshless fingers seized her wrist.

"I've missed you," he said, holding onto her spotted hand.
He looked around at Vuur, Glaciem, and Vjetar. "I've missed
all of you."

He let go of Dawn's wrist.

"Where is your brother, Destan?"

Dawn gulped.

Did he know? Did he know what she and Destan had done?

"Destan has been wandering the earth," Vuur said, "looking for you, Father." His waxy hand rested in his lap.

Erebus touched the burnt side of Vuur's face with his fleshless hand. "He is a good son." There was no sarcasm in his voice because there could be none.

Dawn sat next to Erebus. "How long have you been back, Father?"

"Time rolls by when you are hungry."

"I can get you something." Dawn rose from her seat. Dawn had stopped faking her raspy voice. Now her voice rang out clearly, like a young woman's. It seemed unnatural to her weathered form.

"Oh, can you, my dear. Perhaps a little baker's boy or a wandering traveler."

"The town is abandoned," Vjetar said, "and travelers do not pass through often." His sharp blue eyes pierced the darkness.

"Pity."

Glaciem gripped one of his ashy brown fingers and broke it off with a dull crack. The brown nail fell away. "Here, father."

"I can't eat your frost bit flesh."

Glaciem withdrew the finger and put it in his pocket with his head down.

"Why are you hiding in this hole?" Erebus asked.

When Dawn had touched his face to see him with her sightless eyes, she noted that he was more deteriorated than when she had last saw him. Dawn feared that his eye, un-grounded by any flesh, would pop out and fall upon the floor. Eating rats underground had rotted his teeth and increased his need for human flesh.

Dawn still had the nightmares about Dustpath, and the people lining up to eat from the communal stew. She could still smell the rotting intestines of the bodies.

Erebus slammed the small table with his fist. "Why are you hiding here?"

The butter knife clamored to the floor.

A knock sounded at the door.

Dawn rose from her seat to answer it.

A tall, shadowy form stood in the doorway, but that was all her eyes would allow her to see. Still, she knew it was Fulgur. She could sense his energy.

She moved aside so that he may enter.

"Fulgur, my son," Erebus said, "please sit. We were having tea."

Dawn thought for a moment how absurd it was that they were having tea. After all, they could find no joy in it. They could eat dirt just as well to dissuade their hunger.

Fulgur sat where Dawn had been sitting next to Erebus.

Dawn walked over to the kettle and poured a cup of tea. She offered it to Fulgur, but he refused it.

When was the last time Fulgur had eaten? Dawn wondered. *Was he letting the pings of hunger consume him?*

"What have you been doing?" Vjetar asked.

"Amusing myself," Fulgur said.

"With humans," Vuur said.

When their father was gone, they had made a pact not to mess in the affairs of humans. They would watch from afar but never again try to present themselves as gods. Fulgur had gone against that pact.

"Why are you all dressed in rags?" Erebus asked, staring from Dawn's plain robes to Vjetar's tattered gray shirt. "You look like prisoners. Humans should be making you glowing robes with glass beads and gifting you golden necklaces."

Dawn kept her fine robes and golden necklaces of the past locked away in a chest to remind her of the decadence that killed so many people.

"This is a different world than when you left it, Father," Dawn said.

"I did not leave it," Erebus snapped. "I was imprisoned by one of my sons."

They looked around at each other.

"Destan," he hissed. "He bites the hand that feeds."

Dawn visualized Erebus's arm where the flesh had been pulled away.

Destan used to be his favorite son.

Would he give Destan the fatted calf if he returned or would Erebus condemn him?

"You were supposed to keep this world in line for me. Instead, you've let the humans take over to rule themselves again?"

Glaciem's head seemed to sink into his lap.

Vjetar stared at the ground, now dying with the great tree.

"They brought this world to shambles the first time," Erebus said, "and I cleaned it up. Now, you have let it go to ruin. I've seen vessels flying through the air. Little machines to replace them. Government. There would be no need for shadow leaders if the people had gods."

Vuur stared into the eyes of his father.

Dawn watched his form.

Fulgur focused on his peeling lips, the blood dripping

from the corners of his mouth as if he had just eaten.

"I am the Creator of the Children of Spheres. They must bow before their gods."

Dawn remembered the old days. Humans were their slaves. The Children of the Spheres kept them in line, like sentinels, but they were no less slaves than their ungifted counterparts.

She remembered the first uprising.

The Children of the Spheres armed with their elements attempted to fight against the Keepers. Hundreds of thousands died fighting against their gods.

Dawn had refused to help her father, and Destan hid himself away.

When the battle was done, those who remained cowered in fear. Erebus celebrated with his children, sad that Destan was not there to join them.

Until one day, Erebus disappeared.

His children didn't look for him, didn't wonder where he had gone.

They calmly retired until, over the centuries, the people forgot them.

Dawn didn't want power. She didn't want life. She wanted to sleep, to be restful.

No matter how often she closed her eyes, she could not sleep, could not dream, and could not see anything beyond this world. That was the gift her father had given her.

Now he wanted to be worshiped again.

Dawn had lived in a semi-calm before this moment. Her father didn't trust her. She would refuse to help once again. He said she had more water in her soul than Destan, that her fate was wavering.

"You will show them what we can do," Erebus said. "I

will reveal myself to them after they have seen this show of power. Give them time to digest it."

Dawn could sense Fulgur staring at her. She shifted in her seat.

She still felt his lightning rage the day she scorned him.

She had moved the earth in Jetty Verte.

Their lovers' quarrel had inconsequently freed the prisoners in the underground jail and crushed many beneath the falling earth. Power had consumed her that day.

Since then, it had been decades since she had used her element. It stirred inside her, but just as Fulgur refused to eat, Dawn refused to give into releasing the energy.

They sipped their tea in silence.

Dawn could hear no breathing. She had been used to such silence when they were together, but now it was unsettling.

She wondered how long Erebus had been out of his cage.

It would be like her father to settle a few matters behind their backs before coming to them. He no longer trusted his children.

Dawn heard something wet hit the floor, and she wondered if that was a piece of her father's flesh falling from his bones.

They settled into pairs.

Vuur and Vjetar talked in one corner.

Erebus and Fulgur sat together in silence.

Glaciem read to Dawn from an old book that she kept.

It was the history of Tosia, but it was only a partial history. It told the story of how fate led the people of Dustpath to the Great Tree where they carved their future. It spoke of their vows to live by nature and to never use their elements.

Glaciem had difficulty turning the pages. He could only

use his ring finger and thumb because the other fingers had turned stiff and brown.

His voice rang out youthful and clear.

Sometimes Dawn imagined they were all young.

She could feel her thinning, brittle hair and the deep wrinkles on her face, but she had never seen herself after her hands left the sphere.

Her father was the only one in the room whose face she had seen, and she could never forget it. The skin on one cheek was rotted away so that the sinews beneath were visible. The flesh around his eyes was starting to rot, and he had several bony fingers where the flesh was almost gone.

Dawn looked up from the book.

She was so lost in her thoughts she had not noticed her father and Fulgur leave. She had not heard the door opening or closing.

Dawn placed a hand on Glaciem's arm. "Is Father still here?"

"He and Fulgur left moments ago."

Dawn allowed Glaciem to read for a little while longer to not draw suspicion. Then, she stood from where she sat.

"Where are you going?"

"I need some fresh air," Dawn said. "Now that my plants have died, this room has become stuffy."

Dawn felt the wall to the door. She sensed her father and brother's energy and followed it to the Cliff of Broken Promise.

Dawn leaned against the tunnel-like walls. Through her dull vision, she could make out two forms on the Cliff. Sensing their energy, she knew it was Erebus and Fulgur.

"Don't you want peace, my son?"

"But I'm afraid to die."

"You have been a good son. You deserve to rest. Will you help me gather them?"

"Yes, Father."

From the remnants she gathered, Dawn could not piece together what her father meant. Keepers could not be killed. They could not rest. The eternal slumber was denied to them.

Dawn could see their forms move towards the tunnels.

She snaked along the walls until she was out. Then she walked along the blackened tree branches that made up the pathway.

She moved into the center of town where the Domum Fidei was nestled and up the narrow pathway.

If her heart could beat, it would be hammering.

Once she was satisfied she was far enough away not to be suspected, Dawn slowed her pace to a steady stroll.

She was turned around by the shoulder and pushed against the wall.

She felt static.

"Fulgur?"

"It is so nice to hear that voice," he said.

She felt urgent lips pressed against hers.

She slapped him.

Fulgur pressed a hand against her chest and shocked her.

She thought she felt her heart beat again, but only for a moment.

"What were you and Father talking about?" she asked.

"It was between me and him."

"Don't you think we should all know?"

"If you kiss me with passion, I'll tell you."

Dawn glared at him with her sightless eyes.

"I have to go," he said.

"Where?"

"Not where father has sent me."

"You're disobeying him."

"I'm just making a detour," he said. "There is so much to get settled first."

He touched her face. "You are lucky you held onto the sphere long enough to take your sight, so you can't see what I'm about to do."

17

WAR

The Creator and His Keepers have Taught us that there is no Need for War. War is about Taking Power and we already have It.

SARA rubbed the tattered uniform across the tin surface and squeezed the water out into the wooden bucket. She placed the uniform on the drying rack beside her.

It had been days since Bolton left.

On many evenings, Sara stared at the blank pages Bolton had left her. She allowed her fingers to become marred by the charcoal, letting time tick by, leaving the pages . . . blank.

She looked at her glass ring as she soaked another tattered uniform into the water. The sunlight glanced off it.

Benn stood not far away.

She hated how he stared at her.

He had a habit of watching her every day. Not daring to

speak to her, just watching her.

He should be the one journeying to the Insula.

Sara vigorously washed the tattered uniform, staring down into the slushing water.

A shadow came over her.

Sara looked up.

A chariot blocked the sun.

At first, she thought it was Thatch, but then she saw more chariots in the distance. They were smaller than Thatch's vessel.

"No," she whispered.

The fighters stopped their marching and looked up at the chariots gathering in the sky. They withdrew their weapons, thinking the vessels might land.

"Run!" Sara shouted.

That is when the blasting started.

A missile sailed through the sky down onto the barren plain and exploded. Fire spread out, killing all in its wake. Smoke curled up into the sky and mingled with the fire.

Another missile sailed to the ground and another.

The fighters scattered. Even their spears could not reach the flying chariots.

There were six chariots in the skies all shooting missiles from above.

Jin was barking orders.

Sara ran. They were no match for the chariots.

The bodies of fallen fighters littered the ground. The ground was burnt and smoky where they lay, their bodies red and skin bubbled.

"Not that way, damn it, girl!"

Benn grabbed her hand and led her in the opposite direction.

There was an explosion behind them.

Sara could feel the heat of it.

Jin had gathered the Earth Elementals in his army.

"Now!" he shouted.

They knelt to the ground.

The earth crashed together, causing a quake.

Sara and Benn fell to their knees and scrambled back to their feet. They were headed for the entrance.

The smell of burning bodies rose into the air. They were roasting on the ground. Some were only injured and were trying to crawl away, but the rough ground was hurting their burns as they scraped across the rocky plain.

The earth gathered until it formed into a point, rising from the ground. It shot up, catching the side of one of the chariots and knocking it off balance.

A missile crashed down, its fires burning the flesh of those in its range.

Fire Elementals sent fires at the chariots.

"Come on!" Dema shouted, her tattered uniform ashy from the smoke spreading through the air. Breathing was difficult, and tears obstructed her vision.

Lightning bolts rang through the skies. Lightning formed in the sky above one of the chariots. The bolts seized the vessel, encasing it. The chariot lost function and crashed to the ground.

Dema trucked it to the next vessel, but her fellow Lightning Elementals were losing energy. They could not take down another chariot.

Wind Elementals gathered together. The winds knocked two of the chariots together, damaging the vessels, but missiles continued to sail through the air, killing and injuring those below.

Jin called his men back, but a missile landed several feet away from him. The force of its blasts threw him.

He landed on the hard ground, his arm mangled.

Sara and Benn neared the entrance, but Sara spotted Jin in the distance.

"Jin!"

She tore her hand from Benn's and ran to where Jin had fallen. She knelt beside him.

His arm was bloodied, and the bone protruded below his elbow.

Jin twisted in pain.

"We have to go," Benn said.

"I'm not leaving him here."

"We have to. He'll slow us down."

"I'm not leaving," Sara snapped.

Benn picked up Jin with effort and put his body across his shoulders.

"My men." Jin forced his voice from his throat.

"They're running," Benn assured him. "They heard your command."

Sara was headed for the rock. "There'll be no one to open it."

Benn pulled her to the cliff. "Jump!"

They jumped, the ground below forcing their legs from under them. Jin fell hard on his back. Sara and Benn rolled upon the ground, and got to their feet.

Benn struggled to get Jin back on his shoulders. The old man was breathing with difficulty.

Their feet thundered across the hard ground.

Benn led them down Dustpath Road.

"No!" Sara shouted. "Not to Dustpath. We can't lead them there."

They turned around and ran to the abandoned city of Wyvek. Benn's footsteps were labored with Jin on his back.

"I have to put him down."

"What?" Sara said in disbelief. "We can't leave him here. He's injured."

"Bolton would never forgive me if anything happened to you. You need to go."

"I can't. You're going to leave Jin."

Benn rested Jin onto the ground.

"Stay with him then." But Benn made no move to leave them behind. They were at an impasse.

Sara stared at Benn, and he looked back at her. Jin, helpless, lay between them.

Fighters were running from their Headquarters.

Two of them stopped to come to Jin's aid. They lifted their leader from the ground. One held his shoulders, the other taking hold of his legs.

"Let's go."

They ran in perfect harmony with Jin's body creating a bridge between them.

What was left of Jin's army ran with Sara and Benn through the abandoned streets of Wyvek. They stopped outside an inn and pulled the boards away from the door. Sara tried the handle, but the door would not budge.

"Stand back." Yerish stepped forward and kicked the door in. The door hammered open on its hinges.

After their leader was securely through the threshold, the rest of the survivors rushed into the building.

Yerish shut the door behind them.

No lights lit the abandoned inn, and the windows were boarded up.

No one dared speak a word as they recovered their losses.

Jin was brought into a room and placed upon the bed.

Taryn rushed in and knelt by his bedside. "I need an Earth Elemental in here now. Preferably one who hasn't exhausted all his energy," she commanded.

Fer ran out into the hallway. He returned with Reed.

Sara watched from the doorway.

"I need two straight branches or saplings roughly the length of his forearm."

Reed concentrated. He produced two straight branches and handed them to Taryn.

"Do we have any meli?"

Fer shook his head.

"This is going to hurt, Commander." She took his forearm and bicep in her hands and moved the arm until the bone was no longer protruding.

Jin yelled out in pain.

His sleeve was torn and bloody where the bones had come through.

Taryn ripped the stitching where the sleeve connected to the main part of the shirt. Then she gently pulled the sleeve down until it was over his hand.

Jin winced.

"We need something to clean the wound," Taryn said.

"Fire?" Fer asked.

"That would work."

Fer nodded and went to get Yerish.

"Who were they?" Taryn asked.

"Those were Morica guns," Sara said.

"They were driving those things?"

"They were built for them with missiles to attack their enemies," Sara said. "That's what they used on us."

"How are we supposed to fight that?"

Sara moved aside to allow Yerish through the door.

The large man lumbered into the room.

"We need to cauterize the wound," Taryn instructed. "Hold him down."

Fer pinned one of Jin's shoulders to the bed while Taryn took the other.

Yerish focused.

Smoke rose from Jin's arm as Yerish sealed his wound.

Jin gritted his teeth and tried to pick himself up from the bed, but Fer and Taryn held him fast.

Once the wound was properly tended to, Taryn told Yerish to stop.

Yerish, being long without the use of his element, needed her signal.

Taryn took the two branches and placed them on the sides of Jin's arm. She tore Jin's sleeve into long strips and tied them around the arm and branches until they were securely in place.

Jin was exhausted from pain, and after the ordeal was done, he fell into a deep sleep.

THAT night, Sara found Benn sleeping in the hallway among the fighters. There were not enough beds for everyone so once the bedrooms were full, people took to sleeping against walls. It was better than sleeping outside where they might be attacked.

Sara leaned against a door frame opposite Benn. She nudged his leg with her shoe.

Benn stirred in his sleep, and his eyes blinked open. He looked up at her.

"You weren't going to leave us, were you?" she asked.

"What do you mean?"

"Back there . . . on the road."

Benn shook his head. "I didn't think I was going to make it, but I'm trying to be a better man."

"You should keep doing that."

Sara smiled thin-lipped and nodded before making her way back down the hall. She rested on the floor of Jin's room and listened to his shallow breathing.

SARA was in a room with dying vegetation, turned black. It was falling from the walls and ceiling. Curled leaves were crushed beneath her feet as she walked. The roses smelled like rotting animals. Petals littered the ground.

Suddenly, she felt sick. It was a nauseous feeling. She felt like she was going to vomit. She put her hand on her stomach. The room seemed to move around her, it took some time for things to come back into focus.

She could see the shadows of five others, their backs to her.

"Hello?" she whispered into the darkness, but her voice echoed louder than she intended. She feared her own voice, scared it might summon something from the darkness.

The people in front had their backs to her.

She turned around.

There were five others behind her.

They, too, had their backs turned to her.

She heard a low, dull rumble in the distance.

"You are no longer a Child of the Sphere." A voice sounded. It echoed around her, the words lingering in the air, an epitaph of her doom.

But then the voice rang out, "You are something greater."

A fleshless hand reached out to her from the darkness.

Sara awoke in a cold sweat.

18

THE CALM PEOPLE

There are Those of us who Think Ourselves Better because we are Closer to Our gods. Our gods have Given us the Gifts of Earth because it is the Greatest of Their Gifts. Our People can Move Mountains, Shift Plains, and Cause the World to Tremble.

JIN blinked once, twice.

When he tried to sit up in the old, worn bed, he put pressure on his arm. He winced in pain. He was dizzy with it until it cooled to a dull ache.

Some of his soldiers slept around him on the floor.

Sara was close to the boarded-up window. She was sitting up with her head in her hands, her long hair trailing over her fingers.

The lamp gave him just enough light by which to see her.

Unable to sit up, Jin craned his neck. "Where are we?"

Sara lifted her head from her hands.

He only saw her despair for a moment. Her eyes creased at the corners, and her lips turned up.

"You're awake," she exclaimed, her voice sounding relieved.

"My ears are still ringing. How many of my men have fallen?"

Sara shook her head.

"We need to gather the bodies in the morning." Jin did not know whether it was night or day. The windows were boarded up so well, not a glimpse of daylight could shine through even if the sun was burning in the sky. "We need to bury them."

"It's too dangerous," Sara said. "The chariots could come back. They might have never left. They might be waiting for our return so they can ambush us again."

"Those were Morica vessels."

"How did you know?" she asked.

"Spies like Rodan. We have them all over Vella City. They told me about the chariots, that Atrus had been building them for the Council."

He gritted his teeth.

"You should rest," she said.

"I'll be fine. We have to warn Malachi."

"I'll send someone to warn him."

"No." Jin shook his head. "I'll tell him."

Sara pressed her lips together, but she did not argue with him.

Jin rested his head back down on the pillow.

He became a Resistance fighter when he was only eighteen. He had just met Rodan's mother, Rebecca. At the banding ceremony, she sat regal and thin-lipped, but Jin knew his decision upset her.

In his first year, she was newly made a mother.

Jin's face was the sixth, maybe the seventh face his new-born son saw.

Every moment Jin spent with his son felt stolen.

He often watched his wife's stony eyes and wondered if she loved him. He would take Rodan and go away for days. She would worry, and then he would know.

Rebecca's face pervaded his memory. Her small features and soft curls contrasted with her stern expression. Her delicate hands scrubbed the floors of their little cottage in the woods outside Tosia. She was always working, always surviving.

Her hands were unused to such work. He had taken her from her family in Lumina when he married her. They were children with the fickle love that young people have.

As they grew older, their love turned into a dependency on one another. He more so than she. Jin needed to know she was there in that little cottage waiting for him on these long walks home. He needed to know that she had been faithful.

And she would always be there, stoic.

Rodan's little feet would come trampling upon the wooden floors to meet him. He was more passionate than his mother.

Jin had not seen his wife in many months.

Was she still waiting for him?

Despite the lack of light, Jin could sense the morning. He smelled the heat and dewy morning air.

Several of the fighters awoke from their sleep. Despite being weary from battle, their bodies were set to rise with the morning sun.

The ash and sweat pervaded the air of the musty inn. The

smell was trapped inside.

Sara had fallen asleep where she sat against the wall.

Jin's stomach was empty, and his arm still throbbed. His lips were dry.

The fighters were getting up, their bodies beaten.

He heard a creak from the entrance of the inn, and a flood of light erupted into the hallway. A rush of fresh air invaded the inn, pushing out the distasteful smell.

Jin pushed with one arm until his back was leaning against the headboard.

"How are you feeling, Commander?" Taryn had gotten up from the ground and sat in the small, wooden chair by his bedside.

"My arm's felt better."

"If you're going to sit up, you'll need a sling."

Taryn took out her knife and cut a long, wide strip from the sheet at the end of the bed.

Jin grinded his teeth together as she lifted his arm in the sling to tie the ends of the strip around his neck.

"How far are we from Headquarters?" he asked.

"We're in Wyvek. We ran a few miles at most."

"I want to go to Malachi to tell him what happened. We need food and water. Malachi can help us. Also," Jin winced, "they might have meli."

"I can go back to Headquarters, and get you meli."

"No. You are brave, but it's too dangerous. We go together to Dustpath. Gather the fighters."

Taryn nodded and left the room.

Jin could hear her shouts echo down the hallway.

Sara was awakened. She sat up as two fighters helped Jin to stand. "We're moving on?"

Jin nodded.

Malachi would tell him his people could not fight, but Jin felt a sense of honor, that he should tell Malachi to prepare himself and his people.

His arm felt lifeless in the sling. He had the urge to move it, but he fought that urge. "Only a few fighters. We don't want to draw any attention."

JIN took Taryn and Yerish along with four other fighters down Dustpath Road. They stayed close to the rocky wall and in the shadows to avoid detection.

Jin watched the skies.

The air was deafeningly calm.

Jin's heartbeat was loud in his chest, and his breathing was labored as he fought the pain in his arm. He prayed Malachi had meli.

The dusty path turned green in the distance as they rounded the rocky bend in the road. The trees grew above the ruins.

A fine job Malachi was doing keeping his people hidden, Jin thought with sarcasm.

They journeyed onto the soft grass and snaked between the ruins and the trees.

The people greeted the fighters as they passed, carrying baskets full of food.

Yerish pulled an apple from one of the baskets and took a giant bite. Juice dripped down his chin.

"We're looking for Malachi," Jin announced to a group of passing women.

They looked at him like he had spoken a foreign language.

"Malachi."

"He's with the Great Tree," one of the women said.

They looked fearful.

Their fear reflected Jin's own.

Jin wondered if his expression was riddled with it.

They walked to the great tree in the center of the growing town. There Malachi sat beneath the tree. He appeared to be either meditating or sleeping.

Jin ambled up to him with his group of soldiers close behind.

"Malachi?"

Malachi looked up, his eyes still in a dreamlike state. When he recognized Jin, Malachi got to his feet. He was in no rush despite the urgency Jin felt in his own voice.

"What is it, my friend?"

"Your people need to prepare for a fight."

Malachi looked puzzled. "My people do not fight. That's why we hired your guards."

"It won't be enough."

"What is the meaning of this?"

"Morica attacked us with erupting fire. You and your people could be next. They might see you as a threat."

"My people, a threat?"

"Look what you can do." Jin gestured toward the greenery that lay before them. "They fear Elementals worse than anything. Your people will have to fight. You won't have a choice if they come for you."

Malachi sighed. "We already lost one home."

Jin patted him on the back. "Don't lose another."

"But if they come with the erupting fire," Jin continued. "You need to run."

Malachi nodded. "You can't bring your people here. You might lead them to us, but we can give you food. You can take some on your backs."

Malachi ordered his people to help gather food for their visitors. Jin tried to help them harvest the fruit into baskets with one hand. He stood beside a woman who was pulling grapes from the vine.

Her delicate hands plucked the grapes and popped them into the woven basket at her side.

Jin knelt beside her, pulling at a grape with his free hand.

The woman's head was covered in a shawl to protect her from the sun. The side of her face was also hidden by the shawl.

But there was something about her hands.

The more Jin stared, the more he wondered.

He grabbed the woman's wrist.

She stopped picking.

As she turned her head, the sun hit her face.

"Rebecca!" He stared at her, his eyes fixated on her.

Her face had grown older, older than he remembered, but she was still beautiful. Her soft features betrayed her stern expression.

"Why didn't you come to me?" Jin asked, still grasping her hand.

"Why didn't *you* come to *me*?" she replied.

He let go of her hand.

Rebecca got back to work.

He stared at her. "Have you seen Rodan?" he asked.

"Months ago," she said. "He grew up like his father."

"I couldn't come, Rebecca. I'm sorry. How did you get here?"

She kept working and did not look at him. "When the people left Tosia, I went with them. I heard strange howling at night. I was afraid."

She was buried in her task.

"Rebecca, come with me."

"I like it here."

He touched her shoulder. "Please."

Rebecca's eyes remained narrowed, but she looked at him.

Jin knew that that meant she was warming to him.

"Is Rodan with you?"

Jin shook his head.

Rebecca's hard expression dropped. "Where is he?"

He could read the worry on her face. "He's safe."

"Jin."

"I don't know."

Rebecca's eyes were starting to collect water. She looked away and got back to work, plucking the grapes with more vigor and tossing them into the basket.

Jin grabbed one of her arms. "Rebecca, stop. Stop."

Rebecca cried against his shoulder.

Jin rubbed her back. "He's fine. He's okay."

"How do you know?"

"Because I know our son."

19

THE CHARIOT

Yet, the World should not Fear us for we are Honest and True with Our Gifts and Follow the Laws of the gods.

RODAN watched from the upper windows as the Morica chariots flew into Elementa. The trees were still aflame when Thatch's vessel left the ground. The hulking mass soared through the sky, shuttering for a few short moments.

They had been flying into the night.

Rai was still tirelessly at the wheel as the sun went down.

"I hate that we're going back to Breeze." Farah frowned.

"I thought you'd be happy to see Shift," Thatch said.

"Shift left me for his pride."

"He was afraid," Thatch said. "You know your brother

never likes to face anything, especially the thought of you being gone."

"Oh, stop it, Thatch." Farah shoved his shoulder.

Thatch only grinned.

Rodan watched their exchange. His only family was his
mother and father, and he had not seen either of them in
months. Before they left Tosia when they were looking for
Sara and Bolton, he went to see his mother. But she was gone.
Their little cottage was abandoned.

His mother had not wanted him to go to Elementa to
train. For without him, she would be alone. But his father had
insisted. He was never stern with her, only logical.

She was not an Elemental. She could not begin to understand how to help her son control his element. He needed to
go to Element where skilled trainers could help him.

He was only six years old. Her only child. The child she
raised while his father was away.

But at six years old, Rodan could not even begin to understand what his mother felt.

He did not want to be with her in the woods anymore.
She was overprotective. She loved him too much.

"Rodan. Rodan."

"What?"

"Did you hear me?" Farah asked.

"No."

"I asked if you wanted to eat with us," she said.

"No. I'll just stay up here."

"'Kay, suit yourself."

She and Thatch went to the elevator and rode up to the
third floor.

Decca and Spire had set up house in the engine room.
The hum of the engine kept Canace calm, and they needed

that to manage the Chariot.

Stannum's long fingers leafed through the book Lucerna found in Dustpath. Pages sounded like crickets in the quiet room.

Rai was at the steering wheel.

Rodan could not tell if she was concentrating only on flying or if her mind was on other things as well.

"You handle this contraption well," Rodan said.

"Not as well as its previous driver."

"I wouldn't know anything about that."

"No, you wouldn't." Rai looked angry. Her eyes were narrowed, and her mouth formed a thin line.

Rodan barely knew her. "So, how long have you been flying this thing?" he asked.

Rai was silent for a while.

"A few weeks at most," she said.

"My father taught me to sail in a little boat on a lake in the Crystal Forest. He used to boast to my mother that it was the most natural thing to me in the world. Maybe flying is that for you."

"Flying is flying for me. In my opinion, humans shouldn't do it, birds should."

Rodan pressed his hand into the seat. "I think I will take that dinner with Farah and Thatch." He pushed off the seat and walked to the elevator.

Stannum hummed as he read.

Rodan pressed the button to the third floor.

FARAH and Thatch were laughing at the bar. They drank wine and ate bread and dried fruits.

It looked like Farah was on her third glass.

"So, he says: 'If you're just like the rest of us, let's see you knock me down without touching me.'" Thatch was gesturing wildly as he told his story. "So, I whistled and Thermal comes swooping in. The guy falls onto his back to avoid those massive talons and there . . . I didn't touch you."

Farah laughed like it was the funniest thing she had ever heard.

Rodan looked pass the giggling duo to the loft where Lucerna slept.

She had not wakened nor did she stir in her sleep. In those long hours when he held a wet rag to her head, Rodan wondered if she was trapped in a dreamless sleep, a nothingness.

The thought scared him, to be surrounded by nothing, or to just disappear without thought or feeling, to one day just be gone.

A chill ran down his spine.

He looked back at Farah and Thatch.

It looked like the party started long ago without him.

Sev was there too. Sitting at the bar. He didn't join in with Farah and Thatch. He was misplaced.

Rodan saw him a few times before. Before the Resistance had become fractured, but they had never really spoken.

It seemed odd now. Clearly, he wasn't on the side of Morica, but he had chosen them over the Rebel Resistance. Rodan wasn't sure what he believed. Sev helped Spire and Decca escape from Caleena and that was enough for Rodan not to be suspicious of his intentions.

He went back to the elevator and up to the roof. He walked down the short hallway to the hatch door. Up the stairs, leading out was the roof.

Vassal, Atrus and Pentagon sat up there as the wind rushed past.

Lights bordered the Chariot's edges and illuminated the

roof in the night.

Rodan settled down next to the worn-out villains.

"Go home, stranger," Atrus said. "We've already tried a fourth, it didn't work out so good for us."

Atrus chewed on a tough piece of bread.

"Who says I want to be your fourth?" Rodan asked. "You guys earned a bad reputation for yourselves."

"Did Rai say something?" Pentagon asked.

Vassal looked away.

"She doesn't have to," Rodan said. "I can't imagine she's always in such a bad mood."

"You don't know Rai." Atrus laughed.

Pentagon ran his hand through his bleached hair.

"You're a councilor, right?" Rodan asked.

"Ex-councilor. I'm a wanted man just like these two."

Suddenly, a bright light blinded them. It came from the right side of the Chariot.

Rodan shielded his eyes. "What is that?"

"They ambushed us, those bastards," Atrus exclaimed.

He, Pentagon, and Vassal rose. Rodan followed suit.

Vassal drew his sword.

The light swept around, and the Morica chariot butted itself up against their vessel.

The Chariot shuttered, knocking the four off their feet.

They regained their footing as the Morica vessel lurched from against the side of the Chariot.

Atrus looked down at Vassal's sword. "I don't know what you plan to do with that."

The ship launched against the Chariot again.

"Damn it!" Atrus yelled, maintaining his balance. "That's it!"

He ran for the vessel as it was about to ram into the Chariot again. Atrus leaped over the railing and rolled onto the neighboring vessel.

Atrus grinned back at the others who ran to the edge of the Chariot.

"You're crazy!" Pentagon yelled.

The hatch to the Morica chariot opened. Several guards came out with guns ready. They charged in with their backs hunched and their guns pointed in Atrus's direction.

"The fool," Vassal said before leaping over the railing and onto the other ship.

Pentagon joined him.

Rodan watched the three, their backs silhouetted against the light. Then he jumped over the rail to join them.

Atrus and Pentagon had their guns drawn. Vassal had his sword.

Rodan unsheathed his blade.

The guards released their bullets, and the four slammed to the floor, shrinking into the darkness.

The bullets hammered from their guns, and the shells littered the floor.

Rodan smelled gun powder for the first time.

After several minutes, the bullets stopped.

Rodan heard the guards re-loading their weapons.

"Now," Atrus yelled.

He and Pentagon opened fire on the guards.

There were yells and shouts, interrupted by bullets.

Vassal ran toward the guards. He cut down three men with his sword in less than a minute.

The Morica vessel lurched.

Bullets whistled through the air.

Rodan swept into the group of guards and cut his way

through.

A guard pushed Rodan. Rodan's back leaned over the steel railing. The man launched forward, pushing Rodan's shoulders. Rodan dropped his sword. He reached up his hands and gripped the man around the neck, until he got good leverage. He exchanged places with the man with one swift turn.

With his hands around the man's neck, he pushed him hard. Rodan released him, and he plummeted over the railing.

Rodan picked up his sword in time to buffet against an approaching guard.

One of Atrus's bullets came flying in the air close to the side of his face.

A guard with his gun raised before Rodan, gasped and fell to the ground.

Vassal punched the release button to the hatch door.

The door opened with a hiss, and Rodan followed the worn-out villains to the stairs.

Their feet lighted upon the metal steps. They crept down so they would not be heard.

A guard stood at the bottom of the steps. His back was to them.

Vassal grabbed him and choked him before he could say a word. Once the man hung limp, Vassal placed his body onto the floor.

They entered through the door at the foot of the stairs into the short hallway to the control room.

A councilor watched their vessel from the windows in the hallway. The sound of the door opening distracted him. When he saw them, his mouth opened to yell, but Pentagon rushed him with his dagger drawn.

He sank the dagger into the councilor's neck and chest several times. Blood spattered on Pentagon's clothes. He let the councilor sink to the floor.

Pentagon stared.

"Come on." Atrus patted his friend on the back.

They moved on to the steel door at the end of the hall. The door opened with a screech despite Vassal's care in opening it.

The guards were ready with their guns pointed at them.

A guard was at the steering wheel, and a councilor stood in the corner.

"Drop your weapons," the councilor commanded.

There were six guards in the room, including the one at the wheel.

"Okay, okay." Atrus held his hands up with his gun pointed at the ceiling. His finger was off the trigger.

The others followed suit.

Atrus brought his gun down to the floor.

What the guard could not see was that his other hand, hidden behind Vassal, was reaching into his back pocket.

He retrieved a metal orb from his pocket and rolled it across the floor.

It hit the foot of the councilor and started to tick.

The guards looked down at the metal orb.

"It's time to go," Atrus whispered to his friends.

Vassal looked back at him. "What did you do?"

"Go!" Atrus shouted.

Rodan pushed the steel door open, and they rushed through the door and slammed it shut behind them.

A few bullets rang out and hit the door before a loud explosion filled the room.

Their backs were against the steel door as it shuttered.

"What was that?" Pentagon asked.

They were all breathing heavy.

Then came an uneasy feeling like they were in an elevator that was dropping suddenly.

Rodan watched as the Morica vessel fell away from the Chariot, heading down.

"Damn it!" Atrus said. He scrambled to his feet followed by the others. He pulled the heavy steel door open.

The rushing wind was deafening.

The explosion had blasted the glass out of the windows in the control room.

The bodies of the guards and the councilor were in pieces. There was blood everywhere, and the control panel and the steering wheel had been blown to bits."

"Can you fly it?" Pentagon yelled to Atrus over the rushing wind.

"Does it look like I can fly it?" Atrus shouted back.

The vessel was descending rapidly.

Thatch's Chariot was shrinking into the distance.

"Well, guys, it's been great," Atrus said.

Rodan stepped up to a window. The wind tore through his hair.

"Take each other's hands," Rodan said.

"I think it's a little late to start praying," Vassal said.

"Just do it."

Pentagon took Atrus's and Vassal's hands. Then Rodan grabbed Atrus's arm.

He focused.

It was like all the energy in his body concentrated on one thing and one thing only.

A vine emerged, wrapping around the railing of Thatch's vessel.

Rodan took the other end.

Their bodies swept through the broken window as the Morica vessel fell to the sea.

Rodan and the worn-out villains dangled from the vine attached to Thatch's Chariot. Rodan looked down at the others. "Now, will you take a fourth?"

20

BLOOD STAINS

*Before I am Dead and Gone, I want to Know that I Followed the Right
Path. I feel Sorry for Those who have not Found It.*

MIST veiled the sky.

As Mordecai gazed out his bedchamber window,
he thought he saw something black streak across the
open plain beyond the trees. It disappeared into the wild
brush.

Maybe it was a bear.

Mordecai turned away from the open window. The wind
drifted in, sending sharp chills through his body.

Curious, when he was a boy, the cold didn't seem to bother
him. After his parents died, he would spend days sleeping in
the snow. His body had become accustomed to the luxury of
heat. Now, he couldn't even go out in the spring with no less

than a thick shawl.

He hated how fragile he had become.

He wanted to ravish the cities with his knife to Elemental throats. But instead he moved pawns on a table inside his marble fortress.

Perhaps his blood, now unused to battle and strife, had cooled. He threw the cushion from his chair and sat on the hard oak. He looked at the raised veins in his hands before putting inky quill to paper.

He scribbled the instructions, folded the paper, and placed it under his bed. He knew discussions would turn to Breeze, and he was ready.

His plan had worked. He had gassed the Rebel Resistance out like rats from a hole. But he had not found the traitors.

When his hands were on the spheres, he felt powerful. He had done that without the help of his fellow High Councilors. They were a bunch of old men who knew nothing about hunger and need. They didn't know how to fight for what they wanted. But Mordecai did. He knew what it was to be hungry in the streets, to be without love and family, to feel betrayed.

Elementals were abominations. They created fear.

He had to do something about them.

The mist drifted into his window like it was being beckoned. The pitiful man's screams echoed down the hallway. Mordecai didn't understand what the man meant to Fulgur. Perhaps he was just a plaything to him, to wind up when he was bored.

All Mordecai wanted to do was put an end to it: both the man's misery and the misery he might inflict on others as one of *them*.

Mordecai cringed when he thought about how readily the

spheres had been taken from him. Months of gathering, plotting, and deception to be left with—nothing.

And the failed union between Veil and Sara tormented his soul. Mordecai should have known she would break him. Veil was like fractured glass, and she had tipped him over the edge, leaving only shards on the floor. *What he did . . . What he had become . . .*

Mordecai couldn't form words for the hopeless loss he felt over Veil. Veil had the people's sympathy, their trust. Now all he had was their fear.

Mordecai never wanted a union. He wanted an extermination. To think that Elementals could be trusted, that they could be treated as brothers was nonsense. The High Council was weak for thinking it. But Mordecai—he couldn't say it. He couldn't let them discover his plotting. They would tear him down, expel him from the High Council, and destroy their only hope of ridding themselves of Elemental tyrants forever.

Mordecai looked at his hands. He hated to admit it, but he could feel his body weakening. It was like being trapped in a decaying house, knowing it will one day collapse on him, but finding no way out. He wondered if Fulgur felt like that, but somehow his soul would not leave its tomb.

Mordecai shook his head—that's just the kind of tool he needed: immortality.

That's why he feared Fulgur. The man had not changed in over thirty years since the first time Mordecai saw him. How long he had lived was as mysterious as what he was. Fulgur was not an Elemental. He was something more. Mordecai couldn't even think of how to challenge that beast. He hoped there weren't others. He had to hold onto what he could control.

He hated to think on his mortality.

MORDECAI joined the rest of the High Council at the large dinner table. He preferred when he was traveling. He didn't like to pretend he liked the other High Councilors or that he could even tolerate them.

Surnom sat at the head of the table. *Would he nod off into his own food this evening?*

Jove eyed Mordecai as he took his seat. He perhaps wondered what Mordecai chose to do with that map. If Jove thought Mordecai would more fully confide in him, he was wrong. Mordecai only told the other members of the High Council enough to get what he wanted, but not more. They couldn't contribute to anything beyond what he asked of them.

Mordecai took his seat.

"This is the only time you grace us with your presence, High Councilor Mordecai," Romulus said.

Mordecai hated Romulus. He was a pompous fool. He was only on the High Council because he killed his brother and took all the credit for founding Jetty Verte back when it was a prosperous trading camp. Of course, it was only a rumor that he killed his twin. They were the only two there. Romulus claimed his brother fell to his death through the rifts in the wrinkled plain. Mordecai had stabbed enough people in the back to know not to believe that.

Caduceus chimed in. "Being alone is a good time to think."

"Then High Councilor Mordecai must be the most thoughtful among us," Romulus said.

You've got that right.

Mordecai took a sip of his nectar wine and ignored the

fact that Surnom had yet to raise a glass or a fork. Mordecai glanced in Surnom's direction. His eyes were on him. Mordecai's lack of respect did not escape his attention, but he did not mention it aloud. The other High Councilors waited until Surnom lifted his cup to drink before they delicately started their meals.

A heavy cloak of silence smothered all noise in the great dining hall.

The soundlessness was so thick it made Mordecai's skin itch. It was the same sick feeling he got when he could sense Fulgur's presence. He listened as footsteps invaded the stillness and waited for a knife to drop.

Silverware clamored against glass plates. The High Council stared in chilled silence at the tall, gaunt figure that had entered the room.

Mordecai looked on in shock.

It was not Fulgur.

The tall figure walked around the table and took his seat. His dark roots were growing; the white hair trailed down his back. The whole thing reminded Mordecai of a snowy avalanche, and it was fitting as Veil had become little more to him but a downward spiral, a shell of a man.

Veil was so thin that his robes hung on his bones, and his eyes were sunken like shallow graves.

"What is this?" Surnom's voice came out with a mix of bewilderment that dampened his authority.

"I'm taking my seat."

Mordecai was shocked when Veil's voice came out of the shell. He had almost expected his voice to have withered like his body.

"You think you still have a place here?" Surnom's voice had settled into its old croak. It was from all the dust that had filled it from the second recorded storm in Dustpath.

"I am a High Councilor."

"And an Elemental," Caduceus said. If his body stretched across the table any further, he would pull something.

Mordecai could only see him from the corner of his eye. His attention was focused on Veil. He didn't want to look at the creature that was once his most trusted instrument, but Veil looked like a ghost that had possessed his own rotting corpse, moving it around like a puppet. But Mordecai could see no motive for his return. *Why had he come back here?*

"You have Elemental guards and spies," Veil said. His place had not been set, and he rested his hands where his plate would have been. The fingers had little flesh on them and the bones were visible even in the dimmed light.

"You have not filled my seat," he went on.

There was an air of fear around the room. The High Council had not witnessed the blight he set on Lumina, but they had all heard the gory tale of it.

Although it was a blow to Elementals, it was Morica's shame as well. And if the High Council chose to prosecute Veil for it, Elementals might be unwilling to side with them. However, if they didn't police it, they would be sending all Mirmina the message that the Council cannot protect them. If Mordecai had been able to see this sooner, to stop Veil before he became undone, he could have inspired the people further. He would have been the beacon for all Elementals. It would have shown them that Morica was accepting, and then it would have been like leading unknowing lambs to the slaughter.

"Even his predecessor was a traitor," Caduceus said.

Mordecai tore his eyes away from Veil long enough to see Jove shrink in his seat. What would Veil think of Caduceus's words? The fear was potent.

"I have not come here to escape my crimes," Veil said. "I have control over my element now."

Mordecai cringed. Everything in him wanted to reach across the table and strangle him. He was less than human. Who he was had been sluffed off like a snake's skin.

Despite what Veil had done in Lumina, Mordecai couldn't find reason to fear him. He was a broken man, but not a violent one. What he had done in Lumina was because he had lost control. What they really needed to fear were others like him. Veil could be a real asset against them. They still needed him on their side. Mordecai could convince the people that what Veil did was a result of being burdened with an ability that he had yet to understand. That they would hereby provide services and counseling for Elementals with such struggles. Veil could do a penance as an apology for what he did. The people would soon come to forgive their favorite Councilor and his words would once again sooth their concerns.

"There must be a public trial," Romulus said.

Whispers went around the room as each of the High Council leaned in toward the other, but still all eyes were on Veil. Only Veil and Mordecai did not take part in the harsh whisperings that became a roar.

Mordecai stood from his seat. His heavy chair squealed against the floor. "We don't need to shout this any louder to the heavens," he exclaimed.

The whispering stopped. The High Council turned their eyes to Mordecai.

"What would a public trial do, but incite the people more? We must help them to forget the bad and move on. Veil had been a great asset among the people. I believe they will be quick to forgive. What's more, he can control his lesser self. Which he has proven by sitting calmly among us. He needs only to rebuild his rapport with the people so he can continue to be our beacon."

Mordecai's hand was on his knife as he spoke. He didn't intend to use it, but keeping it within his grip gave him a sense of power.

Veil had more power in him than that knife. He was a worthier instrument to Mordecai now. Why hadn't Mordecai seen it before? The more he spoke, the more he realized. If Veil could be contained, he could be Mordecai's greatest weapon.

"Well spoken, High Councilor Mordecai," Surnom said. "But the people will likely require more than an apology for these crimes."

"And they will get more than an apology," Veil said. His bony hands moved to his lap.

"What will you give them?" Surnom croaked.

"My life."

If the silence could have gotten any heavier than it was before, it did. It was like the very air became heavy.

He's a madman, Mordecai thought, *and here I thought he could be reasoned with, restrained, and contained.*

Veil resumed. "For their loyalty to Mirmina and our cause, to the unification of Mirmina."

"How will you qualify that?"

"Laws and consequences. There must be a vote by all, a vow to uphold what is right."

Big words with no substance. *What is he up to? He doesn't want to die.* And Mordecai knew full well that Veil was never against Elementals parading their powers in the streets. *They could never be our equals so why should they be treated equally.*

"Once that happens, I'll take my punishment. The people may choose for me to die in any way they like."

"I don't think the High Council can endorse such a thing," Surnom said. "As long as you're one of us, you would have to be treated like a High Councilor, and we would have to have a trial."

"And decide what? That I should die." Veil spoke with such calm about his own demise that it chilled even Mordecai. "Wouldn't it be better that I die for something good rather than for a moment of weakness and terror?"

It wouldn't matter. In the end, it wouldn't matter what happened to Veil as long as he was of use to Mordecai while he lived.

21

OLD WOUNDS

Belief. Is it Fear or Comfort?

VEIL was alone in his room. It took every fiber of his being not to let out the darkness, the pure energy, but he had to show the Council that he was in control. He had managed thus far to convince them he would atone. The acknowledgment had surprised and startled Mordecai. Mordecai's hands had shaken against the table. He might have thought that it escaped Veil, but it hadn't. He was watching Mordecai's every move.

Veil wanted to feel a certain depth of hate for Mordecai, but his feelings were conflicted. Despite all Mordecai had done, he was like a father to Veil long before Veil knew Mordecai was capable of such evils. The ultimate betrayal was making him believe his father had killed his mother, to the point of having Veil commit murder, murder of his own flesh and blood. Cronus hadn't been a model father, but he didn't kill Veil's mother. There was no one who hated Elementals more than Mordecai.

Veil wasn't blinded by him any longer. He had seen things in the darkness, that had made him shutter, that had revealed the truth.

But he could not know if the darkness was tricking him. Perhaps it was damning him.

He needed to hear Mordecai say it. Until then Veil could not be convinced.

As Veil walked down the hallway to his room, he saw Jove make his way to the great hall. Veil marveled at the way Jove studied him, like he was a specimen to be examined.

They're having a meeting, Veil thought. This was his chance.

With tunnel vision, he made his way to Mordecai's room. His element heightened his senses.

Veil, unlike the others, knew Mordecai kept a key hidden behind a loosened stone on the wall beside his chamber door.

Veil knocked at the door. "High Councilor?" He put his ear to the worn wood. No sounds came from inside.

His finger pried at the loose stone until he lifted it heavy from the wall. Veil retrieved the key and turned it in the lock. The door swung open before Veil's tall form.

His slippered feet were quiet as he entered the room.

Against the wall was Mordecai's bed with a plain white sheet and pillow. Beside the bed was a desk and chair. An inkwell and paper rested on the desk along with a few books. A jar of dirt sat on the shelf in the corner of the room.

Maybe something in this room would help Mordecai to confess.

Veil made quick work of the shelf, leafing through papers

and turning the books down to the floor as their pages fluttered like the wings of captured moths.

Veil searched the desk. There were letters to Lumina and Elementa, instructions to the guards about tariffs, but little else.

He knelt and checked under the bed. Dust settled in the corner, but the floor was bare. He glanced up. Between the mattress and the spring set was a piece of paper. Veil lifted the mattress and withdrew the folded parchment. His fingers opened the letter and read.

It was instructions . . . for soldiers.

Mordecai was instructing Morica soldiers to attack Breeze and to make sure no Elemental left the city.

Veil folded the letter.

His eyes were distant.

He couldn't tell anyone. If he did, he would never get to Mordecai. Besides Mordecai had resources, he would find a way to go through with his plan anyway.

But all those people?

Veil shook his head.

He couldn't help them. He just couldn't.

Mordecai was a smart man. He would say that Veil was trying to frame him, that he really was a traitor. He had not been in Vella City long. He had not built the trust and confidence he needed to withstand such a blow.

He lifted the mattress and put the note back.

That's what they had gone down to the great hall to discuss. That was why Mordecai was preparing this.

Veil wished he could talk to the soldiers, but they would only fear him. The High Council had not yet revealed that he was once again among them. Surnom thought it would be too soon. They needed to settle other matters and find better ground, to let the dust settle on what happened in Lumina before they could reveal Veil's presence.

Veil left Mordecai's room, he locked the door, and placed the key back in its hiding place. Then he rushed down to the great hall.

"WITHOUT Breeze, we cannot regain favor with the cities," Romulus said. "The people are looking for protectors."

Veil entered the great hall in a rush.

Surnom sat at the head of the table. The other High Councilors assembled on either side of him.

"It is nice of you to join us, High Councilor Veil," Surnom said in his raspy voice.

"I would have joined you sooner if someone would have informed me of the meeting."

"We had been meaning to discuss it for some time now. That was a while before you happened back to Vella City."

Veil took his seat at the table.

The reproving glance from Mordecai did not escape him.

"Breeze has the manpower and the advances to provide the people with security." Romulus continued. "Besides they may already have plans to be the people's protectors. If they did defend the people without us backing them, the people will see them as their leaders. If we endorse their aid, the people will perceive us as their true protectors and Breeze as our soldiers."

"The people of Breeze would never do that." Everyone looked at Veil. "They aren't the kind to help others unless it suits their own interests. That's why they helped in taking down Hephaestus, only because he threatened Tag's daughter. The threat to the people is real, but Breeze has yet to suffer from that. They have no sphere sanctums near the desert.

The danger is not looming within reach of them. I highly doubt you would be able to convince them to be your soldiers."

Caduceus nodded his head slowly.

"Their leader's daughter is one of the traitors," Jove said. "It is only another reason why he would not side with us."

Caduceus leaned over to Veil. "You need to bleach your hair." He glanced up at his dark roots.

"Then we'll offer to pardon her," Surnom said. "We're losing our grip on the cities especially after . . ." He looked at Veil. "We need Elemental sympathizers."

"If they're not with us, they will only harm us further," Mordecai said.

"What do you mean by that High Councilor?"

"I think you all know what we must do if they refuse to join us," Mordecai said.

"You're not suggesting . . ." Romulus said. "To kill them would be a waste."

"It would be necessary," Mordecai said.

"How so?" Caduceus asked.

They'll never agree with you, Veil thought. *That's why you wrote those instructions.*

"When word gets out that they refused us," Mordecai said, "the people will question our motives. They will think Elementals don't trust us to lead. Breeze is a powerful city. Rejection from them could mean even less support from the people. Despite their leader's reasons, they did defend Mirmina against Hephaestus."

"But killing them wouldn't send any better of a message," Romulus said. "If we kill them, the people will fear us and find ways to revolt against us."

"Not if we don't leave any survivors," Mordecai said.

"A bombing?"

Mordecai nodded. "Once they are gone, we won't have to worry about them ruining our plans."

"I don't think destroying the city is the answer," Veil said. "And I wouldn't instruct the men to undergo such a task. Word would get out that we did this. We're not supposed to be in the business of killing innocent people." Veil swallowed. It hit how hypocritical his words sounded in the face of what he had done.

"Our goal is to protect the interests of Mirmina and its people," Mordecai said.

You mean your *interests.*

"That means sacrifices must be made for the greater good," Mordecai said. "I'm presenting this to the High Council because I trust your judgments."

"I agree with High Councilors Romulus and Veil," Surnom said. "If Breeze does decide to join in the protection of Mirmina, we will welcome them with open arms. If they choose to separate themselves from us, we will let that be. We will make an announcement to the people that we asked for their aid, and we were denied. We will say that Breeze does not want to get involved, not because they don't support our cause but because they are still trying to rebuild their city after the attack by Hephaestus."

VEIL watched from his window as Mordecai walked his instructions over to the barracks. The other High Councilors were blinded just as he was. Mordecai had so many puppets to play with.

His body moved through the thin mist.

Veil wished he could make the mist darken and consume Mordecai, but he had yet to hear his confession.

The commander accepted the instructions with a smile.

All those people . . .

Veil gritted his teeth to muffle a scream of rage as he swept his desk clean in fury, knocking the items to the floor. He banged his fists against the desk as he sat in his chair away from the window.

Sara was right about Mordecai. Veil should never have trusted him so blindly. He was evil.

And Sara . . . Sara was gone.

The last time he saw her she was looking into his eyes. They were in Lumina, but in that moment, they could have been anywhere. She understood him. She wasn't trying to use him for power, greed, or gain.

Veil had become so ashamed.

In that moment, he had felt her energy, so good and pure. He wanted to take it with him.

VEIL lifted his head. He hadn't remembered falling asleep. His body was still exhausted from lack of food and rest.

He could sense something . . . *an Elemental?*

Veil closed the door to his bedroom and walked down the hall.

He could feel the energy . . . coldness.

The hallway had never been so icy.

He stopped at a door. It was stronger here. Whoever it was, was behind that door.

Veil reached for the handle. It was cold like he had touched a block of ice.

There was life inside that room. Veil could feel it.

Veil turned his back and slid down the door until he was sitting on the floor. He could feel the cold air creep from the narrow crack.

He took pity on the Elemental locked inside. He remembered being alone in the dark.

22

LEADER

If He Loves us, Why does He want us to Fear Him?

SHIFT watched from the window of the tallest building in Breeze as his father and his workers marched back into the city.

Tag was shouting orders.

Although his son could not comprehend the context of those orders, he could hear his father's shouts in the streets below.

Tag met his son's eyes as he marched toward his steel palace. Tag's feet hammered upon the metal steps. The way his father took the rickety steps, he was lucky they did not collapse.

"Son." Tag patted Shift on the back. "Where's General Riee."

"Dead." Shift walked away from his father's touch.

"Dead?" Tag asked. "Who's been taking care of my city?"

"I have."

"I didn't put you in charge, boy." Tag pointed his finger at his son.

"You weren't here to make that decision."

"You're not ready for leadership."

"Well," Shift said, "I was before I lost my element. That's what you're mad about, isn't it? It embarrasses you. Well, how do you think *I* feel about it?"

Tag kept the stern look plastered on his face. It did not melt with sympathy for his son.

"Well," Tag said. "I'm back now."

"But you're not going to make all the decisions."

"What did you say to me?"

"You're not making all of the decisions anymore. This is my birthright. You're not going to be here forever, old man. It's time I start learning how to lead."

"Like hell." Tag stalked away into the other room and slammed the metal door.

Shift was fuming.

The nerve of that man to deny him his legacy.

He had led his people in his father's absence for weeks, and the city thrived despite the shortage of workers. The windmills were up and running. Shift ordered that the broken ones be repaired.

The steel palace had been white-washed, and Shift made sure the streets were cleaned and the *Lacwanx* sector properly secured.

All issues that his father had not addressed for years.

Now, Tag marched back into the city demanding the seat as leader, like all Shift was doing all this time was keeping it warm for him.

Shift grinded his teeth.

He was not going to let his father treat him like a child.

OVER the next few days, Tag settled back into his position as leader.

Shift tried to keep control over the people. He ordered them to maintain the windmills, to keep sheet metal out of the streets. But when his father spoke, the people listened, and it nullified every command Shift voiced.

Shift's anger grew.

He felt that his father was being contrary on purpose to spite him.

At dinner, they ate in silence, his father at one end of the table and Shift at the other.

Tag was constantly telling him to remove the bronze band from his arm, the symbol of his leadership.

"You look like a damned fool," Tag said.

Tag had his workers hammering away at some contraption in the tower. He worked on it for hours, every day in that room, never coming out except to eat and sleep.

He cared more about his contraptions than his people.

Shift looked out the window.

A shadow hung over the city. A caw sounded through the air.

Shift tilted his head upwards.

It was the great bird, Thermal.

Tag came running out of the steel palace. "There's that big bastard."

Thermal landed in the center of the city and faced the steel palace. The citizens scrambled out of the way to avoid getting smashed beneath his clawed feet. The wind from

Thermal's descent blew sand into Tag's face, but he stood his ground against the great bird.

"What are you doing back here?" Tag shouted. "I thought you were helping Thatch fly his damned ship."

Shift joined them outside. "We lost him in Vella City," Shift said.

Thermal cawed.

"Well," Tag said, "it's back to your nest then."

Thermal cawed and pushed off the ground with his great feet. His wings flapped until he was in the air above them.

"Come down here," Tag commanded, but Thermal paid no mind to the little man.

The great bird flew off into the desert.

"That jackass." Tag ambled off and closed the steel door behind him.

Shift stayed, his eyes watching Thermal until he became a dot against the sky.

He wished Thatch was there. He could have gotten the great bird to stay. But it was mostly because he missed Thatch.

Thatch had told him that his father wouldn't appreciate a thing he did in his absence, and he was right, but Shift didn't do it for him. He did it because he wanted to lead the city. He needed to. It was his birthright.

THE next day, a vessel landed outside of the city.

A guard came to the palace to announce the visitor, but Tag was too busy upstairs. Instead, Shift came down. "What is it?"

The guard was hesitant.

"You can tell me, Quinn."

"It's Morica. A councilor is asking admittance to speak with our leader."

"Don't let them in."

Tag made his way down the stairs. He still had his goggles on. When he took them off, ashy dirt surrounded his eyes in wide circles, but the area the goggles had covered was clean.

"Who's here?" Tag shouted.

"Morica," Quinn said. "They want to speak with you."

"Alright then." Tag nodded.

Shift glared at his father.

Quinn gave the okay to open the gates.

Once the guards opened the gates, the violet robed councilor entered the city followed by his guards. His hair was silvery-white, and he walked with grace.

Quinn escorted them into the meeting room.

Shift followed them and took a seat at the head of the table.

"Who are you?" asked the councilor.

"My name is Shift. I lead when Tag's away."

"Is Tag away?"

The door opened, and Tag walked into the room. He glanced at his son who had taken his seat. Tag still had the dirt around his eyes, and his hands still had grease on them.

He walked down the long room and offered his hand to the councilor. "I'm Tag."

The councilor tentatively took his hand. "I am Councilor Agravv. We have a proposal I think you would be interested in."

"What's that?"

"Morica Council would like to form an alliance with Breeze."

Shift's anger rose. "You can take that alliance and shove it—"

Tag marched across the room and took his son by the

arm. He closed the door behind them.

"We can't make a deal with them," Shift hissed. "It's Morica we're talking about."

"If we don't, how many of my people will die? You don't use your head."

"If we form an alliance with them that means fighting against other Elementals. That means fighting against Farah. They have her on their hit list."

It was the first time he had said his sister's name since she was lost in the Altasi Sea.

Tag's face became fierce. "You think being a leader is all about fixing things. But being a leader sometimes means setting aside less important things for things that are more important. It means making the tough decisions that hurt other people. It means swallowing your pride and choking back your honor. It means messing up and taking the fall. This has nothing to do with your element, boy. It has to do with your attitude."

Tag re-entered the large meeting room and slammed the door behind him.

Shift listened at the door. He did not have to listen too closely because his father's voice boomed from inside.

"I can't accept your alliance."

"We can give you more time to think it over," came the councilor's delicate voice.

"I don't need more time, damn it. I said no. Now take your silk robes and your guards and get out of my city."

It was his father's pride that led him to reject Morica. He was not going to make a deal with someone who was hunting down his daughter, not because they might find her, but because it was an insult to him.

But bringing up Farah made Shift think about her, and

he did not want to think about his sister.

THE sun peaked over the horizon and shined through Shift's window. He looked at his abandoned tracker and communicator.

Thatch might have tried to contact him. He wouldn't know because he smothered the communicator, wrapping it with layers and layers of cloth. He threw it in a drawer and tossed clothing over it.

He never went into that drawer.

He had breakfast with his father in silence.

Then he went out to the center of the city to see if anything was starting to deteriorate without his guidance. Some things he just gave up on.

Sheet metal once again littered the city streets, and one of the windmills' blades was broken. It scraped the ground as the spokes turned.

Sometimes he heard Thermal cawing in the distance, but the great bird never came back to Breeze. He was probably tired of being bossed around by a man so much smaller than him.

Shift could understand. By the time he was fifteen, he towered over his father.

It felt ridiculous to him that he should be led by a man whose stature was as short as his temper. Yet, he was a loyal son, always following his father's orders, and this was how he repaid him.

Farah never put up with the old man.

He smiled as if by accident. Once he became consciously aware of his revelry, he shook the memories away.

Shift looked beyond the gate.

Smoke rose in the distance.

"What in Mirmina?"

Of course, his father wasn't sending anyone to investigate the smoke rising so close to their home. He was building his machine.

Shift grabbed one of Thatch's cubed vehicles and left the gates of the city.

In the distance, he could see a large structure. The smoke was coming from the massive thing.

His heart sank.

The Chariot?

Shift dropped the cube on the ground, and it unfolded until it was the size and shape of a motorcycle, and it ran like one too. It zipped across the desert to the wreckage beyond.

Shift stopped the vehicle a few feet from the smoking structure.

It was the Chariot.

He walked around it, careful not to get too close.

"Shift!"

Small arms reached around his neck. When she was finished choking him with her tight embrace, Farah pulled back.

Shift's vision went blurry for a moment. His mouth was open.

Thatch and several others stood outside the Chariot.

"Say something to me, stupid," Farah commanded. She punched his shoulder.

"I missed you."

23

CONSEQUENCES

Life is a Contract, It is not about Free Will. For It is not Free to Give Choice, and then Say But if You Choose Any but Me, You will Suffer Forever.

THATCH woke up in his old room in his uncle's steel palace. He hadn't slept there in over a month, but there was still a sense of comfortable familiarity about it.

When his mother and father died, Tag took him in and raised him like a son.

He loved machines and contraptions as much as his uncle. He spent hours with him, soaking up his instruction and watching him build things.

Shift had watched from around corners and built things that didn't work.

But Thatch was a natural.

Tag always appreciated that.

As a young boy, Tag would bring him everywhere he went, showing him things. He brought him to D'arkadia when they put up the lights. He was one of the first people to see the D'arkadia beneath the darkness.

He poured over books from the old world, full of blueprints and descriptions of machines. He kept the books piled under his bed until there was no room for any more. He placed them on the window ledges and stacked them against the walls.

He had notes and drawings sticking out from between the pages of several books. He built the Flying Chariot from those books.

Despite Tag's kindness, Thatch still felt like the foster son, not quite belonging. Coupled with the fact that he was not an Elemental, Thatch always felt a sense of detachment. He loved his family, but he did not feel like one of them.

After he had breakfast with the others, Thatch went to the *Lacwanx* sector to find materials to fix the Chariot. The vessel was simply too large for the engines alone to power it. Even with the surge of energy from the Sphere Protector, the Chariot could only operate on its own for a month at most.

That afternoon, Thatch attached a small trailer filled with scrap metal and engine parts to his motorbike and rode out into the desert.

Once he got to the Chariot, he went to work hauling parts in and out of the vessel's engine room. His hands were covered in grease and dirt. Black blotches got on his face and clothes.

The sun creeped below the horizon. From where he stood, he could see the moon rise as the sun set. Thatch breathed in the dry air of the desert. He had missed home.

He thought about all the days he spent out in the desert building things.

His heart skipped a beat.

Morica chariots flew in the distance. Had they led them here?

Thatch wiped his hands on a dirty rag and picked up his motorbike. Thatch drove off to Breeze. He dropped the motorbike off at the gates. He didn't bother to wait for it to fold back into cube form.

"Morica's approaching the city." He told the guards. "You have to warn everyone."

He ran to the steel palace and up the stairs. "Uncle?" he yelled, banging at the workshop door.

There was no answer, although he could hear sounds of metal scraping against metal and Tag yelling commands to his workers.

"Uncle?" Thatch continued to bang at the door.

"What's wrong?" Farah wandered down the hallway.

Decca and Spire walked up with her, Spire with her baby in her arms.

"Morica vessels are coming."

"They followed us?"

"I don't know."

The metal door screeched open.

"What is it?" Tag asked, his voice agitated, the foggy goggles still over his eyes.

"Morica."

Tag looked concerned beneath the goggles. He shut the door in Thatch's face and started yelling orders to his workers. "Alright, we gotta get this thing outside."

"What do we do?" Farah asked.

"We have nothing to fight them with," Thatch said.

"We have our elements," Spire said. "And Atrus has enough guns to arm everyone in Breeze."

"They'll attack the palace first," Thatch said.

"I'm getting you and the baby out of here," Decca said to Spire.

Spire nestled the baby's head close to her.

"There's an inn on the edge of the city," Thatch said.

"We'll go there," Decca said. "Come on."

"Take Lucerna with you. She's downstairs in the second room on the right."

Decca and Spire ran down the metal stairs, their footsteps echoing through the hallway.

"I'll go warn the others," Farah said.

"Wait," Thatch said.

Farah stopped mid-run.

"Tell Atrus to bring as many weapons as they can carry." Farah nodded.

Thatch felt weird issuing orders. He had never been a leader.

Tag emerged again from behind the steel door. "What's the matter with you, boy? Go outside with the guards and watch the gates. When they get close, contact me on this thing." He tossed a communicator to Thatch. Then he shrank back into the room.

Thatch clenched the communicator in his left hand. He burst through the steel door and ran to the gates.

The guards watched the massive vessels with their bright lights. There were six chariots. Thatch doubted they commissioned Atrus for that many.

Before he made it to the gates, a loud explosion sounded.

Thatch was knocked to the ground. There was ringing in his ears. The communicator hit the ground hard and skidded across the metal plates. Thatch got up and grabbed it.

Fire rose around the gates. The guards were dead, and the wide steel door had been blasted off. Three of the vessels landed near the gates, and men got out wielding pistols.

Clenching the communicator in his hand, Thatch ran and hid behind the wall of a nearby building.

He looked down at the communicator. It was smashed.

Bullets and screams sounded from the center of town. The sounds of feet hammering the stone paved streets rang through the city.

Thatch squeezed his eyes shut and prayed for the courage to peer around the corner to see where he could go next. Images flashed through his mind of the Great Raid. If he stayed there too long, they would find him, and he would die just like his parents.

Shaking, he glanced around the corner.

Bodies littered the ground.

Thatch pulled his head back and leaned closer to the wall. He breathed through his nose. His teeth clenched.

He heard more shots and screams. Smoke rose into the air. He gathered the nerve to run behind the wall of the next building. From there, he peered around the corner.

The vessels gathered above the city.

"Come on, men." His uncle's voice boomed.

They were wheeling a metal contraption toward the center of the city.

The worn-out villains emerged from the palace, guns and swords ready. He saw Rodan and Farah in their company. Shift was not far behind. He carried a gun.

Farah commanded Wind to knock down some of the men still in the square.

Rai ran past him. She turned around when she saw him

out of the corner of her eye. Rai reached out her hand, and Thatch took it.

Without saying a word, she shoved a gun sideways against his chest. Thatch took the gun. Rai ran off down the streets.

Loud bellowing echoed down the alleyway.

"Fire!" Tag yelled.

Thatch looked around the corner just in time. A missile hit one of the Morica vessels. The vessel shuttered in the sky and leaned dangerously.

"Again!"

The vessel was now on fire.

The other vessels started raining missiles.

Blood filled the streets, and the smell of smoke became stronger.

Thatch decided to run to higher ground.

As he was making his way through the streets, a Morica guard ran into him from an alleyway. Without thinking, Thatch shot him. It was the first time he had ever shot someone. The man fell to the ground and dropped his gun.

Thatch grabbed the gun and searched the man for any other weapons.

The man's body was limp.

Thatch began to sweat. He wiped the sweat with the back of his hand, smearing grease and dirt along his forehead.

He found a dagger on the man and took it.

Then he ran into the building and took the stairs two at a time until he made it to the roof.

Several of his neighbors were dead in the streets.

Tag was bombing the vessels. One was behind the wall on fire. It had crashed in the sand. There was damage along its sides.

Three more vessels remained in the sky.

The others had scattered.

Farah knelt in the alleyway on the side of a building. She sank her dagger into a Morica soldier and moved on.

Thatch tried to shoot the men from his vantage point at the top of the building. He shot one in the arm and another in the chest before the gun Rai gave him ran out of ammo.

He lifted the weapon he had taken from the guard. It fired rapidly, more than one bullet at a time.

He was blinded by an explosion and dropped to the floor.

When he got back up, Tag's contraption was blown to pieces. The workers who were operating it were dead. He could not see his uncle anywhere.

He saw Shift run into a building.

Thatch decided to follow him. He leapt down the stairs and out the building. Running to the other building, he ducked every time he heard an explosion. The vessels were still shooting from above.

He made it to the building. He climbed the stairs outside. This was where they stored most of the sheet metal and parts. Thatch scaled the railing.

Tag and Shift stood below. Between them was a Morica soldier. He looked to be about eighteen or nineteen years old. He was scared.

He switched his gun from Tag to Shift and back again.

"That's right, boy. Keep that gun on me," Tag instructed.

The man was shaking.

Thatch stepped further out along the railing and tried to get a better aim on the soldier. Something fell from the railing and hit the sheet metal below with a clang.

The soldier pointed his gun at Thatch.

"Hey, hey, back at me, back at me!" Tag shouted. "Thatch, drop your weapon. I said drop it."

Thatch tossed the gun over the railing and put his hands up.

"Now, look back at me, boy. These two. They can't hurt ya. I'm the dangerous one. You point that gun at me."

The soldier pointed his gun back at Tag.

Sheet metal fell to the right of Shift. He had not touched it, but the sound alerted the soldier.

He pointed his weapon at Shift.

"No, point it back at me," Tag shouted, "you point it at me."

But the soldier was too scared. He wasn't listening.

"Point it at me, damn it! Don't you dare point it at my son! Don't you—"

The shot hammered in Thatch's ears.

The soldier had turned around, swiftly . . . suddenly.

Tag stopped. Blood seeped through his shirt.

The boy stared at the body. Smoke issued from the gun in his hand.

Shift ran to his father.

Thatch's feet thundered along the metal railing to the stairs.

Shift knelt. Tag was on the floor. Nothing else mattered.

Shift cried out. His father's head was in his hands.

Thatch kneeled next to them.

Tag's eyes stared upwards. There was no life in them.

Thatch's eyes were wet. His heart had moved up to his throat. His jaw was locked.

The shifting of sheet metal sounded behind him.

Thatch turned around.

Farah stood on top of the pile of sheet metal. She stared at them in shock. "Dad." Her voice came out weak. She saw the boy with the gun.

He ran.

And she ran after him.

Thatch got up.

Shift was about to get up too.

"No, stay here," Thatch commanded. "She's headed for the *Lacwanx* sector. You don't have a gas mask."

"Neither does she."

"I know."

Thatch ran after Farah and the soldier. Once he reached the *Lacwanx* sector, he put on his gas mask. His vision was blurred through the mask.

Rounding the corner, Farah was nowhere to be found.

There was a pit not far from where he stood. Thatch ran up to it.

There was Farah. She wasn't moving. Beside her was the soldier lying in a pool of his own blood, Farah's bloodied dagger beside him.

Thatch climbed down into the pit. He turned Farah over and slapped the side of her face until she came to.

He removed his gas mask.

Farah shook her head no, but he ignored her. He placed the mask over her face and picked her up.

With Farah over his shoulder, Thatch climbed out of the pit.

THE next morning, the streets were still filled with blood. They removed the bodies and prepared them for burial. The battled destroyed half the city. Buildings were damaged; some needed to be condemned.

Morica chariots, damaged from the fight, littered the city. Thatch was certain that some of Morica's fighters fled. *They must have. They knew they couldn't take the city*. These were the thoughts that Thatch used to comfort himself. He had designed the chariots to better the world, not to level it. Thatch learned that his uncle had refused their alliance.

They put Tag in a metal coffin, and Shift and Thatch dug a place for him near the windmills that powered the city. Without the windmills, Breeze would not have thrived, just as it would not have thrived without Tag.

Farah cried against Shift's shoulder as their father was lowered into the ground.

Now they were like him, Thatch thought. Orphaned.

Tears fell down his cheeks as he shoveled the sand over his uncle's coffin.

THATCH surveyed the wreckage. There were seven Morica vessels down. Some of the damage was superficial. He imagined that the chariots must have run out of missiles and the fighters stormed the streets with their guns instead.

He got out his blueprint and searched his stockpile for the right parts to repair the vessels. Thatch needed to work with his hands. He needed to keep himself occupied. It kept his mind off Tag.

It took him half a day to repair two of the vessels that needed only minor fixes. However, the other vessels needed parts he didn't have.

"Need help?" Atrus approached Thatch as he replaced the siding of one of the chariots.

"No," Thatch said. "I'm doing this to help me meditate. I can't do that with you here."

Atrus leaned up against the side of the vessel. "You know, the reason these things fly better than yours is because they're smaller. They need less power to operate. If you had made your vessel smaller, you wouldn't need Thermal to help it along."

Thatch stopped and looked at him. "So, that's what you learned from stealing my work?" Thatch turned back to what he was doing. "The Chariot flew fine without Thermal."

"The engines are overtaxed."

"Look," Thatch said. "I don't know what you're doing out here, but if you're bored, you can help clean up the streets. The best way to get these vessels out of here is to repair them and fly them out. You're slowing down my work."

Atrus stopped leaning against the side of the chariot. He sighed. "I know we were never friends, but . . . Farah and I were. I didn't mean any harm with the whole 'stealing your ideas' thing. I just needed to get away from this place. Start out on my own."

"I'm not putting a good word in for you with Farah."

"I just saw you out here," Atrus said, "and thought I could help. I did build these things after all. I can get arrogant. I never denied that."

Thatch glared at Atrus.

Atrus put his hands up. "I'll let you get back to your work."

You're the reason for all this, Thatch thought. *Building chariots for Morica . . . with missiles!* Atrus was lucky Thatch didn't have Shift throw him out to the desert.

THATCH and Shift sat in the dining room. They hadn't said much.

"Are you alright?" Thatch asked.

"My father's dead."

Thatch had never felt awkward around Shift. They had been like brothers. But he did now. He didn't know what to say to comfort Shift. Tag was Thatch's father too. He had taken him in when his parents died. There was nothing any-one could say. With time, the hurt would numb, but it would never leave.

"What are you doing out there?" Shift asked.

"I'm working on the Morica chariots," Thatch said. "Best way to get them out of the city is to fly them out, but they have to work first. Only Uncle Tag doesn't . . . um . . . we don't have the part I need in the storeroom."

"What part do you need?"

"Five of the vessels need the same replacement part." Thatch reached into his pocket and unfolded his blueprint on the table. "This one." He pointed. "Once I have these. The chariots should fly no problem."

"You could probably find those in the *Lacwanx* sector," Shift said.

"I already checked," Thatch said.

A guard entered the room and delivered an envelope.

"What's this?" Thatch asked.

"His will." The guard gave a quick nod and left.

"You should open it." Thatch passed the envelope to Shift.

Shift ripped the envelope open and read the will. He frowned and tossed the will on the table. He left the room and slammed the door behind him.

Thatch picked up the will.

It was short, to the point, just like Tag always was.

He left most of his assets to Farah and Shift. But below that under successor he had named: Thatch.

Thatch sighed. He folded the will back up and placed it in the envelope.

THATCH knocked on Shift's door. "Shift, open up. Come

on. I want to talk to you."

Shift turned the door knob, opened the door, and walked away.

Thatch walked in and closed the door behind him.

Shift sat in a chair near a small round table by the window in his room. "What's there to talk about?"

"This." Thatch tossed the envelope on the table.

Shift picked it up and rose from his seat.

"This," he said, raising the envelope in the air. "This is an insult. I'm his son. I went into that building for him. That boy would have killed him right then and there if I hadn't showed up." Tears fell from Shift's eyes as he clenched his teeth. "I wanted to save him."

"Shift, he had no time to change that will. You going in there like that. You tried to save him. If he would've lived, he would've changed it."

Shift shook his head. He put the envelope back down on the table.

"He would have," Thatch said. "You are his successor, and that's what we're going to tell everybody, even Farah."

"What are you talking about?"

"We're the only ones who've seen this." He pointed to the envelope. "So, we're going to tell everyone you're the leader of Breeze. It's your birthright."

24

GLASS HOUSES

Doubt is the Worst Thing because with Doubt, comes Lies. You can Never be Truthful with Doubt in Your Heart.

RAI buckled the straps securing Vassal's wooden hand. She placed the lifeless limb on the table beside the bed. She sloshed a rag into the bucket of water. She wiped the cut above his elbow.

It was open and until recently was gushing blood. The wound was now cauterized, but it needed cleaning to prevent infection.

"Why are you helping me?" Vassal asked.

"Because no one else will touch you." There was spite in her voice.

She cleaned the wound and the area around it.

Vassal gritted his teeth.

"You've had much worse." She rinsed the bloody rag in the water. She pulled his arm. "You hit me, and I'll kill you." She sounded sincere.

"I wouldn't."

Rai closed her eyes.

Smoke came from the wound.

"Aww . . ." Vassal groaned in pain.

"That'll clear any infection. Congratulations. You're not going to die."

She reached below the bed and retrieved the wrapping. She wrapped his arm. Blood seeped through the dressing.

She looked at his stump. She remembered when Morica guards hacked Vassal's arm off along with his leg. It wasn't a clean cut. They slashed with weapons unused to cutting through flesh and bone that way.

Vassal followed her eyes. "I don't like to think about it."

"How can you not?" she asked.

"I focus on other things mostly. When I find myself thinking about it, I try to think of the happiest I've ever been. You know when that was?"

Rai got up. "I don't have to sit here and listen to this."

"No, you don't."

She walked away from his bedside and out the door. Rai's feet thundered down the metal stairs.

"Hey!" It was Rodan. He was coming down the stairs from another floor. "They're looking for abled bodies to help wash the blood from the streets. You'd be a real asset."

"I'll come." Rai's voice was hard, without feeling.

"Alright, follow me." Rodan went down a few steps ahead of her.

Rai sighed.

She met Rodan at the well. They filled steel buckets of

water one for each hand and carried them into the city streets.

The streets were paved in stone or steel. They poured the water over them and brushed them down with push brooms.

"How's your day been going?" Rodan tried to make conversation as they worked.

"How does it look?" Rai pushed the large broom forward. The bristles swept the blood into the cracks.

"Are you always this pleasant?" Rodan asked.

Rai stopped. "Look, I didn't sign up for this."

"But I thought you agreed to come out here and help."

"You wouldn't understand," she said.

"Help me to understand."

Why was he prying?

Rai got back to work.

Rodan sighed.

"I didn't want to go back to the Lake," Rai said. "I've got nowhere else to go. I wanted to travel again to get my mind off things, and then the very thing I wanted to forget about is hanging around like lingering death."

"What's that?" he asked.

Rai shook her head. "The leader of the Rebel Resistance."

"Commander Vassal?"

"Commander. Ha," Rai said.

"You two have history."

"That's the understatement of the year," she said. "We traveled together for a long time, Vassal, Atrus, Pentagon, and I. Vassal's a traitor. I never wanted to see his face again."

Rai pushed the broom with aggression.

"When we leave to find Sara," Rodan said, "we can leave him here."

"Your Commander?" Rai was puzzled. Rodan didn't

seem the type to break oaths, but then again, he was part of
the Rebel Resistance so he must have broken the oath to his
former leader.

"It doesn't look like he's commander of anything right
now," Rodan said. "When I saw him on the roof, he was a
shell of a man. I think you did that to him."

"Are you always this perceptive?" Rai said.

"Only on my off days." He smiled, pushing the broom.

Rai felt her lips upturn. She hadn't smiled in weeks.

AT dinner, Rai moved her food around on her plate.

Farah and Shift had not come out of their rooms. They
were still in mourning.

Atrus bumped Rai's arm with his elbow. "You're supposed to eat it."

Rai glared at him.

"If looks could kill." Atrus returned to his food.

Canace was in a bassinet close to the table. The baby
hadn't cried since the battle. Rai had never heard the baby so
quiet and calm.

They moved Lucerna back to one of the bedrooms in the
palace. She still slept in her unnatural slumber.

Vassal looked across the table at Rai.

When Rai caught his glance, she put her fork down and
got up from the table. Without having eaten, she walked
across the room and into the steel plated hallway.

She heard footsteps behind her. She pulled her dagger out
and turned around.

It was pointed right at Rodan's chest.

"Why are you following me?"

"I wanted to check on you," Rodan said. "Did something
upset you back there?"

Rai withdrew her dagger. "I don't know what kind of friendship you're trying to strike with me, but I'm tired of being your distraction."

"My distraction?"

"You want to find her. But I don't see anyone looking, do you? You're stuck here with us, and you can't stop thinking about her."

Rodan just stood there. His face was a mixture of hurt and anger.

Rai didn't wait for him to gather himself. She made her way down the steel steps and to her room on the lower floor.

THAT night, Rai awoke after a bad dream.

She lay in bed. She couldn't help but think about Vassal, of his hacked off hand and leg, and of the night he betrayed them.

After what felt like an hour of thinking of things she had tried to avoid, she saw something out of the corner of her eye.

A bright light shone from under the door. It grew so bright, it seemed as if the sun was shining into Rai's room, but the sun had not risen and wouldn't rise for many hours yet.

Rai got up from bed.

Her sword was at her bedside. She grabbed the hilt and tiptoed to the door. She eased the heavy steel door open, but it still squealed.

Rai gritted her teeth.

The hallway was full of light. It was blinding.

Rai shielded her eyes as she moved toward the source of the light. It wasn't warm like sunlight only bright. The light emitted from under one of the bedroom doors.

Rai pushed the door open.

The light flooded in like water from a broken dam.

Rai turned away afraid the light would blind her permanently.

"Lucerna?"

The light dimmed.

Lucerna stood with her white hair flowing over her shoulders. Her pale blue eyes were startling against her darker skin.

LUCERNA stuffed the bread into her mouth and chewed. She downed the glass of honey mead in two gulps and moved on to the dried figs.

Her mouth crammed with food, she looked up at her observers.

Rai and Rodan sat across from her at the table. Their eyes wide.

"I feel like I haven't eaten in days," Lucerna said by way of apology.

"You haven't," Rai said. "You've been out since we left Lumina."

"Really?" Lucerna shoveled more food onto her plate.

"We told you that your element was untested," Rai said.

"Yeah, but we won, right?" Lucerna asked.

Rai was thin-lipped.

A man with black hair walked into the dining room. He was dressed in a gray jumpsuit that was belted around the waist. "So, she's up?"

"Do we know each other?" Lucerna asked, her mouth half full.

"This is Atrus," Rai said. "We've taken a few rats aboard."

"I'm going to pretend you weren't referring to me." Atrus took a seat at the table.

"Once you're stronger," Rodan said. "You should practice your element. You don't want stuff like that happening to you all the time."

Lucerna nodded and swallowed. "But, I don't really . . . understand it. I feel it, only I don't know what to do with it."

"That can be weird," Atrus said, looking at Rai. "We only know how to walk because our parents show us what to do with our legs. She doesn't even have an example."

"Nonsense," Rai said. "Neither of my parents were Elementals, and I didn't go to a fancy school like you did. I still handle my element just fine."

"Not everyone is as astute a learner as you, Rai," Atrus said. "I heard how quickly you took to flying."

Lucerna looked up at Atrus. "Are you a Wind Elemental?"

"Yeah, how did you know that?" Atrus asked.

"And you're an Earth Elemental?" Lucerna turned to Rodan.

"Yes," Rodan said. He eyed her with suspicion.

"At first," Lucerna said. "I didn't think it was anything. My vision was so messed up from the light. I thought maybe I was just seeing things. But when we were fighting in Lumina, when I allowed my eyes to be hurt by the sun, I saw something. Something surrounding all of you. A light, like haze or mist, or something. The colors were unique. You and Farah have the same color." She looked at Atrus. "Earth was just a guess. Process of elimination."

"So, you can sense when someone is an Elemental?" Rai asked.

"That's impossible," Atrus said. "She just got lucky. Only people who share the same element can do that. And sometimes not even then."

"This is something completely new," Rodan said. "So, it's just radiating off us?" he asked Lucerna.

Lucerna nodded. "Sometimes, the light is stronger and spread out wider. Yours and Rai's is heavier than his." She nodded to Atrus.

"Probably a way of indicating strength," Rai said. "The stronger the Elemental, the denser the cloud."

"Hey," Atrus said. "Maybe it's the other way around."

"I doubt it," Rai said.

AFTER Lucerna had eaten, Rai brought her to Tag's old storage building.

"This should work," Rai said. "There's enough room in here, but no one to get caught in your crosshairs."

"What about you?" Lucerna asked.

"Go easy on me."

"I don't know what to do," Lucerna said.

"What do you feel?" Rai asked.

"Sparks."

"Sparks? Where?"

"All around."

Rai watched Lucerna touch the air with her hand, like she was feeling for something.

"Do you see the cloud around me?" Rai asked.

"Yeah."

"What color is it?"

"Red."

"How strong is it?"

"Deep red."

Rai unsheathed her sword and set the blade ablaze. "And now?"

"Darker. Almost black."

Rai thought for a moment. "Lucerna, what did you see when Farah and the others used their elements in Lumina?"

"Colors, but different from yours."

"Did their colors ever deepen?"

"Yes."

"To black?"

"Yes, sometimes."

The cloud was black, Rai remembered, *but they could all see it. They could see the energy. Veil had wanted them to. And Lucerna . . . she had destroyed it.*

"Lucerna," Rai said. "Can you do something to the cloud around me?"

"I don't know," Lucerna said.

"Can you try? Do what you did to Veil."

"I might pass out again."

"Try to hold back a little this time." Rai stopped forward and held her sword in front of her.

Lucerna's eyes darted like she was trying to remember something.

Then, suddenly, the flames that lit Rai's sword were extinguished. Rai had more trouble holding her sword than she had a moment before. The weight of it felt heavier in her hands.

Lucerna staggered back, but she didn't fall.

"Is the cloud still dark?" Rai asked.

"No," Lucerna said. "It's light and transparent, like glass."

25

FLAMES

Is It True that Sometimes Gifts can be Curses? If That is a Lie, then Why do So Many climb over Our Walls in Hopes that Their gods will Alleviate Them of Their Gifts?

VASSAL didn't like the way Rodan got up from his seat when Rai left the table. His eyes followed him as he left the room.

Pentagon must have seen the look on his face. "Vassal. She's not yours."

Vassal shook his head. "That's not what I was thinking."

"That's exactly what you were thinking," Atrus said.

Spire rose to nurse Canace.

Decca and Sev were talking at the end of the table.

Vassal glared at his companions. Then he went back to his food.

"How long did it take you to learn to eat with your left hand?" Atrus asked from across the table.

"Long enough." Vassal put his wooden hand back on before he came to dinner. The straps that secured the hand to his arm hurt his wound. The missing hand hurt his pride.

After he cleared his plate, Vassal ambled back to his bedroom.

He sat on the cold bed and removed his wooden leg with one hand. Unbuckling the straps was a difficult task, but he managed. He rested the leg against the bed.

He unwrapped the stump and rubbed it with his left hand. It was sore from walking on it for days without rest. He didn't like to take the leg off unless he was in private.

The skin was thin and pink around the bone.

Normally, Marissa helped him with the leg.

He tried to avoid thinking about how he was going to get it on again.

For almost two years, he had lived without the leg. Yet, he still woke up every morning forgetting that he had lost it.

The straps bit at his arm.

He rolled up his shirt.

The bandage was bloody, and the straps were pressing on it. He unbuckled them and let the wooden hand fall off on the bed.

He placed the hand on the bedside table and lay down.

Vassal stared up at the steel paneled ceiling. There was nothing he could do to change the way Rai felt about him.

In her eyes, he was a traitor.

He couldn't even remember that night. He was lying in the road. No leg. No hand. Just bleeding.

His vision was blurry.

In the morning, he woke up in a sick room in Lumina.

People were in beds lined against the wall and filling the rooms. They were coughing and vomiting. He rested on one of the beds, his arm and leg bandaged.

No one came to tell him what happened.

A carpenter made the hand and leg.

He learned to fight with one arm, having to defend himself on the streets from other homeless villains wanting his food.

Months later, he was still on the streets and scavenging for food and odd jobs.

That's when he peered around the corner of an alleyway in the city and found a group of Resistance fighters. He shrunk back, knowing that the Resistance was working for Morica.

He turned to creep back down the alleyway and hide among the beggars, but then he heard something that gave him pause.

"Morica would be onto us." It was a red-haired Resistance fighter. Her uniform was tattered, and her silver band had a thick, black line running through it.

"We can't do this anymore," said another. "Hiding in the streets like wanted men."

"We *are* wanted men."

"They don't know that yet."

"They're dangerous just like Hephaestus."

Vassal came from around the corner. "What you need is a hideout," he said.

The red-haired woman was called Mercedes, and she and the others had broken away from Morica. They were without a training ground or a plan.

Vassal traveled with them and helped them find a hideout among the rocks where they could train. For half a year, they trained. Their numbers grew into the hundreds.

They were careful. They were hidden.

Despite his injury, Vassal was one of Mercedes's best fighters.

They formed a bond.

At night, Vassal would visit Mercedes's tent.

Until he saw Marissa.

It was in Lumina when they were getting supplies. Mercedes feared a rat so she sent Vassal to await the others while they were in the city. There, he saw a young woman in the alleyway. She was foraging through the trash and looking for food.

Her long dark hair was knotted and hadn't been washed. When she looked at him, Vassal saw Rai staring back at him.

He took Marissa with him and brought her to Headquarters.

After that, he never visited Mercedes's tent again.

In anger, Mercedes dragged Marissa away from Headquarters. She was taking her back to the city if she had to drag her the entire way.

Vassal followed her.

Mercedes was halfway to Dustpath inn by the time Vassal caught up with her.

"What are you doing?" he asked.

Mercedes held onto Marissa's arm so tightly, Vassal thought she might break it.

"Let her go," he said.

"You want her. Take her." Mercedes threw Marissa to the ground.

Marissa glared at her and got to her feet.

"What do we have here?" It was a troop of Morica guards. Nine of them by Vassal's quick count. One of the guards unfolded a piece of paper. He scanned it.

Vassal watched the paper fall to the ground. It was a picture of Mercedes. They even colored her hair red for better identification.

The guards drew swords and batons.

Marissa stood behind Vassal who withdrew his weapon.

Swords clashed and batons pummeled against bodies.

Vassal didn't see where Marissa went.

Several of the guards fell.

Vassal's wooden leg buckled from under him. The straps were not secured correctly.

The guard raised his sword above his head, ready to bring it down on Vassal.

Suddenly, the guard fell on top of him, the back of his head bloodied.

Marissa stood there, a bloody rock in her hand.

Vassal pushed the body of the guard off him.

He looked around.

Mercedes was laying on the ground. Blood pooled around her.

Vassal crawled to where she lay. He cradled her head in his hand, but she was already gone. Her blank eyes stared at the sky.

Marissa strapped Vassal's leg back on. She wanted him to leave Mercedes there. He couldn't carry her, but Vassal ignored her and picked up Mercedes's body and brought her back to Headquarters.

They buried her in the hard sand.

Vassal became Commander.

VASSAL looked at his hand and his stump. As he squeezed his hand into a fist, he could feel his phantom hand clenching as well.

He looked out the window. Past the city, there were no lights in the miles and miles of desert.

Vassal closed his eyes.

He was running on both abled legs. He clenched his hands as his feet sunk into the snow. He saw his father's body smoking in the cold.

It wasn't his fault. The Protectors' sanctums were sealed.

His father was a librarian not a fighter.

He told Hephaestus what he knew. He wouldn't listen.

He needed a Water Elemental.

Vassal had tried to stop them as Hephaestus's men dragged his father's body out of the city. They tossed him into the snow.

Vassal tried, but all that came from him was smoke.

They were hacking off his leg. It felt cool when they reached the bone. Blood. Everywhere.

The silver worms glowed from their mouths.

Vassal bolted up from the bed.

He could feel heat.

The end of the bed was ablaze.

26

THE CAPTAIN

Show me the Way for I have Lost My Way. I Thought I was on the Right Path and then Doubt seeped In.

BOLTON stared out across the Lake.

It was calm now, but he still searched the waters and hoped not to be tossed into the watery depths.

He got down into the boat and took off his bag.

The moon's reflection was on the Lake's surface. The darkness between the stars looked deeper.

Taking the two oars, he rowed.

He thought about Sara, waiting for him. That gave him comfort as he rowed his way back to the coast.

Once he made it to the coast, he dragged the boat onto the sand.

His bag felt heavier now after the rowing. He walked a

few feet from the coast and put it down.

He made sure he was hidden by the tall grasses near the Lake. He ate some of the fruit from his bag and took a swig of water. Then he settled among the grasses and slept until morning.

The sun shined on the Lake. The water was a dull brown, lighter than before. A rabbit hopped up to the coast and drank. Months before, the rabbit would have been too scared to drink from the Lake for fear of being pulled in.

Bolton noticed the rabbit and decided to re-fill his canteen.

Through the forest, he headed for Tosia. Bolton wrapped the lower half of his face in a cloth so he would not be recognized in case he came across any Morica guards.

The darkness had spread into the forest like something alive and growing. It crept up the trees and blackened the bark. The ground where it spread had become infertile. The blades of grass lost in the blackness had curled back and died.

Bolton crushed them beneath his feet, unable to find a spot at the entrance where the darkness had not spread.

The door had been left ajar. The roots of the great tree were cracked and broken.

Tosia was empty.

Bolton wanted to get out of there as soon as possible. He walked down the path to the D'arkadia entrance. Strangely, the light from D'arkadia was brighter than Tosia.

Bolton emerged from the wide gap and onto the harder ground.

He remembered when Sara and he journeyed through weeks ago. Now, it was even brighter. He could see the sun peering over the clouds at high-noon. The water from the river looked less brackish.

He walked until he saw the marking left long ago. Talon had pointed it out to him three years before. It marked the half-way point between Tosia and the Crystal Forest.

It was evening by then, and Bolton still had a few daylight hours to travel by, but he decided to stop here and rest for sentimental reasons.

It was in D'arkadia that he really opened up to Sara for the first time.

She believed him about the Insula when most people would have called him a fool. When he was taken to Element at a young age, he was teased about it, so he had stopped telling people where he came from. He said it as a joke at the Element Games. He knew no one would believe it, but she did.

He touched the mark on the ground.

Talon was gone, but Bolton hadn't had the time to process it like the others had. It still felt surreal that his uncle was dead. He released him from Eli's grip. Talon was more of a father to him than his own.

Bolton didn't get to go to his burial. He didn't get to mourn for him.

When he was a child, he found his mother crying over a letter that she had been writing.

He asked her what she was doing, and she told him that she was writing a letter to her mother and father who were dead. She said that once she was finished he could help her send it off into the sea where they would get it.

She nailed the folded letter to a piece of driftwood, and they let it float away on the water.

Bolton and his mother watched the letter drift away.

Bolton wondered if that letter would ever reach the grandparents he never knew. He decided it was more for his mom than it was for them.

Bolton took some food out of his bag and ate.

He didn't like traveling alone. He found that out when he journeyed from Tosia to Lumina a few months ago. Even traveling with those three loons he met in Lumina was better than traveling alone.

He didn't want to be on the road. All he wanted was to settle down with Sara in some little town somewhere where no one was after them, where they weren't on the run because of some crazy tyrant.

He had hoped that that was how he would find her. Someplace quiet. She deserved it after everything that happened.

BOLTON jolted from his slumber.

He hadn't remembered going to sleep.

He looked around.

There was nothing but empty earth, not a soul in either direction. Blades of grass peeked out of the cracks in the ground.

Bolton shouldered his bag and walked out across the plain toward the Crystal Forest.

One night, his mother had told him that if he ever got lost, he was to wait for her in the cave between the forest and the city. There, an old man in a ship would pick them up and bring them back to the Insula like he did before.

All the people on the island told the same story about the Captain who would sail to the Insula for glistenings even though they were worth nothing.

Bolton's memory of their journey to the Insula was vague. He was very young, just starting to walk. He remembered a ship and a captain and the cave they went through to get there.

He was carried on his father's back. His blond hair swept his face.

Bolton found the valley where he and his parents descended.

He was sure of it.

Past the trees, down below where the water fell into a lake was a cave, hidden by wild brush and trees.

Bolton climbed down. He fought through the trees and tall bushes until he made it to the mouth of the cave. He thanked his memory.

It was just as his mother described it, a cave between the forest and the city.

He went into the dark cave. Lightning guided his way.

Light flooded into the cave from the other side. It led to a cape surrounded by the sea. Water rushed up the sides. Rocks made a fall treacherous.

The cape tapered off near the water where Bolton could walk along the sand close to the edge.

There was no sign of a ship.

Bolton put down his bag and searched the area.

Nothing.

Just the sea for miles.

Bolton sat in the sand, his arms on his knees. He stayed there for hours, walking to the edge where the tide came in and sitting back down again, searching the seas for the ship.

Soon it was dark, and no ship had come.

Bolton settled down to sleep, using his bag as a pillow.

In the morning, his lips were dried and cracked from being out in the sun the day before.

He drank some water from his canteen.

The morning sun was glaring, but he saw no ship.

Maybe the captain didn't come anymore, maybe he died a long time ago.

Bolton took to counting his coins. He spread them out on the palm of his hand and felt the weight of them.

He had betrayed Sara for these coins.

The captain better come.

But the day ended with no sign of the captain or his ship.

Bolton was exhausted from waiting and not knowing if what he waited for would ever come. He feared that even if the captain did come, he wouldn't have enough water left to survive the trip. He decided he needed to ration it so he only drank a few sips throughout the day.

Bolton fell asleep. It wasn't night yet, but he was exhausted, and the heat made him more tired. He slept close to the coast where he could feel the cool spray of the sea.

Water splashed his face.

He woke.

Sunlight surrounded a young boy's face.

"Balin?"

"No, that's Turner," said a rough, old voice.

Bolton turned his head. His hair and shirt were drenched.

An old man held an empty bucket over him. "You wouldn't wake up. I suppose you want to travel to the Insula."

BOLTON gathered up his bag and his canteen. He approached the ramp to the ship when the Captain grabbed his shoulder.

"No, no, no. First the glistenings."

Bolton reached down into his pocket and retrieved the glittering coins. He poured them into the Captain's hands.

The old man counted the coins slowly before putting them in his pocket. "That'll do."

Neither the Captain nor the young boy looked like they had bathed in weeks, maybe months. Their teeth were yellowed, and the Captain was missing several.

Bolton boarded the ship.

"You sleep on deck," the Captain ordered. "I trust you brought your own food. We don't cater to anybody."

Bolton nodded.

"Alright. That said. We're off." The Captain swept his hand up into the air, and Bolton wondered if that was the direction he meant the ship to go.

He looked around.

There was no crew.

"Do you need help with the ship?" Bolton asked.

"You don't touch anything," the Captain said.

The boy didn't speak. Bolton wondered if he could. The boy was skinny, and his face was so dirty Bolton couldn't make out his features.

He simply sat in the middle of the ship. As soon as the boy closed his eyes, the ship's sails filled with Wind, and it carried the ship out to sea.

The Captain took the steering wheel and whooped as the ship took off. He continued to yell as the ship crashed through the waves.

Once on calmer waters, Bolton lay on the deck and tried to get some sleep. The night air was cool.

The Captain talked to himself at night. He also talked to the moon like it was his lover. In the morning, the Captain shouted at seagulls with a bow and arrow. He loosed the arrow, and the seagull screeched as it dodged from its death.

Bolton sat up on the deck.

The boy was still sitting in the center with his eyes closed. Bolton looked for his bag. It wasn't on deck anywhere near him nor was his canteen. Bolton got up from where he sat and went to the Captain. "Hey! Hey!"

The Captain had started talking to the seagulls like he was wooing them.

"Where's my bag?" Bolton asked.

"What bag?"

"The bag I brought here with me."

"I didn't see any bag, but it matters very little now."

"What are you talking about?"

"Turner is cooking tonight, Seagull." The Captain continued to talk to the bird.

THAT night, Turner opened his eyes. He moved from his seat in the center of the deck and sat up against the railing near where Bolton sat.

"How long have you been here?" Bolton asked.

The boy did not speak.

"Do you know where my bag is?"

Turner pointed to the cabin.

"Can you go down there?"

He shook his head.

The Captain was sleeping on the deck behind the steering wheel.

The next day, Bolton woke with his lips dry. He pressed his lips together, they felt flakey and rough. His stomach growled. He hadn't eaten since his bag was stolen.

Turner had remained his seat in the center of the ship.

The Captain was still asleep.

Bolton stared at the cabin door.

After several minutes of hunger pings, he got up and crossed the deck to the door. Just as he was about to reach for the handle, the Captain invaded the space between him and the door.

"You can't go in there!"

"My bag's in there," Bolton said.

"What bag?"

Bolton reached for the handle, but the old man spread his arms and knocked Bolton's hand away.

"You're the passenger, not the Captain. Sit down, passenger."

"I'm hungry," Bolton said. "You took my bag."

"Sit down, or I'll throw you off my ship."

Bolton didn't know when they would reach the Insula, but he didn't want to cause any problems. He walked away and leaned against the railing.

The tension in the Captain's shoulders was released, and he walked back up to the steering wheel.

Bolton saw fish in the water, and his stomach growled. He rubbed his dry lips with his hand and flakes of skin fell off.

All he could see was water for miles. Was this man really taking him to the Insula? Did he even remember where the island was?

BOLTON fell asleep with his back against the railing. His growling stomach made it hard to sleep. The pings of hunger kept waking him from his dreams.

His eyes blinked open and before him were fruits and a canteen of water. He recognized the canteen as his.

He grabbed it and gulped down the water. Then he grabbed an apple and ate it to the core. He gathered up the plum, the orange, and the second apple and put them in his pockets. He didn't know if it would last until they reached the Insula.

The Captain stared at the moon.

The young boy was still sitting in the center of the ship.

Bolton didn't know which of them had returned his food to him. His stomach gurgled as it digested the apple. He washed it down with a swig of water and capped the canteen, hoping it would last.

27

BALIN

It is hard to Be a Chronicler because You feel Apart from Everyone who is Not.

B ALIN loved his mother, but she could be overbearing. She was always leaning over his shoulder and watching him from a distance. Sometimes he wished she would leave him alone.

He dug into the ground and pulled out a worm.

The gray thing wiggled between his fingers.

He watched it and examined the segments of its body.

Suddenly, he felt energy run up his arm and through his fingers.

The worm fell limp in his hand.

He had not meant to kill it.

He cradled the small, dead creature in the palm of his

hand and mourned over it.

His mother was watching from her tent. She was fileting fish the men had caught that morning.

Had she seen him kill it?

With the distance between them, Balin didn't think she had.

He dug the hole deeper and placed the worm inside. He smoothed the dirt over it and patted it down.

He felt sorry for the worm, having done nothing. Yet some greater god came to rain brimstone down upon it. Before that, the worm didn't know it was lesser, that something greater could destroy its life in a second. It might have had religion and society and friends. Now, all that was gone because some unsung giant came and took it all away.

He was glad that his mother hadn't seen it. She would have cried like she used to do when he was little.

The very first was a dog.

He was only petting it, and then it was dead, its friendly eyes stony and staring up at the sky.

He wondered if she thought he was evil, that he had meant to kill those things.

He walked over to his mother. All around her was a sharp, fishy smell.

"You could help me with these fish instead of playing in the dirt," she said.

Balin hung his head.

He grabbed the knife at the end of the table and worked alongside his mother.

He hated the way she watched him as he cut the fish. He pretended not to notice her penetrating gaze or the concern in her eyes.

"Are you okay?" she asked.

"Mom, stop asking me that."

"I worry about you, especially now that the Old Scholar is gone."

"You shouldn't worry so much, Ma. I'm fine."

Abby went back to what she was doing, but Balin knew she wouldn't leave it at that.

"I see you tossing and turning in your sleep at night."

"Mom!"

He hadn't been sleeping easy lately. He was having terrible nightmares, but he didn't want his mother to know that. She would only worry more.

"I don't understand why you have to be on me all the time about things." Balin cut the head off the fish and swept it aside with the knife.

"I'll worry about you until I'm dead and then some," she said.

Balin rolled his eyes.

THAT night, all the people on the island gathered round the fire and ate. After they ate, the people danced to drum beats.

Cirtus patted Balin on the back. "Enjoy yourself, boy. Smile."

Balin attempted a weak smile, but it seemed to satisfy Cirtus.

"That's more like it."

Cirtus's bright, white teeth contrasted against his black skin. He clapped while the dancers danced. A woman took his hand, and he joined them.

Balin was glad Cirtus had joined the dancers. He didn't feel like talking. His mother had put him in a bad mood, and he was still angry, angry that the Old Scholar had left him. It had been over a month, and he had not returned.

Who cares if he comes back?

Balin pouted.

His mother was sewing beads on a dress she was making.

Balin's hands were clenched.

Lightning cracked across the sky.

Suddenly, the people stopped dancing and looked up.

Another bolt of lightning erupted.

The people ran.

Balin couldn't control it.

Lightning shot down from the sky.

His mother panicked. She dropped her beading and rushed over to her son. Placing her hands on his arms, she spoke to him. "Remember what the Old Scholar taught you. Just close your eyes and calm down."

Balin shook his head. He closed his eyes, but he could feel the Lightning strike close to him and his mother.

Balin opened his eyes. "I can't."

Cirtus came and grabbed his mother's arm. "Abby, you have to leave him."

His mother shook her head, but Cirtus was strong. He yanked his mother's arm and dragged her away.

She was screaming his name.

BALIN slept by the fire.

The flames had dulled down throughout the night, and in the morning, the dew doused the remaining sparks of fire.

Balin sat up where he had slept.

His mother had not returned. He was alone.

He stood to walk to their tent when Cirtus walked up to him.

"No, no, my little man," Cirtus said. "We can't have you back at the village."

"What are you talking about?" Balin asked. "Where's my mom?"

"She's safe. She's been up all night worrying about you."

"Then let me go see her."

"No, no, no. In time, she will come to see you."

"Come? From where?"

"From the village."

"Where will I be?" Balin asked.

Cirtus pointed to the opposite side of the island.

"But barbarians live out there," Balin said.

"Those are just stories. You will go there so the people can feel safe."

Safe? Balin could send Lightning to the whole island and all by accident.

"I will walk with you there," Cirtus said. "After that, you're on your own."

THEY walked along the coast in silence until they reached the other side of the island. Balin walked with Cirtus through the trees away from the beach.

Cirtus gave him a bag. It contained jars of preserved fruits, several strips of dried fish, and three canteens of coconut milk. He looked at Balin as if he was not sure how to say goodbye. He patted the boy on the back. "Your mother will come soon."

And that was his goodbye.

Balin watched Cirtus walk away. He clenched the bag in his hands.

Static ran through his fingertips.

He didn't want his mother to come. He didn't want anyone to come.

Balin moved out onto the coast and sat in the sand. The

sun was hot on his face. It beamed off his tan skin.

Balin took a jar from the bag and ate the pickled fruit with his hands, taking large scoops of it into his mouth. It dribbled down his chin and onto his beaded shirt. He ran his sticky hand through his hair without thinking.

At nightfall, he slept in the sand and used the bag as a pillow.

Something touched his shoulder.

Balin jolted up.

A face stared at him in the night.

"Mom!"

"They wouldn't let me see you," she said. "They were afraid I would take you back to the village, but I begged Cirtus."

Balin sat up.

"I brought you more food." His mother set a canvas bag beside him. He could tell from the size that there was more in it than the one Cirtus had given him.

His mother settled down next to him.

Balin stared into the dark sea. "They're afraid of me."

"They're afraid of what you can do."

"That's why they banished me."

"No one wanted that." She stroked his hair.

"Then, why am I here?"

"They're ruled by their fear. You can't control this gift you've been given and that scares them."

"Gift? You mean curse."

"Don't say that. Your father had the same gift."

"Well, he's not here."

He could feel his mother's hurt after he said those words, but he wasn't sorry. He walked to the coast and rinsed his hair in the salty water.

28

FAMILY

The Keepers dine Together, walk Together . . . They are Never Apart.
They Call Each Other Brother and Sister, But They do not look Alike.
Yet They are Family.

BALIN walked out across the sand. The hot sun beat on the back of his neck. His hair was stiff from the salt water.

Abby had journeyed through the trees in search of more coconuts. She told him to stay on the coast. She was paranoid about the stories of bandits living on this side of the island. She would call him when she found a tree so he could climb up and drop the coconuts down to her.

So Balin waited on the coast. He walked along the tideline bare-footed so the water could sooth his hot feet.

His body was tense. He had had bad dreams the night

before, and his mother kept waking him, asking him what was wrong.

He felt static in his fingertips, and when he tried to touch the fingertips together, he saw tiny bolts of white lightning between them.

Balin knelt in the sand. He knew what was coming, but he had no power to stop it. The energy was building, and his head felt like it was on fire.

A bolt of Lightning shot up through the air. The sky cracked open like an eggshell.

Balin curled into a ball in the sand as the bolts rained down around him.

His mother's panicked voice rang out, but she couldn't come near him.

Between her screams and the energy building up inside him, his headache worsened. The grains of sand were digging little pits into his knees. His hands pressed into his temples.

Balin's eyes were closed, and the energy around him subsided, but the war inside him remained.

He felt hands grab his arms and help him to his feet.

But he didn't want to stand. He wanted to lay down in the sand until it was all over.

"Focus," said a man's voice. "You need to focus the energy. Imagine it's a small ball inside you. You control it."

"What happened to the bolts?" Balin asked.

"I calmed them, but I need your help, okay?" It was a man's voice. "I need you to imagine that the energy is something small, something you can hold in your hand."

Balin shook his head. "I can't."

"You can. You have to try."

Balin concentrated, but he kept thinking he couldn't do it. He worried about his mother being so close. He hadn't opened his eyes, but he knew she wouldn't leave him.

"What's something you do around the island, something your mom thinks is too dangerous?"

Balin didn't understand why that was important, but he answered anyway. He knew his mother wouldn't like his answer.

"I like to climb the rocks behind the waterfall. They're slippery, and if you fall, you land on the hard rocks."

"And the first time you climbed, was it easy?"

"It's never easy," Balin said.

"But you did it, right?"

"Yeah."

"Because you tried."

"Yeah."

"That's all I'm asking."

"Okay," Balin said.

"Imagine that the energy is pulling back from your fingertips. That it's becoming smaller and smaller."

Balin listened to his words, he tried to remove all doubt from his mind, but that didn't work, so, instead, he became mechanical, only doing as he was taught and not thinking about the seed of doubt sprouting in his mind. Balin could feel the energy receding. It crept up his arms and to his center.

It was different from the Old Scholar's guidance. The Old Scholar had helped Balin to block his power. This man was teaching him how to control it.

Balin opened his eyes.

The man had blond hair and tan skin. There was a deep, white scar running down the left side of his face.

"Benn," his mother whispered.

Bolton turned around. "No."

"Who are you?" she asked.

"My name's Bolton."

Abby touched the place where her heart beat. "That girl wasn't lying."

Abby ran past him to Balin. She hugged him.

Balin grimaced at his mother's affection.

Abby continued her embrace, but turned her head to thank Bolton. "You helped my son."

Bolton smiled, thin-lipped.

Abby let go of Balin and ran up to Bolton. "Let me go back to the village and get more food."

"I can't stay long," Bolton said. "I've paid the Captain to get me here, and I gave him my return fee. He's waiting for me on the other side of the island. He'll only wait until night-fall."

"But you can't leave my son," Abby said.

"I came here to teach him how to control his element."

"It can't be over, can it?"

Bolton shook his head.

"You have to take him with you," Abby said. "I can pay the ferryman. Walk with us back to the village, and I'll get you the glistenings. Enough to bring him back to me after his training is complete."

Balin couldn't believe his mother was asking this man to take him.

Who was he?

He walked with Abby and Bolton to the outskirts of the village.

Abby went ahead to get the coins while he and Bolton waited by the shore.

Bolton didn't say anything to him. He looked uncomfortable. His stance looked awkward, and he kept looking around.

"Who are you?" Balin asked.

But Abby returned before Bolton could answer.

Abby poured more than a dozen golden coins into Bolton's hand. "There, that should be enough."

Balin wondered what they were. Money was irrelevant in the village. Everyone traded.

She went over to Balin and kissed him on the forehead.

"What are you doing, Mom?" Balin asked.

"You're going with Bolton."

"I don't even know who he is."

"He's your brother."

Balin eyed Bolton.

"He's going to take you to the mainland and teach you how to control your element," she said.

"I'm not going with him."

"Yes, you are, Balin. Listen to me. You're a brave boy, but I can't have you sleeping on the other side of the island for the rest of your life. You'll go with him, and you'll come back here when you're ready." Abby was tearing up. "I love you." She hugged him.

She walked over to Bolton. "You bring him back."

Bolton nodded. He turned to walk along the coast.

Balin watched him then looked to his mother.

Abby gestured him along, tears in her eyes.

Balin looked down at his hands. He didn't want to kill things anymore.

BOLTON and Balin boarded the ship.

It was the first time Balin had been on a real ship. He figured that fishing with his friend, Alex, on a small wooden boat didn't count.

He touched the wooden railings of the ship.

"No additional passengers," a gruff voice rang out.

An old man ambled down the short stairway that led to the captain's steering wheel.

"I'm paying his way," Bolton said.

The man held out a dirty hand, and Bolton filled it with coins.

He gave him one too many, but when Bolton tried to reach for it, the old man clenched his hand shut and sheltered it to his bosom.

"That'll do."

Abby had given Bolton and Balin the bags of food that had been meant for Balin's stay on the other side of the island.

"We have to watch our food," Bolton whispered to him as they settled down against the railing opposite a boy who sat in the center of the ship with his eyes closed.

What is he doing?

Balin stared at the boy.

He never moved or opened his eyes.

"Turner, to the main," the Captain yelled.

Suddenly, the sails filled with air, and the ship was pulled forward.

The Captain turned the steering wheel haphazardly. Balin wondered if he needed to turn it at all. Wind commanded the ship.

The boy controlled the Wind. He looked to be around Balin's age, maybe a bit younger. This fact made Balin feel ashamed.

The man who took him from his mother didn't talk much, at least, not to him.

His mother said he was his brother. He had never heard of any brother. Maybe his father took his brother with him when he left the island. Balin was a baby then. His mother told him he could barely walk when his father left, but she never mentioned a brother.

Balin looked at Bolton and decided that maybe he could be his brother. There was no looking glass on the island, but Balin looked at the strands of his own hair and compared the color to Bolton's. Maybe, he thought.

And what was that name his mother had called out?

Benn?

Was that his father's name?

His mother had never called his father by his name and instead only referred to him as "your father." Balin began to equate him with all fathers. He had no individualism to Balin. He was just lumped into that general category that Balin had built up into his mind of what a father was. There was only one anomaly: fathers didn't leave their sons.

Balin wondered if his father had loved his brother more than him because he took Bolton with him. Or, maybe it was because his mother wouldn't let his father take him.

Maybe his mother hated Bolton.

She didn't seem at all affectionate toward him on the island, not like she was with Balin, not like normal mothers are towards their sons.

Was Bolton her son?

Balin turned to Bolton again.

He didn't look at all like his mother, but then again Balin had seen other children that didn't look like their parents.

Bolton caught Balin looking at him out of the corner of his eye.

Balin turned his attention back to the boy in the center of the ship and then to the waves hugging the ship below the railing.

"Have you ever been on a ship?" Bolton asked.

Balin was shocked. He spoke to him. He thought this was

going to be a silent journey. He suddenly regretted that it was not. He wondered if Bolton was talking to him out of guilt.

"No," Balin said. "But I've seen one before. There was a big ship that got wrecked on the island. There's a huge hole in it. We use the wood to build with sometimes. We used it to build Filley's bench when she got old and couldn't walk anymore."

Bolton didn't respond right away, like he didn't know what to say to that, and he hadn't prepared anything or maybe what he prepared to say didn't work.

Yeah, he was feeling guilty.

The conversation died if it had ever really been alive to start with.

Bolton tried to resuscitate it as if doing that would calm whatever he was feeling inside. "So, you've never been away from the island?"

It was a stupid question. If he had never been on a ship before how would he have left the island? He couldn't swim to the mainland.

It was hard for Balin to imagine being the son his father loved and meeting the son he hated, but he did think that he would feel bad for the hated son. Maybe that was what Bolton was feeling.

Balin shook his head. "But I know what the mainland's like. I've heard stories. It's much bigger than the island, and the people live in tall houses that soar into the sky."

"Well, not every place is like that. Some places are smaller with less people, and the houses aren't so big."

"Oh. Well, do *you* live in a tall house?"

"No. I've been traveling so I really don't live anywhere right now. I'm staying with some people. That's where I'm bringing you. These people are like you. They've just started learning to control their elements."

"How many are there?"

Bolton thought for a moment. "More than a hundred."

Balin had never seen so many people in one place.

BOLTON slept with his hand clenching their bags.

Balin couldn't sleep. The movement of the ship made his stomach uneasy.

The boy in the center of the ship hadn't moved. Was he sleeping sitting up?

The Captain slept below the steering wheel at the front of the ship.

Why wasn't he sleeping in the cabin?

Balin stared at the door to the cabin. He wondered if he would feel better inside. Regardless, he wanted to go in.

He looked at Bolton. He was still asleep.

Curiosity took hold of Balin. He tiptoed across the ship, careful to avoid nudging the boy. He opened the door to the cabin.

The door creaked, and Balin looked around to see if anyone had awakened. Neither the boy nor Bolton had moved. Balin couldn't see the Captain, but he didn't hear him stirring.

There were steps at the foot of the door. Balin descended the steps. The door creaked closed behind him.

The room was dark, too dark to see. Balin found the wall and felt along it. He touched a circular structure cut into the wall. Bunched up cloth was stuffed into the hole.

Balin pulled at it until it was out.

Once the hole was free of the cloth, Balin could see that it was a window, a porthole. By the moonlight, it was still difficult to see in the dark room.

Balin thought he could make out a porthole close to the

one he had found. It was also stuffed with cloth.

He pulled it out.

Portholes lined the walls, wrapping all the way around, all stuffed with cloth.

Balin removed the cloth from the portholes until he could see the contents of the room. As he pulled the cloth, he kept slipping on objects on the floor. They made a resounding jingling sound.

The moonlight glanced off piles and piles of golden coins. They were beautiful, but that was all they were worth to Balin. He walked around the piles and marveled at the glittering coins, but when he came around to the center of the pile, he froze.

Nestled in amongst the beautiful, golden coins were the skeletal bodies of three men. Their clothing was like the Captain except more tattered.

Two of them still had their teeth, but the third skeleton's teeth had rotted out either in life or in death.

Balin backed up against the wall.

The cabin door swung open.

The Captain came rushing down the stairs. He grabbed Balin's arm.

Balin struggled, but he was unable to get away from him. The old man was a lot stronger than he looked.

"You're not supposed to be down here," the Captain shouted.

He dragged Balin up the steps and to the deck. Balin tried to pull away from the Captain, but he failed. The Captain dragged him to the railing. He picked Balin up and lifted him over the railing.

The water rushed below.

"Hey, what are you doing?" he heard Bolton shout.

"He broke my rules. I'm the Captain. Listen to me or it's off my ship."

Balin could feel the Captain's grip on him slacken.

"No, wait! I can pay you more," Bolton said.

But that money was to get them back to the Insula.

"More?" The Captain sounded intrigued. "How much?"

"Four glistenings."

"Five."

"Five then."

Bolton reached into his pocket and showed him the coins.

The Captain marveled at the glittering coins. He brought Balin back down onto the deck. He grabbed the coins out of Bolton's hand in a rush.

Balin backed away from the Captain and moved to the center of the ship.

The Captain knelt on the deck, fingered his coins, and breathed through his nose. It was like he had saved up all his energy for that moment, and now he had exhausted it all. Balin wondered if he would die the next day.

THE waters had calmed.

Turner slept where he sat, and the Captain stared down into the sea and appeared to be talking to the fish.

Do they talk back to him? Balin wondered.

Balin looked at Bolton.

Bolton stared ahead, not really looking at anything, but looking beyond to something.

If he wasn't his brother, Balin thought he might as well call him brother. He had saved him twice. He had traveled with this crazy man for days and days to get to him. He was his brother.

Bolton sighed. He reached into one bag and retrieved two

jars of pickled fruits and a canteen of water. He handed a jar to Balin and kept one for himself.

They ate in silence for a while, then Balin spoke. "Who did you leave back there? On the mainland, I mean."

Bolton took a swig of coconut milk from the canteen and passed it to Balin. "My wife."

Balin sipped the milk. "Do you miss her?"

Bolton nodded. "We were just married."

"But you came to the island to get me."

"It was important."

"Why now? Why wasn't it important five years ago, ten years ago?"

"I didn't know you existed."

Balin thought for a moment. "But you're my brother."

"I left the island years before you were born."

So, he didn't leave with our father. Balin was wrong about Bolton.

29

WHAT WE'VE TRAINED FOR

Can they not See? We were fine Before these Gifts. Now that we have Them there is More to Fear.

SARA awoke from her slumber. Her back was hurting from sitting up all day.

The fighters had taken some of the boards down from the windows to let just enough light in to see, but the inn was still dark and stuffy.

Sara peered out the window.

The streets were deserted. All around them were boarded up houses and shops. No one lived there anymore.

Sara turned back and leaned against the wall. She moved her stiff neck around, trying to relieve it.

Sleeping fighters filled the room, but as the sun crept further over the horizon, they would be waking.

They started training in the abandoned town square.

Jin's arm had not healed, but the pain didn't stop him from leading his soldiers.

It had been days since the attack.

Jin had sent soldiers to retrieve weapons and supplies from Headquarters, but he feared another attack so he kept his fighters stationed in Wyvek.

They trained well into the night, every night. Jin was making up for lost time.

Sara still went to Dustpath to train apprentices, but her days were becoming monotonous. She would wash uniforms for the fighters, go train apprentices, help clear the tables after dinner, and she would do these same three things every day.

She wished Bolton was there, that he would return from the Insula. She had no way of knowing if he was safe.

Benn had started taking walks. Day and night, he would walk around the city. Sara wondered what he did on those walks, what he thought about.

Even though he had saved her, she was still suspicious of him. She questioned everything he did in her mind.

She still often found him staring at her. She pretended not to see him.

The fighters were starting to get up. They didn't wake up gradually like most people. When they woke, they stood at attention, ready for an attack.

Sara would watch them train as she washed uniforms.

Jin was more forceful than ever. He shouted commands at the fighters, he had them training well into the night, he had them using their elements far more than Vassal ever had, and he was planning a strategy with Yerish and Fer behind closed doors.

Jin approached Sara while she was washing clothes.

Lately, it wasn't like him to break his focus away from training for anything.

"I need to talk to you," he said.

Sara nodded.

She left the wet shirt in the bucket and walked with Jin.

"The fighters and I are leaving soon," he said.

"How soon?" she asked.

"In a couple of days. I made the announcement early this morning, but I didn't see you in the square."

"Where are you going?"

"We'll be marching on Vella City."

"You're going to battle?" she asked.

"We have no choice. They opened fire on us. They can't be trusted with a truce. We have to attack them before they get to us again."

Sara didn't know what to say. She didn't want a war, but Jin was right. Morica would keep attacking until they were all dead.

"You can come with us," he said. "You don't have to join the battle, but it would be useful to have the woman who fought Hephaestus on our side. You can help my fighters prepare for battle, physically and emotionally.

Sara shook her head. "I can't. Bolton will come looking for me to find me gone. We'll lose each other again. I have to wait here for him."

"I understand," Jin said.

TWO days later, the fighters prepared to leave.

Sara helped them pack food, clothing, and weapons. She packed meli and bandages for those who would be wounded. She patched up uniforms at the last minute.

Benn stepped up behind her. "Are you going with them?"

"No," Sara said. "Are you?"

"No."

The fighters were lining up with bags on their backs.

Jin was walking the line, checking that each fighter had a bag, a canteen, and a weapon.

Sara handed the last uniform to Dema. She didn't see Jin walk up to her.

"Are you sure you're not coming?" he asked.

Sara nodded.

"Take care of yourself," he said.

Jin turned around and marched with his soldiers to the entrance of Wyvek. They would move on to Lumina where they would find a ship to sail to Vella City. Some of the fighters were still bandaged from the bombing. Yet, they marched toward a new battle.

Sara hoped Jin would fight well and come out alive.

In the battle with Hephaestus, she had hoped that every one of her allies would live, but that had been an unrealistic thought.

Sara watched them until they disappeared into the distance.

Sara and Benn stood alone in the square.

Sara felt very small, like the world was planning to swallow her, and that she would not escape. She had the uneasy feeling that change brings to people.

She could feel Benn's eyes on her.

SARA spent most of her time in Dustpath with Malachi's people. She lunched with them, dined with them, and sometimes she would fall asleep on the soft grasses.

Benn never came.

Sara thought he might have moved on.

She decided to go back to Wyvek. She wanted to walk along the road in case Bolton had journeyed back. She was hopeful, but she knew it had only been a few weeks. He could have turned around.

Sara stared at the rocky wall that hid Rebel Resistance Headquarters. The smoke rose in the distance.

They had taken a lot of bodies from there and buried them in Wyvek. Sara had etched their names into stones. Even though she hadn't known them well, the act of painstakingly etching their names gave her the sense that she had known them, and when they were buried, tears wet her cheeks.

She moved on to Wyvek and wondered if Benn was still alive. She felt guilty because part of her hoped he was dead. She thought it might make it easier for Bolton if he was gone.

It was getting darker than Sara had hoped. She didn't give herself enough time to go back to Dustpath before the sun set.

She dreaded sleeping in the inn, but what left her even more uneasy was being on the road after dark. She breathed a sigh of relief when she could see the city in the distance.

When she reached the inn, it was dark and quiet without the snores of over a hundred Resistance fighters.

She called Benn's name once, twice. Getting no answer, she walked into the inn with her arms folded.

"Benn?"

It was still stuffy, despite the door having been opened.

"Benn?"

She opened the doors one by one.

Light flooded the hallway.

Sara hurried into one of the rooms and closed the door. She backed up to the window until she could no longer see the light under the door.

She could hear her own breathing.

The room was dark and unfriendly. She couldn't see if there was anyone in there with her.

Light was aimed at the window. It flooded in from the missing boards.

Sara sat against the wall on the side of the window.

She listened.

Footsteps sounded. The light was taken from the window.

Sara peered between the missing boards.

Two Morica guards stood in the street. They had a pair of long tongs and a jar. They were stalking around like robbers in the night.

One of them pointed.

A long, glowing worm crawled up the wall of a building.

The guard picked it up using the tongs. The tongs were shaking so bad, Sara thought he might drop it, but he managed to place it in the jar, which his companion held open.

Quickly, the other guard screwed the lid onto the jar, trapping the glowing thing inside. The guard held the jar up and shined the lamp light on it.

The glowing worm forced itself against the jar, making the man jump. He dropped the jar, and the other guard fell to the ground to catch it.

He cursed his companion and handed it back to him. The guard placed the jar in the bag at his hip.

The guards looked in Sara's direction, and she leaned back against the wall and hoped they had not seen her.

30

LIKE FATHER LIKE SON

There would be No Need for the Keepers' Laws had the Gifts Never Existed. We were Farmers, and Sometimes, I wish we were Never Chosen to Fulfill the Creator's Promise.

SARA fell asleep against the wall beside the window. The morning light streamed in as she awoke.

Benn stood in the doorway. "Why did you come back?"

Sara sat up from her slumped position. Her back hurt. "I was looking for Bolton. To see if he came back."

"It's a long way to the Insula."

"Wishful thinking, I guess."

Benn walked over to her. He offered her his hand.

Sara took it tentatively, and he helped her up.

"I saw Morica guards last night," Benn said.

"I did too. Do you know what they were doing?"

Benn shook his head.

"At first I thought they were looking for the Rebel Resistance," he said. "But I'm not sure what they were doing here. They left in a rush."

"Do you think they will be back?" she asked.

"I don't know."

Sara hung her head.

"What is it?" he asked.

"I'm worried about Bolton." She fiddled with the ring on her finger. The thick glass almost looked gold.

"He wouldn't be back yet."

"Yeah, I know, but that doesn't stop me from worrying. I want to follow him."

"He left weeks ago."

"No," she said. "I mean on the Chariot. I need to find my friends. They can take us to the Insula, to Bolton."

"There's a reason I asked Bolton to go in my stead," Benn said.

"You don't have to come with us, but will you help me find them?"

"Aren't you afraid I'll play the coward?" he asked.

"Prove me wrong."

Benn sighed. "So, what's the plan?"

"We need someone who can make a communicator on the same frequency as Thatch's."

"How are we going to do that?" he asked.

"I imagine some of Atrus's workers fled to Lumina to find work. We try there first."

Benn shook his head. "No. I can't let you do that."

"What?"

"The guards in Lumina will know your face. They'll take

you away."

"I can cover my face." Sara showed him the scarf she used when walking along Dustpath to keep the sand out of her eyes. She wrapped it around her mouth and the tip of her nose.

"I can still recognize you."

That's because you're always staring at me. "That's because you see me all the time."

That didn't seem to satisfy Benn. He opened his mouth to say something, but Sara interrupted him. "Look, you can come with me or not, but I'm still going."

Benn looked uncomfortable, but he nodded.

IT was windy on Dustpath that day. The sand kept kicking up into their faces. Sara used her scarf as a shield against the sand. Benn tried to keep his eyes closed and his head down.

Dustpath Inn was ahead of them.

Sara knocked on the door.

Solace answered. "Lady Sara! You're okay."

The last time Sara saw Solace, she was being kidnapped by Morica guards.

Solace's leg was bandaged. He caught Sara looking at it. "Wound just won't close up. That's all."

"I'm sorry."

"No need. It was worth it to stand up to those Morica bullies. Come in, come in." Solace moved aside to let them in. "I was just about to have some spiced nectar. Can I offer you a cup?"

Sara nodded, but Benn refused. Solace poured a cup of nectar for Sara. Sara took the cup and sipped the warm liquid.

"Been traveling long?" Solace asked.

"Only since Wyvek."

"Who's your friend?"

"Oh, sorry. This is Benn."

"Looks an awful lot like . . ."

"My son, Bolton."

That made Sara uncomfortable, the way he said it like he and Bolton were on good terms.

"Your son's the spitting image of you," Solace said.

Pride radiated off Benn. But what had he to be proud of? He didn't raise Bolton.

Solace tried pouring Sara another cup, but she put her hand over the mug. "We're traveling to Lumina," she said, "and I wanted to get there before nightfall."

Solace nodded. "Well, if you need a place to stay on the way back, I have the hallway. It's not ideal, but it's something. I know the place looks deserted now, but that's only because my boarders like to go to Lumina during the day. There's nothing to do in Dustpath, no food, no jobs. That's why they travel to the city, but they'll be back in the evening. The inns in Lumina are packed."

Sara nodded. "Thanks."

She and Benn left the inn.

The wind had died down, and the sand had settled back to the ground.

They neared the city. As they walked upon the marble stairs, the roar of the crowd was deafening. People packed the streets.

Sara and Benn weaved through the crowd.

"You said you were looking for who?" Benn asked.

"Workers who can build a communicator."

"Do you know any of them in particular? Can you give me a description?"

"I don't know any of them personally," Sara said, "but I'm looking for a *Lacwanx*. You know what they are?"

"A *Lacwanx*. Yeah, I've heard of them. But don't they live in Breeze. I've heard they never come out from underground."

"Atrus had some of them working for him in Wyvek. That's before they all left." Sara bumped into someone passing out flyers. She grabbed the flyer and read.

Benn was close behind her. "What does it say?" he asked.

"I should have remembered," she said. Tacitum was traveling to Vella City because Morica told the workers Atrus was there. It was probably their way of getting workers to build more chariots for them.

"It says that Atrus is calling his workers to Vella City," she said. "We have to go there."

"You want to go to Vella City to get a *Lacwanx*?" he asked.

"We don't have a choice."

"We do have a choice. We can go back to Wyvek."

"Not with Morica guards patrolling the streets."

"It's too dangerous to go there," Benn said. "You know that."

"We need that communicator."

The people moved like ants in an ant colony. They passed Benn and Sara.

Benn put his hand on Sara's arm to stay with her. "I know you're brave, and I'm not. But I only have one chance of reconciling with my son, and that's by keeping you safe. I screw that up, and he'll never forgive me."

So, that was it. He was trying to make sure Bolton didn't hate him forever.

Sara grabbed Benn's arm and led him through the crowd to the entrance of the city. Once they were there, she tore off her scarf.

"What are you doing?" he asked.

"How strong of an Elemental are you?"

"Why do you ask?"

"Because regardless of whether you're coming or not, I'm going to Vella City. But if you're strong in your element, it would help if you came along."

"Strong, I guess."

"How strong?" she asked.

"How am I supposed to answer that?"

"Show me."

"Not here I'm not."

"Cause a lightning storm in the distance, out there." Sara gestured to the ruins far outside Lumina, away from Malachi's village and Solace's inn.

"Out there?" he asked.

Sara nodded.

Benn closed his eyes.

Lightning cracked across the sky. The bolts came one at a time, until many bolts danced in the distance. As the bolts picked up speed, Benn stood a bit straighter. Sparks pricked across his body yet left him unharmed.

Sara's eyes widened. Next to Bolton and his brother, Benn was the strongest Lightning Elemental Sara knew, but she didn't want Benn to read that on her face. She clamped her mouth shut and narrowed her eyes.

Bolton had showed greater precision in his element, but Benn certainly had the same strength if not more.

How long had it been since he last used his element? She couldn't recall witnessing any lightning storms in all the time she had traveled with him as the Old Scholar. *How could so much power be contained?*

Benn knew much of control. Had he trained her, she might have been able to keep her own element a secret from

Hephaestus.

The Lightning stopped dancing, and Benn opened his eyes.

He didn't even look exhausted.

"Did I pass?" he asked.

"So, you're coming?"

"I can't let you go alone."

"You passed."

Sara wondered if the sandy area where Benn caused the Lightning storm was all glass now. She looked down at her ring. She needed to find Bolton.

31

A City Under Attack

Sometimes I Think we were Chosen because we are Weak. We are the Least of All who would Stand up Against an Adversary.

FARAH sat in her windowsill and stared at the people below. They moved like ants, cleaning up the blood and the bricks and steel of the fallen buildings.

The blasts had made one of the storage buildings too unsafe to let stand, so Shift ordered that it be demolished. He sent out workers operating a huge crane with a heavy metal ball that swung back to destroy what was left standing.

Two weeks passed since her father died. Shift didn't like to talk about it, and she only wanted to talk about it with him.

They read her father's will the other day. His estate was divided between her, Thatch, and Shift. Shift was named his successor.

She was glad her dad came around in the end. She knew he was just being tough on Shift because he wanted him to be a leader someday.

There was a knock at her door.

Farah got down from the windowsill and walked across the room to open the door.

Rai stood in the hallway. She carried a plate of food. "You didn't come down to eat again, so I brought you this."

Farah looked down at the plate. "Thanks, but I'm not hungry."

"What have you been living off of?" Rai asked.

"It hasn't been that long. I came down for lunch yesterday." Farah made a weak attempt to smile.

Rai wasn't buying it. She placed the plate down beside the door and left.

Farah picked up the plate with a heavy groan and put it down on the table. She wasn't in the mood for dried fish. She brought the chair up to the windowsill and sat, leaning her arms against the sill.

She watched Thatch come and go from the gate. He was still trying to fix the Chariot and the Morica vessels that had been damaged.

Orka was flying around the city. Occasionally, she came by and nestled her head into Farah's hair. But she hadn't come back since morning.

Lucerna had woken up, but she couldn't take the brightness of the desert so she stayed in her room and blocked the windows with sheet metal.

Farah swore her hair was even whiter if that was possible. Lucerna had become quieter and calmer since she got her element. Farah preferred the old Lucerna, always happy and curious.

She needed some of that now.

Farah decided she needed to get out. But it was hard. Everything in the city reminded her of her father, and then she would think of some happy memory and cry. She had cried so much her eyes hurt.

She walked down the steel steps and hoped she wouldn't see anybody on the way down.

She was lucky.

Out in the streets, the people were still working. Farah picked up some debris and carried it to the stockpile. All the debris would be reused in the rebuilding and as parts for what would have been her father's new projects. The people wasted nothing.

Farah helped until the sun turned a deep orange. Her arms and back were sore. She was bringing her last piece of scrap metal into the yard, when she heard a caw.

Farah walked around the tall pile. In the clearing Thermal sat, picking his talons with his beak. He was still wearing his harness.

"Thermal?" Farah approached him with caution.

The great bird opened his mouth and cawed at her.

The bird was rude.

"Behave yourself."

Thermal let out another ear-splitting caw. He had been eating out of the city waste and drinking water from the nearby oasis.

"You're the worst. Stay here. I'm going to get Thatch." Farah ran through the streets and to the gate. "Has Thatch been through?" she asked the guard.

The guard pointed to the *Lacwanx* sector.

"Thanks."

Farah ran to the edge of the sector. "Thatch?" She

stepped beyond the point of safety. "Thatch?"

Thatch came riding through with his motorcycle and trailer full of scrap metal for the Chariot.

"Haven't you learned your lesson?" he asked through his gas mask.

"It's Thermal. He's here."

Thatch got off his motorcycle. "Show me."

He followed Farah through the streets to the stockpile. Behind the pile was the great bird, Thermal still picking his talons. When he saw Thatch, he stopped and put his foot down.

Thatch marveled at him. He ran his hand through his feathers.

Orka settled down on Farah's shoulder and looked up at Thermal. Orka chirped, and the great bird cawed. Standing on one foot, Orka scratched her head with her claws.

Thatch stood back and looked up at Thermal.

His wing had healed. He looked healthy.

Farah knew Thatch was happy to see Thermal, as happy as she had been to see Orka again after being away from her for so long.

She petted the soft feathers of Orka's belly.

Farah walked back into the town square. The citizens, exhausted, were ambling back to their homes. For the homes that had been damaged, neighbors were letting neighbors stay the night.

She looked around.

They had cleaned up, but the city was still in ruins. Farah never liked feeling trapped in Breeze, but she frowned at the damage. It reminded her of the Great Raid.

She sat on the only remaining stone bench in the square. Rodan sat beside her.

Orka flew up to her bedroom window. Farah had fruit and water up there for her.

"How are you holding up?" he asked.

"Alright. I guess."

"I know it seems like the end of the world, but—"

"I've had people die on me before." Farah regretted her words. "I'm sorry. I'm used to this. My mom's gone too."

"My grandfather died," Rodan said. "I was six years old and still at Element. I didn't get to go to his funeral."

"It doesn't get any easier." Farah looked at her feet. "Remember what Talon said to me in Jetty Verte? How you can learn from the wise, but you can learn from the foolish too? Do you think my father was a fool?"

"Why would you say that?" he asked.

"Because he made the same mistake twice. Before the Great Raid, he said no to Hephaestus. This time, he said no to Morica."

"Your father was not a fool. He stood up for what he believed in."

"But doesn't that make us fools? I mean, to stand up for what we believe in when it could get us killed."

"No. It makes us honorable," Rodan said.

Farah sniffled. She wiped her eyes with the back of her hand. "I've never wanted to be away from this place so bad." She laughed behind the tears.

"I heard Thatch is almost finished with the Chariot."

Farah nodded. "And now that Thermal's here, he can help fly it."

Rodan put his arm across Farah's shoulders and hugged her. He rose from the stone bench. "Are you coming to dinner?"

Farah shook her head.

FARAH climbed the steps to her room. Shift walked down the hall leading away from the dining room. She broke the silence between them. "I haven't seen you all day."

"That's because you don't come up for dinner," he said.

"I was thinking about Dad."

Shift lowered his head.

"Why don't you want to talk about him?" she asked.

"You know I don't like to talk about that stuff."

"That stuff?"

"Why are you doing this?"

"Because I want to talk about him."

Shift put his hand on the doorknob to his bedroom.

"Don't you dare run from me," Farah said.

"I'm tired."

Farah scowled. "Every time I try to talk about Dad?"

"What do you want to talk about?" his voice was agitated.

Farah started crying. "He's dead, Shift."

Shift took his hand off the doorknob. He walked over and hugged his sister.

She cried against his arm. Her small frame shook as she sobbed.

Feet thundered up the stairs.

It was Thatch. Rai was not far behind him.

Shift released Farah from his embrace, and Farah wiped her eyes on her sleeve.

"Sorry, but there's something you should see," Thatch said.

They ran up the stairs and looked out the big window. In the distance was a white glow coming like a wave toward the city.

"What is that?" Farah asked.

Thatch shook his head.

"We need to get out of here," Rai said.

"The best way out is the Chariot," Thatch said, "but we couldn't possibly board everyone in the city."

"Then it'll just be us," Rai said.

Farah frowned. "We're leaving everyone?"

"What choice do we have? I'll get Thermal," Thatch said. "Meet me at the gate."

"I'll warn the others," Rai said.

Thatch was half-way down the stairs. Farah turned to leave with Rai, but Shift stood staring at the white mass.

"Hey, let's go." Farah pulled his arm, but he wouldn't move.

"I can't go. This is my city. I need to protect it."

"Shift, this is a mistake."

Shift looked down at her. "But I'm owning it."

"Farah." Rai was at the foot of the stairs.

With hesitance, Farah let Shift's arm slip from her grasp. She joined Rai on the stairs and took one last look at her brother. He was starting to look like their dad.

FARAH and Rai banged on doors as they raced down the hallway.

"Spire!" Farah shouted.

Holding Canace, Spire rushed out of her bedroom. "What's going on?"

"We have to go, now!" Farah said. "Something is coming for the city. Meet us at the gate."

Spire hurried down the steel steps.

Rai pounded on Lucerna's door while Farah alerted Rodan. Lucerna came out, shielding her eyes from the light in the hallway.

"We have to go," Farah said.

Rodan nodded.

Farah opened the door to her room. Orka sat on her perch, but when she saw Farah, she flew to her and landed on her shoulder.

They ran down the stairs.

"Wait!" Farah stopped on the landing. "Aren't we going to warn Atrus, Vassal, and Pentagon?"

"Leave them," Rai said.

"We shouldn't—"

"There's no time." Rai grabbed Farah's arm.

Rodan remained in the hall above the stairs.

"What are you doing?" Rai asked.

"Vassal's my Commander." Rodan turned back and ran down the hallway.

"Idiot," Rai said under her breath.

Rushing down the stairs, Farah, Rai, and Lucerna skipped steps along the way. They emerged from the steel palace.

Thermal flew toward the Chariot.

Thatch and Spire waited at the gate. "Where are the others?"

"We don't have time," Rai said.

"Rodan?" Spire asked.

"He's going to warn Vassal," Farah said.

"Decca!" Spire hugged Decca as he approached with Shilo at his side. "Something's coming towards the city. We have to get out of here."

Thatch threw three steel cubes onto the desert floor. They unfolded until they took the shape of motorcycles. Thatch got on one and Decca and Spire, holding Canace took another. Shilo grabbed the third.

"Wait!" Farah stopped them. "What about Rodan?"

Thatch reached into his pocket and threw down three more cubes. "We don't have time to wait. If they get out, they'll take the bikes."

Farah looked back toward the city.

Thatch took her arm. "They'll be fine."

As the cubes unfolded, Farah took a seat on the back of Thatch's bike, and Rai picked up her own.

THE motorcycles kicked up the sand, as they raced to the Chariot. Thermal, still in his harness, waited outside.

"Come on, Farah. I need you to help me with his harness," Thatch shouted.

The glowing mass wavered below the horizon.

Thatch pulled the latch at the Chariot entrance, and the hatch door opened. They piled in, and Farah, Thatch, and Rai rushed to the elevator.

They ascended to the roof. The glowing mass loomed closer and picked up speed.

Thermal leaned down, the buckles of his harness close to the Chariot.

Thatch took one strap made of tempered steel and leather while Farah and Rai took the other. They looped it around the mechanical pivots that directed Thermal and secured it. Thatch took the second set of straps on the left side and Farah took the right. They pulled them through the railing of the Chariot. Rai helped Farah buckle the last strap and pull it tight.

Thermal cawed.

While Farah and the others were on the roof, Rodan and the three worn out villains skidded through the sand on their motorcycles. They scrambled to their feet and rushed for the open hatch door.

The white mass licked the sand. Farah had seen those things before, the little white worms.

Rai went down to the control room.

Farah backed away from the railing. The Chariot jolted, knocking Farah and Thatch off their feet.

Thermal struggled in his harness. He cawed into the sky.

"What's wrong with him?" Farah asked.

"I don't know," Thatch said.

Rai tilted the Chariot upward, directing Thermal's harness, but the great bird slammed the vessel back down again.

"Thatch, you have to do something," Farah said.

"Thermal," he yelled over the roar of the wind. "We have to get out of here."

But the great bird still struggled in his harness. The glow was over the horizon and getting closer.

"It's okay," Thatch said. "But we have to go!"

Thermal dug his feet into the sand and screeched into the air.

Thatch ran to the great bird and reached his hand over the railing. He petted Thermal's soft feathers. *He's not going to listen to me.*

"Rai," Thatch spoke over his communicator, "release the harness."

"Are you sure we can fly without him?" Rai's voice buzzed over.

Thatch paused. "No, but we don't have a choice."

The straps of the harness snapped away from the Chariot. Thermal kicked off the ground and flew out across the desert.

Thatch watched the great bird go. *Goodbye, Thermal,* he thought. "Alright," Thatch said over his communicator. "Let's get out of here."

The Chariot rose, hovering above the air. They were above the white mass. Thatch looked over the railing. It was like a white, glowing sea covering the desert. The Chariot zoomed, and like a dam had broken, the glowing worms engulfed the city.

32

THE PEDESTALS

*But They said that They Chose us because we are creators. Because we
create Life with Our hands. We Tend the fields and Encourage Nature
to Grow. And that in turn, we Deserved the Gift of Earth. But we were
Blind, Blind Followers and that's what They really Needed.*

RAI flew the Chariot out over the ocean. No one was in
the control room with her, except the robot Stannum.
Stannum clicked his fingers over the great book. He
was parsing through volume three. The robot had indexed
and filed volumes one and two in his brain.

No one told Rai where they were going. She was free to
fly wherever.

She was glad to be alone. Though she had her own room
in Breeze, she only used it to sleep, and on the road, or should
she call it the sky, she had people around her all the time. It

was becoming a burden to have no time to herself.

The elevator door opened behind her.

"You were going to leave us back there, weren't you?" It was Rodan's voice.

Rai focused on the skies.

He took Thatch's empty seat.

"I wanted to leave Vassal," she said.

"Yeah, I got that." A twinge of sadness dampened his voice.

The guilt centered like a weight in her chest.

"You know, you were right," Rodan said. "I am using you as a distraction, but it seems like you need a distraction too."

"I do just fine stewing in my anger." She saw him out of the corner of her eye. It looked like he was getting more comfortable.

"How did it feel to steal from a Sphere Protector?" Rodan asked.

"Why are you asking me that? Didn't you and your friends take five spheres from their sanctums?"

"Well, four actually. Spire did the Water Sphere by herself, but I wanted to hear how *you* felt about it."

"Guilty." Rai was silent for a moment. "And powerful."

"Powerful?"

"Like I could make the world kneel."

"Is that what you want?"

Rai shook her head. "No, but oddly enough, it was what I wanted then. I've never felt that feeling since."

She didn't know why she was opening up to him. Maybe it had been so long, she wanted the release. She barely knew him, but that made it easy somehow. What she did know about him made it easier too. She knew he was scorned. And she knew what he was looking for.

"It's funny," she said. "I steal a sphere, and I'm branded and beat in the street. You steal four, and you're sang a hero."

"Life isn't fair."

"No, it's not." Rai felt the sorrow in her voice. Too much for the conversation. Ashamed, she tried changing the subject and hoped he wouldn't notice.

"So, you're a Resistance fighter?" she asked.

"Rebel Resistance."

"When did you join?"

"I joined the Resistance after the battle with Hephaestus."

"You mean after the great Bolton went missing?"

"I wouldn't call the man great by any means," Rodan said.

"He's all they talked about on this vessel for days. I barely knew the guy so I was just annoyed."

Rodan laughed.

"So, he stole her from you," she said.

"Stole is a strong word. She was never mine to begin with."

"Why didn't you stay with her instead of running off to that fighters' club?" she asked.

"She never got over him."

"And you never got over her."

Rodan looked out the window. "No, I guess not."

"Tough."

"What about Commander Vassal?"

She hated how he called him Commander. "What about him?"

"Was your experience like mine?"

"Not unless Sara stabbed you in the back."

"What happened?"

"I rather not talk about it."

The elevator door opened. Farah, Spire and Decca came in followed by Vassal, Pentagon, and Atrus.

"Where are we headed?" Farah asked.

"I'm just flying," Rai said.

"What were those things that attacked the city?" Decca asked.

"I've seen them before," Rai said.

"Yeah, we saw them in Wyvek," Farah said. "And in the Fire Sphere sanctum."

"What are they?" Pentagon asked.

"They have something to do with the sanctums," Rai said. "I saw them leaking from the pedestals."

"Then they're the essence of the spheres," Spire said.

"What?" Rodan asked. "I thought the essence was inside the spheres."

"The essence flows from the spheres into the pedestals and throughout the land," Spire said. "It's the only way new Elementals can be born. Otherwise, the element is lost."

Atrus nodded. "So, long story short: We need to put the spheres back?"

"I don't know if that will stop the problem," Spire said.

"What do you mean? It seems simple to me: Stop up the pedestal and the little worms can't get out, right?"

"But what about the ones that are already out?" Farah asked.

"We might not be able to do anything about them," Rai said.

"But we need to stop any more from coming out," Rodan said. "The only solution is to replace the spheres."

"But what if Morica takes them back?" Farah asked.

"It took an army of skilled warriors and Elementals for

Morica to break into the sanctums," Vassal said. "Even if they had the manpower, they need it in case of attack. Besides, the other High Councilors don't approve of Mordecai's venture. That's why he kept it from them."

"So, which sphere do we return first?" Pentagon asked.

"The Water Sphere," Rodan said.

Rai had predicted his answer before he gave it. *He thinks by returning the sphere, he can give Sara's power back to her. That would be a good way to win her heart.*

RAI landed the Chariot in Jetty Verte. They would rest the night before journeying to the Sphere Sanctum.

Rai took the elevator to the roof. She sat and looked up at the clear night sky. She hated sleeping in enclosed spaces. Any chance she got to sleep under the stars, she took it.

The hatch door opened behind her.

Rai turned, expecting to see Rodan, but it was Vassal ambling toward her.

Rai stood.

"Just getting some fresh air," Vassal said.

Rai approached the hatch.

"Where are you going?" he asked.

"Back to the control room."

"You don't want to sleep?"

"I'm tired of sleeping."

"That's funny. You barely get to," Vassal said. "Please, stay. I have something to tell you."

Rai put her hand on the pummel of her sword.

"It's a shame you think you need that," he said.

Rai eyed him.

"I wanted to show you something." Vassal snapped his fingers, and a flame hovered in the air.

Rai withdrew her sword, flames erupted around the steel. "You're an Elemental."

Vassal rolled his hand into a fist, and the flame extinguished.

"What else are you hiding?" she asked.

"I wasn't hiding. I haven't been able to do that in years. And then, one morning, my bed was on fire. This means something."

"It means you lied about who you are," she said, "but I already knew that."

"I remember."

"What?"

"That night. I wasn't myself, Rai."

Rai tightened her grip on her sword. "Don't you do that," she said through clenched teeth. "You're not allowed to play the victim."

"I don't remember much, but I know I wasn't myself. I know that. I've been having these dreams and now this. Flames erupted from his hand."

"Step back."

Rai's eyes were wild.

"You want to stab me again?" Vassal moved to the side, and Rai watched, moving with him. "I didn't come up here to frighten you. I wanted you to know the truth."

Rai groaned. "The truth?"

"You never let me explain."

"Why should I?" she asked.

"Because there's always another side to the same story. Think about it. Weren't you shocked when it happened? You think it's because I'm such a good liar, but maybe it was because of something I had no control over."

Vassal took a step towards her.

"No," Rai shouted, holding out her sword.

Vassal calmed the flames until they were extinguished.

Rai swung the sword at him, and Vassal raised his arm. The sword embedded into the wood. Rai pulled back, releasing her sword.

She walked backwards to the hatch door, her sword still raised against him.

Vassal made no move towards her.

Rai pulled the latch, and the door opened. She closed it as soon as she was through, watching Vassal's body disappear behind the steel.

She was breathing heavy, but her adrenaline was pumping.

She pulled the panel off the wall and tugged at the wires until she saw sparks. She tried the latch. The door wouldn't open.

THE next morning, Rai awoke to someone shaking her shoulder. Startled, she jolted up into a sitting position.

"Hey, it's okay." Rodan's brown eyes met her darker ones. "You slept here all night?"

Rai had fallen asleep in the hallway between the elevator and the door to the roof.

Rodan looked up at the wall where Rai had torn out the wires.

Vassal must have stayed on the roof all night. He couldn't climb down. But she didn't care.

"Taking out some aggression?" Rodan asked.

"You could say that."

Rodan helped her up. "Thatch is going to be mad."

"I don't see why. I gave him a project." Rai massaged the back of her neck.

"Here, let me get that for you."

Rai glared at him.

"Please?"

She rolled her eyes, but she moved her hair to one side.

Rodan rubbed his hands together until they were hot and placed one on the back of Rai's neck. The warmth soothed the sore muscles.

"Better?" he asked.

Rai nodded with her eyes closed. She did need a distraction.

33

SCYLLA

We went Against Them Once. We Found out we had Bred Monsters. Monsters to guard Their Gifts.

LUCERNA petted Orka's feathered head. The little green bird tilted her head towards Lucerna's hand.

"Wow," Farah said. "She must like you. She's not normally like that with other people."

"I like her."

Orka chirped and flew to Farah's shoulder.

Farah sat next to Lucerna. "It's weird seeing you with that white hair, and your eyes used to be so dark."

"Yeah. I haven't quite gotten used to it either. But it's better when it's dark like this. During the day, I can't see a thing. The light blinds me."

"Isn't there any way to control it?"

"I wish I knew." Lucerna was pensive. "One day, back when I was still in Tosia, I found a speckled lizard with horns on its head. It was beautiful, but it wasn't like any of the other lizards. It was always alone."

"But it's not like that. You might be a night owl now, but you'll always have us."

Lucerna smiled, but it was a tired smile.

She had been having bad dreams, but she didn't want Farah to know that. In her dreams, she saw the white worms and there were others like her, not Light Elementals, but somehow, she knew they had something in common. They never spoke to her. It was like they couldn't see her. She could see them in the darkness, but she always forgot who they were when she woke.

IN the morning, Rodan called everyone to the control room. Thatch was fixing the wiring that Rai had pulled out. No one had seen Vassal. Lucerna walked into the control room with her eyes closed. The morning light hurt them.

"We have to go into the Sphere Cave to set the Water Sphere," Rodan said. "It comes down to who's going."

Canace whimpered.

"Spire has to stay with the baby," Decca said.

"Decca, I have my element," Spire said. "You should stay with Canace."

"No," Decca said. "A child needs its mother."

"And its father." Shilo patted Decca on the back, and walked up to Spire. "I'll make sure he comes back."

Shilo didn't match Decca's mass. But Lucerna was starting to see how they might be brothers. Though they hadn't seen each other in years, they used the same mannerisms, like the way they grabbed a hold of your shoulder when they talked to you and made you feel like you had been friends for a long time.

"Pentagon and I will go," Atrus said. He was lounging in Thatch's seat while he was away. "Pent, doesn't have an element, but he's starting to learn how to use a gun."

"Starting?" Pentagon said.

"I'll go," Lucerna said, her eyes still closed.

"She hasn't mastered her element," Spire said

"She'd be our best weapon." Rodan unhinged himself from the wall.

"Not if she passes out in the cave," Spire said.

"I can see in the dark," Lucerna said, "much better than any of you. Caves are dark, right?" She couldn't see them, but she could feel the tension in the room.

"She's right," Rodan said. "Farah, you in?"

"Did you have to ask?" Farah tossed the large volume back onto Stannum's stack.

Orka chirped.

"You're staying here, Orka," Farah said. "You have to protect Thermal. You remember what Talon said. There are monsters in there that don't turn to ash with the lift of the sphere."

LUCERNA felt someone put a hand on her shoulder.

"It's alright." It was Decca.

Lucerna kept her eyes closed as they entered the cave. The sun was blinding. She could see it through her eyelids. She put her hand over her eyes for extra protection.

"We're in the cave now," Decca said.

Lucerna lifted her hand and opened her eyes. She could tell by the way Farah was holding her hands out in front of her that she couldn't see.

A bright light burned. Lucerna guessed that it must be Rai, setting her sword ablaze.

Not far from her, their faces hidden by the light, was Atrus and Pentagon. They carried strange metal weapons they called guns.

Rodan gestured to her to move to the front. She would guide them.

Lucerna could see every crevasse of the cave wall as if it was in the light of day. The ground of the cave was mucky. Lucerna lifted her foot. Black ooze painted her boot.

"What is that?" Farah asked.

"Darkness," Lucerna said.

"Like with Veil?"

Lucerna nodded, forgetting they could barely see her.

The cave was like a labyrinth. Every time they turned one corner, new possibilities arose.

"There's another fork in the road," Lucerna said. "Which way?"

"Keep going right," Decca said.

Lucerna turned right only to be met with more options. Soon, she became tired of asking which way, so she just kept going. Suddenly, Lucerna stopped.

Rodan ran into her. "What's wrong?"

A shadow, so deep her eyes could not penetrate it, hovered in front of them.

Lucerna closed her eyes.

A man, wearing a long gray robe and holding a sphere, stalked into the cave. Two men, carrying a glass pedestal, trailed behind him. Around their necks were iron collars attached to long chains.

The man in the long robe held the ends of the chains and

pulled the men along. He walked into the depths of the labyrinth, and Lucerna followed them.

Somehow, she knew why the man was here, like in dreams where the dreamer understands things she has not experienced. He had given his son a great gift, and he was wasting it. He feared he would try to destroy the sphere. So, he ripped the pedestal from its foundations and was carrying it to a new home.

As the man walked, the darkness trailed from his steps.

Lucerna followed close behind him.

The chained men put the pedestal down upon a high rock. The pedestal bonded with the earth.

The robed man's face was tortured. The skin was peeling back, and in places, the muscle underneath was visible. His long, yellow fingers wrapped around the sphere. He placed it on the pedestal.

Energy flowed into the ground.

Lucerna felt her body being thrown to the floor. She looked up.

Above the sphere was a creature with six arm-like appendages, all sharp as spears. Its face was spiked and scaly like a sea creature. A spike sat right above its small, gray eyes. Its mouth was open, baring two rows of sharp teeth. Scales covered its body. They were bluish-gray except for the pinkish skin on its belly. Its tail fin fanned out in the wide expanse. Its body was ghost-like, transparent.

The creature floated in the air like it was on water.

"Scylla," Lucerna whispered under her breath. She didn't know how she knew that name.

It opened its mouth, and a sound somewhere between a screech and a rattle issued forth.

Rai had her fiery sword raised against it, blinding Lucerna. But the flames of the sword extinguished.

Lucerna opened her eyes.

They were fighting the creature in the dark.

Farah sent Wind, and the monster's body jolted against the back wall.

Hearing where its body hit, Pentagon and Atrus opened fire on it. The bullets tore into the body of Scylla. Every bullet that hit its mark, sent blue-violet blood spattering against the back wall.

Scylla screamed, but once the bullet assault was over, it pulled itself up from the wall.

Farah was climbing the large rock to the pedestal. She had the Water Sphere in her hands. But Scylla floated back to the center. Its large fin swept across Farah's arm, cutting it with its sharp spikes. Farah dropped the sphere, and it rolled down the rock to the floor.

Lucerna saw where it fell, but Scylla was looming above it. Lucerna reached for the sphere, but Scylla's large tail fin skirted the air above it, and Lucerna pulled back in fear.

White worms clung to the walls like leeches.

Her companions were swinging their weapons and focusing their elements in the wrong direction.

"Over here!" Lucerna yelled.

Scylla's head turned. It was looking right at her.

Decca ran at its body and sliced through a large section of its tail with his dagger. He lost his balance and fell against the opposite wall. Decca groaned as his head hit the wall.

Shilo darted to where Decca had fallen. His sword was raised to Scylla as he slashed against the beast's body.

Lucerna was still on the ground. Something cool crept up above her fingers, and her clothes were getting wet. The cave was flooding with water. Lucerna stood and leaned against the back wall.

Decca was coming towards her, his back to the wall. He was breathing heavy.

Farah assaulted Scylla again, the Wind pinning the creature to the back wall, almost pinning Decca with it.

Rodan lurched forward, his sword in his hand. His hearing was good. Scylla's spiked tentacle whistled through the air, and he sent a branch from the ground to block it. The ground was cracked where the branch grew. The branch curled back.

Rodan raised his sword against the monster. But he wasn't quick enough.

Scylla plunged a spiked tentacle through Rodan's stomach. Rodan's sword dropped to the ground. His body keeled over. Scylla pulled the tentacle away, and Rodan hit the ground. He rolled onto his back. Blood issued from his wound.

"He's hurt. Rodan's hurt," Lucerna shouted.

"Rodan!" Farah's voice rang out.

"Where?" Decca asked. He was by Lucerna's side.

Lucerna grabbed his muscled arm and pulled in the direction of Rodan's fall. "There."

Decca got to his knees and felt the ground until he found Rodan. He lifted him from the ground. Blood stained his shirt.

Their feet sloshed through the water on the cave floor.

Scylla screeched.

"Let's go!" Decca shouted.

Rai's sword was ablaze, and the others ran towards it. Lucerna was blinded. She had to wait for Rai to turn the corner before she could pursue.

Scylla hovered above her.

The wall of the labyrinth appeared to be moving. Lucerna

screamed as the shadow followed her. She tripped.

The shadow lunged for her, and Lucerna put her hands up to shield herself against it. Light erupted between Lucerna and the shadow. The shadow disappeared, unable to hold its form. The Light spread, dissipating the mucky dark substance on the ground.

The sphere rested near the pedestal. A foot of water covered it. Lucerna crawled from the drier spot down to where the water pooled. She reached down into the water. Her fingers were inches from the sphere.

Scylla turned to her and screamed.

Lucerna could sense the energy around Scylla. It was a deep blue, almost black. Lucerna focused on it, and the color became lighter.

Scylla screeched and whipped its tail, but Lucerna was light and quick.

She snatched the sphere and hugged it to her chest. She climbed upon the stones atop which the pedestal sat. She reached up and was aided by the sphere's pull. It snapped back onto its pedestal.

Lucerna slipped on a wet stone and was thrown down into the water, which was now several feet deep.

She heard Scylla scream again, but she dared not turn back to look at the monster. Like the other Protectors, if Scylla turned to dust, it would be back.

Lucerna pulled herself up out of the water and ran through the labyrinth. The light at the cave's entrance blinded her. Lucerna covered her eyes.

Her companions were still breathing heavy. Lucerna was also out of breath. She ran faster than her companions. She was only slowed down by her efforts to set the sphere.

Someone patted her on the back.

"I couldn't get the sphere on the pedestal," Farah said between breaths. "How bad is it?"

Rodan groaned.

Lucerna imagined his body writhing on the ground in pain, and Farah kneeling beside him, the panic in her eyes matching the panic in her voice. Lucerna wanted to tell them she had set the sphere, but after she caught her breath, all attention was on Rodan. She would tell them later, she decided.

"We have to get him to the Chariot," Rai said.

Someone took Lucerna by the arm. "Let's go." It was Decca's voice.

Without her vision, Lucerna's other senses were heightened. Their feet padded against the soft grassy ground as they raced to the Chariot. Her clothes and hair were heavy with water. It had even invaded her boots and soaked her socks. The humidity in the air was thick on her tongue as she breathed it in. She could smell the rustiness of the blood dripping from Rodan's wound.

34

RUST

We could have Refused our Punishment. We could have Refused to Eat from the Communal Stew, to Eat of our Dead. But we did Not because the Backbones of my People are Weak.

RODAN blinked in and out of consciousness. One moment, he would see the sun, the next, darkness. His head felt light, and he could taste blood in his mouth.

Two pairs of hands carried him. Hands were at his shoulders and feet.

"You're going to be okay," Farah's voice echoed in his head. She said something else but he couldn't quite make out the words. *Was it something about Sara?*

Rodan grew dizzy.

He opened his eyes.

The ceiling of the Chariot loomed above him.

But they had been outside only moments ago.

Rodan felt like he was looking down a tunnel where he could see the light at the entrance, but the sides were dark and fuzzy.

Farah's face was at the end of the tunnel. "Rodan, can you hear me?"

Rodan tried to respond, but he was so tired. His lips felt too heavy to speak.

"Hey, keep your eyes open for me, okay?" echoed Farah's voice.

His lids felt heavy.

"No, Rodan, come on."

He felt softness under him. There was pressure on his stomach. It felt like his skin and tissues were being ripped and clawed.

He looked down.

Rai was applying pressure to his wound. Blood gushed over her hands.

Farah ran up to him with clean, dry rags. She handed them to Rai, and Rai continued to apply pressure.

He groaned and coughed.

The air was drying his mouth out.

His head was spinning. He was having trouble keeping his eyes open.

Then everything went black.

HE was cradled in his mother's arms. His mother's face looked much bigger than he remembered it. A small, fat hand reached up to touch it. He tried gripping his hand, but his movements were slow and unpracticed.

He loved everything about his mother, the smell of her hair, the softness of her embrace.

He was born in the summer. The sun was hot, hotter than most summers.

He was ripped from his mother's arms. His fat, little hands had grown larger and his fingers longer.

People walked all around him.

He felt the soft grass beneath him. He made the blades grow.

A girl watched from the window. She was the most beautiful thing he'd ever seen.

He met her near the water.

Her eyes. Her smile.

He vowed to follow her.

His feet were weary, and his vision blurred.

He saw her with his best friend.

His anger was hot like the summer.

His friend took off his mask in the tower.

He felt the petals of the flower touch his hand, soft like his mother's embrace.

Steel clashed against steel. He was sweaty and exhausted, but still his Commander pushed him. The pummel of the sword hit him in the mouth. He tasted blood. He smelled rust.

A black line was painted through his silver band. The black paint dripped down onto his shirt.

He was among his enemies, their purple robes skirting the ground as they walked. He heard conversations. He wrote back to his Commander. The ink spilled and dripped onto his shirt.

The billows of her nightgown graced his face. He felt the warmth of her body as he helped her down from the vine.

He felt the stab of steel as he kneeled.

He saw her face.

She offered him meli, and in his fever dream, he had imagined she came just for him.

He heard a cry.

It was Spire's baby, cradled in its mother's arms.

There was humming. A soft rhythmic humming.

The Wind whipped his face so roughly that he had to close his eyes against it.

Spire was gone. Her baby was gone.

In their place was a red-haired woman, wearing a long coat lined with sheep's wool. She looked like Spire, but her long, rust-red hair trailed down her back like blood.

The Wind wailed.

She reached out a pale, white hand to him.

Rodan reached for her, but the Wind was unbearable. Rodan could barely keep his balance. The roar was deafening. It was like the whole room was shaking.

Rodan opened his eyes.

It was quiet.

He was on a hill. In front of him was a shadow in the shape of a man. It was so dark, Rodan could not make out his features.

Then came the humming, quiet at first and then growing louder.

Something roared in the distance. It sounded like it had teeth.

He reached out to touch the shadow, and it wavered like water. It wailed, and darkness spread. It spread throughout Mirmina and across the skies.

Rodan blinked.

He was standing right before the hill, before the shadow. The darkness emerged from it like shadow warriors, but their feet were solid, thundering upon the land.

Rodan put his hands to the ground. He felt the earth move. It took all his energy to do it, and then he was gone.

35

EARTH

That is Why the Creator was Not Afraid to Gift to us the Greatest of His Gifts. He Knew we would Not Move the Earth Against Him.

FARAH pressed the damp rag against Rodan's head.

The sun had risen and set and peeked over the horizon again, but Farah hadn't left his side. At night, she slept at his bedside and, in the morning, food had to be brought to her because she wouldn't come down to get it.

"Please, don't die on me," Farah whispered as she moved the rag from temple to temple. "I've lost too much already."

Rodan's breathing was irregular. There were times when no breath escaped his lips, and then he would gasp, sometimes slowly, sometimes rapidly. Farah would hold her breath when he stopped breathing, waiting for the gasp to come.

He groaned in his sleep. His eyelids were squeezed shut

as if he were struggling with bad dreams.

Blood stained the bandages.

"How's he doing?" It was Rai.

Farah marveled at how quiet she could be. "No change."

Rai knelt beside her at Rodan's bedside. "I can take over."

Farah shook her head.

"They're talking about going down to the dungeons to set the Earth Sphere," Rai said.

"I can't leave him," Farah said. "What if he wakes up?"

Rai took the rag from Farah. "I won't go down there again."

"Oh, you mean . . ."

Rai wet the rag in the small bowl under the bed and wrung it out. "Just thinking about it makes me nauseous. I'll be of no use down there. I'll end up getting someone hurt."

Farah stood. "I'll go. You'll protect Rodan?"

Rai nodded. She placed the cool rag on Rodan's head.

Orka sat on her perch beside Farah's bed. Her eyes were closed, and one foot was nestled into the feathers of her belly.

Farah walked up to the little, green bird. She petted its head until it opened its eyes. "You be good, Orka."

The little bird stretched its wings and chirped.

FARAH walked into the control room.

Thatch leaned forward in his seat. He was nervous about something.

Vassal stood by the window with his arms folded. Farah didn't know how long he had been out on the roof before Thatch fixed the wiring.

Stannum was clicking away as he read the large book. Spire rocked Canace and tried to sooth her cries. Decca had his hands on Spire's shoulders. Pentagon paced the room. Atrus leaned against the back wall. He smiled when Farah walked in.

"What are you guys talking about?" Farah asked.

Pentagon stopped pacing.

"Going down to the Sphere Room," Decca said.

"Everyone's a little nervous after what happened last time," Atrus said.

"But we have to go," Farah said. "Rai's right. As long as the spheres are off their pedestals, those white worms will keep coming."

"We don't even know what they really are," Pentagon said. "We're risking our lives to set the spheres, and we don't know what we're fighting."

"You saw what they did to Breeze," Farah said.

"We didn't stay to see the aftermath," Atrus said.

Farah suddenly felt ashamed.

What had happened to Shift?

When she came back, would she find his body eaten by the white worms?

"We need to go," Spire backed Farah. "Regardless of what those things are, we're upsetting the balance by leaving the spheres off their pedestals."

"The balance is more important than our lives?" Atrus asked.

"The balance is important to all our lives," Spire said.

"We need a plan then," Pentagon said.

Farah lifted her head. "There's a hole above its head."

"What?" Atrus asked.

"Above the Protector's head, there's a hole to let the light in. Roots grow all along the ceiling and the walls. I'm a good climber."

"But the Protector could attack you from above," Spire said.

"Not if it's distracted," Farah said. "We could split up. The group can distract the Protector while I climb down into the Sphere Room."

"I don't think that's a good idea," Atrus said. "You'll be in the middle of everything."

"We need to get in and out of there fast," Farah said. "It's the best way."

Pentagon looked at Atrus. "It's a good plan."

Atrus did not look pleased, but Farah didn't care. She knew it would work.

THE hatch door opened. Farah emerged with Decca, Shilo, Atrus, Pentagon, and Vassal. Grasping the Earth Sphere, she led the way to the dungeon.

They crossed the grassy plain in the heat.

Vassal was falling behind. He was stiff, and he kept rubbing his leg. Farah didn't slow her pace for him nor did she feel any sympathy towards him.

After the Great Raid, men and women loss limbs. Her father developed mechanical appendages. They often malfunctioned, and the amputees would lose control of them. People stopped wearing them and resorted to wheelchairs or working with one arm.

But Vassal's injury did not warm Farah to him. She trusted him about as much as she trusted Atrus.

Atrus walked beside her, which was too close for Farah.

She quickened her pace, hoping he would get winded and fall back, but Atrus used to race her through the desert in Breeze. He was a good runner. He could always keep pace with her without losing his breath.

Farah sighed to signal her distaste, but Atrus didn't seem to notice or care.

Suddenly, Farah stopped. She put her hand out to stop the others.

"You don't want to fall into there. Look." Farah knelt beside the hole in the ground. Everyone, except Vassal, knelt to gaze into the great gap.

The Protector's body was broad with leafy vegetation all round. Vines curled out from its mass. Its sharp teeth dripped venom like a snake. White worms crawled on the ground around it.

"I hate this one," Atrus said.

"You guys go through the dungeon," Farah said. "I need you to distract it while I climb down into the Sphere Room."

"I could do it," Atrus volunteered. "You know I'm a better climber than you."

It wasn't true. Atrus was a good climber, but he was teasing her.

"Diverging from the plan will only cause us to make mistakes," Farah said.

"Let's just go," Vassal said. "I don't want to relive this any more than you do." He ambled to the entrance of the dungeon.

Decca patted Farah's back a little too hard. "Good luck." He and Pentagon followed Vassal.

Atrus smiled at Farah, thin-lipped. "You be careful in there."

Farah was still angry with him, but she couldn't help but feel a tinge of emotion. She had known Atrus for a long time, and she was glad he still cared for her.

"Hey," Farah called.

Atrus turned back.

"Whistle when you have his attention."

Atrus nodded and ran to catch up with the others.

Farah waited for the signal. She stared down at the great Protector and hoped she would get used to its frightful size and sharp teeth and be less afraid.

No such luck.

She heard the whistle. Orka whistled like that sometimes.

Farah placed the Earth Sphere in her satchel secured to her hip. She dropped down through the hole, careful to keep a grip on the edge. She swung her feet and tangled them in the roots growing along the ceiling. She gripped the roots and climbed down.

Bullets rang out from Atrus's and Pentagon's weapons.

Vassal was closer, swinging his sword at the Protector. He sliced through a few vines, eliciting a screech from the great beast.

Decca had his dagger raised. He was beside Shilo. Although Shilo was a much smaller man, Farah couldn't help but notice a similarity between the two. The way they moved. The way they both made the same grimace when they felt pain.

Farah continued her climb.

The worms darted toward them. Pentagon and Atrus aimed their weapons down and shot at the worms. The worms crawled up Vassal's legs. He screamed.

The Protector's vines flailed, hitting Farah.

Farah lost her balance and fell from the ceiling. She landed hard on her back, the white worms all around her. She scrambled to her feet and struck the worms from her chest.

The Protector screeched.

Farah looked up, and she swore the eyeless creature could sense her there. She ran to the Sphere Room. Roots were growing along the door, sealing it to the frame.

Farah took out her dagger and started tearing into the roots. Vines grabbed her around the neck. Something ripped through the vines.

It was Atrus's dagger.

The vines fell away, and Farah got back to work cutting the roots. Atrus helped, cutting the one far above Farah's head.

The Protector screamed. There was so much pain in its voice.

Atrus yanked the door opened.

Worms snaked out from the pedestal like water from a tap. Glowing worms caked the walls and floor like they were feeding on it.

Farah removed the sphere from her satchel and approached the pedestal. She had to step upon the worms. They were soft. Some of them fizzled when her boots touched their spineless bodies.

Farah clasped the sphere.

The worms leaked out of the pedestal. There was no waiting for them to stop. Farah placed the sphere on top of the pedestal, blocking the worms' escape.

36

THE WORMS

Is this what We wanted? Power, Grace, and Progress. Written into History I'm sure. Everything we Ever wanted.

SHIFT watched from his father's tower, his tower, as the glowing mass approached the city. *I must save my people,* he thought.

He ran down to the streets.

The citizens of Breeze were still removing the debris and repairing broken buildings. They didn't know about the danger. The gates of the city hid it from them.

"We need to ready the canon," Shift commanded.

"The canon, Sir?" It was Armandis, one of Tag's top mechanics and most trusted soldiers.

"Yes, now!" Shift said. "Bring it outside the gates."

"What's going on, Sir?" Brodin asked.

Several others overheard his command to Armandis as well. They crowded around Shift.

"There's something approaching the city," Shift said.

"What?" a young woman asked. Shift knew her. *Karina.* They were the same age. She had two children now. He imagined she was worried for them. Especially after recent events.

"It's something I've seen in my travels," Shift said. "Something that might be dangerous."

"What is it?" Brodin asked.

"I don't know!" Shift said.

Several men and women wheeled the canon outside the city gates. Shift followed them. People rushed to the shelter of their houses. Others stayed to watch along the top of the gates.

"Do you need me to ready the men?" Armandis asked.

"No," Shift said, "I don't think this is something we can battle with blades and bullets."

They couldn't see the worms over the horizon.

Shift wiped the sweat from his brow. *Maybe they'll stop in the desert? Do these things have sentience? What would they want with the city?*

Then, Shift saw it.

Light glowed over the horizon. If he hadn't been looking so closely, he might have mistaken it for the sun glancing off the sand.

In a rush, like a wave, the worms came.

Billions. Trillions of them.

Shift took an instinctual step back. He let out a gasp. He hoped his men hadn't heard it. He gulped, wanting to ensure his voice was clear and firm when he said, "Ready the canon!"

The men loaded the cannon with bits of scrap metal and explosive grenades. The grenades were volatile and not even

Tag had trusted them.

The wave was about a hundred yards from the city.

"Fire!"

The canon exploded.

Shift's ears rang, but he could still hear a muffled high-pitched chorus of screams, like a colony of mice squeaking behind a wall.

"Fire!"

This time Shift covered his ears to shield them from the blast.

A segment of the wave was hit, but it was still coming, less than fifty feet from the city.

"Do we have more canons?" Shift asked.

"No, Sir," Armandis said. "The rest were damaged in the battle."

What am I going to fight them with? Shift wondered. *What would my father do?*

"Armandis, send a few men to gather every Elemental in the city," Shift ordered.

"Yes, Sir."

"Fire!" Shift shouted.

Screams echoed in the distance.

Shift turned around. Men and women in gray jumpsuits stood behind him. Armandis ordered his men to close the gates.

"We need to push them," Shift said. "Now!"

The Wind Elementals of Breeze closed their eyes. They focused on the wave. Shift could sense the energy pushing out in the space before him. He stared out into the desert helpless.

He had never directed a battle before. He wasn't like his father, shouting orders. He felt more like he was playing dress up, only *pretending* to be his father.

We can push them back, but then what? They will keep coming. My Elementals aren't strong enough to eject them from the island. It's too many miles wide. The worms will come over the walls of the city. This is it.

"Fire!"

Shift stopped bothering to shield his ears. He felt numb all over. He might as well be deaf too.

The canon fire failed to put the smallest dent in the wave. The worms were still coming in great numbers. The Wind slowed them, but it wasn't enough.

The worms were strong. Shift could not only sense that, he could see it. Fifty Wind Elementals, and they were still coming.

The men stomped them under their heavy boots. Screams issued forth.

Suddenly, there was a deeper cry.

Shift looked around.

It was Armandis. The worms were snaking up his legs, to his chest, and into his mouth. His eyes went white. No iris, no pupil.

Armandis withdrew his dagger. He sliced into the throat of the man next to him. The man shrieked in surprise and held his throat. The blood cascaded over his hands.

Armandis went on to the next man and stabbed him in the chest. Armandis stopped. His back arched in an unnatural way, his chest smoking. He collapsed to the ground.

The gun shook in Shift's hand. It surprised him that he had met his mark. He didn't become leader to kill his own men, but the white worms were invading their bodies.

They attacked each other.

Shift knelt to the ground. The worms were at his knees. *I've failed. Just like my father said I would. And now I'm going to die.*

Thatch will have to come back and rule the city anyway.

A caw sounded through the air. A great shadow shielded the sun from Shift's eyes. *Thermal.*

The wind swept the sand across Shift's face as Thermal landed. The great bird landed a small distance away as if he was being careful not to step on the worms. Thermal turned his beak to the sky.

He's beautiful, Shift thought, *I hadn't noticed that before, but he really is.*

Thermal cawed into the air.

The worms crawled up his body.

I was already dead, Shift thought. *This is going to be overkill.*

But he noticed something different about how the worms rushed to Thermal's body. It wasn't like they were snaking towards it, but more like they were being pulled.

Their bodies didn't slither. They were stiff, like a dead body being dragged. They were pulled from the bodies of the people and into the mouth of Thermal.

Shift stood.

The great bird, Thermal, raised his feathered head to the sky. The worms' bodies glittered under the desert sun and encased Thermal like a silver suit of armor.

Shift didn't know how long he stared. He imagined the others were staring as well. But the idea wasn't important enough for him to tear his eyes away from the image before him.

The last of the worms flooded into Thermal's body, and the great bird lowered his head. He looked down at the people and the city with eyes more intelligent than they were before.

His body, too, had changed, but it only added to his beauty and magnificence. His feathers were golden-tipped. The tips looked metallic. The once gray feathers of his belly brightened to an opulent green. His feet had darkened to a rich black. His talons were like thick glass. His eyes were a golden-amber. Sparks of energy lighted across his body.

He was something to be worshipped.

SHIFT looked across the desert. It was quiet. There was no indication that a couple days before, the sands had been swept by powerful, glowing worms.

Shift was unable to understand why Thermal could do what he did, but then again Shift hadn't fully understood what the worms were in the first place.

But they could turn his men against him and his people. They were dangerous, and Thermal stopped them. Shift was indebted to the great bird.

Thermal soared through the sky. Fire issued from his mouth, and Lightning zinged beneath his feet.

He was never able to do those things before, Shift thought. *Somehow absorbing the worms had changed all that.*

Shift ordered workers to fix the Morica chariots left among the wreckage. Now that the city was safe, he needed to find Thatch and Farah. They couldn't fight Morica alone. Morica had attacked his city, and he had to make sure they paid for that. Thatch had started on a few of the vessels and had managed to fix some others before he left.

Thatch had shown Shift the blueprint. Shift had pretended to be interested. He didn't want to think about his father's death.

Shift remembered the part he needed, but only vaguely. He didn't have the blueprint to refer to. That was probably with Thatch. His father's harsh criticism had turned him away from building things. He should have stuck with it. That's what the people of Breeze did, they built things.

He didn't know how to describe the part to the men or what it was called, but he would know what it was if he saw it.

Thatch said he couldn't find the part in the *Lacwanx* sector. *Had he checked the underground?* Shift wondered.

What am I thinking? Shift thought. *I can't just waltz into the Lacwanx's home. They might kill me.*

But I'm living on borrowed time now anyway. Thermal didn't save me and my city so we could sit back and let the world handle itself. What happens out there affects all of us. And those worms. Thermal didn't consume all of them. There is something greater to be afraid of than Morica's puffed pigeons.

SHIFT donned his gas mask. He didn't tell the workers where he was going. They might want to go with him, and Shift was afraid *Lacwanx* would be more aggressive if he brought in a troop of his men.

He entered the *Lacwanx* sector.

Shift's breathing was loud beneath his gas mask. He could see the pollution in the air. Well stationed guards used Wind to stop the air from invading the city. During the battle, the air had drifted through the streets, making the people who inhaled it sick.

The *Lacwanx* could breathe the noxious air, but no one knew why. It wasn't like *Lacwanx* were lining up for people to examine them. They didn't trust humans or as they called them: *Menslike.*

The *Lacwanx* had gathered metal parts from the wreckage, anything that would be of use. They brought these parts down to their home underground.

No one, to Shift's knowledge, had ever journeyed down to the *Lacwanx's* home and came back alive.

Shift was deep into *Lacwanx* territory. He stepped over the debris. He wasn't sure how to get down to the underground. He guessed there had to be an opening somewhere.

Shift had only been to the *Lacwanx* sector once before. He was a child, twelve or thirteen, and his friends dared him to. He was Tag's son; he had to do it. So, he did.

Shift stepped on a pile of sheet metal. The ground didn't feel right. The metal wasn't thick but malleable. It folded under his weight.

Shift fell into the hole.

SHIFT didn't know how long he had been out. He blinked. The sun beat down on him, but darkness engulfed him.

He stood.

Tunnels branched away from him. Sheets of metal covered the walls. *Lacwanx* surrounded him. They were short in stature. Not one of them was taller than Shift's waist. They had spears made of steel parts and other materials.

"Kleb ena tu leha lana, Menslike?" The *Lacwanx*'s voice came out deep and knurled. It was not the voice Shift expected to hear out of a creature so small.

He wanted to know why Shift had come.

Shift learned to speak *Lacwanx* when he was a child, but he rarely used the skill.

"I need something from you," Shift said in *Lacwanx*.

The room filled with laughter, but the *Lacwanx* kept their weapons pointed at Shift.

Shift never saw a *Lacwanx* without his gas mask on. They had defective faces. Some had three eyes or no eyes. Others had masses growing on their faces and teeth that jutted out too far.

Shift tried not to show shock on his face.

The conversation continued in *Lacwanx*.

"You come to bribe us with meli," said the first one who spoke. He had what appeared to be two mouths, one in the front and one off to the side. His eyes were an uncomfortable space apart.

He must be their leader, Shift thought.

"Meli?" Shift asked, "Why would I bribe you with meli? I just need to see your storeroom."

"What makes you think we will show you our works?"

"I'm not trying to steal your work," Shift said. "I need a special part. I can't find it anywhere else."

"Why should we help you? You came with nothing."

"You're right," Shift said. His dialect was off, but he hoped they could still understand him. "Because I knew I had nothing you would want. But I know you know the city was attacked a couple weeks ago."

"And?"

"The people who attacked us," Shift said. "We plan to attack them back."

"What do we care for the battles of *Menslike*?"

"The people of Breeze don't bother you. We don't wage war with you. We don't meddle in your affairs," Shift said. "But these people who we're attacking. How do you know they will treat you the same?"

There was silence.

Shift thought he saw a scowl on the leader's face, but he wasn't sure because of the two mouths.

"I can tell you," Shift continued. "Unlike the men of Breeze, these men will attack you. They are afraid of anything different. They would try to eradicate you before you attack them."

"*You* are not men, *we* are men. We survived. You are only *like* men. You are not men."

"Fine," Shift said, "but my people won't attack you. You know this. You've lived in harmony with us. If you let us protect our city, we can keep those men from your doorstep."

"What if your enemy comes in, and *Lacwanx* take the city."

"You want to make that gamble?" Shift asked. "It won't end that way. I promise you."

The *Lacwanx* put his little finger up in the air and brought it down. The other *Lacwanx* lowered their weapons.

"We will show you to our works, *Menslike*. You will only take the parts you need. Then, you will leave, and you will never tell your kind that we allowed you this."

"Agreed," Shift said.

The crowd of *Lacwanx* parted, and Shift followed their leader.

The tunnels were winding, and there were many paths. Alone, Shift would have gotten lost in such a place. He wondered if the reason no one came back from the *Lacwanx* sector was because they simply got lost and starved to death.

He glanced around at his companions with their sharp-tipped spears. They would never let anyone out alive.

They came to a large steel door. It took two *Lacwanx* to open it. Behind the door were piles and piles of metal and other materials. The room was the size of a small town.

I'm never going to find it in here.

"Don't be long, *Menslike*. Find what you're looking for before the sun goes down."

"How will I know when the sun goes down?" Shift asked.

The leader pointed to a device high on the wall. It had a dial and pointed to symbols on its face. "When the arrow points left, you are too late."

SHIFT watched the dial on the wall. His time was almost up. He was getting a headache, looking through piles of junk.

Lacwanx must collect everything, he thought.

He saw a few contraptions here and there, but the *Lacwanx* leader had nothing to worry about. Shift couldn't even begin to guess what any of them did.

Thatch would be so jealous right now, he thought with a smile. *It's almost wrong that it should be me who is allowed down here. It's a waste really. I can't appreciate any of this.*

Shift was starting to think he would never find the parts he needed.

He was going through another pile when he felt something nudge him in the back. It was the long-tipped spear of a *Lacwanx*.

"That's it, *Menslike*. Your time is up."

But Shift's eyes were on something in the pile in front of him. *Why didn't I see it before?* He picked it up and laughed. It was the part he needed. Shift was sure of it.

He looked at the dial. It was all the way to the left. His time *was* up.

"It's time for you to go. You got what you wanted."

"No," Shift said. "I need four more like these." He showed the *Lacwanx* the part he was holding.

"Your time is up."

"Yeah, but will you just listen to me."

The leader walked up. "He is listening to you, but what you say doesn't matter now. We had a deal."

"The deal was that you let me find the parts I need," Shift said. "Or the next time Morica storms in, they'll take the city."

"Find four more of this part," the leader ordered his followers.

Shift was amazed. In less than a few minutes, they were

dropping the parts at his feet. It had taken him hours just to find the first.

The pollution had put them at a disadvantage in terms of their facial deformities, but had it made their eyesight better?

Shift placed the parts into his bag and shouldered it.

"You have what you want, *Menslike*, now leave and never tell anyone you came here."

37

FAULT

I have been Asked to Chronicle for the Creator. I am One of the Only of my People with the Gift of the Written Word. I Fear what would become of Me should I Refuse, but Everything I am wants Me to Refuse.

RAI watched Rodan groan in his sleep. She hated feeling sorry for him. She didn't want to get to know him. She made the mistake of getting close to someone once before.

Footsteps sounded on the stairs leading up to the bedroom loft.

It was Atrus. He lay out on the bed next to Rodan's. "You missed quite a show."

Rai hadn't wanted to go down to the dungeon for two reasons. One was the sense of entrapment she felt down there. The other was Vassal.

She hadn't told anyone about what happened on the roof. She was still processing that Vassal was a Fire Elemental. She wondered why she hadn't sensed it before.

Rai could sense when another Fire Elemental was near. She could feel the energy like heat throughout her body, but Vassal hadn't given off that heat. Or maybe he had, and she had mistaken it for something else.

"We did this, you know," she said to Atrus.

"Yeah, but people do lots of things for money."

"We're responsible."

"You need a drink." Atrus got up from the bed. "So do I for that matter. I've been around death too much." Atrus eyed Rodan.

Rai followed his gaze. "I suggest you get a drink then," she snapped.

Atrus put his hands up in surrender as he walked backwards towards the bar.

Rai turned back to Rodan. His face appeared redder, and he was starting to sweat. He groaned through clenched teeth. Rai felt his head. He was burning up.

She unwrapped the bandages around his stomach. The wound was festering. The opening was gaping with white pus leaking out. The skin surrounding the wound was angry red.

Rai ran down the stairs to the bar. She grabbed the bottle of alcohol out of Atrus's hand.

"Hey!"

Farah walked in from the elevator. "What's wrong?" she asked as Rai ran back up the stairs.

"It's infected."

Farah raced after her.

Rai poured the alcohol on the open wound.

Rodan's back arched off the bed. He grimaced, and his

eyes squeezed shut.

Farah's hands clapped over her mouth.

Blood bubbled down Rodan's side.

"He needs fresh bandages," Rai said.

Farah left and returned with fresh strips.

"I'll lift him up. You move the bandages under his body." Rai lifted Rodan, and Farah weaved the bandages through the gap between the bed and his body. Rai applied the fresh bandages to the wound and tied up the ends.

"Will he be alright?" Farah asked.

"If the infection clears. Will you stay with him?"

Farah nodded.

RAI took the driver's seat.

Thatch sat at his blue screen and stared at the pulses of energy lighting up at each sphere sanctum.

"Where to?" Rai asked.

"We should go to Demlama."

"What fun." Rai pushed the steering wheel forward. As the Chariot picked up speed, Rai tilted the wheel back, and the vessel ascended into the air.

It was a short journey to Demlama from Jetty Verte without having to journey through the forest.

Rai landed the Chariot in the snow.

"How are we going to get over there?" Thatch asked.

Rai had melted the ice bridge after their last visit.

"You're going to have to fly me over the sphere sanctum," Rai said.

"What?"

"I'm jumping down."

"Alone?"

"Yes, it will be easier that way," Rai said. "I'll be in and out."

"I can't see that happening."

"I'm fast. I can do this without anyone else getting hurt."

"I built this thing," Thatch said, "but Shift was always the pilot. I'm not that good at flying."

"I'm not asking you to fly. I'm asking you to hover."

"What do I tell the others?" Thatch asked.

"You don't tell them. I'm doing this one alone. Can I trust you?"

Thatch was hesitant.

"Can I trust *you*?" Rai asked.

"Yes . . . yes."

"Alright, take the wheel. Just hover until I drop from the hatch. Then land the Chariot on the other side of the bridge."

Thatch nodded. He gripped the wheel.

Rai took the spheres from Stannum's side and placed them in her bag. She raced to the elevator and went down to the engine room. She released the latch and punched the button to open the hatch door. The door opened.

Rai was a few feet above the snow when she jumped down. She landed on her feet, sinking into the slush. Thatch pulled the vessel away, and Rai waved to him from below.

Withdrawing her weapon, she trudged through the snow to the sphere sanctum. Her breath proceeded her like fog. She could feel the heat from the flames surrounding her sword.

She opened the doors to the sphere sanctum and walked inside.

Her sword met the wooden handle of an axe as the skeletal guard brought it down on her. Rai heaved forward and knocked the guard off his feet. She brought her sword down on him, scattering his bones across the floor.

She walked down the hallway and saw Clara's statue. The

glowing worms clung to it. Their bodies looked stiff like the cold had frozen them.

Rai placed the Frost Sphere in Clara's outstretched hand. Inside her monument was the pedestal, sending energy throughout her marble body.

Commotion came from the great room.

Rai peered around the corner.

At the long table were undead warriors. All along the table were bowls of food long turned to ash like a feast after a victory that never came. At the head of the table was a black skeleton.

He raised his glass, and the warriors followed suit. Their fleshless jaws moved, but their tongues had rotted long ago, making it impossible to talk.

Although they didn't have lips to smile, it was an obvious feast of merriment. A long, purple runner decorated the table.

Rai stared.

The black skeleton turned toward her and glared at her with its hollow eyes. He pointed, and all the warriors turned their fleshless faces towards her.

Rai ran to the entrance hall. The doorway to the outside was in front of her, but she needed to place the Wind Sphere.

Rai rushed down the opposite hallway to the Sphere Room. She entered a large circular room. It was cold. Icy wind issued from the hole in the back wall where the marble had been blasted through.

Across the expanse was the Sphere Room. The marble door was shut.

Rai raced to it, pulling open the heavy door.

White glowing worms flooded out, wrapping around her feet. They were on the walls, floor, and ceiling of the small room, and more were issuing forth from the pedestal.

Trying not to think about the white worms, Rai rushed into the room and capped the pedestal with the sphere, sealing the exit point for the worms.

When Rai turned back, the skeletal army was blocking the exit. They raised their steel weapons, and their toothless mouths were opened to their soundless screams. The black skeleton was at the forefront.

Seeing no other way out, Rai hurried to the hole in the back of the room. The temple sat right along the cliff, and only a sliver of snowy earth graced the back of the building.

Rai snaked along the side of the building. Her eyes were glued to the treacherous abyss. Mist covered the bottom of the gorge.

She was almost to wider ground. Rai's foot slipped. She felt a moment of heart-sinking terror. Both feet were over the edge, and her body slid in the snow. She raised her sword up over her head and brought it down into the frost. The fiery blade sank past the snowy surface into the icy ground.

Rai hung from the handle of her sword. As she struggled to pull herself up, the skeletons that pursued her had fallen into the abyss, but the others were moving fast.

Rai got to her feet in time to yank her sword from the ground and meet blades with a skeletal warrior. She knocked him off balance, and he fell.

The more Rai moved along the temple wall, the wider the ground before the edge of the cliff became until she could see the entrance of the temple.

The black skeleton and his army had emerged. He pointed to her and screamed his silent scream.

Rai ran to the edge where the ice bridge used to be. The gap between was too wide. She would never make it. She heard the clamor of weapons behind her. Rai felt the heat of her sword. She looked down at her blade.

She backed up and ran towards the edge. Leaping over the wide expanse, Rai raised her sword over her head. Her feet missed the ground, but her sword sank into the side of the cliff.

She gripped the handle and grinded her teeth. Her feet kicked along the side of the cliff. Finally, her feet found a secure ledge. Steadied by the ledge, Rai pulled herself up over the edge and grabbed at the snow.

A hand took hers and helped her up.

"What the hell were you thinking?" It was Atrus. "I never thought you had a death wish."

Rai brushed the frost from her clothes. "We're responsible for this. I'm just paying my dues."

"Yeah, that's right, *we're* responsible. Not just you. Next time, we do it as a team." Atrus held out his hand.

Rai swiped it away with the back of hers. "We're not a team anymore."

RAI stepped into the control room. Thatch sat at the blue screen. Stannum had powered down. His tiny, metal arms hung at his sides, and he floated in mid-air, unmoving, like he was sleeping. Atrus leaned against the back wall with his arms folded.

The elevator door opened, and Farah stormed in. "Are you crazy? Setting a sphere by yourself."

"Two spheres." Atrus held out two fingers.

"They were my responsibility," Rai said.

"I took the spheres once too," Farah reminded her. "This is just as much my responsibility as it is yours."

"But you replaced them," Rai said. "Now that's what I must do."

"You should have waited for me," Farah said. "What were you thinking: set two spheres, and then it doesn't matter if you live or die?"

Rai couldn't help but marvel at how much Farah cared.

"We're going to D'arkadia, and this time I'm setting that sphere with you." Farah shook her head and stormed back out of the control room.

"So, you set both the spheres?" Thatch asked.

Rai nodded.

"How many were there?" he asked.

"The worms?"

"Yeah."

"Too many to count," Rai said. "It looks like the cold slows them down, but there were so many."

Stannum lifted his metal head and shook it until something rattled inside.

"I need to rest," Rai said. She went up to the cabin room.

On the loft, Rodan was still in bed. The blood on the bandages around his stomach had dried a dull brown. Beads of sweat were on his head.

On a bed across the room was Vassal. He was rubbing his leg. He was uncomfortable.

Rai settled in the bed close to Rodan's. She watched Vassal struggle until she fell asleep.

WHEN she awoke, Rai walked to the elevator and went down to the control room. Farah stood beside Thatch. She pointed to something on the blue screen.

Rai didn't know how those machines worked and didn't bother to. Pentagon and Atrus were talking in the corner. Stannum was once again hibernating like an animal. Of all the machines Thatch had worked on, Stannum was the most difficult for Rai to understand. Sometimes it could be more human than machine.

"You ready?" Farah turned to Rai.

Rai nodded.

She wanted to get off the Chariot and away from Vassal. She knew he hadn't slept the night before. He must have tossed and turned well into the daylight hours because, in the morning, he was knocked out with his wooden leg dangling over the side of the bed. Rai doubted a thunderstorm could wake him.

She wondered if she should tell Atrus and Pentagon that Vassal was an Elemental. It was just one more lie atop many. But they were starting to trust him again, and that could be dangerous for them.

Rai didn't hate Pentagon or Atrus, but being close to them meant thinking about the past.

Still, she couldn't help but laugh inside when Atrus made one of his snide comments or smiled when Pentagon looked irritated by Atrus's crudeness.

She had traveled many miles with them, laughing and smiling. Her father had kept her hidden from the world into her early adult years. They were her first real friends. It was with them that she had the best times of her life and the worst.

Sometimes she would sit up at night and feel lost.

She looked at Pentagon and Atrus.

"We're coming too," Atrus said.

"Don't get in my way." But when Rai turned to face the elevator doors, she cracked a smile.

Atrus and Pentagon met Rai and Farah in the snow.

"It feels weird," Pentagon said. "Not long ago we ripped the spheres from the pedestals. It felt destructive and wrong. This feels right."

"We only do what's in our interest," Rai said.

"You can say that again," Atrus said.

Farah frowned. "Let's just set the sphere and get back to the Chariot in one piece without the road show."

Atrus put up his hands in surrender.

Their feet sank into the snow as they walked towards the Crystal Forest. The closer to the trees the snow became, the more it thinned out.

Farah turned around. "Can't you guys walk any faster?"

"You're like a machine," Atrus said. "What I don't understand is how those short legs get you so far."

Farah huffed.

Rai shook her head. She was in no mood for Atrus's banter. The icy wind was in sharp contrast to her body temperature, and she was reserving her energy, so she couldn't use her element to warm herself.

She looked over at Pentagon.

He hadn't said a word. He had his arms crossed over his chest. His fingers dug into his arms. Pentagon wasn't used to the cold. His tan skin was a product of the sunny environment he grew up in on the coast of the Placid Sea.

He came to Dustpath when his parents went missing after a typhoon struck their village. Many fled, and so much was washed away. Pentagon never found his parents.

His arms relaxed as they approached the Crystal Forest where the air was warmer, and the snow faded into green. The crystals at the base of the trees glowed like fireflies. The light had heat in it, like the heat that comes off something living.

Farah stopped and listened. "I don't hear them."

"The Muses?" Rai asked.

"Something's wrong."

"We have no time to think about that now," Rai said. "We set the sphere and get out of here. No road show." She walked ahead of Farah, but kept looking back to see if she was following.

When Rai stopped at the mouth of the cave, Farah was close behind Atrus and Pentagon. Water filled the opening and receded into the depths of the cave.

"We go in through here," Rai said. "Last time, rocks fell and blocked the front entrance. Now there's only this one."

"I'm not picky," Atrus said.

Rai touched the sides of the opening to help her into the water below. She jumped in with a splash. The water was up to her chin.

Farah paddled to keep her head above the water.

They swam deeper into the cave. The deeper they got, the shallower the water became until they were walking upon damp rock.

The pedestal was bare. No white worms. Only a few months ago, Sara, Rai, and Farah had taken the sphere from its pedestal to join the other half. Farah removed it from her bag.

Rai drew her sword. She was ready should the Beast come out from the shadows.

Farah held the sphere out.

"Wait," Pentagon said.

Farah stopped. "What?"

Rai felt her heart drop. She looked around and waited for something terrible to come.

"I know this is what we came to do," Pentagon said. "But if we set that sphere, won't there be more Elementals like Veil. They could destroy entire cities. What happened in Tosia—"

"That is not for us to decide," Rai said.

"Then who decides it?" Pentagon asked.

There was silence.

"It was us," Pentagon said. "We took the spheres. We decided. There are no gods to stop us. No one to interfere. No one to rain lightning down on us if we disobeyed."

"You're deciding this now?" Farah said.

"No," Rai said. "That's not like him. He thought about this before we left the Chariot. Maybe even before we left Jetty Verte."

"It's the right thing to do," Pentagon said.

"And what do you suggest we do about those worms?" Atrus said. "Soon they'll be coming out of that thing. They attacked my operation in Wyvek. Maybe they would destroy cities."

"We could stop it up with something else." Pentagon looked around the cave. He picked up a jagged rock about the size and shape of the sphere. "Set this."

Farah took the rock from Pentagon and tested the weight in her hand.

Rai didn't like it, not that she had a soft spot for Dark Elementals, but Hephaestus had given Fire Elementals a bad name too. She feared someone would place a rock where the Fire Sphere should be. The idea made her skin crawl.

"What if a Dark Elemental is born who can't control his element like Spire's baby?" Pentagon asked.

Farah was still looking between the sphere and the rock, like the decision rested with her.

Rai held her tongue. Her eyes held her distaste, but Farah didn't look there.

Farah lifted the rock higher than the sphere. She placed the Dark Sphere into her bag, and instead set the rock on the glass pedestal.

"That's that then." Atrus sighed.

Rai stared at the rock upon the pedestal. It was wrong. The feeling of foreboding carried with her all the way through the cave until it fell back into the corners of her mind.

Then, the rock fell.

Farah placed it back on the pedestal, but it fell off again. Farah turned the rock over as if she could inspect why it wouldn't stay on the pedestal.

"Try it again," Pentagon said.

Farah placed the rock back onto it. A force ripped the rock from the pedestal. The rock slammed against the cave wall and broke up into pieces.

"Whoa." Atrus backed away.

"Find another rock," Pentagon said.

"Come on, Pent," Atrus said. "It's not working. You don't want it to throw the next rock at us, do you?"

"Put the sphere on it," Rai said. "It won't be right otherwise."

Farah looked down at the Dark Sphere and sighed. She placed the sphere on the pedestal.

INSTEAD of going back to the control room with the others, Rai continued to the cabin. She told Farah she wanted to take a nap before they went on to Wyvek to set the Lightning Sphere.

Vassal sat at the bar. He was drinking.

"Rai." He called.

Rai ignored him as she continued towards the steps, but he ambled towards her and reached for her arm. He realized the drink was still in his hand so he twined his arm with hers.

"Stop ignoring me, please," he said.

"You look like a fool."

"I feel like a fool. Like a puppet that somebody played with."

"You're not a puppet. You made your own decisions."

"Did I?"

Rai shrugged away from Vassal. He lost his balance and stumbled to the ground. Rai didn't look back at the dejected man.

She walked over to the bed where Rodan lie. She took his hand. It was warm, but not with fever. "Had we not taken the spheres in the first place," she whispered, "you wouldn't have been in that cave."

Rai glanced at the black band about her arm.

She remembered the angry faces of the people yelling and throwing things at her the day she took the Lightning Sphere to pay for her mother's medicine. She was just a child. There was so much shame in it. But there was anger too.

When she took the spheres two years ago, she felt a sense of revenge. The conquest took away the guilt because she accepted her role as a sphere thief. It was the wrong thing to do, and she was wrong for doing it.

38

IN THEIR FOOTSTEPS

*What could He want Me to Chronicle? Why would He who is Eternal
need to Ensure that a Message survives Time?*

BENN looked across the Lake. No boats were anchored
to the coast. He heard stories about this Lake when he
lived on the mainland. A creature would bring you
down into the depths of the Lake. Bodies below the water tangled in grasses and vegetation so they couldn't rise to the surface.

Benn peered into the water like he was looking into the
eyes of a ghost. He thought he could see one of the bodies.
Then something crossed his field of vision.

"Look there!" Sara said.

Another fish darted across the water.

Splash.

Sara jumped into the water. Her head bobbed above the surface as she kicked her feet beneath it. "We can swim across."

"Swim?" Benn asked. "In the Lake de Somnia?"

Sara looked around. "What other choice do we have?"

Benn sighed. He stepped out into the Lake and waded in the water until it was up to his chest.

"Can you swim?" Sara asked.

"Yeah."

"Well, come on then." Sara swam across the water.

Benn followed. If there was one thing he could do well, it was swim. Soon, he was swimming alongside her. He tried not to think about what could be lurking under the water.

A dull orange glow reflected off the surface. The day was coming to an end.

Benn's arms were growing tired. It had been a long time since he swam so far, and he wasn't a young man anymore.

The coast was in sight.

Sara swam ahead of him.

Benn wished he had not wasted so many years of his youth. He made it to the coast. Sara's outstretched hand helped him to his feet.

He looked back over the water.

A feeling of pride settled inside him in that instant. He wanted to share it with Sara, but she could not feel it, and even if she could, she would not celebrate it with him.

Sara sat. Exhaustion had finally taken her. She pulled the canteen of water out of her wet bag and drank.

Benn settled down where he stood. Now that she was sitting too, there was no shame in taking a break.

Sara's eyes suddenly harbored a look of panic. She reached into her bag and retrieved soaked pages and muddied charcoal. She unfolded the pages, and one by one rested them on the shore to dry.

Sara's glass ring gleamed in the moonlight.

Benn thought of Bolton.

He had asked him to travel hundreds of miles to help Balin.

Balin was the son he raised, but he never knew Benn's true face. The boy was strong and innocent. He reminded him of Bolton when he was a boy.

He hoped Balin didn't hate him too.

Sara lay down, and, without saying a word, she closed her eyes and fell asleep.

This girl faced the monster he couldn't. It was no wonder that his son loved her.

BENN opened his eyes. The sun was on his face. He looked around, his eyes still blurry with sleep.

The spot where Sara slept the night before was empty.

Maybe she decided he was slowing her down.

But then he spotted her, filling her canteen, further down the coast. She must have taken a walk while he was asleep. Ana used to do that when she wanted exercise.

Benn stretched as Sara approached.

"Are you ready?" She shouldered her bag.

He grabbed an apple out of his bag before putting it on his back. As the Old Scholar, his appetite was almost non-existent. Now, he was hungry all the time, but not used to eating. He had to remind himself that a rumbling stomach meant time for food.

He bit into the apple, and the juice ran down his chin. He wiped it on his sleeve as they walked through the forest to Tosia.

His grandfather had always been hard on him for being a coward.

His father was a Lightning Elemental, but he had left the family to study young Elementals. Benn hadn't known much about his father's work, but he knew it involved powerful Elemental children.

Neither his grandfather nor his mother possessed the gift of Lightning.

But that only made it worse for him.

His grandfather would say that gifts were meant to be used and that a coward couldn't wield such a weapon.

His grandfather's father before him had been a Lightning Elemental, and his mother had confided in him that his great-grandfather had hated his son for not being a Lightning Elemental. His great-grandfather died long before Benn was born.

His grandfather would whack him in the back of the head when he didn't want to do things.

Most of all, he hated the forest.

When his grandfather went hunting, Benn stayed home with his mother and watched her knit. He knew more about knitting than hunting.

One day when he was eleven years old, his grandfather had enough. He dragged the boy out with him on a hunt. They journeyed deep into the forest.

Benn was afraid. At eleven, he was a skinny boy who knew nothing about the world. He had a collection of colored stones that he dropped along the way, worried they would get lost in the woods and not be able to make it back home.

But his grandfather put his bow on his back, and turned around to face his grandson. He had to knelt to match his height. "No grandson of mine will fear his shadow. You see that bear."

Benn hadn't seen the bear. It was off in the distance. Now he could see it. Its large body loomed behind his grandfather.

It looked like it was sniffing something on the ground.

"You have your bow."

Benn clenched his bow.

"Go on."

He reached behind his back for an arrow. His hands were shaking. He had heard of a bear that ate a little boy in their village. What if his arrow missed, and the bear came after him? Would his grandfather protect him?

He was trembling so bad the arrow fell from his hands.

"Pick it up!" his grandfather yelled.

The bear growled.

Benn lost his nerve. Ignoring his grandfather's shouts, he ran through the forest. He didn't know where he was going. He had lost the pretty stones.

"ARE you alright?" Sara asked.

They were at the door to Tosia.

"I'm fine."

"I can't be losing you like that," Sara said. "Morica is after us, and you have to stay focused. I may need your help if we run into any guards."

What Sara didn't know was that Benn froze up at the sight of danger. He couldn't use his element. He would be of no use.

He stepped into Tosia. The walls and ground were blackened and cracked under his feet. He feared the ground would give way, and he would fall somewhere beneath the great tree to be lost forever.

Maybe that was why Sara had brought him on this journey, just like his grandfather, to get rid of him. He was an old man, but running was another of his best skills. All the time in the world couldn't take that away from him. He was too practiced in it.

They reached the entrance to D'arkadia. He had heard stories of the Beast, but those were all fables. They were half way to the Crystal Forest when the sun set.

Sara put down her bag. Benn sat across from her. "So, when we get this device . . ."

"A communicator."

"This communicator, then we'll signal the flying machine. Then what?"

"We'll find the Insula."

"Only one man can get to the Insula. We should be going to him."

"The Chariot will get us there faster."

"But your friends won't know where to go."

"They made it there before." Sara refused to look at him.

"That was because of Balin. If Bolton's helping him, he won't be releasing that kind of energy. We'll never get there on that."

"Do you know what blind faith is?" she asked.

Benn didn't understand what she was getting at.

"Blind faith is when you believe in something without proof. Sometimes you need that when there is no other way," Sara said. "We don't have the glistenings to pay our way to the Insula. Thatch will figure out a way to get us there. It's our only chance."

"But you're risking everything."

"I need to know Bolton is safe. I need to know he is on the Insula and not in one of Morica's cages. If given the chance,

I'd risk everything for that again and again."

Benn lowered his head. Ana's screams echoed in his memory.

Benn reached into his pocket and pulled out a colored stone. The stone was a symbol of both cowardice and courage to him.

AS he ran through the woods, he came upon the row of pretty stones he had dropped along the way. He looked behind him. His grandfather was nowhere to be seen.

He could follow the stones home. Picking one up, Benn weighed his options.

If he returned home to the safety of his mother and her knitting, his grandfather would soon come home and find him there. He would be beaten for disobeying, and how many more times would his grandfather bring him out into the woods to die?

Maybe his grandfather was glad he had run off to get lost. His grandfather could return to his mother and say he went missing, that there was nothing his grandfather could do, that the boy ran off because he's a coward who knows too much about knitting.

His mother would be sad at first, but soon her mourning would end. Maybe his father would come back, and they would have another son, and his parents would be happy. That boy would be brave and strong and everything his grandfather wanted.

Returning would spell his death. Even if his grandfather let him live, he would be endlessly tormented by his high expectations of him, and Benn would never reach those expectations.

As much as Benn wanted to be in the warm arms of his

mother, he didn't want to face the wrath of his grandfather.

It was easier to walk away.

Benn pocketed the pretty stone and journeyed deep into the woods.

NOW that he was older, Benn wondered if his grandfather's resentment of him was because he hated himself. His grandfather didn't love him because he wasn't a Lightning Elemental, and Benn was a constant reminder that he wasn't. He needed something to hate Benn for, and his cowardice was that something.

Bolton hated him for his cowardice too.

Benn rolled into a ball.

Sara was already asleep. Her body knew and understood the road in ways his body didn't.

He needed to prove to his son he wasn't a coward anymore, that he could step up when he needed to.

He fingered the smooth surface of the stone.

That's what his sons needed from him: courage. All the apologies in the world weren't going to bring Bolton's mother back or erase the years of deceit Balin had suffered, not knowing his father had been there for him all along.

Benn still questioned his grandfather's motives in bringing him out in the woods that day, but his grandfather would have taught him something that would have changed the course of his life.

He wished he had shot that bear.

39

LIKE US

I tied a Blade to My Ankle, concealed. I might Find use of It when I Encounter the Creator.

THE sun shone through the thin veil of clouds. The light sparkled on the river, sending diamonds down to the forest.

Hoping to wake Benn, Sara let out a loud yawn. He blinked a few times, and his eyes opened. Sara waited while he sat up and rubbed his eyes.

"We should move on," Sara said. "We're only a day away from Vella City."

Benn did not look pleased. Sara hated the way he frowned, so much like Bolton.

After taking a swig of water from her canteen, Sara put her bag on her back. She was determined to make it to Vella

City by noon the following day.

She set off at a quick stride. Benn was having trouble keeping pace with her.

Bolton had to know Sara wouldn't wait around while he journeyed to the Insula. Sara was not fit for the sedentary life. Since she was a child, she dreamed of life beyond the walls of Element. She wasn't going to waste that now.

It was almost sunset by the time the forest was in sight with all its many crystals glowing at the base of each tree.

But then, Sara's vision went blurry.

The thundering of her and Benn's feet echoed in Sara's ears. It sounded like it was coming from far away.

Something emerged from the trees. Blurry, white worms crawled towards Sara and Benn. They darted across the plain like snakes.

The edges of Sara's vision went black, and the darkness closed in.

SARA sat on the edge of a cliff by the sea. The warm breeze wafted through her hair. The salt of the water stung her nostrils. Her arms were wrapped around her legs, and her feet were bare as if she had been sitting, perhaps relaxing for a long time.

Red flashed out of the corner of her eye.

Sara turned her head.

There was a little girl. Nine, maybe ten years old. She had long, dark hair. When her hair hit the light, there was red in it. A spray of light brown freckles sprinkled the bridge of her nose. She sat with her legs under her, looking at the sea.

"Who are you?" Sara asked.

The young girl turned her dark brown, almost black eyes to Sara. "Your sister."

"I don't have a sister," Sara said.

"He made us sisters. But he didn't choose me. He has another plan for me. There are other sisters and brothers waiting for you. You're just like us."

"I don't under . . ."

Sara felt herself falling.

Everything went black. Except for a light coming towards her.

Sara tried to step back, but she backed up against a wall she couldn't see.

The white worms were coming.

40

ENERGY

To Those who read this, It is Sometimes a Dreadful thing to be Chosen. One may get the Pride of having Done something Great, but one also has the Fear of having to do It.

SARA blinked. The ground beneath her was soft. She rolled onto her side. Crystals surrounded her.

Benn sat across from her. He foraged in his bag for food. As he bit into a plum, and the juices ran down his hand.

"What happened?" Sara rubbed her head.

Benn swallowed the bite of plum. "You fainted."

"I fainted?" Sara whispered.

"Did you eat before we started for the forest?"

"I don't remember."

"Here." Benn reached into his bag and retrieved an apple. He offered it to Sara.

Sara took it. "We should keep going."

"No way. We'll stay here until morning," Benn said.

"We couldn't have gotten far with me blacked out like that."

Benn ignored the insult to his strength. He was not his younger self. "We got far enough."

Trees blocked the sky. "Is it still daylight?"

"Doubt it. It was almost nightfall by the time I got us to the forest. The moon's up. I could see it just over the horizon before I entered the trees."

Sara didn't like this at all. Half the day wasted. They could have covered more ground had she been strong enough to go on. But she felt fine now.

She took a bite of the apple.

The flesh was soft and mealy. It was mush in her mouth. The fruits of the Earth Elementals didn't stay fresh as long as normal fruits.

It left an unsettling feeling in Sara's stomach. She put her hand there.

Benn tossed her the canteen of water.

Sara drank, hoping the water would settle her stomach.

"You'd better put that hood back over your head," Benn said. "I believe Morica guards pass through here."

"You would imagine right." Sara placed the hood over her head. The fringed fabric tickled her face.

The chill from Demlama drifted through the forest though the snow could not bear the warm glow of the crystals.

"You've traveled through the Crystal Forest before?" Sara asked.

Benn kept his head bowed. "I lived here."

"Here?"

"There's a village to the east. My mother and grandfather

lived there. My grandfather used to hunt in these woods. There are bears, you know."

"I've never seen a bear."

"You don't want to." Benn turned towards the forest. "We're probably too far west to see bears or any other animals for that matter. My grandfather used to say living things didn't venture west because that's where the Maledixit lives."

Maledixit. Bolton had told Sara the story of the Maledixit; it used to be a man before it ate its human companions.

"Is that why you told Bolton that story about the Maledixit?" she asked.

"I would have never told Bolton any story about a Maledixit. I would have scared myself."

Hephaestus must have told him that story.

BENN had fallen asleep where he sat against the tree.

Sara lay on her back, but she couldn't sleep. The crystals glowed around her. The instruments of the Muses ceased their melody.

She sat up.

The woods were quiet.

Sara got to her feet and walked to the lake.

Someone stood at the water's edge. Sara shrunk behind a tree.

The figure was twelve feet high. It had a feathered head. A golden stringed harp was at its feet.

Founten.

Sara stepped from behind the tree. "Why aren't you playing?" she asked.

Founten turned around. His expression was unreadable.

Founten's mouth was beaked. Silvery feathers decorated his head. His great eyes bulged, the lids curled all the way back. His pupils never left the very center of his eyes.

"I couldn't hear the music," Sara said.

Without moving his great beak, a voice echoed from Founten. "We are in mourning for a fallen brother who has returned."

"Who?" she asked.

"You call him, the Creator."

"Of the Elementals? What do you mean he has returned?"

"He walks Mirmina, free from his cage."

Sara didn't understand. She knew very little of the Creator. Spire taught her a little history, but often Sara focused more on her element than anything else. Now, she wished she had listened.

The way Founten made it sound, it was like the Creator wasn't a mortal man, but something else entirely, something that needed to be caged.

Sara cringed at the thought of the creature in the dungeon of Omega Ray.

But why did she think of him?

Surely, that decaying monster had nothing to do with the Creator of the Element Spheres.

Founten looked beyond. The Muses gathered on the opposite side of the lake. They did not carry their odd, little instruments. Their animal-like faces were expressionless, but their sadness was like a warm, damp blanket, making the air heavy with emotion.

Why would the Creator's return bring them such grief?

Sara remembered Bolton's return.

Had they thought the Creator was dead? Did they mourn him only to find that the world had lied, that he was alive, and that the heavens had played a cruel trick on them?

Founten turned his feathered head towards her. Though he would not harm her, his height was terrifying. It was hard to stand next to him and not be afraid.

"There's something you learn when you die," he said.

Sara waited for him to finish. The silence lasted too long. If she tried to hold her breath, she might faint again.

But Founten continued, and the world stood still for him. "All energy that exists has always existed."

What did he mean?

"Look at your hand," Founten commanded.

"What?"

"Look at your hand."

Sara did. Shallow valleys and ridges crosshatched her palm. The pattern reminded her of the scarred land of Jetty Verte.

"What do you see?" he asked.

"My hand," she said.

"Do you think it's solid?"

"Yes."

"It's not. It's energy."

Sara turned to him. "What do you mean?"

"Your hand. It is tiny pulses of energy held together and, every time you touch something, that energy rubs off on it and remains with it until it is transferred to something else. The forest, me, you, them." Founten pointed to the spirits that were gathering at the opposite edge of the lake. Milbill and Omar were among them. "We're all energy that is passed on. It's what the Creator understood that we did not."

"Why are you telling me this now?"

Founten bent down. His great head was eye level with hers. "Because he has returned for you."

"Why?" How could she have any significance to the Creator? She couldn't even use her element.

"Look into the water and see." Founten gestured to the lake and invited Sara to kneel at its edge.

Sara knelt.

Reflected at her was not her own reflection but the reflection of someone else.

His skin was dark. His eyes were piercing. On his head, he wore a feathered headdress of plucked owl's plumes. The top of the headdress was decorated with large owl eyes and a beak that hung low in the middle of his forehead.

Sara became one with the man in the water. She could see through his eyes like she was staring at her own reflection.

41

THE BEAR

*I was Met at the Door by the Keepers. Their Eyes are Youthful though
Their Bodies are Not. Besides the Chosen, they are the Only Ones al-
lowed into the Dark Palace.*
My Soul sank.
Perhaps I will Never Leave this Tomb.

FOUNTEN'S image reflected in the water of the lake.
His face was painted in thin featherlike strokes of alter-
nating yellow, blue, and white. His large, dark nose was
painted yellow like an owl's beak. His brown eyes, lighter than
his skin had a touch of maroon in them. Atop his head was an
elaborate headdress of owl's feathers with large, orange,
wooden eyes. His dry, black hair came down in strings on his
bare chest where white paint was mocked like feathers.

Founten enjoyed quiet places away from the rush and

rumble of his village. He needed places to think, to hear his own thoughts and reflect on others. When he was alone, he felt one with the trees around him. He didn't like to join in the raucous banter of his brothers. He only exerted himself for the hunt and nothing more.

But his responsibilities led him away from the lake. A great hunt was beginning.

He walked back to his village and entered through the gates, twigs tied together meticulously by the women of the village with bits of twine.

Women, washing clay plates, greeted him at the entrance. They would soon take part in blessing the hunt.

In the center of the village stood three of his hunting companions.

Milbill was on the left. The red squirrel skin went down to his shoulders. Omar was on his right. He wore boar skins, and he was as nimble as a lizard, but his voice was deep like the croak of a toad. They waved their long, blunt sticks at the Bear, not meaning any harm.

The Bear was thin, but muscled. His skin was lighter than the others, almost pink. They called him the Bear because he never backed down. His given name was Erebus because his mother died giving birth to him. He wore bearskins with a large bear head that sat atop his crown. The bear had black fur with a row of sharp teeth hanging from his severed jaw. Erebus had killed the bear on a hunt.

As was his nature, he ignored Founten's advice. Founten had told him to leave the bear alone and that they had plenty of venison for their village. Erebus wouldn't hear it. He took his spear and crept down to the stream where the bear was drinking. He thrust the spear in its side. As the bear rose, the spear broke. Half of the weapon was still embedded in the muscled flesh.

Ready to attack, the bear rose on two feet. Its massive shadow, more than nine feet tall, hung over Erebus like a death omen. All fifteen hundred pounds came thundering down upon him. The bear's deadly jaws were open wide.

Erebus knelt as if in a defensive stance.

Steel flashed.

The bear growled, and its hulking mass sank down onto Erebus. The bear had collapsed.

Founten called for the others.

Together the four of them pushed the bear aside with a labored heave.

Erebus gasped for air. In his hand was the bloodied dagger he embedded into the bear's throat. Thick blood was in his hair and on his chest like red paint.

Erebus refused to leave his kill.

They had to send for others from the village to help them carry it, but by then Erebus had skinned it to the shoulders and severed its head.

The skin draped down Erebus's back. It served him well in the winter.

He was unafraid of Milbill and Omar. Avoiding his swing, he grabbed Milbill and tossed him to the ground like he was one of those dolls the women made for their young. He came at Omar. Omar, dodging and laughing, swung at the Bear with his stick while Milbill got up to defend.

The Bear pushed Milbill aside. He grabbed the stick from Omar and raised it against him. Omar wasn't laughing anymore.

The Bear rushed at him with the stick. Omar backed up, trying to avoid it, only to lose his footing and thunder to the ground. Milbill was still getting up when the Bear hit him in the back with the stick, knocking him down again.

Now the Bear was laughing, pummeling his companions with the stick until Omar rushed for his legs, tripping the great Bear to the ground.

Founten didn't like to get in the middle of things. But there was the blessing and hunt to get underway.

The hunt was sacred. It was the life blood of the village. Without it, the people would starve. They could not hunt the animals that drank from the lake in their forest because they drank of the spirits of their ancestors. No one understood how the spirits lingered in the lake, but they lived by that belief.

The five hunters would journey far to the snowy dunes to find food for the village, and then they would have to carry it back.

Founten stepped forward. "Stop this!"

The Bear was still on his back laughing as he wrestled the stick back from Milbill, but Milbill and Omar weren't playing the game anymore. They stopped and turned to Founten.

Founten's shadow loomed in the firelight, stretched even taller than he was. "This is not the time for play. Where's Athanati?"

Omar pointed to Founten and Athanati's tent.

Founten left them to find his wife.

He lifted the folds of the tent and entered.

Athanati sat with her eyes closed in meditation. Her wolf head headdress rested beside her so that her long, black hair was free of any covering.

Her large, dark eyes hung below a tall brow. Her nose was flat and wide and lips large as orange slices.

The hunt would begin when the moon rose, but Founten didn't like to disturb her when she was praying to her gods. After all, they would need their help during the hunt.

Founten turned to leave, but his wife's eyes popped open.

"You weren't leaving without me?"

He turned back to her. "Never."

Athanati smiled and rose from her mat. She kissed him surprisingly.

"You know that is bad luck before a hunt," he said.

"I prayed to Tutus for safe passage and to Kynigi for a good hunt. What do we need of luck?"

"It is a harsh winter." Founten lifted the tent for Athanati to walk through.

The people of the village had gathered to witness the blessing. Mothers brought their babes from their beds in the middle of the night.

Founten was glad to see Milbill and Omar waiting near the fire for the blessing. Even the Bear had heeded Founten's command and awaited the ceremony.

Founten and Athanati joined them.

The Mother emerged from her tent to give the blessing. She wore a violet headdress with a beaded band across her brow. The beads were made of fish bones. Her old eyes were light blue, so light the pupils were almost white. Specks of black paint decorated her dark cheeks. She carried a wooden bowl of a red concoction. Only the Mother knew what it was, but it tasted bitter and sharp.

Her young apprentice, Foititis, followed her. Foititis was chosen out of the newborn daughters born on the Mother's thousandth full moon. Two other daughters were born that night. They were all taken to the cliff on the plain where the Mother sat with them. She chose one to be her successor. The others she tossed to the sea.

The Mother returned with her successor who she named Foititis.

The Mother and Foititis approached Founten. The Mother anointed Founten's forehead with the blood-red mixture. She did the same for Athanati, Milbill, Omar, and Erebus.

The Mother stepped back, facing them.

Her full lips did not move. Instead, Foititis spoke for her. "May Kynigi bless this hunt."

Founten did not believe in the gods. He had seen how fortune could turn her head with favor or ill with no regard for the gods or the prayers of the people. His father would say that was because the gods did not favor them or had ignored their prayers, but Founten had always been inquisitive and thoughtful even as a child. *Where were the gods? Why were they so fickle with their children's lives?*

The Bear accepted the blessing. He was highly religious, praying to the gods every day. Founten could sense him praying to his gods now, thanking Kynigi for her blessing and perhaps asking Dynami for strength.

The red liquid dripped down Founten's nose and tickled his cheek, but he dared not wipe it away for fear of insulting the Mother.

Children clung to their mothers' skirts as they watched the hunters leave the village.

The hunters were armed with their bows, daggers, and staffs. Leaving their fate in the hands of the gods, they left without food or water. It was disgraceful for a hunter to sneak out with food from the village.

They hunted on the snowy dunes that stretched all the way to the frozen sea. It would take forty moons to get there. Because it was forbidden to hunt the animals of the forest and golden plains, they would not eat until they reached the depths of the snowy dunes.

Founten was tired of hearing the banter of Milbill and Omar. They were the youngest of the group and had been hunters not above a year. On the first day of the journey, they were all talks and jests until the hunger set in to sober them.

The Bear didn't seem to be bothered by their raucousness. Founten admired how he could go inside himself and find sanctuary. Founten needed the sanctity of the forest.

Athanati walked in her austere silence. Founten loved how high-browed and regal she was. If she had been born on the Right Moon, she would be the perfect Mother. The people would follow her with faith, and she would lead them to their gods.

ON the seventh day, their stomachs tightened. They found a little pocket of water on the golden plains as they journeyed, but now that they had made it to the fields of snow, the water was frozen and their lips were dried and cold. They were trying to preserve the water from their canteens that they had filled on the fields.

Milbill shook his canteen. The water had turned to an icy slush.

"A little further," Founten urged. The hunt would begin in the snowy dunes near the frozen sea; it would be many miles before they would see a beast and eat its flesh and drink its blood, but Founten's urging was a sign of hope.

The Bear grunted. Hunger was making him more irritable. The journey was always the same. Milbill and Omar had become quieter, each concentrating on his own hunger, and Athanati remained calm, taking her discomfort in a silence that was never broken.

"We'll make it pass the fields of snow down the valley to the dunes," Founten said.

"We don't need a tour guide," the Bear said. "The journey's far. We'll be hungry and tired like always. We don't need the foreshadowing."

He walked pass Founten, sinking his long feet into the snow.

Athanati wrapped the shawl tighter around her shoulders. She was struggling with the cold more than usual. It must have been because she fasted the day before the hunt in hopes that the gods would look more favorably upon them.

As they trekked through the snow, the expanse of whiteness was infinite. They were in a white, endless abyss.

Despite his great headdress, Founten's face was numb, especially his nose. At first, the cold had caused it to ache. Then the ache dulled, leaving it without feeling. His fingers felt the same. The nails had turned purple. He rubbed them for fear they would blacken. Once they blackened, there would be no hope. They would fall off like dead tree leaves.

Perhaps Athanati was feeling the cold more than usual because it was colder than usual. This winter had been harsh even in the great forest where snow did not touch the ground. The air was colder as it drifted from the snowy dunes and the frozen sea.

The clouds prevented them from seeing if it was night or day, but their feet did not lie.

It was time to rest.

There was no shelter in the icy fields, just miles and miles of snow.

Milbill pulled something out of his pocket and grinned. On the ground, he placed three round stones and a handful of tiny balls made of wrapped twine. The toys were part of a game the children played in the village.

Milbill drew a circle in the snow and spread the balls out

within the circle. He drew a larger circle around the smaller.

He picked out the three stones from the smaller circle. He handed one to Omar. He tried handing one to the Bear, but the Bear had turned away from the grinning mouse.

Milbill aimed his stone at one of the balls in the circle, trying to knock the ball out of the smaller circle, but careful to keep it within the larger one. If the ball was knocked out of the smaller circle and into the larger one, he could keep it, and it would be his point.

Founten watched them play their game without interest. They were so childlike, not understanding the seriousness of the hunt.

They were chosen after two others, Sofos and Liti, had died. A great boar attacked them. Tusks speared Sofos in the stomach, and Liti, who tried to save him, got the same.

The Mother said their spirits were absorbed into the forest. Founten didn't quite understand what that meant. The Mother fasted in the forest, drinking only the blood of Sofos and Liti before choosing Milbill and Omar to take their places.

The red liquid had long dried on Founten's face. It was starting to crack and fall away from the frost.

IT had been thirty days. Their stomachs were groaning loudly. One groaned, and the others followed in close chorus. Their steps had become lazy.

Founten sat in the snow. He took his bag from his back and pulled out a few pieces of narrow cedar, a bunch of sticks, and a stone with a sharp point, like the head of a spear.

He placed the sticks in a pyramid pattern. He rubbed the cedar with the stone, taking out the shavings of the inner bark. He created a tinder bundle with the shavings. He took one branch and a bit of base woods. He rubbed the branch between his hands with one end of the branch rubbing into the base branch until smoke rose and an ember sparked. He placed the base branch into the bundle and blew on it until fire rose. He placed the tinder into the nest of sticks. The fire burned the sticks and rose into the air.

The others sat around it. Milbill placed his canteen close to the fire so the heat would melt the ice inside.

"We're getting close to the dunes," the Bear said. "We normally see at least a rabbit by now to hold us over. The gods did not look favorably upon us."

"Nonsense," Athanati said. "We are too quick to blame the gods for our misfortune."

The Bear grunted. Then was silent. He was combative, but with Athanati, it was different, he would not go against her.

MILBILL and Omar fell asleep around the fire. The Bear snored. Founten rested on his back under the starless, moonless sky.

Athanati was stirring. Founten had thought she was asleep too.

She leaned up on one elbow and turned to him. She took one of his hands and placed it on her stomach.

Energy pulsed.

"I'm with child," she said.

Her growing belly hid beneath the folds of her clothes. Founten had done less than fulfill his husbandly duties. He was surprised to find his wife was so blessed, but she had gone against their creed. Pregnant women were not supposed to take part in the hunt.

"But . . ."

"I knew you would stop me," she said, "that Mother would stop me. You need me on this hunt."

Athanati had always wanted to be a mother.

Founten held his breath. The Bear's snore ceased. A grunt sounded, and the drone of the snoring continued.

IN ten days, they made it to the snowy dunes. They climbed up the rocky wall of the valley. Athanati's steps were labored. Founten was careful to be there should she fall.

The dunes were great white mounds of snow. This was where the hunt would begin.

They hunted in groups. Athanati walked toward Milbill and Omar.

"Wait," Founten stopped them. "Athanati, you come with me this time. Erebus can go with Milbill and Omar."

Athanati shook her head. "This is the way it has always been." She joined her usual companions, and they made off across the snow.

Founten went with the Bear. Erebus was in a foul mood. He was hungry.

They walked for miles through the expansive snow. There were no beasts to hunt. They returned to the camp empty handed as did Milbill, Omar, and Athanati.

The next day, they tried again, and settled down to another supperless night.

The Bear was a quiet companion. Founten liked that. Only when he was challenged, did the Bear roar.

That night, they huddled around the fire, their stomachs tight and empty. They rubbed their hands together and blew hot air into them. Their stomachs were audible.

"I'm starving," Milbill said.

"This is not a place for children." Erebus was pale-skinned, an outcast. If he hadn't been a hunter, he would have been shunned. His differentness made him tough.

Omar reached into his bag. He pulled out a piece of salted meat.

Breathing stopped. The wind whistled.

The meat was dark. The salt had kept it from freezing.

Milbill marveled at the meat, the life source. "Where did you get that?"

"From the village," the Bear said. He grabbed the piece of meat, wrenching it from Omar's hands and threw it across the snowy plains.

Omar's mouth was agape.

The Bear settled back down as if nothing happened.

"YOU know it's forbidden," Founten said. "It is bad luck to take a life when life is growing inside you." Founten lay down on his shawl. The cold crept through the shawl and chilled his body to the bone. There was no sanctuary from the cold.

Athanati slept across the fire from him. Her face was visible through the flickering flames. A hulking mass was behind her. It was the Bear in his great headdress with fur dropping down over his shoulder.

He nudged her, and Athanati's eyes flickered open. She turned to him. He presented her with the meat he had thrown to the snow. The Bear was going against his gods.

Had he heard them the night before? Did he know Athanati was with child?

He held the meat out to her, but Athanati was as stubborn as he was. She refused the meat, turning around to go back to sleep.

The Bear stalked off. He tossed the meat far away from the camp. He knelt in the snow.

Was he cursing the gods?

THE next day, they broke off into two groups to try the hunt again.

The Bear and Founten walked in silence looking for signs of wandering beasts. As the day drew to a close, the Bear stopped in his tracks. "We need to go back. Back to the village. The winter has been too harsh. There is nothing for us here."

"It is disgraceful to return without food for the village."

"Screw disgraceful. We're dying out here. Your pregnant wife is dying out here."

"How did you know about that?"

The Bear didn't answer.

The snow was coming down in flurries so thick they couldn't see.

Something roared in the distance. The Bear ran towards the sound. Founten tried to follow, but he got lost in the thick snow. Erebus's tracks disappeared, covered up by the falling snow.

Shouting was out of his habit, but he shouted the Bear's name. "Erebus!"

Shouting without answer, he walked for miles. His feet were numb, and his legs were tired. The others must have made it back to camp long ago.

When Founten returned to camp, Milbill and Omar were asleep, but Athanati sat up. When she saw him, she rushed over to him and hugged him tight. She looked over his shoulder. "Where's Erebus?"

"He didn't make it. I lost him in the snow."

But Athanati didn't stop peering into the distance. "You're wrong. Look!"

Through the thick snow, a dark figure was approaching.

The closer he got, the more they could make out his white skin against the black fur of the great bear. Erebus swooned, but regained his balance.

Founten rushed to him.

Blood dripped from a large gash in his shoulder right below the neck. It looked like a bite. Teeth had torn through the muscle, revealing bone.

Suddenly, the Bear opened his jaws and bit into Founten's neck.

Athanati screamed, running towards them. Her screams were lost in the flurry of snow.

Founten had fallen to the ground, facing her.

The Bear knocked Athanati into the snow. She fell against an exposed, jagged rock. It bit into her side, and blood issued forth into the snow.

Facing Founten, Athanati lay in the snow. One side of her face sank into the ice. Red snow spread before her.

Gushing and screaming echoed from the camp.

Blood warmed Founten's neck.

Tears were in Athanati's eyes. She was crying. "No! No!"

Founten was becoming light headed. It was like he was looking through a tunnel that was getting narrower and narrower.

Athanati's cries grew more and more distant, and then, there were none.

42

ATHANATI

I look back at the Hundreds of My People who gathered to Watch Me enter the Tomb. Did they Know what was in store for Me? Would One of them have gone in my Place?
I am not a Man to Say that Someone Must Do It, so Why not Me?
I step aside and let Heroes do their Work.
So Why am I compelled to do this Task?

ATHANATI lay in the snow and watched her husband die. Her tears froze on her face.

A shadow hung over her. The Bear threw off his headdress, and it sank into the snow behind her. Erebus walked around to Founten's body, laying in the snow.

Blood painted Erebus's shirt, and, up against his pale white skin, blood circled his mouth. Thick blood dripped from his lips into the snow.

Erebus knelt next to Founten's body. Was he going to pray to the gods, to ask forgiveness? No. He opened his jaws.

Athanati had never seen a man open his jaws so wide. She could see every tooth in his mouth.

He sank down, biting into Founten's neck.

"No!"

Erebus ripped off his shirt and sank his teeth into his flesh. He chewed off a bit of flesh and took it in his hands, mushing it into his mouth. Pieces fell into the snow.

Athanati shut her eyes against the bloody feast, but she could still hear the smacking and ripping and feel the spray of blood across her face.

Eventually, the chewing stopped.

Athanati dared to open her eyes. She couldn't look at what was left of her husband. Erebus stood above him. His teeth were bloody.

Athanati's bag and her weapons were back at camp. She couldn't search her husband's body for a blade. She couldn't bear to look at him.

"Kill me!" Athanati screamed. Her hand was over her belly. Blood was issuing from her side. She didn't have the strength to stand.

Erebus looked at her.

Were those tears?

"Kill me!" she cried.

But Erebus couldn't kill the blood of his blood, it was his child in her womb, not even animals did that. He ran off into the snow, blood trailing behind him.

Athanati's cries echoed in the distance. A burst of water leaked out onto her legs. Pressure built at the base of her stomach and tightened. The tightening grew into a cramping.

Athanati screamed.

She had hoped now that the baby would not be born, that it would die inside her.

As the pressure built, she removed her pants. She grinded her teeth as she pushed.

Normally, women of the village gave birth standing up, but Athanati didn't have the strength to stand.

She pushed.

High pitched crying filled the air.

The pressure was released. Blood and fluids mingled down her legs.

Athanati reached from under her legs and held the baby. It was warm and smarmy. A girl.

Athanati cradled her head in her hand. She was small. She wasn't ready to be born. Athanati wiped the fluid from the baby's face. The baby had a pale face and blue eyes.

Once in her mother's arms, the baby's crying stopped.

Athanati started to cry afresh. The baby wouldn't survive. More and more blood issued from Athanati. She would not live to care for her child.

"Baby," she cried. "Baby."

She found the rock under her and pulled it from the ground. It was as heavy as her heart. She raised it above her head, above her newborn daughter.

Her eyes looked up at her mother so trusting.

Athanati brought the rock down. The rock, still wrapped in Athanati's fingers, rested far from the baby's head.

The baby cried and so did her mother.

She cradled her in her arms and reached around for the Bear's headdress. She wrapped it around herself and the baby.

Athanati slept with her baby in her arms, and she did not wake. The baby's cries echoed into the distance.

43

NOT MY KIND

Fear grows within Me. If I were to Clench my Quill any tighter, It would Snap between My fingers.

RAI had fallen asleep by Rodan's bedside. Her hand was on his. She was shaken from her sleep. She awoke with a start.

"I'll wait with him for a while," Farah said.

They had landed in Wyvek the night before. After landing the Chariot, Rai was supposed to get some sleep, but she found herself watching Rodan sleep instead.

She jerked her hand from on top of his. "Sure."

Farah sat in the chair beside Rodan's bed.

Rai walked down the steps to the bar. She grabbed a piece of bread from the bar and bit into it. She drank from the bottle of warm nectar wine.

Pentagon and Atrus sat at the end of the bar. They ate in silence. Rai had forgotten the last time she saw Atrus quiet.

Something was up.

"What's going on?" she asked.

"I'm not going in there," Atrus said.

"Isn't this your set-up? Didn't some of your men die here?"

"That's right." He took another swig of honeyed wine.

"That's the cowardly thing to do," Rai said. "I've never known you to be a coward."

Atrus rose from his seat and spread out his arms. "Well, I've never known you to be a bitch. It's a new day."

He was drunk, but it still stung.

"How many times have I had your back?" Atrus asked. "We fought together."

Pentagon got up from his seat and grabbed Atrus by the shoulder. Atrus shook him off and approached Rai.

"Now you act like *we* were the traitors," Atrus said. "Like we weren't betrayed too."

"What's the meaning of this?" Vassal stepped between Atrus and Rai.

"Speak of the devil," Atrus said.

"I don't have time for this." Rai walked to the elevator. She pressed the button to the control room.

The door opened, and Vassal stepped in.

How was he so fast on a wooden leg?

"What?" Rai asked. "Have you come to tell me now how it wasn't them? It was you. That I shouldn't take it out on them. So you can look like some kind of victim or martyr?"

"I know this is hard for you."

"Don't play that game with me. It's hard for *you*. You're a traitor. You should've just stayed that way. We can never be friends, and lovers, hah! What do you think you're doing here? Because you're wasting your time on me."

The elevator opened to the control room. Thatch was at his seat.

Rai stormed in. "I'm going in alone."

"Farah didn't like that last time," Thatch said.

"Well, she's with Rodan. Pentagon and Atrus are strung out. They've had too much to drink at the bar."

Thatch looked at Vassal who walked up beside her.

Rai followed his eyes. "No."

"Go with Decca and Shilo then. They're down in the engine room with Spire and the baby."

Rai turned her back on them and went back to the elevator.

Down in the engine room, loud crying echoed through the cavernous space. It was Canace. Rai followed Canace's cries through the labyrinth of engines, gears, and piles of scrap metal.

Spire was rocking Canace, but the baby continued to cry. Hoping to settle her tears, Decca cooed at her.

Lucerna was standing nearby. She had wanted to hold the baby, but Spire wanted to calm her first. Lucerna had taken refuge in the windowless place during the day because the sun hurt her eyes.

The Wind rushed against the Chariot. Lucerna had been practicing her element by sensing Canace's energy and trying to quell it, but the baby was strong.

Lucerna had easily extinguished the flames from Rai's sword. Yet, this baby was a challenge. Rai. How much more powerful would the infant be when she grew up?

"Let me hold her." Decca reached for his child and took her in his arms. The crying stopped, and Canace gazed up at her father.

Spire's face was a mixture of feelings Rai didn't understand.

"Where's Shilo?" Rai asked.

"I think he's on the roof." Decca rocked Canace.

"I'm setting the Lightning Sphere," Rai said. "I was hoping you and Shilo could be my backup."

"*I* could be your backup," Lucerna said.

"Fine."

"Wait," Decca said. "I can get Shilo. You can never have too many people on your side."

More people only means more betrayals. Rai shook the thought from her mind. "Alright then. We'll wait for you outside."

"We're going now?" Lucerna must have been disappointed she couldn't hold the baby.

"It will be in, out, and done." Rai retrieved the sphere from her bag and handed it to Lucerna. The remaining spheres were with Farah. Rai had managed to slip this one away from her.

"Come on," Rai said.

Lucerna followed Rai to the exit. She shielded her eyes against the evening light. They waited for Shilo and Decca.

"Rai," Lucerna said, "Something interesting. The haze around Canace, it's always black, deep, strong."

"She's powerful," Rai said.

"It's like . . . no matter how many layers I pull back. It's still dark." Lucerna gazed into the distance. Lucerna could see things Rai couldn't, perhaps Canace's energy looming overhead. The Wind had kicked up again.

Decca and Shilo emerged from the Chariot. Shilo patted Decca on the back and laughed. They were both smiling.

Their faces turned serious as they approached Rai and Lucerna.

RAI pushed the doors open to the temple.

The smell inside was putrid. A half dozen bodies had been rotting inside for days. The Rebel Resistance had removed the bodies, but not the smell.

Couldn't they have at least left the door open to air out the place?

When they got inside, Lucerna's hand moved from her eyes to her nose. "What is that?"

"Death," Rai said.

The doors to the inner room were open.

"Man, is it eerie in here," Decca said.

"Let's go," Rai said.

"Wait." Shilo grabbed Rai's shoulder.

Rai frowned, feeling his hand there.

"What is that?" Shilo asked.

"That's those worms, brother," Decca said.

Glowing white worms snaked around the statues. Their bodies were fizzling with energy.

"Damn it." Rai stepped on one close to her feet. She sent Fire. The worms squealed in a sickly chorus.

"We need to get to the sphere room," Rai said.

"Go with Lucerna, and close the door," Decca said. "My brother and I will handle these."

Rai wasn't sure how Decca and Shilo were going to fight those things with swords. But she needed to get the sphere on its pedestal. *Might not make them disappear, but it'll stop new ones from coming.*

She and Lucerna ran into the next room and closed the door behind them.

No energy ran through the channel to power the elevator.

The platform was frozen at the front of the second-floor loft where the Sphere Room was.

"I don't know how to work this thing," Rai said. She had used a rope the first time. "Here. I'll get you up there." She squatted and cupped her hands together.

Lucerna put one foot into Rai's hands, and Rai lifted her, allowing Lucerna to reach the elevator. She pulled herself up.

She reached her hand out to Rai.

"You're not strong enough. You still have the Lightning Sphere?"

"Um-hum." She patted the bag at the side of her hip.

"If you see the Sphere Protector," Rai said, "Get out of there, okay?"

Lucerna nodded.

Rai leaned her back against the wall. When she had broken into the temple years ago, the great beast stood over her. It had shocked her. Energy tethered the sphere to its pedestal, and she pulled it away.

The people beat her in the street.

And her mother died anyway.

She had been no one until she stole a sphere. Then she became the girl with the black band. Her life had been defined by sphere stealing.

Putting them back seemed . . . separate from her identity.

She touched the black band around her arm. Vassal had never asked her about it.

Lucerna was on the broken elevator. "I don't know what's wrong."

"What do you mean?" Rai asked.

"The sphere . . . it just fell from the pedestal."

"Let me see it."

Lucerna reached down to show her the sphere. It didn't

glow as brightly as the others.

"That's not the Lightning Sphere," Rai said. "Drop down."

Lucerna held onto the edges of the platform and let her body hang. With only a few feet to fall, she let her body drop. She landed on her feet on the main floor.

She was animated. "There were so many white worms. All over the walls just like in the Sphere Cave. I didn't see the Protector."

The doors of the inner room burst open. A figure had entered, a tall gaunt man. *Fulgur.*

She only called him a man for lack of a better term. Whatever he was, it was something *not*-human.

Decca. Shilo. Had he killed them?

Rai's heart stopped. There was nowhere to hide.

She stepped in front of Lucerna. Her blade was ablaze and ready, but it wouldn't help.

"I didn't come for you. I came for her." He pointed a long, crooked finger at Lucerna. "I need her. She was my sister's pet."

A bolt of Lightning shot into the air and hit Rai in the chest. The sensation was like a rubber band had snapped just beneath the surface of her skin. The blurred image of the Sphere Protector walked across the room.

The horse was made of Lightning. Sometimes the Lightning formed a horn on the top of its head, but not this time. Its white eyes stared back at her.

There was no fear there. Only loneliness. Hundreds and hundreds of years of loneliness in its eyes. Years without love or contests. Life was of no value because it never ended. Life was loneliness.

"Not the first time you were touched by Lightning." The

voice came from far away.

Light flashed at the corners of her eyes. She shut them. When she opened them, she was kneeling on the ground. The elevator raced up and down. Lightning filled the energy channels.

Lucerna was gone.

The doors of the inner room swung on their hinges. Decca and Shilo marched into the room. Their swords hung at their sides.

Something was wrong about them. Their strides were stiff and unnatural. Their eyes were . . . white.

Shilo raised his sword against Rai.

Their blades met.

Steel zinged against steel, as Rai swung to touch blades with Decca. She struggled under the weight of Decca's blow, but she managed to push. She staggered backwards.

The two brothers were closing in on her. Decca barreled towards her. Shilo darted to her right.

Rai matched blow for blow. Then, Decca knocked her to the ground. His sword clamored against the cold marble. Rai rolled out of the way just in time.

Her sword arm was starting to get fatigued.

She sent Fire into Decca's face, but the flames were weak and dissipated quickly.

I'm getting too tired. But I can't stop. I'll die.

They ran at her.

Surging with adrenaline, Rai threw flames at Shilo. She rushed into Decca, sword against sword. She pushed back as hard as she could.

Decca stepped back. His foot went down into the energy channel, which was still zinging with Lightning.

Decca staggered to the ground. The white worms spilled

out of his mouth like they were evacuating a burning building.

Rai gulped. Then screamed.

Shilo had embedded his blade into her shoulder, her sword arm. He yanked it away.

Hot blood ran down her arm. She turned around and backed away from Shilo's next blow.

In rapid succession, she sent blasts of Fire in front of Shilo, forcing him to back further and further away from the flames.

He stepped into the energy channel, and the worms left his body.

Rai sent flames after the worms, and half-smiled at their screams. She grabbed her bleeding shoulder and winced. She rushed to the temple door. *Was it possible that Lucerna was still here?*

Rai stopped. Her feet skidded across the marble floor.

Bolts of Lightning ran like bars against the temple's entrance.

44

HEARTBEATS

*All other Nations have been Forgotten. All other Rulers have been
Killed. Mirmina is United. Yet, It is United in Fear.*

FARAH sat at Rodan's bedside. The sky turned black. No
matter where they were, they were always under the
same sky. She hoped that somewhere her dad could see
it too.

Orka was nestled on her perch.

Farah should have given Shift a communicator before
they left and made him promise to listen for her call. What
had become of her brother? She didn't like to think about it.
She wanted to tell Thatch to turn around and go back to
Breeze. But then what? To find her brother dead? She didn't
want to bury anyone else. And either way she would be bury-
ing him.

Rodan's breathing was shallow.

Where was Sara? She was like a sister. She and Farah had traveled many miles together. They laughed and told stories. But Sara had wandered off never to be seen again.

What's more, Bolton came back after years of being dead and then disappeared.

It was an anticlimactic reunion.

Atrus was still drinking at the bar with Pentagon. They were starting to sing now. One of the songs they drunkenly claimed to have sang on their voyage to rid the spheres of their sanctums. They both sung the chorus, but only Pentagon knew the other lines. That's when Atrus finished off his drink.

He was making a fool of himself. Atrus never could hold his liquor well.

Farah rolled her eyes, but when Atrus twirled with his arms around an imaginary girl, a laugh escaped her lips.

She turned back to Rodan and became sober. *How long had the sound of his breathing ceased?* Farah could no longer see the rise and fall of his chest.

She put her ear there.

Nothing.

45

THE NEW KEEPERS

In Only a Few Seconds, I have Imagined that I would Die in a Thousand Different Ways.

SARA'S reflection stared back at her. Founten stood as he was before. His boundless nocturnal eyes were startling in the glow of the crystals.

"What does this mean?" she asked.

"When Erebus ate us, he knew we would not be gone," Founten said.

"What happened to you?"

Founten turned his great owl head. "We returned to the forest in our true forms."

"So, that's it then," Sara said. "He used energy, storing it into the spheres to give us power. But how did he find a continuous source."

Founten's feathered hand touched Sara's chest.

"He used people?" she asked.

Founten nodded. "But those people are betraying him. He needs new children now."

"Sara?" Benn walked from among the trees. "Who were you talking to?"

Founten was gone, and she still had so many questions.

"We need a communicator," Sara said.

"I know," Benn said. "You've been saying that."

"We need one now. I have to talk to the others." Sara rushed away from the lake.

Benn wrapped his hand around her arm. "What's wrong? You look crazed."

"I need a *Lacwanx*."

Benn followed her. "We should wait until dawn. This is crazy."

"You want to wait until dawn? I'll do it myself."

The sky was still dark through patches in the trees. The glow of the crystals lit their way.

SARA'S feet dragged as she approached the waterfall. The walk had sobered her. Benn had caught up.

The gates of Vella City appeared through the trees. Four guards stood at the gates. Many more sentinels stood watch throughout the city.

From the higher ground of the forest, they could see over the city gates.

"I don't see any *Lacwanx*," Benn said.

"They must have *Lacwanx*," Sara said. "Atrus didn't supply them with that many chariots."

"Maybe he lied. He was a thief, right? They lie."

Sara shook her head.

"Even if there were *Lacwanx* in there, what then?" Benn asked. "The place is riddled with guards. At best, we'll make it a few feet from the gates. They'll recognize you and take you prisoner. Never mind what they'll do to me or Bolton when he tries to rescue you."

Sara took a deep breath.

Realization hit her.

She didn't look for her communicator. When she fell, she didn't look for it. It could still be there in Omega Ray. It was a long shot that it still worked. But maybe.

"You're right," Sara said. "There are too many guards. But not in Omega Ray."

"Why Omega Ray?"

"It's where I dropped my communicator. I think. I was out of it. But I always had it on me. It could still be there."

"Do we have enough food to travel all the way to Omega Ray?"

Founten had journeyed beyond the mountain to the snowy dunes. She had made that journey with him in her mind. Relative to that, this journey was nothing.

"We'll have enough," she said.

Benn shook his head. "We should go back to Dustpath and wait for Bolton."

"I'm going to Omega Ray." Sara made it final.

Benn sighed but said nothing.

JETTY Verte had changed since Founten and his companions crossed it. The ground was no longer smooth. It was wrinkled, like the face of an old man.

Founten said the Creator had returned, Erebus, the black Bear. But why was he afraid? He said energy could not be created nor lost, so what had he to fear? He would always live in one way or another.

Sara didn't understand it.

She had always thought of the Creator as an aloft being in the clouds. She imagined he formed the spheres as a gift to the lessor creatures below him long before anyone could remember. She was surprised to find that he was once without power, that he was weak, that he killed his friends.

Sara and Benn set up camp just outside the forest.

It was nice to see the stars.

Sara rolled up her bag and laid her head upon it. She didn't remember falling asleep.

Upon the cliff was the little girl, her hair tousled by the breeze. She was gazing out to the sea. She didn't seem to notice the figure standing beside her with the head of a bear. His true form.

Sara jolted up. Sweat was on her brow. A few strings of hair were matted there.

She was thankful she hadn't awoken Benn. She didn't need him questioning her about her nightmares. She was having them more and more now. Something was coming.

THE next morning, Benn was up before Sara. As she was opening her eyes, he was shouldering his bag. "I was about to wake you. If you want to make it to Omega Ray before our food runs out, we'd better make use of every bit of daylight."

Sara yawned, rubbed her eyes, and grabbed her bag from under her head.

She had a fitful night.

She kept seeing that young girl, sometimes with the Bear, sometimes alone. In a few flashes, the girl was with others, but their faces were shadowed.

Sara shouldered her bag and joined Benn.

The mountain was in the distance. They had a long way to go.

BENN chewed an apple to the core.

Sara marched ahead of him despite her tiredness. She had gone days without restful sleep.

"You should have been born a Fire Elemental," Benn said.

"Why's that?" Sara played along.

"Fire Elementals rarely lack energy. They're full of passion. They want to change the world. Ana was like that." Benn changed the subject. "Water Elementals find ways around problems. They don't confront them head on."

"What would you know about Water Elementals?"

"I met a few in my lifetime. They always thirsted for the freedom of the open road. I guess you share that in common. They don't have structure so they either succeed or lose themselves completely. Always reflecting what they see. Good memories. They're able to see something and project it back perfectly. They easily let their emotions get the best of them."

"And what about Lightning Elementals?" Sara eyed him.

"Spontaneous, assertive, volatile."

"You're none of those things," she said.

"No, but my son is."

"You haven't known him for that long."

That shut Benn up.

But the silence it created was uncomfortable. Benn walked behind her with his head down and sulked over the years missed with his son.

At first, Sara felt no sympathy for him, but she was starting to feel guilt.

She couldn't wait for Bolton to return, so she could go

back to hating Benn instead of feeling sorry for him.

He was right. Bolton was volatile and rash. He left her. He could have held out longer, stayed with her longer. Benn forced his hand. Every second he waited, his little brother would be without a safety net to catch him when he fell.

Sara didn't want to think about Benn anymore. Maybe it was a mistake to bring him. She hadn't needed him once along the journey, and she doubted she would need him now.

They had passed the inn. In another day, they could make it to the base of the mountain and begin the climb.

Sara dreaded that climb through the cold, but it had to be done. She left her communicator in Omega Ray. She just had to look. When she and Bolton left the city, she had been too scared to stay a moment longer. She wasn't thinking about the communicator. She was thinking about that thing in the dungeon.

Sometimes she saw it in her nightmares too, the man with the rotting face.

She had never had nightmares so intense. She woke up still believing they were real, like memories.

She didn't know how she got there. Omega Ray was miles from Tosia. Yet, when she fell from that cliff, she landed into the chasm outside the city.

The closer they got to the mountain, the colder it grew. Sara hadn't planned to journey all the way to Omega Ray, so she hadn't packed anything warm enough.

She crossed her arms over her chest.

The first time she climbed this mountain she had an army. She wasn't thinking about the cold then. Her mind was focused on the battle. She imagined so many ways that it could go, and the true battle reflected not one of them.

The main lesson she had learned was to avoid high expectations of anyone or anything. She'd rather be surprised when things go right than disappointed when they go wrong.

Her boots sank into the snow. Her legs were getting heavy. She had to swing her arms to propel herself forward, removing the extra protection they provided against the cold.

She wished she was a Fire Elemental. Their blood was hot. They were easily exhausted in the heat. The cold was their domain because it cooled the hot temperature of their bodies.

The day was wearing down, but Sara kept walking. She was tired of it. She wanted to get it over with and arrive in Omega Ray. But trying to take on the mountain in a day was fruitless. The winds were blasting. It was a harsh winter.

"Stop." Benn put his hand on Sara's shoulder. "That's enough for today. I don't need you passing out like you did in D'arkadia."

"I'm fine." Sara tried to walk away, but Benn tightened his grip.

"You know I'm right. Water is never stubborn."

"Alright," Sara said. "We'll sleep. But if I wake before you, I'm continuing up the mountain without you. You can catch up."

Benn sighed. That was all he was going to get out of her.

SARA woke before sunrise. Clouds covered the moon and stars. Benn's steady breathing drifted through the cold air.

Sara reached into her bag and pulled out an apple. She took a bite. It turned to mush in her mouth. She made good on her promise to leave Benn. Shouldering her bag, she ate the apple as she walked up the steep slope of the mountain.

By evening, she had reached the gates of Omega Ray. She

turned. Benn was nowhere in sight. Maybe he decided to turn back? She wouldn't be surprised. She didn't miss him either. He had become a burden.

Sara trekked up to Hephaestus's stone palace. The roof was torn off, and the columns that had held it up had crumbled. The marble floors were cracked.

She searched the ground. No communicator.

She didn't want to, but she descended the steps to the dungeons. The evening light still flooded into the entry way, but darkness shrouded the rest of the dungeon. There was no way she was finding the communicator down there. She would have to search the ground on her hands and knees. The fear would cause her body to tremble, making the task even more difficult.

But what else could she do?

"You're back."

Sara turned around.

It was the old man with the teardrop scar and the glowing arm.

"I'm Destan. Do you remember me?"

"I do," Sara said. "You scared us. Ranting something about letting him out and not explaining yourself."

Destan took a step closer to her, and Sara backed away into the darkness of the dungeons.

Shadows hid her face.

"I just want to explain. Will you come out?" Destan took a few steps back and spread his arms as a sign of peace.

Sara was hesitant, but she came out of the darkness into the early morning light.

"It took me years to learn how to seal that door, and you opened it in seconds. Only a Keeper could do that."

Keeper. That word was scattered throughout the books Lucerna discovered. The Keepers came to Dustpath with the Creator. When they took the Lightning Sphere from Wyvek, Talon had said it was the Keepers who knew they had come to take the sphere. Learning about the history of the spheres was a common part of a young Elemental's education, but Sara was trained to defend herself. Spire had neglected the more academic lessons.

"What do you mean *Keeper*?" Sara asked.

"I know what you're here for. He chose you."

"Who chose me?"

"The Creator. To replace me."

"I don't understand."

"You won't. Not yet." Destan stepped closer, but Sara stood her ground. Not that she had grown comfortable with him, but she had to hear what he had to say. "Your element, Water . . . there's a reason why it hasn't manifested itself again."

"I'm listening."

"When the sphere was broken, the energy seeped out, like a soul leaving the body. Without the soul, the body is useless."

"So, once the energy is put back, then I can use Water again?"

"The energy can't be put back. It has moved on. New energy must take its place."

Destan pulled something from his cloak and held it up to her.

It was the Water Sphere. It had grown from bright blue to gray, like the skin of a person who died.

"How did you get it?" Sara asked. "Have you seen my friends?"

Destan shook his head. "I found it abandoned in the

Sphere Cave. There was still enough energy left for me to sense it. I had to go through hell to get it, but I had to know."

"Know what?"

"Hold it."

As he placed it in her hands, he held it there. "Don't hold on too long." He let go of the sphere.

As soon as he did, a rush swept through Sara's body like a wave had crashed over her. Then, the tide pulled back. It was like her very being was being pulled into the sphere.

She closed her eyes.

Around her, buildings were rising, breaking through the ground as it cracked open. It was a city with lights and structures higher than those in Lumina. The roads were paved, and music and the sounds of engines filled the streets.

In the distance, Talon stood, but his sword was not at his side, and she knew why. It was still down in that dungeon where she left it. He approached her through the mist.

Suddenly, Sara was crying. Her mother and father were walking towards her too. All the people who had died. They were approaching her. Their figures were transparent.

And there was Rodan. He was among the dead, but his body was more solid.

"No, Rodan!" Sara tried to scream, but her voice sounded far away.

Her soul was joining them.

Then, she was falling. The sphere slipped from her hands. Arms gripped her waist. Her body hit the floor hard.

"He's a liar. Whatever he promised you was a lie." Benn was on the ground beside her. "He tricked me, told me I could see my son again."

Destan had disappeared.

She was breathing heavy. "I saw . . . Rodan."

Benn helped her into a sitting position. "Don't worry about that right now. Are you okay?"

"It was like the energy was being sucked out of me."

"It didn't take it all," Benn said. "I stopped it."

"What?"

Across the floor was the Water Sphere. Sara rushed over and picked it up. The color had returned, a little duller than before, but no longer gray. Energy swirled inside.

46

FAVORITE SON

*If I Die, what would It Matter? I am Only Important because He
made Me Important.*

DESTAN met his father deep in the snowy dunes beyond Omega Ray. His father called it the darkest
place in Mirmina. Destan didn't understand why.

From the snow, he knew it was cold, but he could no
longer feel cold nor heat.

His father looked like a huddled bear in the snow. His
black cloak clung to his body. It wasn't to protect him from
the cold, but to hide the bits of skin that were lost, rotting from
his body like he was a walking corpse decaying before his
eyes.

No warm breath came from their mouths.

"She's my replacement." Destan's voice no longer had

the ability to hold disdain. It came out more evenly than he intended.

Erebus turned to him.

His father looked different when Destan locked him in the pit. The flesh around his eyes had been intact. Now, Destan feared his right eye, unfastened by flesh, would pop out and lie frozen in the snow. His cheek was so badly rotted bone was visible.

His father was hungry. He had that look in his eye.

"I saw her hold the sphere," Destan said. "Her essence was strong. It didn't take much . . ."

"That is because some of you still remains." Erebus' voice was rough, perhaps from hundreds of years of not speaking, of being alone in the dark, of living off the flesh of rats.

"But you want to get rid of that?"

"I did it for you, my son," Erebus said. "Your existence was always a burden."

"For me? Or for you?" Destan asked.

"You have suffered in pain. I wanted you to be free of all that. You were always my favorite son."

It was true. Destan had suffered. He wanted nothing more than to join the ones he lost in the flood that took Omega City. But he needed to take care of his father first.

"I tried to destroy you. I'm still trying," Destan said.

Erebus's eyes narrowed like spearheads. "That's because your loyalty is like Water—wavering." His words came out like lashes from a whip.

Destan backed away.

Hunger had mixed with the anger in Erebus's eyes.

Why hadn't his father eaten? What was he saving his hunger for?

"I gave you a gift," Erebus said, "and you treat it like a

curse. None of my children appreciate what I have given to them. So, I will take it away. I will give it to others who will be loyal and steadfast." There wasn't any anger in Erebus's voice. He spoke like it was just the natural course of things to rid himself of his children, of the only people who he had known for thousands of years.

"She won't be like that, not after she sees what you are, how you created us."

"You don't know what I am."

Had his gums rotted enough for his teeth to fall out? Would he make his children pick the flesh apart for him, or would he make them chew it up and spit it into his hungry mouth?

"You are not a god," Destan said. "You are a demon."

His hungry jaws open wide, Erebus lunged at his son.

Destan side-stepped him.

Erebus stumbled into the snow. His eyes piercing, he turned to Destan.

"I guess it doesn't matter if you devour me since you already have my replacement," Destan said. "How did you do it? You told me I would live forever."

"Energy can be transferred and traded and used again and again," Erebus said. "That's all you are. That's all that makes you walk and talk and feel. What happens to our bodies when we die? They rot in the ground to become food for lesser creatures. Our essence without a body can do whatever it wants . . . can move on beyond this world or stay stuck in it. But there are no gods to greet us when we go, no one to guide us."

"How do you know that?" Destan asked.

"Because I've seen the darkness, and I prayed for it to go away. It never left me. I don't want to be a floating, wayward mist of wandering energy. I don't want that to be all that I am."

"What more is there?" Destan shouted. "What are you now, but a wandering piece of rotting flesh, your spirit trapped in a sphere? What more could you ever be?"

Erebus's peeling lips pulled up into a smile. "Much more."

47

KNIFE IN THE BACK

I began this Chronicle hoping to be Absent from It. But the More I Wrote, the More I Understand that I was Inevitably Part of It.

LUCERNA'S white hair moved in the breeze. Never in Fulgur's life since he dedicated his soul to the sphere had he marveled at another living being. But she was his salvation. She was what would keep his restless body from its slumber.

Fulgur's long, cold fingers inched towards Lucerna's snowy mane.

She turned, and he withdrew.

Her eyes were quizzical and afraid. She didn't know where he was taking her or why. She didn't understand she was a pawn in a game Destan started and Fulgur would finish.

She was so young.

Dawn said he had no more feelings, but he sympathized with this poor creature the way he would for a bird with a broken wing.

A hawk was staring down at his prey. But how could the hawk feel sorry for the hunted?

Would Dawn cry? Would she mourn the girl's youth like she mourned her own?

Why did she believe she still had feelings and he didn't? He dedicated no more of himself to the sphere than she did.

She loved this girl like a daughter, and he would steal her innocence. No, it would be the sphere, the sphere that Dawn helped Destan create that would steal it.

Moonlight hit Lucerna's hair and shined on the water.

He could see the bottom. There was hope. But hope would come and go. Such a fickle thing.

His father had chosen his replacement. Fulgur didn't know who it was. If he did, Fulgur would snuff the life out of him so his spirit could not fill the sphere, pushing Fulgur's out into lonely nothingness.

He would rip open his chest and let the spirit leak out. That wouldn't stop his father from choosing another. His life was on the clock again. He never felt more alive.

Fearing for his life had suddenly made it valuable.

He led Lucerna down into the boat. He rowed across the water with the strength of a young man who was used to labor. He rowed into the night, never tiring. No gasps of breath escaped his lips.

When they reached the bank, he helped her out of the boat.

The boat rocked in the water. The birds were singing it a lullaby as the water settled.

What Fulgur felt inside was anything but calm. He hated

the boat. He had never hated before. His hands rocked it until water splashed into it.

Lucerna gasped, shocked by his sudden reaction, passion that seemed without reason.

His replacement would be like that boat, like Fulgur once was, calmed to boredom with no reason to live. He suddenly felt unwanted, like his spirit was slowly returning to his body.

No, it was still in its glass tomb, safe inside the sphere room now.

The hands of his replacement would grab hold of the sphere, having invaded his sanctum, his sanctuary, pushing out his soul.

Fulgur closed his eyes.

He grew up with the corn.

His mother and father harvested it. He couldn't see their faces anymore, but he knew them. The sound of his father's voice and the feeling of his mother hugging him close.

His father smiled at him. It was strange to think of him as his father, having so long called Erebus father. Sometimes he pictured Erebus in his place, and that made the whole scene eerier: Erebus with his skin rotting away among all that . . . life.

The smell of sweat and corn mingled. The roughness of his woven shirt, stained green and brown, tickled Fulgur's skin. The stalks grew for miles and miles.

He would ride down the street in his father's cart, carrying corn cobs still in their husks. He was happy, waving at passers-by who knew his family like their own.

The people were faceless now.

He was content. It was never exciting, but it was never boring. It was life.

He didn't concern himself with whether he would live or

die. Everybody died, and no one concerned himself with it.

Every day, he would work, go to the market, and work some more.

His hands became strong, his shoulders broad, until he was lifting more than his father, working longer, and harder. His father didn't seem to mind. It was Fulgur's destiny to replace him, like all sons replaced their fathers.

It happened when he was in the corn field. The sky lit up, blinding him, once, twice, many times.

Burning.

Bolts of light struck the ground like spears being thrown from the sky.

Should he run? Or be still? What would prevent the crooked, burning lines from hitting him next?

His father screamed in pain, but Fulgur didn't move. He didn't want to die.

The screams faded.

The light, like a blade, tore through the stalks of corn and cut them from the ground.

People were cut down too.

Their bodies dropped. They shook as the light, like a rope, tethered to their bodies until they died.

The light went through Fulgur. It snapped all over his skin. His organs were cooking like there was a fire inside him. Everything went black.

FULGUR blinked. Smoke rose in the air.

He turned around.

The corn that had grown in the distance and covered the land was gone. The stalks lay blackened on the ground like fallen men.

In front of him were *real* fallen men. He didn't want to

look, didn't want to see their blackened bodies still spasming on their backs.

His face was dirty from lying on the ground. He wiped the dirt away with his hand. He walked over the stalks of corn, afraid to find his mother or father.

But he never did.

His tears ran like a valley through the dirt. It was the first time he feared death.

He didn't know where he was going. He just knew that he wanted to get away, far away from the horror.

Night fell as he walked.

A man stood ahead of him in a dark cloak. He stopped in the middle of the road like he was waiting for him.

He couldn't be waiting for me. No one outside the village knew him. He was probably just a traveler lost in need of directions on this dark night.

In a show of normalcy, Fulgur nodded to the stranger.

Once he was past the stranger, the man spoke. "Did you see the storm ahead?"

Fulgur stopped.

Of course, that's why the man feared to go further. He was afraid of the storm.

But its mere mention sent images flying through Fulgur's head and smells of smoke and fried bodies.

"Yes," he managed.

"Did you see how it lit up the sky?" He wasn't afraid. The stranger was marveling at it. *How could he marvel at something so terrible?*

"I was in it," Fulgur said.

"Were you? But you appear unharmed?"

Fulgur didn't want to talk to this man, this man that marveled at his misfortune.

He walked along the road.

"Wait! Can you spare some food for an old traveler?" His white teeth, sharper than the average man's, shone in the night.

"Sorry. Everything is lost."

"No, not everything."

He held something up in his hands. It shined in the night like a star.

Fulgur was drawn to it. "What is it?"

"Your salvation."

"What do you mean?"

"Take hold, and you will never have to fear death again."

Fulgur did not believe this man, yet he was drawn to the sphere. He was a simple peasant boy being had by this old man and his trinket. But the pull was so strong, he could do little else but focus on it. After all, his world was gone. He took hold of the sphere.

It was heavy in his hands.

Suddenly, he felt all the pain and sadness pull away from him. He felt his mother and father far away now, disappearing into the distance. Their spirits were walking away with the others, and he was left, holding the sphere.

He was content again.

As the sphere left his hands, its energy pulled toward him, not willing to let go. It swirled inside the sphere, alive.

"Come," the stranger said. His hand gripped Fulgur's arm. The hand was bony, cold, and unkind. But he was his father now.

In the moonlight, the skin of Fulgur's arm looked spotty and wrinkled like a brown paper bag.

Maybe it was the way the light was hitting him?

It was midnight when he met his brother and sister.

Destan sulked in the corner of the room. Vines and flowers covered the room and blocked the light from a small window. A garden dungeon.

But Dawn was there. She was beautiful like a painting. Her hair was like the moon, silvery white. He could see himself in her pale blue eyes.

FULGUR shook his head. He and Lucerna were nearing Tosia.

He would have to be careful. If Dawn saw Lucerna, his plan would be ruined. She would force his hand, convince him that now was not the time.

Fulgur wondered if his father was still there.

Fulgur pulled the hood over Lucerna's head, covering her snowy crown.

This was the place where his father had told him the truth, his plan.

But why him?

Now that Destan had betrayed him, had Fulgur become his father's new favorite?

Not if he wanted to replace him too.

Had he forgotten Fulgur did not want to die?

Or maybe, Erebus thought Fulgur's life had become a burden, that boredom had sank in and now it was time. Maybe he thought Fulgur would help him fulfill his plot. Perhaps the threat of replacement was to force Fulgur into obedience. But hadn't he always been an obedient son?

No, he wanted a new order.

Fulgur felt abandoned. He felt this feeling before—after the storm struck, like he didn't have a family anymore.

He couldn't die for his father.

Suddenly, he felt like he was in the corn field again, alone in a storm, lightning striking the ground so fast, he didn't know where to turn.

Am I doing the right thing, or is this a test?

They made it to D'arkadia. Fulgur removed Lucerna's hood. Her hair was silvery white like the moon.

48

CHOSEN

As I entered the Dark Palace, I was Overwhelmed with Shadows, translucent Darkness that, Somehow, I felt Only I could See. I had Lost Many Over the Years—Parents, Brothers, Sisters, Friends. They were All here or, at Least, Their Shadows were.

SHASHI was tired of the nightmares.

She would wake up with thick vines wrapped around her, almost choking her.

There were figures in her dreams, dark figures and a little girl with black hair that turned red in the light. The girl would hold out her hand to her, and that hand would become the hand of a creature with rotting flesh. She feared the little girl and her welcoming words.

She wanted the dreams to stop.

Without Bolton mentoring her, it became harder to control her power.

Her mother cried sometimes.

Malachi had taken a special interest in her and her dreams. Prophecies he called them.

But they were just scary dreams.

Sometimes the little girl had a bloody mouth. Sometimes she was sitting next to a man with a bear's head.

Shashi stopped telling her mom about the dreams because they only made her cry worse.

"Hey, you wanna help us pick oranges from the Osage tree?"

Shashi stared at the children in front of her. Her mother told her not to eat the oranges of the Osage tree. The fruit was tough, and she could choke on it. "Um . . . we're not supposed to eat it."

"Who said anything about eating the fruit?" Tot said, a boy with messy hair who never listened to his mother. "We're going to soak them so we can eat the seeds."

"The seeds?"

"Yeah, the seeds won't make you choke," Yari said, proud she knew something someone else didn't.

Shashi didn't have many friends. But this group was offering her a chance. If she said no, she didn't know when a chance like this would present itself again.

"Okay," Shashi said.

Tot gripped the lowest branch of the tree and pulled himself up. The others followed his lead. High in the tree, they reached for oranges and threw them down.

Shashi climbed onto the first branch. When she reached the third branch, the ground blurred beneath her. Her head swam, and her hands were so clammy, she feared they would slip from the branch.

"Shashi, throw down some oranges," Tot shouted. "The seeds are small. We're going to need a lot of them."

Shashi clung to one branch. The next branch loomed above her head, but she decided against climbing. Oranges hung on the lower branches.

Shashi crept along the branch while clenching the one overhead.

She reached up and out to the orange hanging above her. She strained her fingers, and her fingertips grazed the fruit. It twirled on the tree like a dancer. Almost there. She reached for it again with more enthusiasm this time. She could get it. Just a little more.

Slip.

Her heart fell into the pit of her stomach. The bark fell from the tree as her feet rubbed against it. Her head jerked back. Under her body were thick vines, securing to the branch like a hammock.

Sighs of relief went around. The children cheered.

A smile glowed on Shashi's face. She had done it. She had passed the barrier into friendship.

There were gasps.

Was she falling again?

No, the vine was still secured to the branch above her.

What was that sound? Like a breathy whistle. *Where was it coming from?*

High in the tree, Tot was struggling to breathe. The vines securing Shashi were wrapped around his throat. The vines grew along each branch.

Yari rushed down from the tree. She was breathing heavy, her eyes large. She fell from a lower branch and hit the ground.

The people of Dustpath, alerted by Yari's cries, gathered around the tree. Tot's mother and father stood below, screaming for her to stop. Please. Stop.

She was afraid that by staring at Tot as he struggled to rid himself of the vines, she had made the people think she was doing it on purpose.

Shashi shook her head, saying "no" to the crowd. No, she wasn't doing this on purpose.

Her own mother was there. Below. Tears were in her eyes. She was the only one who knew.

Tot struggled for air and clawed at the vines around his throat. His nails missed a few times, scratching at his own skin until it bled.

His father, a dagger in his mouth, climbed the tree. His knuckles were white as he gripped each branch. Shashi had never seen someone climb a tree so fast. He reached his son and cut the vines from around his neck.

Tot gasped for air. He gulped it down like it was the last time he would get the chance.

Wasting no time, his father urged Tot to put his hands around his neck and hold on tight. With the vines still squirming along the branches, his father climbed down the tree with Tot on his back.

His mother was waiting below to meet them. When her husband reached the final branch, she helped Tot down from his father's back and hugged him. Tears were still in her eyes.

Afraid of Shashi, the people backed away as roots grew along the ground.

Shashi had never seen fear in people's eyes like that.

But she had *heard* fear before.

Her mother had hidden her eyes from the destruction in Tosia, but she could still hear the frantic stampeding feet and the screams. She had heard those same screams today.

"I'm sorry, mom."

Her mother was combing her hair. The comb was driving through her curls rougher than usual. But maybe that was her imagination.

"It wasn't your fault, baby."

The strokes became gentler.

"I couldn't stop. It wasn't on purpose."

"I know."

Shashi cried. "Do you?"

Her mother turned her around and pressed her fingers into her arms. "I do. You know I do."

Shashi nodded as the tears fell.

Tears formed in her mother's eyes, but she didn't say anything. She let her tears dry up. Once the tears dried, her mother turned her back around and continued to brush her hair.

Shashi didn't see the point. She wouldn't be able to face them now. She wanted to stay here in their home where no one else could see her.

Her mother smoothed out her hair. "There. Like gold."

Shashi turned her head. "I'm not going out there, mom."

Her mother paused for a moment, then stroked her hair. "You don't have too, sweetie."

"I'm never going out there again."

"Don't say that."

"How can I? They hate me."

"They don't hate you. They're afraid of what you can do."

"How can I make them not afraid of me anymore?"

"Show them it's safe."

"But I can't. I can't control it."

Her mother smiled, thin-lipped. Her eyes were full of worry. "You will someday. You just have to try."

HER mother wouldn't let her stay in the house from more than three days. She had braved the eyes of the people, and she thought it was time her daughter braved those eyes too.

Shashi didn't understand what was good about having the fearful stares of the people upon her. She was angry at her mother.

She tried to ignore the stares. People shuffled away from her like she was a wasp and they feared being stung.

She gripped her mother's hand.

She hoped she didn't see Tot or his mother or father. "Mom, let's go home."

"It'll be fine, sweetie."

They walked to the fields where people grew and gathered fruits and vegetables.

Her mother knelt in the blueberry patch and gathered the berries into the basket at her hip.

The people were giving them wide birth.

Shashi thought she saw Tot's mom. She focused on the berries. She pinched one between her fingers and pulled it from its home. She dropped it into her mother's basket.

She busied herself with the berries until the sun was low in the sky.

Her mother wiped the sweat from her brow.

Because the well was dried up, they couldn't wash the berries in water. They had to use juice to rinse them.

Her mother dumped some into the community basket and kept the rest for herself and Shashi.

The fruit juice rinse gave the blueberries a hint of orange favor. The citrus smell wafted through the air as the winds of

Dustpath swept through the trees.

"Mom, I don't want to go back."

Her mother knelt in front of Shashi. "Sweetheart, you have to show them it's okay. They'll come around. But first, they have to feel safe. If you hide away, they'll only become more afraid when you do come out."

"But what if I never come out?"

"And never breathe fresh air or have any friends?"

"I don't want any friends, Mom."

There was sadness in her mother's eyes.

"I guess it would be okay if I tried again tomorrow," Shashi said. "Maybe they won't stare at me as much then."

"WAIT, you'll fall," Shashi said.

The girl with the black hair with the reddish gleam was walking along the edge of the cliff.

"You'll fall."

"If I do, I'll fall forever." Her voice was clear and bright, what finches would sound like if they had voices.

"Do you want to fall . . . forever?" Shashi asked.

"There are a lot worse things than falling forever. Don't you think?"

Shashi nodded.

"Why do you think people are afraid of you?"

The ground was grassy. "Because I can't control my element."

The little girl continued to walk along the cliff. "Do you want to have control?"

Shashi nodded.

"Why?"

"So they won't be afraid of me anymore," Shashi said.

"Do you ever think maybe they're supposed to be afraid

of you?"

Shashi shook her head. She was confused.

"Are you afraid of bears?"

Shashi nodded.

"Why?"

"Because they could hurt me," Shashi said.

"How?"

"Because they're stronger than me."

"Aren't you stronger than them?"

"I guess so."

"Then maybe they're supposed to be afraid of you."

SHASHI jolted up from bed.

She clenched the woven blanket up to her chin. She looked at her hands.

Bolton taught her to feel her element like her own hands. She could control her hands. Her element was like an extension of herself.

He told her that whenever she got scared or mad or even happy, she needed to channel that energy.

She could feel it in her palms, right below the surface. She was scared.

Shashi closed her eyes. She focused on the energy, focused on pushing it back into the center of her being. The world stopped around her.

HER mother was picking grapes on the vines in the southern part of the village. The grapes were drying up, having not been attended to. Without water, it was difficult to keep the plants healthy. Most would die in a couple of days. The Elementals would have to grow new ones daily to keep the food supply up. It took a lot of energy. Of the hundreds of people, only thirty-four were Elementals and not all were very powerful. Some were children. If several crops died in one day, there wasn't enough energy to go around.

There weren't many people picking from the grape vines. The fruits were going bad. Shashi suspected her mother chose to gather here to save her some stares, but Shashi didn't care about that anymore.

Let them stare.

She kicked over some loose dirt near the grape vines.

Her mother was busying herself with the harvesting.

Shashi knelt and put her hands on the ground. She closed her eyes and remembered the fear from the night before. She used it.

She could feel the roots growing deep in the soil. Soon tender leaves touched her palms. She lifted her hands and opened her eyes.

Small berries were growing from the plant.

She let out a gasp of excitement, and the plant continued to grow. She turned her head.

Her mother was staring in the distance.

Shashi turned back and closed her eyes. She drew the energy back to her core.

The strawberry plant had stopped growing. The berries were big and ripe. Shashi picked one and took a bite. It was the best strawberry she had ever tasted.

SHASHI pulled the covers up to her chin.

Her mother entered the room and sat on her bed. "Sweetie, I need to talk to you."

Shashi nodded.

"I saw what you did back there. I was thinking maybe you shouldn't."

"But, mom, I'm learning to control it. I'm just doing what I was taught. It took me a long time to realize I can do it by myself . . . but now I think I'll be alright."

"I know, baby, and I'm proud of you, but maybe now's not the time for you to start using it. If the people see you doing it, they might be afraid."

"But maybe they're supposed to be afraid."

Her mother paused. ". . . but if they're all afraid, then when I'm gone, you won't have anyone."

"I won't let them see."

Her mother placed her hand over her daughter's. "You know where we come from. For years, we have repressed our elements. We thought it was bad to use them."

"Mom, you think it's bad."

Her mother smiled, her lips forming a thin line across her face. "That's not what I'm saying. It's just . . . sometimes people do things that are not necessarily good or bad. It would be better if you didn't use your element for a while. It would make people less afraid."

"But didn't you say if I hide, they'll be more afraid when I come out again?"

"You don't have to hide."

"But what if it builds up so bad, I won't be able to control it?"

"You can do this, sweetie. Just like we've done it for hundreds of years."

Shashi nodded. Her mom needed her to.

"You'll try."

"I promise," Shashi said.

Her mother kissed her forehead and pulled the blankets up to her chin. "Goodnight, sweetheart."

* * *

THREE days passed since she used her element.

Shashi could feel it just beneath her skin like an insect that had burrowed its way in there and was struggling to dig its way out.

Her strawberry plant was still alive. It stayed alive longer than any plant in Dustpath without water.

Her mother had taken her to the center of the village where the apple orchard was. The dried up well was not far away.

Near the well, Malachi talked to Dorsey, one of the most powerful Elementals in the village. Malachi pointed to the well, and Dorsey nodded.

All the strongest Elementals gathered, but they couldn't get the well working again. Malachi said the water was too deep down in the ground. It would take a lot of power to dig down that deep.

Her mother was picking the low hanging apples.

Shashi was too short to reach any of the apples on the tree so she picked them up from the ground. Some were rotten. She didn't put those in the basket.

Tot was eating an apple a few trees away. When he saw her, he turned away and skipped towards the corn fields.

Shashi sank her teeth into one of the apples. It was mealy. All the fruit tasted like that after the first day. But there were so many people in the orchard the day before, her mother didn't want her to suffer the stares.

Shashi didn't tell her mother she didn't care if people stared. Her mother's only hope was that Shashi continued to control her power, so other people wouldn't fear her.

Shashi wanted her mom to have that hope. It was important to her.

Shashi finished the apple and dropped the core to the

ground. She continued to pick up apples from the ground and place them into her basket.

She could still feel the energy under her skin.

She was angry that her mom thought it was best not to use her gift. After all, it wasn't something everyone had. It was something special.

Maybe people were supposed to fear her.

Roots grew along her palms and down her fingers. "No, no," she whispered. She balled her hands into fists, crushing the roots.

The energy was leaking over the edge.

Her mother was wrong. She had to let it out sometimes, or it would overwhelm her.

Shashi stared at all the people in the orchard and the people passing back and forth near the well. There were too many of them.

They would run in fear, and her mother would be sad. She would cry like she did last time.

Shashi had to do something. She had to let the energy out and at the same time make sure the people would not run in fear. She had to keep it under control.

How could she make the people see that her strength was a good thing? How could she make her mom see that?

Shashi closed her eyes and walked with her palms at her sides.

The ground was rocky and hard beneath the sand. Miles and miles of rocks, cracking and separating. The rocks pummeled against the hard sediment breaking it down, driving the earth out to the sides.

The ground moved beneath her feet.

People were running.

No, don't run.

Wait, the footsteps were getting louder. They were running *to* her.

Hands held her arms. Her mother's voice shouted.

One single rock fell.

Splash.

Water filled the well from underground and forced its way up and up.

Shashi opened her eyes.

Her mother was in front of her, still holding onto her arms, but she was looking away from her toward the well.

She was gasping from all the shouting.

People stood around, frozen. Others were there who weren't there before. They had come to see her.

Malachi was near the well. He picked up the wooden bucket from the ground. The bucket was attached to a rope connected to the well's overhang. Malachi dipped the bucket into the well, and hand over fist, lowered the bucket down by the rope.

The bucket hit the water with a splash.

Malachi pulled the bucket up heavy with water. He dipped his hand into it and drank. The water was fresh, cool, and clean.

Malachi approached Shashi and her mother.

Her mom scrambled to the side, her hand still wrapped around Shashi's left arm.

The people gathered around to see her.

Malachi knelt to Shashi's level. He smiled so wide, tears issued from his eyes. He laughed, picked Shashi up, and spun her in the air.

49

JACOPO

More Overwhelming than the Shadows was the Feeling that I did not Belong to Myself anymore. That I was the Creator's Tool.

JACOPO stared across the desert at the green village.

His army of thirty men had grown into the hundreds. Hundreds of hungry mouths without sanctuary in the desert.

Gerwald stood at his side.

"We can take from them, you know," Gerwald said.

"And have to take care of their women and children?" Jacopo asked.

"We could leave them in the desert to die."

Jacopo could see blood in Gerwald's eyes. He didn't like to see it there.

He shook his head.

"Hephaestus always left widows and children to fend for themselves," Gerwald said.

"Am I Hephaestus?" Jacopo said with a sneer.

He and Gerwald had grown up together, under Hephaestus's rule. Since they were boys, they had been good friends. They treated each other like brothers.

"Our men need food and water if we're going to march on Vella City," Gerwald said. "We need to be ready. There's only one way to do that."

He was right. They needed provisions for the road, more than they could steal from Lumina without alerting Morica guards.

"Hephaestus spent time torturing women and children and leaving them to die. He was a baser man."

Gerwald sighed. "We are at your command."

Jacopo looked upon the green expanse. "Gather the men. Tell them to raid the village. To take food and water."

Gerwald nodded and left to alert the men.

A cat rubbed up against Jacopo's legs.

He picked her up and stared into her orange eyes. "Oh, Fotia, you are getting skinny. The fruits of the Tosians will nourish you. Just as soon as I come banging at their doors with my fiery fists."

JACOPO'S army lived in the ruins of Dustpath. Some of the buildings no longer had roofs so the sun assaulted the skins of his warriors, turning them a reddish-brown. Sand would often stick to their sweaty bodies where the blankets had been kicked away in the night. The sand would leave rashes where it was rubbed between elbows and armpits.

That morning they woke from their sandy beds to march upon the green village in the distance. They were armed with weapons of steel and their elements. Many of the men had worked for years under Hephaestus. They fought and pillaged every day. They were hungry for war.

"Men," Jacopo shouted. "Today, we journey to the green village, not to wage war, but to take food for our journey to Vella City. Take all you can carry and only harm those who get in your way. Leave the women and children. Save your thirst for battle against the Councilors."

The men cheered and raised their weapons. Jacopo's fire red cloak swept the sands as they marched. Each footstep sank only to be refilled with sand as if they had never been there.

When Hephaestus ordered them to kill, he would instruct them to leave the survivors, but often the children were unable to survive on their own.

When they neared the village, Jacopo called for his men to halt. He gathered his most trusted soldiers, including Gerwald, the only one he trusted with his life.

"We cause a distraction first," Jacopo said. "Get them to run. Tosians aren't used to war. They won't fight. They will run."

"What should we do?" asked Turk, one of his commanders.

"You see that tree over there?"

They focused on the giant tree in the center.

"They're growing that tree like they did back in Tosia. We set it on fire and watch it burn," Jacopo said.

Gerwald and the other men nodded.

They focused on the tree until it erupted into flames. The ashes of the leaves swept through the air.

Gerwald yelled. Thinking that was their signal into battle, the other soldiers ran in with their weapons raised.

"No!" Jacopo had lost control of his army. Their thirst for

blood was too strong.

He looked around for Gerwald. He was running toward the village. Jacopo could see him distinctly from the mass of men. He looked . . . like a leader.

He and his commanders followed them into the village.

The people were screaming. Some weren't running. Some of the men were defending their home with wooden pikes they had pulled from the ground. The same pikes had served as fences for their gardens.

Others were carrying buckets from the well to put out the fire assaulting the great tree.

None of this did Jacopo expect. The Tosians were very different people than he remembered.

The scent of blood mingled with the smoke.

His people were using their weapons, killing the men.

A skirt brushed against his leg. A woman was running with her child clenched to her chest. Fire had spread among the crops. The green was turning to black. People screamed, and the smoke caused Jacopo's eyes to water.

This was not what he wanted.

He wandered with his arms at his side through the mass of bodies and blood.

His soldiers were easily doing away with the villagers, but the crops were burning uncontrollably. What they had come for was being destroyed.

The Earth Elementals were exhausted and went down like regular men. They were untrained, their elements untested in combat, only fit for growing crops.

The sky was turning amber.

Jacopo spotted Gerwald.

He was shouting commands, encouraging the soldiers to fight till their bodies were soaked in blood.

Maybe the blood will put out the flames?

An old man was on the ground. Blood poured out from a wound in his chest. A woman knelt beside him and screamed his name: "Malachi!"

Her arms were bloody to the elbows. Her eyes were shut so tight they squeezed the tears out.

Gerwald had his weapon raised, a blood-stained dagger.

A young boy had come upon him with a pike. The boy could barely lift it. There were splinters in his arms.

Gerwald sneered. He lashed out at the boy. His blades slashed into the boy's neck.

The young boy held his neck, trying to stop his life from coming out. The blood gushed over his fingers like water from a breached dam. He collapsed onto the ground.

"Enough!" Jacopo yelled "Enough!"

The air that had once been filled with a chorus of slashing steel, flashes of fire, and screams settled into an uncomfortable quiet.

The survivors ran away.

Only two remained. A little girl was crying over her mother who was slashed in the fray. The woman's eyes were affixed to the sky. They were glassy. An older woman was trying to pull the young girl away, but she wouldn't come. She clung to her dead mother for dear life.

Jacopo's men had frozen with their weapons.

"Leave!"

He saw Turk.

"You stay."

Jacopo looked at the crying child.

There was nothing here. The crops burned to the ground.

"Take her."

Turk approached the little girl. He wrenched her away

from her mother.

"No." The older woman slammed her fists against his arm. Despite her age, she was a beautiful woman.

The little girl cried.

JACOPO had ordered his men to guard Gerwald. He placed him in a ruined building far from the others. Jacopo was his friend, but when he looked at Gerwald, he saw Hephaestus in his eyes.

There was no room for two leaders.

What if the men turned to him?

Gerwald wasn't stupid. He was acting out against Jacopo because he knew the men wanted blood. If he would give it to them, they would follow him.

Jacopo couldn't have that. He needed his army more than he needed his friend.

The little girl sat in the corner. She refused to eat or speak. The woman glared at the men. They liked to stare at her. Maybe it was irresponsible to take them along. But their village was gone, and that was his fault.

He should have kept more careful control of his men. He should have kept more control over Gerwald.

The men were alerted by Gerwald's yell. They knew it was a signal.

Had Gerwald poisoned his men against him from the start? Had he told them to attack on his signal?

Jacopo had trusted him with the message, had trusted him to alert the men of the upcoming raid. Had he told them to fight instead?

And then Gerwald killed that boy and watched his blood soak into the ground.

Jacopo knew what he had to do with Gerwald.

THE men gathered around the stake. They had piled wood all around it from the burned trees of the village. Some of it was already charred to ash. But it didn't matter. The flames would start from the center.

Gerwald was tied against the stake. He didn't struggle in his binds.

Jacopo stared at him.

His friend.

One of his commanders.

They used to make dolls of straw when they were children and light them on fire with their elements.

Jacopo had to make a point. His other soldiers were watching.

"Gerwald, you disobeyed my command. For that, there can be only one penalty."

His whole army was tainted, but he couldn't kill his entire army for insolence. Gerwald would have to be an example.

Gerwald his friend. His threat.

Jacopo looked into his eyes.

Gerwald knew why he was doing this. He would have done it himself. He would have killed Jacopo once the men sided with him. He couldn't have anyone threatening his leadership either, even his friend.

But he was just fooling himself, making it a decision of survival rather than what it was: a decision of power and power alone.

Gerwald would do many things, but he would not kill his brother. He had lied for him, cheated for him, fought beside him. Gerwald was a snake in the grass but a snake without venom.

He was a threat to his power, but not his life.

Gerwald didn't have to say anything.

Though his eyes showed no regret, a part of Jacopo wanted to go back to setting fire to straw dolls, back to a time when having power and keeping it was simple because straw dolls don't talk, don't lead, don't go against their commanders.

And straw dolls catch fire so easily.

Jacopo focused.

Gerwald's heart filled with heat until the center of his chest burst into flames.

He screamed uncontrollably, the way a man screams when he is crying and screaming at the same time. His tears rolled down into his open mouth as the flames spread across his body.

He burned. Slower than a straw man and more violent.

Jacopo stayed by the fire until the embers died. His friend was no more than a black corpse. Jacopo wanted to cry, but he didn't know who was watching. He could blame it on the smoke.

HIS men prepared to leave for Vella City. They had packed their scant belongings with what food they could take from the village.

The little girl had not spoken. The older woman held her hand.

Jacopo wished the child was happy. It had been so long since he heard a child's laugh. It would be ironic in times like these, and the irony would make him smile despite his fears.

He feared the High Council and its army. Unlike his own, theirs was stronger. His army had disobeyed him once.

What was a man to do when he couldn't rely on his own army? He had killed the only man he trusted with his life.

50

THE PIT

When I began this Chronicle, when I was a Much Younger Man, I Always Imagined that Despite the Horrors of the Dark Palace, Upon Entering the Chosen Must have a sense of Completeness, like the World had come Around Full Circle. But that is Untrue, Upon Entering the Dark Palace, I Felt that I had Found the Catalyst for the End of the World.

THE ruins of Omega Ray lay around Lucerna like fallen soldiers.

"Why did you bring me here?"

"So, we wouldn't be interrupted." Fulgur revealed a glass orb from beneath his cloak. His long, bony fingers wrapped around it.

Madam Dawn had told her the story of the spheres.

Long ago, there was a man engulfed by darkness. He

walked the earth alone. His days were filled with monotony. He had learned to talk to himself. Sometimes the despair made him cry out. The guilt over an unknown crime was heavy on his shoulders.

"Why do you want that?" Lucerna asked.

Fulgur moved towards her.

In the stories, the dark man always saw a flash of light. It cracked across the sky. Hungry for something besides the darkness, he ran to the light. He tripped along the rocky ground until he came upon the plain where the light struck. He waited, but the light did not return.

As morning came, the sunlight glanced off something in the ground. The dark man scrambled to the earth and dug away at the hard sand. His dirty fingernails hit something more solid. He continued to dig. He pulled out a structure of solid glass.

Fulgur held up the glass sphere. "I needed it."

"But why? It's useless."

The glass was heavy as the Creator lifted it upon his shoulders. He brought it deep below the ground where the earth was hot, so hot it was molten. There, he melted the glass and used tools to shape it into seven distinct spheres.

He abandoned the remaining glass and brought the gleaming spheres into the light.

Fulgur towered over her. "You may think so, stupid girl," he said without passion. He shoved the sphere into her hands.

"I don't want it!" Lucerna dropped the sphere.

It went rolling across the ground.

Suddenly, a stinging slap landed across her face. Her neck whipped to the side, and warm blood issued from the corner of her lip.

"You are just a pawn, a maggot, crawling around thinking it's here for some greater purpose. This is your purpose."

With wide, quick strides, Fulgur retrieved the sphere from the ground. Just as quickly, he was back. He held the sphere up to Lucerna's face. "This was made for you. Or something like you. You're an instrument of our whims."

"Our?"

"My brothers and sister."

"I don't understand."

"Of course you don't."

Lucerna tried to back away, but Fulgur grabbed her arm with his long fingers. "Right now," he said, "you're not strong enough to do anything."

Lucerna shook her head.

"This," Fulgur held up the sphere. "This is your power. Focus your energy here, and you can stop him."

"Who?"

"My father."

Lucerna didn't know what to say. She could run, but how far would she get? If she held onto the sphere, what would happen then? It would be best to buy herself some time, to distract him. "Stop him from doing what?"

She could read in Fulgur's eyes that he was frustrated even if it didn't reach his tone. She realized he couldn't force her. He would have done that by now if he could.

"Do you know what he is?" Fulgur asked.

Lucerna shook her head.

"Pure dark energy. He's held that same form for so long, he's starting to decay from the outside in."

"He made you what you are?" Lucerna asked.

"Worse. He took what I was."

A chill ran down Lucerna's spine.

"What is he going to do?" she whispered, afraid of her own voice in the open air. She had the undeniable urge to turn around to check that nothing was behind her.

"He wants to take more. He's tired of his children. He wants to replace us."

"What will happen to you if he does that?"

Fulgur's eyes were distant. "I don't know. I guess I'll find out what dying feels like."

"But everyone dies."

Fulgur's face became stern. "Gods don't die."

"If that's true. How can he do this?"

Fulgur didn't want to explain himself to a maggot, but he was desperate. How much more could she get out of him?

"A never-ending source of energy." Fulgur was done explaining. "Take the sphere."

"I don't want to."

"Take it!"

"What would I become?"

"Lost." Fulgur's eyes darted away from her. "But you'll save us all."

Lucerna turned to see what he was looking at. Even with Lucerna's capable vision, it was black. She had never seen darkness so concentrated. It didn't move.

Lucerna turned back to Fulgur. The fear in his eyes was immeasurable. He was holding her arm so tightly, bruises were already forming. "You must take the sphere!"

"No!"

Fulgur pulled her away and dragged her across the stone floor down the steps to the dungeon. The torches weren't lit, but Lucerna could still see. Cells lined each wall.

Fulgur pulled her into one of the cells where the wall was crumbling. Deep grooves in the wall formed a circle.

He touched the wall.

The grooves glowed so brightly, Lucerna had to look away. "What is this?"

The wall began to separate, cutting the circle down the middle. Fulgur shoved the sphere in her hands and before she could think of dropping it, he shoved her inside the wall.

Lucerna stumbled onto the floor. Her head was leaning over the edge of the first stone step.

The wall was closing.

She scrambled to her feet and ran to it, but it was too late. It was shut tight. She beat the stone wall with her fists.

Lucerna looked at the stone steps. She wasn't sure how far they went down because darkness drowned them. Having nowhere else to go, Lucerna journeyed down the steps. The further down she journeyed, the more steps she could see, but still no end was in sight.

Her legs were becoming tired, and she hadn't eaten. She leaned against the wall and sat on the steps.

There was squeaking and scurrying below.

Rats maybe?

Those kinds of creatures could always find a way out of places like this. If she stayed here all night, she would only become weaker and then it would be harder to get out.

The steps led down to a tunnel. Stone lined the gritty walls. Water dripped down from the stones. *Will my thirst become so great, I'll have to lap up the water from these walls?*

The smell of rot drifted through the tunnels. Lucerna knew the smell well. When her village was burned to the ground by Hephaestus's men, they left the bodies. They decomposed in the sun. The smell wafted all the way to the ditch where her mother had hidden her. She didn't remember her mother, she didn't remember her village, but she remembered that smell.

As she turned the next corner, the tunnel opened to a small chamber. Lucerna discovered the source of the smell: a pile of dead rats. But not only dead rats.

Live ones were climbing the pile and eating what meat was left on the bones of their decaying brethren.

Rats don't die like that. They don't pile themselves into a ceremonial heap. They wouldn't have crawled there to die either.

Someone must have arranged them in that way. That means that someone was living here.

Across the room was another tunnel. Either that person was still there or he found a way out. She prayed she wouldn't find a dead body. But the tunnel ended unceremoniously, like someone's idea of a cruel joke.

Lucerna slumped onto the floor.

On the walls were etchings. There was a drawing of a bear and a man chasing it, killing it. There were hundreds of these etchings.

Lucerna followed them along the wall, leading back to the chamber.

She came across one that was different from the others. It was a creature with sharp teeth. *Another bear? No, not a bear, but what?*

51

SHORE

I do not Remember If the Keepers were at My back. But Something beckoned Me like a Heartbeat drumming in My ear.

BOLTON gripped the railing of the ship. It wouldn't be long now before they reached land. The cliff was misty in the distance, but it was close.

Bolton turned his head to check on his brother.

Balin's head was resting on his bent arm. His eyes were closed, and he was breathing gently.

Bolton had seen a lot of people get sick on ships, but not Balin.

Bolton always thought he could take the ocean better because he had lived on a ship in his early years, but maybe it was something in his blood, in Balin's blood too.

The kid looked like him, like his father. The same blond

hair, that look in his eyes like he was indefinitely amazed. He wasn't old enough to have much of a jawline, but Bolton imagined it would be like looking in a mirror when he grew up.

After the Captain had hoisted the boy over the railing, Bolton couldn't take his eyes off Balin. He couldn't sleep for fear the Captain might do something to him.

Whatever the Captain was trying to hide in the cabin must have been terrible. For once, Bolton didn't want to know. He just wanted the ship to dock, so he could be back on land.

He wanted to go back to the Rebel Resistance, to Sara.

The ship rocked against the shore.

"Land, ho!" the Captain yelled.

Balin rubbed his eyes.

When they had hit land, he grabbed his bag and rushed to the railing beside Bolton. "So, we can go now?" he asked.

Bolton nodded. "Let's get out of here."

Bolton didn't wait for the Captain to pull down the ramp. He grabbed a length of rope hanging from the railing of the ship and climbed down. He took one last look at Turner.

Balin climbed down behind him.

The Captain's head poked out over the railing. "Leaving so soon, without even a word of gratitude."

Bolton gave a quick wave to the Captain just as Balin's feet hit land. Then, they turned and walked away.

WHAT would happen to Turner? He was some sort of apprentice. Would he turn out like the Captain? Crazy as a loon?

Bolton wished he could help the boy, but he had Balin to worry about now.

They didn't need to be on that ship a minute longer.

They journeyed up the rocky slope to the cliff overlooking the sea. In the distance was Vella City, sitting higher above the sea.

"What do you know about dad?" Balin asked.

Bolton was taken aback by the question, though he had considered that Balin might ask it. How much could he tell him? Did he want him to hate his father like he did or, was it already too late for that?

"What do you want to know?" Bolton asked.

"I don't know. Stuff."

"Like what kind of stuff?"

"Well . . . what does he look like?"

"Like you."

Balin's eyes narrowed, puzzled.

"What's wrong?" Bolton asked.

"I don't know what I look like."

"No one's ever told you?"

"Well, yeah," Balin said, "and I've seen my reflection in the water and all, but I've never really saw myself, like other people do, you know."

Bolton remembered when he gave Sara that mirror. She had never seen herself. She was so enchanted that she looked like her mother.

Would Balin marvel that he looked so much like his father? Or would he hate it like Bolton did?

"Sorry," Bolton said. "I don't have a mirror on me."

"Do *you* look like him?"

Yeah, an exact copy. "I don't know. I guess so."

"Do you know where he is?"

He didn't want to lie to Balin about that. "Yeah."

"Is that where we're going, to see dad?"

"Is that what you want?"

Balin thought for a moment. "I don't know."

Balin didn't have the same hatred for his father that Bolton had. He had too many questions to hate him. Curiosity wouldn't let the boy hate him. Benn was the only one who could answer all his questions.

Bolton had decided long ago he didn't care about his father's excuses. He had no questions for him, only disdain.

"My mom doesn't like to talk about him," Balin said. "It makes me mad sometimes. The other kids have dads, but I didn't. I just wanted to know what he was like and why he left me. Now, I'll be able to ask *him* that. I never imagined I could do that."

What was Bolton supposed to say? *Kid, your dad was a coward who watched his wife burn to death and left his two sons.* He would hate him then, but what would that do for anybody. It would just hurt Balin to hate his dad.

"Right now, we should focus on getting back," Bolton said. "The more we linger in one place, the faster we'll run out of food. Besides, we're close to Vella City now."

"Is that good or bad?"

His brother had been isolated, like Sara was in Element. He had to explain everything to her, and she trusted him. Now, Balin trusted him.

"The Councilors in Vella City hate Elementals," Bolton said. "So, yeah it's bad. We have to get out of here before we're spotted."

"How far do we have to go before we meet up with dad?"

"Miles and miles. It'll take us weeks to get there with few breaks."

"And your wife is with him?"

"Yeah."

Balin followed close to Bolton, trying to match his pace.

He was only a half-step behind.

They weren't far from Vella City. Bolton was hoping to make it to the Crystal Forest before nightfall, but that didn't look like it was going to happen. The sun had set, and Balin's feet dragged. His eyelids were drooping despite his efforts to keep them open.

The ship ride had made them more lethargic than if they had traveled by foot.

Against his better judgment, Bolton put his hand out, stopping Balin. "Let's rest here."

"But I thought you said we shouldn't take too many breaks."

"You're dragging your feet, and you can't keep your eyes open."

"I'll be okay. I can keep up, I swear," Balin said. "Give me another chance." He wanted to get to Wyvek to see his dad. He didn't know how far it was. He just wanted to close that space between them.

"Soon it'll get so dark," Bolton said, "it'll be hard to see."

Balin slumped to the ground and sighed.

The buildings of Vella City reached into the sky on the distant cliff.

Not distant enough.

The night air was chilly as winds blew in from Demlama. Balin curled up, not used to the cold. Bolton had nothing to cover him with, so he listened to him shiver until he fell asleep.

SOMETHING sharp and familiar stung Bolton's nose. A flash lit behind his eyes. And another and another, like gunfire blasting off in quick spurts.

Bolton's eyes shot open.

Bolts were hitting the ground around him. Sensing the

Lightning, he rolled away in time, before a jolt hit the ground where he had been sleeping. It was like lightning had become rain.

He focused, quieting the bolts, lessening their number. But he was not able to stop the storm.

Balin, stood, his eyes closed, talking to no one.

He's sleeping.

Bolton scrambled to his feet. "Balin! Balin!" He shook the boy.

Balin's eyes popped open. "Bolton."

Lightning hit him. And all was black.

BOLTON'S eyes blinked open. His head hurt. He must have hit the ground hard.

The sky was clear again, but he could smell the heat of Lightning in the air.

Balin was gone.

"Balin?"

Bolton stood, holding his head in one hand. He had fallen on the rocky ground, and his body ached.

"Balin?"

No answer.

"Damn it!"

No footsteps patterned the rocky ground.

The kid was gone.

Bolton's head was screaming. He stumbled toward the forest.

If Balin was still on the cliff, Bolton would be able to see him by looking across the plain. He must have gone into the woods.

But why? Did someone take him?

Vella City loomed in the distance. How many people saw

that lightning storm?

Bolton walked faster until he was jogging. So many possibilities entered his mind. Most of them he didn't want to think about.

The ground became softer as the rocky cliff faded into the woodland. The shade of the trees made his shadow disappear.

Dare Bolton scream out Balin's name?

The lightning storm. Surely Morica Council would have seen it. Morica guards might be patrolling, but would they know him? He could say he was hunting with his brother. Without a bow or a knife?

What if they find Balin first?

"Balin!" His voice scared him.

The trees gave him less comfort then the cliff. On the cliff, he was exposed, but in the forest, his enemies could be hiding anywhere.

And he had more than just himself to protect.

"Balin!"

A blond head turned in the distance to face him. Bolton spotted him. Balin was crouched on the ground, motionless like a wounded animal. Bolton crouched beside him.

Why did you leave?

A twig broke.

Bolton grabbed Balin by the shoulder and drew him down with him closer to the ground. Their bodies were barely hidden by the sparse greenery.

The feet of Morica Resistance fighters trampled past them. Their dirty boots sprayed mud into their hair and faces. The fighters were headed for the cliff.

Once they were past them, Bolton and Balin got to their feet.

"Come on let's get out of here," Bolton whispered.

Bolton led Balin deeper into the forest toward D'arkadia. They wouldn't make it there before dark, but he wanted to get as much distance between them and Vella City as he could.

The crystals became a more prominent part of the forest the closer they got to D'arkadia. They had been designed long ago to keep the beast away from Vella City.

Bolton stopped when they were far from the city.

Bolton tried to tousle the dirt out of Balin's hair, but he only spread it around, making Balin's blond hair brown.

He laughed. A few weeks ago, he didn't know he had a brother. Now, the thought of losing him had put him in panic. Risking his own safety to find the brother he had just met days before. Seeing his light blond head among the trees was like seeing the shore after a shipwreck.

"You want to tell me what happened back there?" Bolton asked.

Balin shook his head.

"You were asleep. It wasn't your fault."

"I could have gotten us both killed," Balin said. "You're better off without me. The whole village was afraid of me. Why shouldn't you be?"

"I'm not," Bolton said.

"Why?"

"Because I'm responsible for you."

"That shouldn't make you any less afraid."

"Look," Bolton said. "I don't need you running off like that. I can teach you to control your element, but only if you let me."

"The Old Scholar couldn't help me, and he was like a hundred years old or something. He gave up on me, and he left."

"I'm not going anywhere." Bolton looked down at this kid, his face all dirty and his hair messed up. He had been abandoned twice. It wouldn't happen again.

"Why do you think you lost control?" Bolton asked.

"I don't know. Maybe it was that dream, I guess."

"What dream?"

"That one I keep having."

Bolton waited.

"It's stupid," Balin said. "Who talks about their dreams anyway?"

Bolton didn't say anything.

Finally, Balin looked down and said, "It's always the same, well kind of, I'm in a dark room with five other people. Their faces are shadowed, but I know they're like me."

"Elementals?"

"No, I mean, yes, but that's not the only reason they're like me."

"What else?"

"They're, um, different than other people. I close my eyes because I'm scared. I've never been so scared of people who are like me. And then there's this man standing right in front of them all, in front of me. He's looking right into my eyes. And he's saying, 'My children.'"

"How often do you have this dream?" Bolton asked.

"Almost every night. I don't remember when it started."

Bolton was puzzled. He recalled Shashi telling him about a dream she kept having. The dreams were so similar. "Did you use your element in the dream?"

Balin nodded. "He told me to. And I did. I was afraid of what would happen if I didn't. He said he chose me."

52

SECOND COMING

*In the Depths of the Shadows, Everyone had a Human Form. And As I
Looked, I Noticed the Dark Tears in Their Eyes.*

MORDECAI looked out his window over the gray
skies of Vella City. It had been weeks since Fulgur
had interrupted his thoughts.

He was like a ghost, haunting him. He had appeared that
night, the night Mordecai escaped from the cage, but it had
the ordinary effect on his memory. He couldn't remember the
day he escaped without remembering all the years he spent
locked away. This duality carried with him every time he was
in the presence of Fulgur.

Without the chill it sent up his spine seeing him, Mordecai
had time to focus on other things.

He was far from the oldest High Councilor. Surnom was

entitled to first refusal on all the decisions made by the Council. So, if Mordecai wanted something done, he often had to go behind the Council's back to get it.

And he was prepared to do that.

There was a knock at his door.

"Come in!"

Jason, the commander of the Resistance fighters, came in. He had a deep violet uniform, almost black. He had taken off the brown one of a true Resistance fighter and now donned this uniform. It marked him as a soldier of the Council. His narrow blue eyes seemed to glare. His lips were pressed together, like he was fighting back the words he wanted to say.

"You called for me, High Councilor?"

"I did, Commander. Please, sit down." Mordecai gestured to the chair in the corner of the room near his writing desk.

As the Commander sat in the chair, Mordecai took a seat on the bed.

"I wanted to talk to you about kingdoms," Mordecai said.

"I'm sorry, High Councilor I'm afraid I know little about that subject matter."

"It's to be expected. After all, this land hasn't seen a unified kingdom since Demlama fell.

"In the past, before Clara and Bennet's tiff on the cliff, before Elementals, Demlama was more than it is now. It was a great city among the snow with buildings that towered over the stars. Every city bowed to Demlama for that was where their king resided. His name was Rogard, and no one sneezed without his permission.

"When the snows fell, and Demlama tumbled into the abyss, the people forgot they had a king. They forgot their history."

Mordecai wet his lips, which had begun to crack in the cold air.

"What happened then?" Jason asked. There was no curiosity in his voice. His lips were parsed, but he wanted to say, "Get to the point, old man."

"It isn't about what happened next. It's about what happened before. Before he was king of Demlama he grew his army and cut down his enemies until the people recognized him as their overlord."

"High Councilor . . ."

Mordecai stood swiftly, like a viper striking. "You pledged your allegiance to the Council."

Jason eyed him like he would a venomous snake. "I did."

"How are kingdoms created?" Mordecai asked.

"Power," Jason said.

Mordecai took a step closer. "How is power created?"

"War."

"Then we must have war if we are to have power."

MORDECAI knew nothing of war, but he knew about killing. Mordecai was young in the days when the Resistance was called the Antistasi. He was fifteen years old and found in the blood of the Elementals he had slaughtered.

He had killed Elementals before. After his parents died, it was all he ever thought about doing. But, he had always attacked individual Elementals, never a family.

This time he targeted a husband and wife who had a small boy. He watched them for days from the road. The boy reminded him of himself as a child, not knowing the world was against him. He watched them live their ordinary lives.

This could be the antithesis of all his heartache.

He did it at nightfall when they were still asleep. First, the father. Then, the mother. The father didn't open his eyes when Mordecai slashed his throat. He lay there gasping and gurgling. The mother screamed, loud enough to wake the child. She bled from the belly as the blade sliced into her.

Mordecai had meant to keep the boy alive, to create another version of himself on their side. Not because he wanted revenge, but because it would give him solace to know there was someone with the same sadness in the world.

But he couldn't do it.

He watched the boy's tears drowning his fear.

He couldn't leave him with that emptiness.

SURNOM would not approve of Mordecai's plans, but collecting taxes for empty promises of protection was not going to earn him power.

He hated Surnom.

He didn't like the way the old man's leathery skin fell just below his chin and gathered there in a flap that moved as he walked. He disliked the effort of having to repeat everything twice to him.

When he was a Councilor, he always hated bowing to him. It took everything in his being not to slap him instead.

He had once alluded to the fact that he didn't think Mordecai was a hard-worker. He tried to stop his appointment as heir to High Councilor Geris.

The old man was talking out of his ass.

Mordecai had fought tooth and nail for everything he got. But the old man would say anything to keep him off the High Council. Mordecai despised him for it.

Many times, he imagined putting his blade through Surnom. He had imagined murdering the whole High Council, but that would not bring him power. The people would wonder how the Council expected to help them when they couldn't even help themselves.

No, he would bring the people something they had to bow down to: brute force.

He slipped sparklings into Jason's hands.

He would keep his secret and train his men for war.

Once the war was won, he could slit the throats of the other High Councilors. As for the Resistance, he paid them well for their loyalty.

The best city to attack first would be Lumina. The other cities were abandoned, and the scattered villages were of no consequence to Mordecai.

He needed to eliminate any traitors.

Mordecai downed his last glass of wine. There was so much to think about, he needed quiet time in the library.

JOVE slammed his book shut when Mordecai entered the room. He shuffled his papers together.

Mordecai turned the corner before Jove had finished. "What are you hiding?'

"Nothing," Jove said.

"Then why do you look so guilty?"

The silence was deadening.

Suddenly, Mordecai's face cracked into a smile and then cackling issued from his lips. "Ever serious." He sat beside Jove. "Let me see. *The Origins of Elementals*," Mordecai read. His finger traced the golden letters. "I didn't think we had that one."

"Just reading up," Jove said, "in case, they attack us."

"Well, I don't think we have to worry about that. What are those papers?"

"My notes."

"May I see them?" Mordecai asked.

Jove shook his head and got up from his seat. He shuffled away.

"I thought we were friends," Mordecai shouted after him. He laughed. He turned the book toward him and lifted the front cover. The first chapter was titled: *Creation*.

"The Creator fired the glass that created the spheres in the depths of a cavern filled with molten rock," Mordecai read.

Where did he find a cavern of molten rock?

Fairy tales.

Mordecai flipped through the pages. *Darkness*. "Dark energy is the glue that holds the world together. If it were to expand, it could create a continuous source of energy.

"Who wrote this garbage?" Mordecai slammed the book shut.

Mordecai stumbled to his room. He collapsed on the bed and soon fell into a drunken slumber.

HE was in a room surrounded by flames.

A long arm stretched over a stone throne. "I see you have come out of hiding, coward."

Mordecai's bare feet touched the stone floor. Despite the flames, the floor was so much colder than the chilly, marble floors of Vella City.

"You tried," Mordecai said, "You tried to have what Rogard had. Where you failed, I will succeed."

"Then your world will crumple just like Rogard's did," Hephaestus said, "just like mine did. Because with power comes the absence of power, and with the absence of power, comes the thirst for power. It is a constant interchange. It is never-ending."

Light erupted in the sky. At first, he saw it behind his eyelids.

Mordecai sat up in bed. He turned around and grabbed the window sill. Using it as leverage, he pulled himself up.

What in Mirmina?

Lightning was falling from the sky like rain. It stretched out as far as the lesser cliff. The bolts were stronger there.

Fear grew in his belly. He had never seen power like this before.

Mordecai jumped back as a bolt struck close to his window. He threw on his robes and flew down the hall.

As the lightning danced upon the ground, he ran to the Resistance barracks. He tore the door open. He grabbed the shirt of the first fighter he saw.

The boy's eyes grew wide. His mouth flapped open uselessly.

"Where is Jason?" Mordecai asked.

"In the archery room."

Mordecai let him go.

He didn't know where the archery room was, but he decided he didn't want to waste any more time waiting for that boy's lips to flap back and forth.

Sweat was on Mordecai's brow as he marched down the wide hallway, yelling "Commander! Commander!"

Jason emerged from one of the rooms, arrows still on his back and bow still in hand.

"Send men to the cliff," Mordecai ordered.

"Why?" Jason asked.

The barracks didn't have any windows. It was well insulated against the cold. How stupid was that? Their protectors were shut off from the outside so that when the threat came, they would be the last to know. But then again, Surnom didn't make the best decisions. How could a ninety-year old man with half his brain eaten away make the best decisions?

Mordecai grabbed Jason by the arm and pulled him toward the door.

Jason's reluctant feet followed.

Mordecai pushed the door open. "You see!"

Bolts hit the ground in rapid succession.

"If these bolts hit my men," Jason said, "they're dead."

"You have Elementals, use them." Mordecai couldn't believe the words came from his mouth. "Don't you see, this is the next Hephaestus."

53

WATER ELEMENTAL

I started to Wonder—How Many of These People, People I had
Known, had Died in Obscurity? There was Not One here Who I had
not Cried over and Envisioned Them in a Better Place. Was This the
Better Place to which They had All gone?

IT rained as Sara cried. Big, thick drops of rain that beat
down hard on Sara and Benn like hail.

Sara had made Benn help her to search for the communicator in Omega Ray. She searched all over the city. Sara
forced Benn to walk down with her into the dungeons. He
sparked Lightning for her to see by, but still she could not find
her discarded communicator.

Their clothes were heavy, and their boots were filled with
water and mud.

The rain was causing the land of Jetty Verte to melt. It

had become a muddy, slippery swampland.

"Stop this!" Benn shouted as the rain thundered down.

But she couldn't. All her emotions, untapped came flooding through. Sara wasn't strong enough to dam them up.

She clenched the Water Sphere in her hands. Weak energy swirled inside.

"Stop, I can help!"

Sara's hair clung to her face. The rain obscured her vision so she could only see the blurred image of Benn. She could have mistaken him for Bolton. Their voices sounded alike too.

"How?" Sara cried. The longer she stood in one place, the faster her feet sank in the mud. "All you do is remind me that Bolton's gone, and you're responsible."

"Why did you ask me to come if you won't accept my help?" Benn extended his hands.

Sara reluctantly took hold of them and closed her eyes. When he spoke, it was like Bolton speaking to her. The energy drew back and coiled up inside her.

Everything was going to be alright. He was coming back.

The cool wind, unobstructed, hit her face. There was still moisture in the air, but the heavy rain was gone.

Sara opened her eyes.

Her hands were gripping Benn's forearms. The Water Sphere was between them. Mud was growing up around it. She hadn't remembered putting it down. It must have slipped from her hands.

The horror of losing it took hold of her, and Sara grabbed it up from the ground. Mud fell from the glass sphere and plopped back to the earth.

Sara and Benn were ankle-deep in mud. They pulled their feet from the mud and slopped toward the forest where the ground was drier.

Sara's muscles were sore from hauling the heavy clothes that slumped on her body. She shivered as the breezes of Demlama drifted through the trees. The winds must have been heavy to have traveled so deep into the forest.

Benn took an apple from his bag and ate.

"I saw all the people I lost," Sara said. She was staring at the ground, but her eyes were distant.

Benn swallowed the bit of apple. "I did too. I saw my wife. I thought I would see Bolton there too."

"But why?" Sara asked.

"Because part of you was joining them," he said. "I heard her in my head sometimes—my wife, Ana. Like she was right there. It's the one thing I miss, hearing her voice."

"When did it stop?"

"When my soul left the sphere and returned to me," he said.

"You could only hear her? You couldn't *see* her?"

"I couldn't truly be with her," Benn said. "It felt like the part of me the sphere took was trapped. It was like I was looking from behind the glass, I was shouting, and she could hear me, but I couldn't be with her."

Sara gulped.

Rustling sounded in the trees. A small creature emerged with a gun in his hand. A *Lacwanx*.

He spoke in a language Sara didn't understand. Farah spoke it. She wished Farah was here now.

The *Lacwanx* was shouting, gun pointed at Sara and Benn.

They put their hands up.

"We don't understand you," Sara said. "Do you speak *Lacwanx*?" she asked Benn.

"What? No," he said. "We came out here to find a *Lacwanx*, and you can't communicate with it?"

The *Lacwanx* spoke a string of words, one of which Sara understood. *Meli*.

"Can you help us?" Sara asked. "We need a communicator." She held her hand to her ear, trying her best to show him what she was talking about. "We need one to signal a flying ship." She weaved her hand through the air.

"*Meli!*" the *Lacwanx* shouted.

"I don't have any meli," Sara said.

"*Vella City!*" the *Lacwanx* shouted. He waved his gun at them.

Sara and Benn backed up.

"That way," Sara pointed in the direction of Vella City.

The *Lacwanx* darted off in the direction Sara pointed. Once the *Lacwanx* was gone, Sara and Benn relaxed their arms.

"So, that went well," Benn said.

Meli? Maybe that was what Atrus was giving them. "He asked for meli," Sara said. "Why would he want meli?"

"He's probably addicted to the stuff," Benn said.

"Addicted?"

"Meli is highly addictive," he said.

Sara shivered. "I need to dry out my clothes before I catch my death." Sara left Benn and walked to another clearing. She removed her wet clothes and rang them out as best as she could, before hanging them on the lower branches of a nearby tree.

She sat huddled, naked among the trees.

She saw Rodan there among the dead. Did that mean that something happened to him? Goosebumps ran down her arms and legs.

Sara rose.

Voices rang through the forest accompanied by marching

footsteps.

Sara peered from behind the foliage.

Soldiers.

They were marching toward Vella City. Sara didn't rec-ognize any of them, but maybe they were part of Jin's army. The Rebel Resistance had friends on the outside.

Although he may have been delayed in Lumina, Jin would have made it out. Finding a boat traveling out of the city was difficult, but he must have made it to shore by now.

These soldiers may have meant to meet him, to attack at the same time. They had a little girl with them. Her face was hidden in the folds of a woman's skirt.

Sara stepped back into the clearing and grabbed her clothes. They were still wet and difficult to put back on.

She was out of breath by the time she reached Benn. She pointed, her wet sleeve hanging from her arm.

"What?" Benn asked.

". . . Soldiers . . . in the forest."

"What soldiers?"

"Jin's men."

"Here?"

Sara nodded. "We have to help."

Benn laughed nervously. "You're not serious?"

"We're here. I have my element back. I can help."

"You can't just go out there. You're not ready for that."

"You mean *you're* not ready," Sara said.

"I've never fought before. And . . . I . . . I can't let you go out there."

"I could change the tide," Sara said. "It might mean the difference between Jin living and dying. If Rodan is gone—"

"It wouldn't be your fault. And saving Jin is not bringing Rodan back."

It was the least she could do. She should have been there. Her best friend died without her. "Your fear is getting the best of you."

"You're not afraid?" he asked.

"I am afraid," she said, "but that's not stopping me. Are you coming?"

Benn shook his head.

54

ALL MY SINS

Then I saw Him. Never had I Looked Upon Him so Closely Before. And Now I Regret that I wanted to be so Close to My gods.

JOVE watched Veil out of the corner of his eye. He had observed him during the entire meal with that same look of fascination.

When he met him alone in the hallway, Veil stopped him. He had not meant to seem imposing, but Jove's eyes darted to and fro, like a caged rabbit looking for a way out.

"Why are you looking at me that way?"

"I'm sorry, High Councilor Veil. You just startled me." Jove's voice was firm, but his eyes still looked afraid.

"I mean, the way you keep looking at me from across the table."

Jove glanced away, perhaps looking for a councilor or a

guard who could draw him away from Veil.

"Please, High Councilor," Veil said, "I want to understand. Many more look at me the way you do, and I want to know how I can dispel their fears."

Jove gulped. "You don't know what you are, do you?"

Veil eyed him. "I'm an Elemental, is that what you mean?"

Jove shook him. "You are an Elemental, there's no question about that."

"What are you talking about then?"

Jove took Veil's arm and led him around the corner. There, it would be harder to hear them from the great hall where servants were clearing the table.

"You're a Dark Elemental," Jove said in a harsh whisper. "That's very rare. Even when the sphere was intact, there are no recorded accounts of Dark Elementals. We don't even know the extent of your powers."

"How do you know all this?" Veil asked.

"I have books."

"You study Elementals? In your books . . . is there any way to rid yourself of your element," Veil whispered.

"Apart from destroying the sphere, no. And even if you were to crack the sphere, which takes an immense amount of strength, conceivably your element would come back once the sphere is mended. There is no way to get rid of your element, not that I'm aware of."

Veil sighed.

"Will you come and talk to me about your element?" Jove asked. "I would love to make a record of it. It will be helpful for future generations to understand what it is."

"Perhaps," Veil said. "But in the meantime, High Councilor, you should go to your library and barricade yourself with your books."

VEIL reached for the handle when the door swung open.

"Veil?"

"High Councilor," Veil said.

Veil walked in despite Mordecai's disapproving look. Veil had sensed a massive amount of energy coming toward the city . . . Elementals.

He had to get Mordecai's confession. It was now or never.

"You haven't spoken to me since I came back to Vella City," Veil said.

"I don't know what you mean," Mordecai said. "I have said many words to you."

"Not to me. And not outside the presence of the other High Councilors."

Mordecai looked at him reprovingly. "I hadn't really noticed. I thought you needed time to yourself after everything that happened in Lumina."

Veil towered over Mordecai. Mordecai was a tall man, but Veil was a good foot higher.

"Do you fear me now?" Veil asked.

"Fear you? I pity you. You're one of them now." His words were flat and unmoving.

"Like you pitied me when my mother died?"

"Your mother died when you were just a boy. Bringing up her memory now does nothing to advance us."

"That's not how you felt when you brought up her death to convince me my father killed her."

Mordecai smirked. "What is this?"

"My father was a shell when my mother died. He surrounded himself with images of her. He couldn't have killed her. He went looking for her. He brought her to live with him."

Mordecai laughed. "He only looked for her to find you. Because he couldn't father another child. Because he needed an heir. He wanted her out of his life the moment she came here, that's why he left her in the first place."

"That's not what I saw!"

"What you saw?" Mordecai asked.

"I saw my mother's murderer. I couldn't remember. I blocked it out, but I remember now."

"You remember." Mordecai spoke the words like he was dispelling something vile from his body. "Your father was blinded by that woman. He would have never advanced to the High Council if she still lived. And you would not have been his successor."

Energy consumed Veil's body. It was full of rage, like the emotion could be quantified. That is how it built inside him, like a solid living thing.

Screams echoed through the city.

Mordecai pushed past Veil. "Get out of my way, boy!"

In that moment, Mordecai's existence was small to Veil, and he rushed to the window.

Smoke curled in the sky, and the walls of the city were compromised. Soldiers were pushing forward, leaping over the walls, their hands aflame.

Veil went out into the hallway.

Mordecai was gone.

He wandered down the hallway in search of the traitor who killed his mother.

When he came to the door where the Elemental was being held, Veil stopped. He looked at the marble barrier for a moment and then kicked the door. He kicked again and again until the heavy door gave way.

He couldn't help the prisoner further. He had to find Mordecai.

55

SIMPLE LIFE

The Creator is a Horror to behold. His Skin wished to Unclasp Itself from His Body. His Lips Wag Loose from His Teeth. His Skull Rejects His Eyes.

SHASHI clung to Rebecca's skirt. Hers was the only face she knew in a crowd of dirty soldiers. It frightened her how their white teeth shone against their dark, soot covered skin.

When she was around them, it always smelled like something was on fire.

She was especially afraid of the taller, brooding one with the cat. She only ever saw him laugh when he was drunk. The strange thing was Rebecca seemed to walk closer to him. As if she couldn't sense his dark past.

Shashi didn't want to see the light behind his eyes. He was

the man who led these people to attack her village and to kill her poor mother.

Why should he get to be good?

"Stop!" Jacopo commanded. "We move in when I say, understand?"

The soldiers grunted and nodded. They were like animals.

Tall buildings peaked through the trees: Vella City. She had never seen it before, but her mother had described it to her: a marble city on a cliff.

Shashi looked up at the dark men. They were going to attack this beautiful place.

Jacopo was whispering among his soldiers. They had pushed Rebecca and Shashi aside to get closer to their leader.

Shashi wanted to ask Rebecca, "What are they going to do?" but she feared her own voice, that it would alert them of her presence. She didn't want them to look at her.

As Jacopo's men drew away from the circle, they clapped their hands in ritualistic affirmation. It seemed brutish.

"Now!" Jacopo shouted.

His men rushed upon Vella City like a wave. Shashi and Rebecca were being pushed and jostled, unable to fight the impending flood.

They were running to the entrance of the city. Jacopo's men were climbing the city walls. Blood pooled from the bodies of the first few guards they slaughtered.

Shashi wanted to cry and run, but Rebecca wasn't moving.

Screams and sprays of blood misted in the sky.

Another army, dressed in tatters, made it over the south side of the wall. *The soldiers from Dustpath?*

She shook Rebecca's skirt, urging her to look. She looked,

but turned away quickly.

Fire lit up the sky and dark smoke rose against the blue. The moisture in the air was turning the black smoke into a dull gray. Then there was that distinct smell, like overcooked meat.

Shashi vomited so forcefully, she let go of Rebecca's skirt. On her hands and knees, she watched the puke pool onto the earth.

Shashi swayed as she rose to her feet.

Rebecca didn't comfort her like her mother. Her eyes were glued to the battle before them, beyond the gates where the cliff rose high across the sea.

The smoke had made the sky carrion-black with a lesion of bright moonlight scarring the benighted heavens. A rupture of stars shone through where the smoke faded to gray.

Sprays of poppy-red blood decorated the sky. Across the cliff, soldiers were on the marble floor painted in blood, gushing from angry wounds. Mangled councilors lay prostrate in their bloodied robes.

Mixed with the fury of fire, spent swords were mangling and gashing their enemies under the smoky sky. Distant coughing echoed through the night along with a tempest of fiery arrows and a storm of lances. Metal clashed against metal, and lightning erupted into the sky.

Metal armor rang in bright notes, contradicting the symphony of screams, screams that only came from a man when he was being burned. Making up the harmony was the snapping and shattering of bones as the sea of enemies crushed together like one wave crashing into another.

A sickly odor drifted from the battle field.

Shashi was cold to her marrow. The blood was rust on her tongue. She closed her eyes, struggling against the death.

Rebecca's hands were pressing into Shashi's arms. She was shaking her. "Shashi, stop!"

The ground trembled and roared. The marble buildings could not stand. And so, they fell to the earth.

56

KILLER

It is a Wonder that Such could be capable of Thought. It is a Walking Corpse, not Only capable of Human Thought but of Godly Thought.

MORDECAI looked out across the pagan-black sky. He had his dagger gripped in his hand.

The rising smoke blocked moonlight from peering into the cavernous marble structure. Blood, still hot, spread like magma across the battle worn, marble floors. It showered down from gaping wounds and sprayed across the faces of the warriors.

Mordecai's soldiers were dealing about as many blows as they were receiving, and they were matched by the two invading armies who wore the tattered uniforms of the Rebel Resistance and the blood-red draperies of Hephaestus's followers. They pounded and battered Mordecai's army, and they were returning blow for blow until the soldiers spread out. Now neither army stood united, and Mordecai could no longer tell who was winning.

The large marble room was open to the staircase. There were no doors.

Mordecai would not go gentle.

A storm of spears went rasping and hissing into the smoke-ridden skies. Men were screaming and slipping on the blood-swamped floors. Steel swords clashed against metal chest plates when they didn't sink into flesh. The skies were a web of lightning and the wind rushed against the windows.

Mordecai avoided the broken glass that littered the floors.

The invading armies were splitting and splintering his forces. Shouts and screams echoed down below. The councilors were slaughtered in their shiny robes.

Mordecai gripped his icy, steel dagger. His hands were cold. His life counted on death.

Stampeding feet thundered up the stairs.

Mordecai would not run. He would kill the Elemental scum that dared attack his city. His hands were brittle. They shook.

There were four of them. Their eyes were red with hatred and battle-hungry. They looked at his pretty robes with disdain.

The window behind him had broken, and the wind whipped at his face. The smoke cleared just long enough for the pale light of the moon to glance off their angry swords.

Mordecai rose his dagger above his head, but he couldn't stop his hands from shaking. Had he not been in the barracks, he would have been in his room, safe behind a barred door.

He wouldn't have to bang on the doors of the citadel, begging to be let in.

He saw fire. Rising between them. Floating in the air, godless.

The septic smell of death stung his nose.

He wasn't there.

He was watching himself in a room filled with his enemies. But he wasn't himself, not in his body. He was standing outside himself. His flesh could no longer trap him.

A mist filled the room.

There was a low, inhuman growl like a hellhound.

The men turned to the staircase.

Avoiding the lingering fire, Mordecai drove his blade into the side of one of the men. He got on top of him and stabbed him until sprays of blood decorated the front of Mordecai's robes. The saltiness of the blood tempted him.

The others raised their weapons against him. He waited for the ball of flames to come careening towards him to put him to his fiery death. But in a flash of fur and teeth, the cracking and crunching of bones filled the room.

Mordecai backed up to the window.

The bodies of the men were mangled and bloody. Blood gushed from their necks, and their bodies were crushed. Limbs were scattered on the floors. They were like broken dolls.

The eyes of the sordid beast stared into Mordecai's. There was pain there.

The room filled with darkness, so dark that Mordecai could no longer see the failing moonlight. It was utter blackness.

Mordecai was in a room. There were no longer bodies sprawled across the floor. It was an earthen room when the Council used to live below the ground.

She was decorating the walls with tiny flowers. She had

kept her secret for so long, from the others, from her husband, but Mordecai knew. He could sense it the day Cronus brought her here. She was one of them.

His dagger was behind his back as he approached her.

Without ceremony, he drove the dagger into her back again and again, wildly, madly, and without remorse.

Her screams were drowned by the gurgle of blood in her throat.

Mordecai turned, a mix of sweat and blood on his brow, to see a pair of young eyes peering at him from the doorway.

He knew he killed his mother. That he had raised the bloody knife because she was vile and because Cronus couldn't.

"Veil."

Mordecai had had little time to think about his failed protégée, but he sensed that mess of fur was him. He still had human eyes.

Mordecai cried.

The marble floor was anointed with entrails and baptized in blood.

The beast's fur was matted in it.

SUDDENLY, the battlefield was silent.

"Veil." Mordecai's voice sounded weak to him, weaker than he would have imagined.

He had lied to him. Veil's young mind had blocked his mother's death from his memory, and Mordecai had made him believe his father had done it.

MORDECAI wondered how long the beast had to think on how he killed his mother and why, how long he had to hate him for it.

Something black rose from the ground. Then, he felt the sharp, needle-like gashing of teeth and the drip of warm blood down his neck.

57

TEAR IT DOWN

And then He Spoke . . .

BY the time Sara arrived, the soldiers had exhausted the wall. The Council's forces were weak. Morica was foolish to command that their warriors lack elements. It was like fighting fire with a fork.

The moonlight ruptured out against the smoke.

Sara couldn't help but cough. Did Jin and his soldiers go over the south wall? They were too far away.

It must have been him.

Sara ran to where they had breached the wall. She wasn't sure where the other invading army had chosen to attack, but she could join Jin.

Stars dotted the skies like eyes peering through the smoke. In the shadows of the trees, a child and her mother stood near the forest. *No, it couldn't be. Who would bring a child to a fight?*

Sara made it to the far side of the wall. *I understand why Jin chose this section.* A long fissure ran down half the marble wall. The gap it created was just wide enough to get a foothold.

Sara was no stranger to climbing.

She used the gap in the fissure to hoist herself up to the top of the wall where her fingertips gripped the inner edge of it. Her arms were over the ledge to her elbows. Pulling herself up, Sara swung one leg over the edge then the other and dropped to the marble floor.

The clash and roar of the battle rang in the air.

Sara found her way through a maze of marble buildings to the center of the city where a blood bath pooled. She didn't see Jin, but she saw his people and there were others Sara didn't recognize.

They were carving through the enemy. It wasn't the buildings that were burning. It was the bodies.

Men were screaming and groaning.

Swords were clashing.

The three armies were like the sea during a storm.

Jin's army was skilled and, with their elements, they outmatched the Council's army. The other army fought like ravenous birds, disgracing the corpses that they left behind.

These two armies share the same cause, but not the same barracks.

A man raised his sword against Sara.

Before he could get within inches, the water was leeched from his body and pooled around his feet. His skin wrinkled, and his body shriveled up like flaky tree bark. He collapsed where he stood.

Never had she manipulated Water with so little effort. After a moment of surprise, staring at the crumpled man, Sara ran to the tower. She threw the door open.

There was no one inside.

Good. She didn't have a weapon of steel, and she needed to save her energy for what she was about to do next.

She made for the stairs.

Suddenly, the ground shook and the tower shuttered.

That was strange.

She continued up the marble stairs until she reached the top of the tower where she could see the smoke rising over the horizon.

The wind was terrible.

Lightning blighted the sky.

Soldiers were invading the building. Windows were breaking. The screams were different from up there. They faded like a distant howl.

Something black and dreadful tore through the door of one of the marble structures. Sara couldn't quite make out what it was.

The cold, north wind from Demlama chilled her to the bones.

The raging sea was before her. She called it to her. The waves obeyed her command and surged over the marble city. The waves gathered until they were one great wave, hovering over the buildings.

No sun cast the wave's dark shadow.

Silence hung in the air like death.

The soldiers stared up at the wave.

Sara was surprised at how well she could concentrate on the wave and the people below, of how effortlessly she could hold such a massive upsurge and have time to search for Jin's face in the crowd.

"Water Elemental," someone shouted.

And the wave came crashing down, careening into both

friend and foe.

Sara had no time to warn them. She could no longer control the giant typhoon.

It rushed against the buildings, smashing people into the marble on the far side of the city. It didn't touch the center of the city.

Jin was okay.

A tremor rocked the city.

Sara knelt as the building shook.

A fissure ran through the ground below.

Sara rushed to the stairs as another jolt shook the tower. Its force pushed her against a wall. She ran, tumbled, and skipped down the stairs as more quakes shook the earth.

When she made it outside, everyone was running, some were crouching as if they were too scared to move. The tower swayed as the ground shook. Sara ran from beneath its shadow. Parts of buildings were falling from the sky.

She ran to the far side of the city were there were fewer buildings. The falling fragments toppled the soldiers who were running towards the wall.

Sara was running toward the cliff. The waters rushed before her and the treacherous rocks sat below. Behind her, buildings were collapsing into the bay of blood.

She had never seen so much dust and smoke. It obscured her vision until she couldn't see anything in front of her.

The ground rocked.

Sara's heart was in her throat as her feet left the ground. She reached up and grabbed, hoping to get a hold of something. Her fingers bit into the edge, and her body buffeted against the stone of the cliff's face.

Sara hung there between life and death, praying that another tremor would not assault the ground.

And it did.

A huge chunk of the cliff's face tumbled into the sea not far from Sara. Her fingers pressed into the marble edge as her body dangled. Her heart hammered against her rib-cage.

The shaking had stopped.

She tried to pull herself up, but she couldn't get a proper foothold.

The air was still.

"Hey!" she screamed until her voice was hoarse.

The north wind cleared the smoke.

A weathered hand reached down and gripped her arm. Then another grabbed her elbow.

It was Benn.

He pulled her up and over the edge.

Sara's legs still dangled over the sea, but her upper body was sprawled upon the marble floor.

Benn was breathing heavily. He sat on the ground beside her. "I heard you screaming. Running in here like that . . . was stupid. What did you get out of it?"

Sara coughed, the ash and sea salt were still biting her nostrils. The sun was warming her back. Sara got to her feet. She blinked against the brightness and walked away from the cliff.

Benn followed her.

She could tell by his hands that he had used his element. They were sooty and smelled ashen.

Sara's wave had cleansed the south side of the city, but many bodies still littered the city's center. Blood spread across the marble floors and sunk into the cracks.

The pungent smell wafted in the air. Metal glanced off the sun. Sara could taste the blood, metal, and smoke.

A councilor's bloody robes hung from the window of a

crumbled building. A great fissure ran through the Council Palace. Across the sea of dead bodies emerged Jin and some of his soldiers.

Sara nodded to Jin.

His smile was ironic in the sea of death. "Welcome back, Water Elemental."

58

NO MORE

I expected His Voice to Croak Out from His Lungs as He Choked on the Plenitude of Dust and Ash. But His Voice was Smooth and Deep. It Fostered an Atmosphere of Trust Among the Lurking Shadows.

JACOPO'S face was bloody and soot-covered. It wasn't his blood. Rebecca waited among the trees. She hadn't run. He had the urge to smile, but it was tempered by the distaste in his mouth.

His army had fallen. He could not find one man. Each one had either died or deserted.

The sweat ran down his face, but it was not enough to wash away the ash and blood. From the look on Rebecca's face, he must have looked like a demon. But Rebecca didn't say a word.

She reached into her dress pocket and retrieved a handkerchief. She wiped off his face so he wouldn't have to blink through the soot. The cloth ran along his jawline and down his neck, and in that instant, he caught her eyes.

He kissed her.

It was impulsive, and he instantly regretted it. There was something beautiful about her waiting for him.

Rebecca backed away from his touch. "What are you doing?"

Jacopo was dizzy from battle. "You only live once." He groaned at his own response.

Rebecca helped him into the forest. He liked her arm wrapped around his. He had nothing left but her.

Rebecca led him to the water. Jacopo drank and washed his face.

Rebecca was walking away.

"Wait, wait. Where are you going?" he asked.

"Away. You've lost your army. It will be quite easy for me to walk away now."

Jacopo was confused.

She very easily could have walked away while they were in battle. It looked like the little girl did. Or maybe she had her hidden somewhere. Maybe she only stayed to make sure they were free, that he wouldn't go after them.

"I trust you'll let me leave freely," she said.

"No, wait. Don't·go. I don't have anyone."

Rebecca turned and continued on her way.

Jacopo rushed for her, his face dripping. He grabbed at her arm and caught hold. "I don't have anybody."

Rebecca turned to face him.

I look pathetic.

But she didn't speak. She didn't berate him. She was considering.

Jacopo shrank back to the stream.

Rebecca didn't move for some time.

At first, he thought she would try to leave again, but then she slowly walked towards the stream and sat beside him.

"Why did you stay?" he asked.

"You begged me to."

"No, before that," he said.

"I thought I saw someone I knew. But that doesn't matter now. He didn't come out. He's probably dead." Rebecca was staring into the water.

"What about the little girl?"

Rebecca shook her head. "I told her not to go. When the buildings started toppling, I was shaking her, telling her to stop. It was like she was in some sort of trance . . . And then, a man came. He was standing far off on the south end of the trees. All I could make out was the dark shape of the man. It looked like he was beckoning to her. She went to him. I told her to come back. She wouldn't. I ran to her and put my arms around her, but the ground shook. I let her go."

Jacopo sighed and took a gulp of water. He let the rest of the water fall from between his fingers. "I had a bit of nostalgia back there." Jacopo smirked. "That wave. I felt like I was back in Omega Ray."

"The Water Elemental is back. What will you do?" she asked.

Jacopo looked at Rebecca with blood-red eyes. "I'm going to kill her."

59

You're One of Us Now

"Child," He Spoke. "Welcome."

JIN stood in the sea of bodies. His white teeth glanced off the sun. He seemed unbothered by the putrid smell all around them. His soldiers looked worn and tired.

"Shall we travel together, back to headquarters?" Sara didn't want the silence to linger anymore. She was feeling awkward and strange among the dead.

Their bloody footsteps decorated the white marble floor as they walked to the forest. They met up with the rest of Jin's surviving army, no more than a few dozen fighters.

Some had deserted. Once the earth had shaken, those who could fled. But the remaining soldiers were loyal to Jin. Among them were Yerish, Dema, Fer, and Taryn.

As they walked, Jin knelt next to the bodies, even the bodies of his enemies, some of whom he had known when he joined the Resistance. He whispered over them.

How can I tell him what I saw when I touched the sphere? What did it mean? It scared her. She wished she could see Rodan and prove herself wrong.

They walked through the forest. Their feet dragged. Sara felt like her arms would fall off. The bones of her fingers cracked when she balled her hand into a fist.

"Are you alright?" Jin watched Sara flex her fingers.

Yerish had an angry cut on his left forearm running all the way down to his wrist. Taryn had patched it up with the sleeve of her shirt.

"I'll be fine," Sara said.

Benn shuffled behind her.

She could feel him watching her back. She was surprised he had braved the battle. He must have been there when the last tremor struck the earth. Did he cause the lightning that had flashed against the sky?

The light from the crystals was becoming dimmer. They were on the edge of the forest facing D'arkadia. The space was becoming less empty. Now that the light had penetrated the darkness, grasses and sprigs had begun to grow. The stream was running clearer, and more grass grew around it.

They went to the stream to wash their faces.

Dema had waded in the water waist deep. She stood there as the gentle current washed the ash and blood from her clothes. Fer removed his shirt and dipped it into the water, ringing it out. Benn stooped by the edge.

"So, what will you do?" Blood painted Jin's face.

"What do you mean?" Sara asked. "We won."

Jin shook his head. "Something's happening. Something

much bigger."

"I don't understand."

"On my travels," Jin said. "I've seen him, waiting in the shadows, watching us like puppets."

"Who?" Sara asked.

"I don't know. But whatever it is, we'll do better facing it together."

"What are you saying?" Sara searched his eyes.

"You're the Water Elemental. People will flock to you. If we hold the cards, no one can stand against us."

Sara didn't like the fear she heard in his voice. What did Jin see? "So, you think I should build an army."

Jin nodded. "We have more to worry about than councilors and guards. And even so, we have yet to take them down in Lumina."

"But all those people," Sara said.

"Don't worry about that right now. We'll think about that once we have men behind us."

Sara looked out into the cool stream. All she wanted was to go back home with Bolton. Had he gone back to Dustpath only to realize she was gone? Would he know where to find her?

Benn was still leaning over the water, staring at his reflection like he could draw Bolton out from it.

THEY rested near the stream. Sara let her eyes close, and soon she was far away. She was on the cliff. She saw the dark red, almost black hair of the little girl. She was playing with something.

Sara walked over to her. "What's that?"

The little girl held up the wooden pieces. One was in the shape of a beast on all fours and the other was a woman. "This is you, and this is Veil."

Something glistened in the sun.

She picked it up from the grass. "And what's this?"

"The knife you're going to kill him with."

Sara woke up in a cold sweat.

She was breathing heavily, but she couldn't recall what had frightened her.

Jin and the others were breathing steadily in a deep sleep.

The light of the moon was bright. Sara reached into her bag and retrieved her paper and charcoal. The charcoal traced the lines of his jaw. Light strokes did quick work of his hair and hard sketches created the contours of his face.

No sound interrupted her. Her breath came fast and quick at times, other times she forgot to breathe. When it was all finished, her hands were black with charcoal.

The fighters were ready to go in the morning. Yerish's bandages were clean and re-wrapped. Everyone prepared to go north to Tosia.

Sara wasn't sure where they were going, how it would work into her final plan or, for that matter, what that plan really was.

She knew what Jin was afraid of, at least, she had seen him too, the dark man. She had seen him in her dreams, and she couldn't tell him that.

They started the quiet walk to Tosia.

Stomachs were grumbling and feet were still dragging.

Benn hung his head.

"Thank you," Sara said, walking beside him.

"For what?" Benn asked.

"For saving me."

"You would have done the same for me."

Sara quickened her pace and stopped in front of him.

"That's right. I would have." She tried to make eye contact with him, but he kept his eyes pinned to the ground. "Because you're a good person."

Benn laughed.

"I mean it," Sara said. "I've seen more good in you than I've seen in most people."

Benn picked up his head.

"You need to show Bolton that," Sara said. She moved away from him and caught up with the others.

Tosia was still abandoned, but much of the darkness had retreated, leaving only rotting bark and empty houses. The great tree's dying leaves littered the ground. They were crushed under the feet of the visitors.

Sara couldn't believe that this was what had become of the Tosia she once knew. She had seen it on her way to D'arkadia, but seeing it before didn't make it any easier.

The door to the Domum Fidei, the House of Faith, was opened, just a small gap flooded in darkness.

With his good side, Yerish shouldered open a shop door. He and Taryn went inside and retrieved some glass jars of preserved fruit and stale bread. They handed them to the others. Yerish handed one to Sara. They went back for more.

Sara opened the jar and ate with her hands. Fer did the same. The juices ran down his fingers. Soon, they were all eating out of the jars and sitting in a circle in front of the Domum Fidei.

"We could sleep in the abandoned rooms," Fer said.

"Are you sure we shouldn't sleep out here, together," Yerish said.

They looked to Jin. "We'll be fine in the rooms. Besides when was the last time you slept in a bed?"

The circle of worn warriors laughed.

"At least two to a room," Jin said. "No one stays alone tonight."

* * *

SARA roomed with Taryn and Dema. She couldn't sleep. She stared out the window across the street to the Domum Fidei. She looked at her hands, at the glass ring on her finger.

Sara glanced back to the window. Out of the corner of her eye, something shadowy entered the Domum Fidei. The gap in the door had grown wider.

Taryn's dagger was on the bedside table. Sara grabbed it. She left the room and closed the door behind her.

Gripping the dagger, she ran across the street to the Domum Fidei. Sara peered through the dark gap. It was hard to see inside, but she could make out the dark shapes of the furniture.

She crept into the room.

The door to the back chamber was open. Going inside, she held the dagger above her head, ready to strike.

Her eyes were wild in the dark.

The bookcase was pushed away from the wall revealing the gaping hole that led to the tunnel where Sara had found the spheres.

Cries and deep sobs echoed from the tunnel.

"Hello?" Sara's voice bounced off the barren walls. She stepped into the tunnel. Her hands were becoming clammy, and it was harder to get a good grip on the handle of the dagger.

A light emitted from the depths.

Sara went to it.

Sprawled upon the floor was Veil with his back against the stone wall. Beside him was a lantern and leaning against the wall was the painting of his mother and her journal.

His black hair had grown out, and he had crudely cut what was left of his long, bleached white locks. Tears dampened the collar of his shirt. He was a mess of blood and dirt.

"Veil." Sara knelt beside him.

He looked up as if startled. "Sara." He reached up and touched her face. "You came back."

"Veil, . . . what are you doing down here?"

"I was reading my mother's journal." He placed his shaky hands upon the bound leather. His face was pale.

"Let's go outside and get some fresh air," Sara said.

Veil smiled. "I haven't breathed fresh air a day in my life."

Sara didn't know what to say. "Then let's go outside," she settled on.

"Do you think it will make a difference?"

"What do you mean?"

"Do you think it will bring back my mother or take away what I did to my father?"

"I'm sorry," Sara said.

"Do you think it will change what I am?" Darkness spread from his fingertips and blackened his hands.

"We can help you control it."

Veil shook his head. "No one can." His hand gripped Sara's, the one that held the dagger, and he brought it to his chest.

Sara looked down at the dagger and up at Veil.

He was broken. He could never be the man that he once was. That man was dead already.

Tears fell.

"I can't," Sara said.

Veil whispered as if others could hear, "You are the one good thing I've ever had." He took the hand the gripped the dagger and plunged it into his chest. Blood dripped from his mouth and mingled with the tears down his neck.

Sara cried, a screaming desperate cry.

Veil's hand dropped from hers, and she held the dagger.

She drew it from his body. She touched his cheek, and ran from the tunnel. She ran out of the building and into the street.

Water erupted around her. Sara closed her eyes and put her hands over her head. She screamed, "Stop it!" The Water crashed down to the floor.

Dawn was in front of her. She stopped for a pale, dark moment. Then she said, "You're one of us now."

60

Ungrateful

My Voice found Itself. "For What am I here?"
The Creator stood Taller than Me, Taller than Any Man I have Ever Met.
"I Need you to Chronicle My Past so I can Know My Future."

SARA sipped the strong tea. It had a bitter taste and dried her mouth out as she drank it. She sat on a plush cushion. The overhanging leaves of Dawn's home were dried and rotting. Every now and then one of them fell from the ceiling. Sara shielded her cup so that they could not fall inside.

"We never thought this would happen," Dawn said.

"That what would happen?' Sara asked. She blew on her tea to cool it.

"That our father would try to replace us."

"Replace you?"

"The Keepers of the Spheres."

"I don't understand what that means."

"You will," Dawn said. "In the beginning, there was our father. Then he decided to create his children. You see, he harnessed all the elements."

"That's impossible."

"Not for the Creator. But to possess all the elements is a great burden. It makes you weak. Your energy needs to be divided among the seven spheres. So, he made us. Each born of a separate tragedy."

"Why a tragedy?" Sara asked.

"Because . . . you have to be willing. Our tragedies were enough to convince us we needed him."

Sara had forgotten about her tea. "I can't be a Keeper of the Sphere. I've never even met the Creator."

"You're not a full Keeper yet. Destan was the Keeper before you. You and Destan share the sphere. Some of his soul escaped when it was broken. It shouldn't have happened that way, but Destan has always wanted something more. He thought we were abominations. He thought his father was the supreme abomination. When you held the sphere, you gave part of yourself to it."

"So, the Creator wants to replace Destan."

"No, not just him, all of us."

"But why not just get rid of Destan? Why would he need to get rid of you all?"

"Because it's not just Destan who was ungrateful." Dawn's sightless eyes fell on Sara. "It was he and I who made the Light Sphere. Lucerna was always meant to be its Keeper. That's why I raised her. But I wanted her to grow up, to live. I don't want her to give her soul to the sphere too soon."

Sara searched her mind. She had so many questions.

"Wait. You don't think you're an abomination?"

Dawn shook her head.

"Then why would you side with him against the Creator?" Sara asked.

"Because I found out something I wasn't supposed to."

"What was that?" Sara asked.

"My father was a murderer."

A chill ran through Sara's body. The coldness settled in her bones.

Dawn put down her cup and continued. "The tragedies, every one of them, he started. That's why they kept getting harsher and harsher. He was gaining strength with each element he gave away. He wanted us to want to be with him."

"That's terrible." The words slipped out of Sara's mouth. "What is the Dark Element?"

"Pure energy," Dawn said. "He creates what this world is built on. He is the catalyst for all our powers. When you call Water, where do you think that energy comes from? But there is only so much stored up."

"Stored up? Where?"

"In the Aethers."

Sara was silent.

"You can't stop him," Dawn said.

Sara looked up into Dawn's sightless eyes.

"I know that's what you were thinking," Dawn said. "Even if you build your army now, he could grow one ten times the size in minutes. Still, without Lucerna's spirit encased in the sphere, we all feel the burden of the element. All our souls, including my father's, are feeding it. But if Lucerna were to become a Keeper, her element is strong enough to kill my father."

"Kill him?"

"Essentially. Lucerna's ability . . . it could eradicate his energy. That's what it does. It destroys energy."

"But I thought energy could not be created or destroyed."

"Maybe before there were gods," Dawn said. "If she can't control it, an explosion of light would expel all darkness, the energy of the universe. It would destroy the glue that holds our world together."

61

In Between

His Words were a Mystery to Me. Why would Someone Immortal need to Remember the Past? Did the Memory Wane While the Body stayed Intact? Or Perhaps for The Creator, It was Different. Unlike His Keepers, His Body was Decaying Before My Eyes. Perhaps His Mind was Decaying Too.

FARAH pressed her ear to Rodan's chest.

Pentagon was passed out at the bar.

Atrus ambled over. "What's wrong with him?"

"Do you think I would know that?" Farah shouted. "Come on," she whispered, "Come on," urging Rodan's heart to beat.

Rodan let out a ragged breath and his eyes popped open. He jolted up in bed. "I saw Sara. I saw her."

Farah put her arms around him. "Don't scare me like

that." She released him.

"I saw Sara."

"What are you talking about? In a dream? You were here the whole time."

"It was like a dream," he said, "but not exactly. It was her that I saw. It was only for a second."

"He's gone." Atrus shook his head.

"Shut up!" Farah snapped at Atrus. "You have a fever," she said. "You're going to see things."

Rodan sighed. "I'm telling you. It was her. I don't understand it, but I know. She was somewhere cold . . . maybe Omega Ray."

"Look, I'm going down to the control room to talk to Thatch. I'll tell him what you saw, but I don't think he'll agree to fly all the way to Omega Ray on that. You have to rest." Farah pinned his shoulders back down to his pillow. "Promise?"

Rodan nodded.

Atrus settled down in the opposite bunk.

Farah waited for Rodan to close his eyes. Then she went down to the control room to talk to Thatch. She told Thatch what Rodan had seen.

"And he wants us to go to Omega Ray based on a dream?" Thatch asked.

"He says it was more than a dream," Farah said.

"We just came from that way. We must set the spheres. If we don't do that, who knows how much more agitated the Protectors will get."

The moon glowed outside.

"Where's Rai and the others?" Farah asked. "It's been a while."

The elevator doors slid open. Rai ambled in with Decca

and Shilo, their arms slumped on either side of her. They looked like drunk men. Vassal, Pentagon, and Atrus rushed to her aid as the men's bodies fell away from her.

"Where's Spire?" Rai asked.

"What happened?" Farah asked.

"I wanted to return her husband to her," Rai said. "He's lucky to be alive."

"Where's Lucerna?"

"Gone."

"What?" Farah asked. "Gone, where?"

"Rai, you're hurt," Vassal said, putting pressure on her shoulder to stop the bleeding. Rai cringed.

"Fulgur . . . took her."

"Who's Fulgur?" Thatch asked.

Farah shook her head.

"That man . . . I told you about in Lumina, Lightning Elemental or whatever he is."

"Why would he take her?"

Rai sighed. "We took the wrong sphere. I should have felt it wasn't the Lightning Sphere, I didn't. The sphere's gone too."

"Which sphere?" Thatch asked.

"I think it was the Light Sphere. I'm not sure."

"We've got to get this thing in the air," Farah said. "Maybe we can see them from above."

"No." Rai was defeated. "He trapped me in the temple. By now, they would have taken cover."

"We can still try," Farah said. "Thatch, come on."

Thatch pressed his lips together.

"She can't fly," Vassal said. "We need to get her bandaged up."

"I'll drive," Atrus said, "but first I have to get this big lug upstairs before he breaks me." His head motioned to Decca semi-unconscious body.

THEY brought Decca, Shilo, and Rai to the cabin room. Spire sat at Rodan's bedside, one hand with a rag on Rodan's face and the other arm, cradling Canace. "Decca!" She stood from where she sat as Atrus brought Decca into the room and laid him on one of the beds. Pentagon rested Shilo on another. Spire ran her hand through Decca's hair. "Decca, can you hear me?"

He turned his head to hers, but didn't answer.

"He got knocked out," Rai said. "Sorry." Vassal helped her to one of the beds. Rai sat as he rushed to get gauze to wrap her shoulder and water to wash the wound. When he returned, Rai said, "Do *you* have to do this?"

Vassal looked over his shoulder. The others were tending to Decca, Shilo, and Rodan. "I guess so," he said, turning back to her. He grabbed the hem of her shirt.

She scowled at him.

"Come on, Rai," he said. "Like it matters between us."

"It does now," she said, but she lifted her arms, wincing from the pain in her shoulder.

Vassal lifted her shirt, brought it up over her arms, and discarded it on the bed. He swashed the rag in the bucket of water, and washed the blood away. "I'm going to have to cauterize the wound to make sure infection doesn't spread. Don't hit me." He grabbed her shoulder and sent heat into it.

Rai gritted her teeth. A shadow of a smile wisped across Vassal's face. "You were waiting for that, weren't you?"

Vassal smirked and reached down to pick up the bandages. He wrapped Rai's shoulder.

For a moment, Rai forgot she hated him, that she didn't

trust him. She felt like she did two years ago, when they were on the road together, when they were something more than friends.

"I thought you would have gotten drunk," Rai said, "like those two clowns." She motioned to Atrus and Pentagon.

Atrus slapped Shilo's face. Pentagon was pulling Atrus away with a cup of water in his hands.

"I only drink when I'm happy," Vassal said.

"You must have been very happy two years ago."

"The happiest," he said. The wrapping was finished, and he stood and walked away.

ATRUS sat in the driver's seat and turned on the controls. "Up?" he asked.

Farah nodded.

Atrus and Pentagon had gone to the temple to set the Lightning Sphere. It served to sober them.

Atrus tilted the steering wheel.

Once the Chariot was in the air, Farah pressed her nose against the glass. "Go out further. Did Rai say what direction they went?"

"No," Atrus said, "she said she blacked out. She couldn't run after them because Lightning barred the door."

Farah leaned her back against the window. "I don't understand why he would take Lucerna or the sphere."

"Rai said he works for Morica. That's why he wanted the sphere." Atrus tilted the wheel forward, and the Chariot hovered down to the ground again.

"Can't we follow the sphere?" Farah asked.

"Its signal is too weak," Thatch said. "The energy inside has been fading since we left Omega Ray."

"So, then what?" Farah asked. "We just let him take her?"

Thatch stopped scratching his head. He laughed. "What are we supposed to do?" He looked up at her. "You can't always do something. Sometimes you're helpless and human. Everybody is."

Farah had never heard that edge in his voice. "Why are you acting like Shift?"

"Because . . . we've been traveling all over Mirmina, trying to help everybody else. It's not our job to set spheres." Thatch put his head down. "Uncle Tag's dead. He's dead because we got in Morica's face. And you know what? We can't do a damned thing about that."

Thatch stood.

"Thatch, I . . ."

He marched to the elevator, and the steel doors shut.

FARAH sat on the roof of the Chariot. Footsteps sounded behind her. She dried her eyes.

Thatch sat beside her. "I'm sorry for what I said back there. He was your dad."

"He was *your* dad too." Farah rested her hands on her bent knees. "I guess I'm always trying to fix things because it makes me feel . . . I don't know . . . like I matter. But losing Lucerna, that's something *we* did. I just thought . . . we have to find her because she's our friend."

Thatch nodded. "Yeah, I overreacted."

"I'm not saying that. We're all overworked. I miss home, and I'm sure you do too. And I miss dad." Tears welled up in her eyes.

Thatch put his arm around her shoulders. "You're a lot like him. There's no one else more stubborn with so much fire in her spirit."

Farah laughed.

Thatch cracked a smile. "We'll find Lucerna, and we'll find Sara. And once this is all over, we'll go back to Breeze and meet up with Shift. It'll be like after the Great Raid, a clean slate."

She nodded.

FARAH met Atrus at the bar.

Decca and Shilo had sat up to eat. Now, they were resting. They didn't remember what happened after they entered the temple.

Atrus was still a little out of it.

Where was Pentagon? He and Atrus were joined at the hip.

"Do you want to join me?" Atrus held up a bottle of spiced wine.

"I think you've had enough," Farah said. She bit into her apple.

Atrus sighed and put down the bottle. "I apologized to Thatch for what I did. And he forgives me, more or less. But you . . ."

Farah turned to him. "I see it this way. Once a cheat, always a cheat. If you have the capacity for that, you can always fill that space with something. I'm never going to trust you. So how can I be your friend?"

"How do I earn your trust back?"

"You can't." Farah turned back to her apple.

Atrus left the bar with a groan. He had to get the Chariot back into the air. They still had one more sphere to set.

Farah watched his back as he walked away. She settled down into a bunk, and rested her eyes. Blankets rustled in the dark.

Rodan shifted in his sleep.

Farah rose from bed and approached him. He turned over and cringed. She shook him. "Rodan!"

He opened his eyes.

"You were having a bad dream," she said.

"No, not a bad dream."

"Did you see her again?"

Rodan shook his head. He lifted himself up and settled back against the headboard. "I saw a tree . . . A big tree, and I could see inside it. Inside were organs, veins, and blood. And the branches were reaching out to the sky, spreading life, energy."

She tried to push him back upon the pillow.

"Farah, I think something's going to happen to me."

Farah stared into his eyes. "Why would you say something like that?"

"I think I saw my death."

62

EXTINGUISHED

I was starting to Believe My Blade would do Nothing if I Had Mind to Use It.

VASSAL peered outside the windows of the Chariot as it sailed toward Caleena. Flying made him sick. If Morica wasn't after him, he would have gotten off this flying contraption back in Wyvek and traveled on foot from there. But where would he go?

Elementa was under attack by a Sphere Protector, Morica guards crowded Lumina, and Tosia was abandoned. He knew nothing of the lesser villages nor where to find them. He couldn't just wander through the forest until he happened upon them. With his leg, he needed constant periods of rest.

He missed having someone to care for him, but he never thought of Marissa. Whenever he thought of Rai, he'd set something on fire. He couldn't control it. He hadn't used his element in many years.

Rai sat in the driver's seat. She had insisted she was fine and she was a better driver than Atrus. Vassal watched her with distended emotion.

He didn't talk much to anyone anymore, not even Pentagon or Atrus.

And he was having nightmares.

Back in Wyvek, he was a leader, here people walked around him like he was invisible. How was Jin handling things?

Vassal could have walked to Headquarters, but he chose not to. The shame of leaving them was too great for him. He was afraid his fighters would think he had turned his back on them, just like Rai did. Better they think him dead.

Spire cradled her baby in the corner of the room. Vassal didn't like the intelligent way the baby looked at him, like it knew something about him. It was so powerful it could crush this vessel. The force of its will could topple it into the sea.

Smoke rose in the distance. The forest was ablaze, and fires rose from Elementa. Rai landed the ship along the docks of Caleena. Her shoulder still hurt, but it was getting better. She had refused meli, saying they should save it for Rodan. She'd never needed it before.

It was a hard landing, and Vassal braced himself to avoid falling. He thought Rai might have landed that way because she knew he was watching.

"Are you coming?"

Vassal looked up.

"We're going to need you if that Protector shows its face," Atrus said.

"Yes," Vassal said. "I'll go."

Rai was looking at him. Did she expect him to confess that he was a Fire Elemental? They needed him more than they knew. He was surprised Rai hadn't told anyone about him.

Pentagon patted him on the back. "Let's go."

Rai and Farah led the group to the chapel. They walked through the deserted town. Curtains were torn from doors, and houses had been looted. Broken glass littered the docks, leading to the hill.

"I understand why Decca and Spire wouldn't want to see all this," Farah said. "This was their home."

"And now it's not," Rai said. "Don't let it depress you. We have to get in and out before the Protector comes back."

"I wonder if Element burned to the ground," Atrus said.

Farah rolled her eyes. Her pout was distinctive.

Vassal had seen the same look in Rai's eyes, many times. Her braid hit the middle of her back as she walked. Her hand was on the handle of the sword at her side.

The smell of burnt bark wafted through the air. The trees before the chapel were burned, and no leaves remained. The bark of the trees was blackened. Their trunks stood like naked scarecrows.

Beyond that, the temple was scorched and empty. There were black marks where the fiery hooves of the Protector stamped the marble staircase. The torches atop the columns surrounding the temple were extinguished.

Inside, marble sanctum was blackened. Broken statues littered the floor. A statue of the Creator was broken in half. His skin was smooth and unblemished. He was aged, but aged a great deal better than most old men.

Vassal picked it up and fit the pieces back together. His father asked him to kneel and pray with him once. It was in this very room next to that statue.

"When this is all over, we'll run away to the Dark Lands," he had promised.

Vassal closed his eyes.

"Are you okay?" It was Pentagon.

Vassal dropped the statue. The figurine broke into several small pieces. Ignoring Pentagon, he followed Rai and Farah into the tunnel that led down to the Sphere Room.

The large door at the end of the tunnel was ajar. Seven symbols glowed above the doorway. There was a great fissure in the floor and cracks branching away from it. They had to jump the tear to get to the other side of the room.

Vassal jumped, but with only one leg, he hadn't leapt far or high enough. His body buffeted against the side of the fissure as his fingers pressed into the marble floor. Pentagon and Atrus grabbed his arms at the elbows and pulled him up.

The fall didn't seem to faze Rai. She was digging in her bag for the sphere. "Here," she held it out to Vassal, "would you like to do the honors?"

What was she trying to do? Vassal was still a little breathless from the fall. He didn't know whether to accept or decline.

He took the sphere. It was warm. Fire swirled inside. Vassal wanted to let go. The energy inside him drew itself out from his fingertips.

The little girl with the dark reddish hair stooped in the corner of the room. She was picking something up. It was a bear's head. Its mouth was gaping open.

Suddenly, the room in front of him was empty, but he felt a presence behind him. Vassal turned around. The room was flooded with the soldiers from the sphere raid. Standing among them was his father.

Vassal thought he had forgotten his father's face, but seeing him now, he knew it was him. He hadn't aged since his death. He looked to be the same age as Vassal.

As the energy flowed out of him and into the sphere, a separate energy drifted away from it. Fire surrounded him.

Everything went dark.

"VASSAL! Vassal!"

Rai slapped him again. He picked himself up from the marble. Blood dripped from the corner of his mouth. Farah stood in front of him, holding the sphere.

Flames still blazed.

"You're an Elemental," Pentagon said, breathlessly.

Vassal searched the floor. "What happened?"

"You were going to burn us alive in here!" Atrus said. "We're lucky Rai knocked you out. When were you going to tell us you're an Elemental?"

Something shook the ground. The gap in the floor glowed with light.

"We have to go," Rai said. "Farah, give me the sphere."

Farah handed the sphere to Rai.

Rai wrenched open the door to the Sphere Room. White worms crawled from the pedestal. They filled the room. They crept from the glowing fissure.

Rai crushed the worms as she rushed to the pedestal. She smashed a few against the pedestal as she brought the sphere down on them, sealing their entrance.

They ran from the sphere room.

"But what about that gap in the ground? They're coming from there too," Farah said.

They kept running. The end of the tunnel glowed. Vassal stopped to rub his leg. The cloth around his stump had slipped, and it rubbed against the wood.

Pentagon stopped.

"Go!" Vassal shouted.

"You need help," Pentagon said.

"Get out of here!" Vassal screamed.

Rai turned around. She threw a fireball at the approaching worms. The ones in the front of the procession squealed in the fire. They turned black and curled up.

Putting Vassal's arm around her shoulders, she helped him along.

"Come on!" Farah yelled from the other end of the tunnel.

Atrus was close behind her. Pentagon looked back at Vassal and Rai. The white worms were inches from their heels. They ambled through the doorway.

Farah shut the heavy door, blocking the white worms. She leaned against the door as her breaths came in short, tight gasps.

Rai ducked from under Vassal's arm.

After Vassal took off his leg and repositioned the cloth to cover the stump, they walked back to the Chariot. What Morica flags that were left wafted in the breeze. The sea was dark under the night sky.

Rai walked closer to Vassal, but he could still feel her coldness.

"Thank you," he said, just loud enough for her to hear.

"We're even," Rai said.

"What?"

"You saved me from that dungeon. You led me out of there. Now we're even." Rai walked past him.

VASSAL crept into the darkness. It didn't chill him like it did before. Figures stood there. He wanted to know who they were.

Just as light was about to reveal their faces, everything went blindingly white. It was so bright, Vassal had to wait for his eyes to adjust.

He stood on a cliff over the sea, and the little girl sat there, staring out into it.

"Do you know what this came to be?" she asked.

Vassal shook his head. Though she had not turned around, she knew.

"Can't you see it?" she asked.

The Great Tree rose from the ground, and darkness crept along the cliff. Instead of the sea, before it was a misty nothingness.

The little girl was facing him. Her bottom lip was trembling. "This is where she fell." She was at the cliff leaning over it. "Look down."

Vassal walked to the cliff and peered over its edge. His feet left the edge. There was pressure against his back as if he had been pushed. The air was sailing around him, whistling in his ear.

He turned his head.

Beside him, falling just as fast was a woman. Her face was turned away from him. Her black hair whipped through the wind as she rushed past them.

She turned her face towards him.

Her eyes were . . . hollow.

63

IRRADIATIO

I withdrew My Paper and Inkwell. My Pen was Clenched in My hand. And I settled Down to Write.

THE hem of Jove's robe was bloody as he walked along the rocky ground of D'arkadia. He was on his way to Lumina away from the battle-ripped Vella City.

One arm was heavy with books, the few he could carry. The other arm held a rope. More books, wrapped in worn cloth, were bound by the rope and dragged behind him.

His lips were cracked and bleeding. The hand that held the rope was calloused. Blood soaked his silk slippers, not meant for travel. The soles were wearing thin.

The Great Tree was in the distance, rotting from its foundations.

The cold was coming in from Demlama.

Jove wrapped his cloak around his shoulders. In his other hand, he clenched a jar. Something glowed inside. He concealed the jar beneath his cloak and continued on his way.

His blood was more suited for underground. That was where he lived most of his life. He loved a girl down there, Oni. When he was a younger man, he would visit her every day to hear stories about the world above.

His wife found out about her. She told him she would find out who she was. Jove, fearing what his wife would do, dressed Oni in rags and gave her a broom so she appeared to be one of the many servants.

When his wife saw her, she pretended not to know her. But she knew Jove was trying to hide Oni. She asked that Oni serve their house.

Oni was miserable and unhappy, and Jove saw that. He revealed who she was. His wife cut Oni's face so she was not beautiful anymore. She let her go, and Jove promised to never speak to her again.

He wrapped the cloak more tightly. He still thought about Oni, especially after his wife had died. Where had she gone when they came from beneath the earth?

His foot caught an uneven break in the ground, and Jove fell to his knees. The moon was above him. A scar ran through it. He traced the scar with his finger, like Oni's face.

IN the morning, he awoke, curled into a ball on the rough ground. He got up. Though his arms were heavy, he picked up the massive books and continued on his way.

He walked onto Tosian soil. The vegetation that used to grow outside the city had died. Dried leaves littered the ground like corpses.

He passed through the entrance. The city appeared to be

abandoned. He walked through the streets. The sealed doors and dying flowers marked the city.

"Get down!" Rough hands wrenched his arms behind his back. His books fell to the floor.

People were coming out from the stores and houses, soldiers. The soldiers who had bound his arms behind his back forced him to his knees. "What are you doing here, Councilor?" someone demanded.

Jove closed his eyes.

"We should take him to Jin. See what he wants to do with him."

Jove was roughly brought to his feet.

They brought him to a room and forced him into a chair. Jove waited with his head hung until someone else entered the room. It was a middle-aged man with browned skin. His blue eyes shined against the leathery flesh. A young woman followed him. *The Water Elemental.*

Sara was the first to speak. "Why did you come here?"

Jove chose his words carefully, "I'm trying to get to Lumina. An army attacked Vella City, and I have nowhere else to go."

The man, whom Jove believed to be Jin, the leader of these men, eyed him.

"I have no motive other than survival. I couldn't stay there. The stench would have killed me," Jove said.

They think I am going to Lumina to warn the rest of the Council about what happened in Vella City. They don't want to lose the upper hand. "Please . . . I beg you," Jove said. "I just want to live."

Sara and Jin left the room. Jove turned as they walked out the door. He hung his head.

It felt like hours before Jin came back. Sara wasn't with him. Jove didn't know whether that was a bad sign.

"We can't let you go to Lumina," Jin said.

"What are you going to do to me?"

"I think you know that if you try anything, any one of my soldiers could kill you easily."

Jove gulped.

Jin nodded to the soldier behind Jove. His binds loosened and fell away as the dagger went through the rough cord.

"We're eating outside the Domum Fidei," Jin said. "You can join us."

THEY watched him.

Jin handed him a jar and hard piece of bread. Jove looked around for something to eat with. The soldiers were reaching their hands in and licking the juices from their fingers.

Jove tentatively opened the jar and dipped his hand inside. He tried to eat as daintily as possible.

The others still eyed him with suspicious glares. Jove tried to ignore them.

He didn't like being on the streets with the soldiers. He would hurry back to his room, passing them on the way. He kept his head down.

He ran into someone.

It was a tall, broad man surrounded by his soldier friends. He stared down at Jove. Jove waited for a blow to land.

But instead the man taunted him with a fake bow. "Pardon me, High Councilor."

The others glowered at him. Jove walked away, careful not to bow his head too low.

It was hard to sleep surrounded by the enemy.

And he couldn't bathe. The stream that ran along the Great Tree wasn't an option because that was where the soldiers bathed and went for water. If caught there, he didn't know what they would do.

He spent many hours in his room and stared at the wall with no books to read and no paper to write on. The only time he came out was to eat. He thought about running but Jin had soldiers all over Tosia day and night.

He heard that a group of them burned his pretty, but stained robes. He now wore the plain cloak of a Tosian. The material was coarse.

His capturers were Elementals. He saw them training in the streets. It was like watching a circus where the animals were in charge.

Everything he knew about Elementals, he had learned from books. He had never met an Elemental in the flesh, at least not that he knew of. Except for Veil. What had become of him?

His father spoke of Elementals in fairy tales when Jove was small. His mother didn't like it, how his father revered Elementals. They used to fight about it all the time. Jove could hear them from his room. And he didn't understand then why his mother was so frightened of them.

When he was a young man, a fire burned down the hall where the Irradiatio studied Elementals. He and his father were not involved, but that day, his mother gave his father a choice: stop studying Elementals or she would leave for good.

His father couldn't stop any more than a painter could stop painting. Jove's mother left that day, and she never came back, not even when they went underground.

The air below the earth was bad for his father, and he missed his mother. He died there already encased in the dirt.

His father left Jove with a fascination for Elementals, and his mother left him with a fear of them. He feared they might decide to burn him next.

He opened the jar, and the sugary scent met his nose. He was getting sick of eating preserved fruit. He missed steamed perch and the savories of Vella City.

He missed his library.

He looked up into the crowd. They had stopped watching him so closely. With the brown, frayed cloak, he didn't even look like a High Councilor anymore.

But one was watching him.

He caught Sara's eyes. She looked at him like he was a specimen under a microscope. She got up, walked over to him, and settled down beside him. "The uneasiness doesn't pass," she said.

"Yes, it does," he whispered. "You just haven't experienced it long enough to know."

"Most of my life, I've been uneasy."

"You haven't lived long enough." Jove put his head down. "I . . . I'm sorry."

"Is there anything I can do to make things better for you?" she asked.

"I want my books."

"Follow me."

Sara led him to a room. On the table, his books were piled up. Some still had the cloth wrapped around them. Jove ran to them and pulled one from the top. He opened it and touched the pages.

Sara walked around the table to face him. "Why are they so important to you?"

"They have a place in my father's legacy. I've been studying them all my life."

"What are they about?"

Jove picked up his head and looked at her. "You." He tore his eyes away from hers and looked down at the pages.

"These books are about Elementals. My father was part of a radical group, a sect of Morica called the Irradiatio."

Sara edged around the table. "I know who they are."

"Then you know that the Council never approved of the Irradiatio, but still members of the sect went on to study Elementals. My father and his father were part of that. And so am I. I've lived under the eyes of the enemy all my life. That's how I know it gets easier."

"But why do you study us?"

"Because you're fascinating."

Sara broke his gaze and ran her hand down the volumes of books, sitting like a paper tower on the edge of the table. "What do they say about us?"

"Too many interesting things to say in one conversation. You're welcome to read them."

"What do they say about the Creator?" Sara asked.

"Irradiatio have been around for centuries, we've gone by different names. We've been around for as long as Elementals have walked the earth.

"Long ago, the Irradiatio found a tooth deep in the caverns of Locust Point, which used to be a site of volcanic activity. The tooth was believed to have belonged to the Creator."

"Locust Point?" Sara asked. "I've never heard of it."

"That's because it has never been found again," Jove said. "Some say it was originally discovered in lands beyond Mirmina, the Dark Lands. The tooth was analyzed, and a set of data was extracted from it. That data was preserved in one of these books. Using the data, the Irradiatio discovered that all Elementals share a certain sequence of that data with the Creator."

"What does that mean?"

"A common trait," he said. "What's more, they found an

exact bloodline. Matching the data found in the Creator to a direct descendant."

Sara walked across the room and then back to the table. Her eyes were thoughtful. "So, if the Creator at one time possessed all the elements then his direct descendant . . ."

". . . could be any one of you."

64

EXPANSION

"For Thousands of Years My Body has been My Curse, has been My Tomb."

CANACE stared into her mother's eyes with such a look of understanding it sent a chill through Spire. She cradled the baby in her arms. The others had returned from the chapel.

"Did you place the sphere?" Spire asked.

"It's done," Rai said.

Decca put his arm around Spire's shoulders. "Where will we go?"

"I say we fly on to Dustpath," Rai said, "maybe meet up with the Rebel Resistance. Keep a look out for Sara and Lucerna."

Farah pressed her lips together.

"Okay then," Thatch agreed.

Rai took her seat at the steering wheel. Soon the Chariot was in the air and flying towards Dustpath.

"How are you doing on those books, Stan?" Farah walked over to the buzzing robot.

"Analyzed and archived," Stannum droned.

"Anything we should know?"

"Just a bunch of prattle mostly," Stannum buzzed.

"What do you mean by that?" Thatch asked.

"The first volume is informative, describing the Keepers as the souls of the spheres. Their spiritual energy fuels your elements. Apparently, they live longer than any of you. Perhaps . . . not longer than me but . . ."

"And the rest of volume one?" Spire asked.

"It's all an account of when the Creator and Keepers lived in Dustpath. The Builders treated them like kings. They lived in the fanciest palaces and were revered and feared by the people."

"The remaining volumes?" Spire asked.

"That's where the rubbish comes in," Stannum buzzed. "The author rambles on and on about a plan . . . it's very repetitive actually."

"Whose plan?" Pentagon asked.

"The Creator's." Stannum blinked his big orange eye. "He wanted to use darkness to expand the space around us. According to the volumes, seemingly limitless energy flows all around us. Seemingly. The Creator desired more power. He thought it was the way to cure his disease.

"No one in the village knew what it would do if the Creator gathered enough power to stretch outside this world, but the author feared it would result in one of three possibilities:

"One, the Creator's plan would work, and energy would

expand beyond the reaches of Mirmina.

"Two, the energy would block the sun. Everything would eventually become cold, too cold to sustain life.

"Or three, the energy would continue to expand until it had nowhere left to go. At which point, it would collapse back on itself, turning back time. Until we don't exist anymore."

The room grew quiet.

"But that's rubbish, right?" Atrus said.

"It would not have worked." Stannum continued. "In regard to curing his disease anyway. His disease was biological. He was bitten by a Maledixit."

"So, the Creator's element is the energy?" Thatch said.

"Yes." Stannum's eye blinked. "What you perceive as darkness is really pure energy. It is the only way your mind can interpret it, but being a Dark Elemental I am sure the Creator can see it much differently."

"There's no sign of anyone." Rai looked down onto Rebel Resistance Headquarters. "It looks like they might have moved out."

Vassal ambled over to the window. The tents were collapsed, and the grounds were empty.

Spire rocked Canace. "There's no point in staying here."

Wind battered against the Chariot, almost knocking everyone to the floor. Rai looked back at Canace as the Chariot was buffeted by the Wind again.

Spire cradled her baby. She wasn't crying. "Stop Canace. It's okay, it's okay."

The Wind picked up.

Pain shot up and down Rai's arm as she fought with the steering wheel. Spire and Farah closed their eyes, trying to settle the Wind, but it was out of their control. The Chariot was jolted to the east, and everyone in the control room was tossed.

Thatch gripped the arms of his seat, but Rai was tossed to the floor. Spire was kneeling on the floor with Decca's arms around her and the baby. Shilo tried to help, but his body was pummeled against the wall.

Vassal held onto the back of Rai's chair. Pentagon and Atrus braced themselves against the wall, where Stannum had landed like a used can. His light had gone out.

Farah scrambled to her feet. "Rodan!"

"Farah, don't go up there!" Rai yelled. As the Wind rocked the Chariot, Rai tried to reclaim her seat at the steering wheel. Finally, she made it. She was trying to land. "Come on. Come on."

The Chariot pummeled to the ground. It flipped twice before settling into the dust.

CANACE was crying. Spire cradled her head in her hands. Decca lay by her side. Spire shook his arm. "Decca. Decca." Her voice was weak.

The others were rousing. Rai was slumped to the side still in her seat. Thatch was on the floor near Stannum. Pentagon's arm was twisted behind his back. Vassal was lying face down, trying to lift himself up with his good arm. Atrus was on his back with his hands on his head.

Decca opened his eyes. He stood. "Are you okay?"

Spire nodded.

Decca rubbed the baby's head.

"It was her," Spire said.

Thatch was at the elevator. He tried pressing the button, but the door wouldn't open. "Farah! Farah, can you hear me?"

"My head is splitting," Atrus groaned. "Pent?"

Pentagon hadn't got up. His arm was mangled behind him.

"Farah?" Rai ran at the doors with her sword. She managed to get the blade through the slit in the two metal doors. She pried them open.

The elevator had started to go up before they crashed. They could see Farah lying on the ground through the gap above them.

"Boost me up," Rai said.

Thatch squatted, cupping his hands. Rai put her foot in his hands, and he boosted her up to the platform. From there, Rai used her arms to pull herself up. "Here she is."

Rai brought Farah's body down to Thatch. She emerged from the elevator, pushing away from the shaft which led down to the engine room.

Thatch patted Farah's face. "Farah."

She opened her eyes. "What in Mirmina? What happened?" She looked up at the others.

"We crashed," Thatch said.

"How are we going to get out of here?" Vassal asked.

"There's a ladder on the side of the elevator shaft. It leads down to the engine room where I should be able to open the door manually."

"What about Rodan?" Farah asked. "He's still up there."

"The elevator is blocking the ladder. But if we can get back into the elevator, on the ceiling is a latch, the hatch opens to the elevator shaft where we can access the ladder and climb up to him."

Rai and Farah climbed back into the elevator, Thatch waited for them in the control room while they climbed down. Decca pulled the lever as Thatch instructed and used the pulley to manually open the doors. The hatch door shuttered open. A loud squeal issued forth right before it hit the ground, breaking from its hinges.

SPIRE rocked Canace. She knew everyone on board was blaming her. She didn't know how to teach a baby to control her element. She was learning everything as she went along. Her mother died long before she could teach her to be a mother. Having that, plus a child so powerful in her element was too much for Spire.

She should be a happy mother, instead she would cry sometimes when she was alone. She didn't want Decca to see.

Atrus was finished bandaging up Pentagon's arm. It hung in a make-shift sling. "There. Now your arm should heal back straight."

"Should?"

"Well, I'm not a doctor." Atrus slumped down next to him. "My head feels like someone took a sledgehammer and smashed it repeatedly."

Vassal was looking up at the Chariot.

"It's alright," Decca whispered to Spire. "No one's blaming you." His hand was on her shoulder. Spire placed her hand over his.

Rai and Farah emerged from the Chariot. Thatch and Shilo were close behind them, helping Rodan along. Spire handed Canace to Decca. She approached Rodan. "Is he alright?"

"Just a cut on the head. He'll be fine," Rai said.

THEY sat around the fire. The desert got cold at night. The Wind had settled to a gentle breeze. From the energy, Spire could feel Canace was causing it. When she wrapped the baby tighter in its blanket, the breeze became stronger.

Rai and Thatch had retrieved food from the Chariot.

"I guess it's on foot from here," Rai said.

"And you were getting good at flying," Atrus said.

Rai pushed his arm, but Atrus only laughed.

"It will be like old times." Pentagon smirked.

Vassal stared into the fire.

Rodan was sitting up for the first time in days, but he barely spoke. He was pale and still looked like he was on the edge between life and death. Farah was looking at him like he might break.

"You can't fix the Chariot, Thatch?" Farah asked in a voice that said she knew the answer, but was hoping she was wrong.

Thatch shook his head. He cradled Stannum's broken body in his hands. "I'll be lucky if I can scrape up enough materials to fix Stan here. The Chariot, that would take months."

"I'm sorry about your ship," Spire said.

"It's okay. The Morica chariots are better anyway." He looked at Atrus.

Decca rocked Canace. Spire looked down at her hands. "You can't help her to control it?" Rai asked. "It's dangerous."

"It's not a problem of control." Rodan held his side. "She can control it. She meant to do this."

65

SHADOW ARMY

"Often Times, I shuttered at What I Must do."

DAWN watched the shadows of the fighters gather in the center of the city. Her sight was limited to shadows.

Someone touched her shoulder.

Dawn turned around.

She smelled the heat.

"How did you get in here?" she asked.

"They're easy to trick," Fulgur said. "Have you seen Destan?"

"Not in a good long time."

"You're lying to me. Destan told you about our replacements."

"He did," Dawn said.

"What are they doing there?"

"Trying to fight shadows."

"Fools," Fulgur said.

"What are *you* doing here?"

"Rebelling against my father, like you did once. I just need to find my replacement so I can kill him."

Dawn turned to Fulgur.

"Don't look at me like that," he said. "Like you have any compassion for ants."

"What have you done, Fulgur?"

"If Destan had any sense, he would kill her." Fulgur pointed to Sara. "That's the new Water Keeper, isn't it?"

"She thinks she can make a difference," Dawn said. "You know, if you kill your replacement, Father will find another. The best thing we can do now is try to get back into his good graces."

"What do you think happens to us once we are replaced?" Fulgur asked.

Dawn shook her head. "I don't want to find out."

"Where are the others?"

"Vjetar and Glaciem are with me.

"Vuur felt something last night," Dawn said. "He went off into the woods. He hasn't returned."

"When will you see Destan again?"

Dawn grabbed Fulgur's arm and led him away toward the Cliff. "Look," she whispered. "We're going to find Father, all of us. Destan refuses. But the best way to make amends is to do it together. What Destan and I did might only make things worse. Are you with us?"

Fulgur stared into her eyes. "I'm with you."

Dawn led Fulgur back to her home where Vjetar and Glaciem were waiting. Fulgur looked at them. "Brothers."

"You came back," Glaciem said.

"I grew tired of humans."

"It can grow tiring watching them make mistakes," Vjetar said.

Their faces never changed expression.

"Fulgur is joining us," Dawn said. "If only we could convince Destan to do the same."

"You're too easy on him, Dawn," Glaciem chided. "He should know his place."

"Well, even I have gone astray." Dawn looked at Fulgur. "But we're together now."

"What about Vuur?"

"He knows we went to find Father," she said. "He'll follow."

They walked through the center of the city. Sara and her company stopped to look at them.

"Who in Mirmina?" Yerish breathed, watching their ancient forms.

"Dawn," Sara shouted. "Where are you going?"

"To join our father. I hope you understand."

"I don't."

Dawn continued along with the others.

"I don't," Sara shouted.

"Remember what I told you," Dawn said. "Don't try to fight him."

Branches grew from the ground, enclosing Sara and the others in a wooden cage. Dawn needed to slow her down. She couldn't stop their father, only his true Children could dissuade him from their destiny with the use of force.

Dawn had to find Lucerna. She wasn't confident Sara would do what needed to be done. It required great sacrifice. Sacrifice Dawn was now ready to give.

Sara would be fine. She had the power of a Keeper of the Sphere. She would find a way out of her cage. Dawn had to find her father before that happened. Dawn arose from Tosia with Fulgur, Glaciem, and Vjetar by her side.

Vuur emerged from the forest. They nodded to each other, and Vuur joined them. He snapped his fingers, and flames erupted at the entrance to the city.

The Keepers walked away without looking back.

THEY didn't need food, water, or rest. The Keepers could walk night and day and never tire.

Dawn could sense her father's presence deep in the cold valley. She knew he had gone to Omega Ray. Together they climbed the mountain. It was cold, but they didn't feel it.

Dawn's feet touched the top of the mountain first. They looked down into the valley, down to the city below.

Shadows were rising. They stretched like human figures as far as the eye could see. Hundreds and hundreds of men.

The Keepers descended. They walked into the valley without fear. The wind swirled around them, and a great beast roared in the distance. There was a muddy patch when they entered the valley. It stunk of filth and excrement. Giant boulders faced the eastern side of the valley, and through the boulders fetid, swampy water ran through like a dying river.

Dark shadows guarded the falling stone gates of the abandoned city, they watched as the Keepers entered, but did not oppose them.

"Father knows we are here," Vjetar said.

The shadows moaned like they were dying.

"Father was always one for theatrics," Glaciem said.

He stood among his army.

"Father," Dawn spoke.

Erebus turned around and looked at his children. The eye that had been threatening to fall out finally had.

"We've come to help you."

Erebus put both hands on the sides of Dawn's face and kissed her forehead. His lips were dry and rough.

"What are we to do, Father?"

Erebus drew her face away from his lips. "I need to harvest your energy."

"DAWN!"

Dawn opened her eyes. She wasn't sleeping. She couldn't. But her mind was far away. Sometimes she liked to imagine she was sleeping. She would close her eyes and force her chest to rise and fall.

She heard her name whispered again. She looked to the window. Standing outside was a man with a teardrop-shaped scar on his face.

"Destan!" Dawn went to the window.

"He doesn't suspect you?" Destan asked.

"No. Come inside." Dawn went to the door and opened it for Destan.

"Where have you been?" Destan asked.

"After I saw you," Dawn said, "I came back here. I needed to know what Father was up to. He's been gathering strength."

"I know," Destan said. "He has shadows everywhere. You must be careful."

"Have you heard from Lucerna?"

"No, I haven't seen her since I was instructed to give Sara the sphere. I'm glad I did. Father would have seen her."

"Do you know where she is now?" Dawn asked.

"I don't. She's not with Sara anymore, but she could still

be with her friends or she might have returned to Lumina."

"It's imperative you find her. I delayed Sara in Tosia. Vuur used his element, but Sara is stronger than she ever was. She'll get out alive, but I didn't get a good idea of where she plans to go next. Sara can lead you to Lucerna. But you must bring Lucerna here. Sara's element is strong, but her emotions are as well. She'll never do what needs to be done."

"You're staying here?" Destan asked.

"I'll keep an eye on Father. He's distracted. He won't know what we're doing. But you must move fast. I don't know for how long I'll be able to draw his attention away from us."

"Dawn . . . be careful."

"I will."

Destan hugged her. It was unlike her other brothers to embrace her. Dawn no longer had the urge for closeness, but Destan always had. She admired that in him.

Destan disappeared into the darkness. Dawn had been careful when talking to him and Sara. Fulgur could hear her. She could smell him. If there was one man she could trick it was Fulgur, now her Father . . .

She hoped Destan would hurry.

Their plan might be risky, but it was all they had.

Dawn wanted better for Lucerna, but she would have to save them all. To do that, she had to martyr herself in the worse way possible, not to die, but to live . . . forever.

66

"I Bestowed Those Gifts upon You Not because I wanted to, But because I was Instructed to."

SARA put her fingers through the branches.

The flames were spreading.

"Move!" Yerish shouted. He cut at the branches with his blade, but they were thick. It would take a lot of hacking to get through them. The others followed his lead, hacking at the branches. Meanwhile, the fire was growing and spreading toward the center of the city where they were trapped.

Sara focused.

A forceful wave drowned the flames, but the smoke remained, forcing loud coughs from the soldiers.

Jove was watching glassy eyed. "It's okay," Sara said. "Get up." She put a dagger in his hand. She hacked away at the branches. Jove did the same.

The sap from the branches leaked down their blades and onto their hands. They breached an area wide enough for them to pass through. They escaped into the forest with as much food and supplies as they could carry.

SARA sat with her back against a tree. Jin stooped in front of her. "You did well today."

Sara smirked. "Just another day."

The fighters were resting up. Some of them had walked to the stream to refresh themselves.

"What did that old woman mean when she said not to fight him?" Jin asked.

"The Creator," Sara said.

"What's wrong with her? Is she insane?"

Sara gave Jin a searching look. "No, things have been happening . . . things I can't explain." Sara shook her head. "I've seen him, Jin. I saw him when I was lost in the pit. She told me what he was. We must be prepared for anything. Right now, all I can think about is getting back to Dustpath. I think that's the best place to gather everyone together. The people there can provide us with food, and we'll be among friends. I know Malachi would welcome us and anyone with us."

"You're right."

Jin got up and walked over to Yerish. He patted him on the back.

Benn sat next to Sara. "You're getting better at that."

"I don't know what the sphere did to me, but I feel stronger."

"No, I mean being a leader again. Jin's looking to you for advice."

Sara shook her head. "This is the part I don't like."

"Why?"

"Because I don't want to be responsible for what happens next. Most of these people will die fighting, and maybe, just like last time, I won't matter."

"Because last time what you did didn't matter?"

"Hephaestus's death had nothing to do with me. It was the Aether. It killed him."

"Who brought the Aether there?"

"Bolton."

"And who brought Bolton there?"

Sara's eyes searched the ground.

"You can do this," he said.

Sara looked up at Benn. "Thank you."

"Alright, to your feet everyone," Yerish shouted. "We're going back home."

TIED to the dock at the edge of the Lake was one boat. Five wouldn't have been enough to carry them all. Taryn didn't think twice, she dove into the Lake, and the others followed. The water was warm. The crickets were making music. The sun glanced off the water, creating spectrums of colors.

Sara closed her eyes as her body glided through the water. Bolton was home. They were together. It was the first time anyone had a good dream crossing the Lake.

Yerish took her hand when she reached the edge and helped her up. Most of the fighters were on the opposite side. They sat and waited for the others.

Dema passed her a jar of fruit. Sara gladly accepted. She took her canteen from her waist and drank. The sun was disappearing into the trees like a guilty child hiding from punishment. Sara didn't remember falling asleep.

SHE was on the Cliff of Broken Promise. The waterfall was dry, and the flowers had died. A young girl sat at the edge of the cliff. Her dark hair covered her face as she leaned over something. The girl was moving her hand in a rough manner.

Sara walked closer.

She was drawing something on a piece of paper. The charcoal dirtied her fingers.

"What are you doing?" Sara asked.

The little girl looked up. Charcoal covered her face. Sara could see her drawing more clearly. It was the face of a bear.

"It's our father."

Sara sat next to the little girl. "What do you mean by our father?"

"I told you before. We're sisters."

Goosebumps ran down Sara's arms. "What's your name?"

The girl continued drawing, making the fur around the bear's face longer and blacker. "You'll see me soon, but you won't know. I can make myself look any way I want in dreams. So can you if you let your mind wander. Have you ever wondered how you got to Omega Ray from here?"

"Yes. I was wondering that. I thought maybe I just couldn't remember journeying to Omega Ray."

The little girl laughed.

"What?" Sara asked.

"It's funny how you all do that. Make up stories so the pieces of the puzzle fit together. You can shape them anyway you want as long as they fit."

"Okay, so what's the real reason I fell from the cliff and ended up in the chasm."

"Our father did that. He wanted the Builders to remember her."

"Who?" Sara asked.

"His lover. She crawled all the way from the snowy dunes to warmer ground. To protect her baby. She was in so much pain. She jumped. No one ever found the baby."

"But how can he do that?"

"He can bend space," the child said. "He can join two places together."

"What else can he do?"

The little girl looked up at her, wide-eyed.

SARA woke up startled. She looked around. Jove was sitting by the Lake. His cloak was still damp. "What are you doing?" Sara asked.

Jove stood and turned. His head was bowed. "Nothing, I . . ." A jar rolled along the ground in front of him. It was glowing. As Jove rushed forward, Sara picked it up.

Inside was a glowing worm. Sara remembered the Morica guards who came to Wyvek that night. With a pair of rusty tongs, they imprisoned one of the worms in a jar.

Sara stood and walked towards Jove. "Where did you get this?"

"I told you. I'm studying Elementals. Those things are coming from the sanctums. I asked the guards to deliver one to me . . . for my work."

"What do you know about them?"

"Nothing."

"Why are you lying?"

"I . . ."

"Tell me," Sara whispered, careful not to wake the others. "They made you what you are."

Sara waited.

"They're energy from the spheres," he said. "They travel through the earth and are delivered through all living things. They are the origination of your powers. Something is drawing them back from the ground."

"What?"

Jove shook his head.

IN the morning, they arrived at Wyvek. The city was still boarded up and abandoned. They marched onto Dustpath. Sara hoped Bolton would be there waiting for her among Malachi's people.

When they came upon Malachi's camp, everyone stood still. Bodies littered the ground. Sara knelt where she stood. Jin came to her side. He knelt next to her.

Sara was crying. "Was he here? Was he here?" she chanted.

"Sara." Jin put his hands on her arms.

"Was he here?" she said louder.

"I don't know."

Sara stood.

All the vegetation had died. Many of the bodies had been burned. Men, women, children. In the center of it all was Malachi. His body was decomposing in the heat.

SARA helped to bury the dead. She forced herself to look at each face. They carried the bodies into small graves they had dug in the village where the ground was softer. Once they were done, everyone was sweaty and exhausted. They prayed over the bodies.

Sara walked to the edge of the village, facing the road. Jin found her there. "We didn't find him. He wasn't among them."

"Some of the bodies were burned."

"I know," Jin said, "but I'm confident Bolton's wasn't one of them."

Sara pressed her lips together. "I should have been here. I should have stayed."

"No," Jin said.

Sara wiped her tears. "The Council did this?"

"It looks like the work of a group of Fire Elementals."

Sara sighed.

Jin got up, ready to walk back to camp. "I hope you join us."

"Just give me a minute."

Jin nodded and strode away.

Sara took a deep breath and closed her eyes. A pool of water appeared in front of her. She used the water to wash her face and neck. She let the water drip off her chin and back into the pool.

THE next morning, Benn handed Sara a jar of preserves. "Be careful, it's hot."

Sara put the jar down on the ground, shaking out her hand.

"Sorry, I don't feel the heat as hot as you do. I thought it would be good if you had a warm meal."

"You sent Lightning through this?" Sara asked.

Benn laughed. "I put it over a fire." Benn sat and took the top off the jar for her so the preserves could cool enough to eat.

"What do you think they want from me?" she asked.

"You mean Jin?"

"The Rebel Resistance."

Benn thought for a moment. "Well, I think they want a unifying factor. Someone to bring the people together. Jin sees you did it once. Why not again? If you could do that, the Council would be too scared to go against us."

"I think we have bigger problems than the Council," Sara said. "If some of them survived the attack, it would be a long time before they could build another army. Most of the High Councilors are dead. I saw the bodies. Jin has to trust me if he wants me to be his unifying factor."

"I don't think he'll have a problem with that."

She twisted her ring around her finger.

"You miss him?" Benn asked.

Sara nodded.

After the meal, Sara wandered back to the road to wait for Bolton. Jin settled down beside her. "I think it's time we talk about what we're going to do next."

Sara kept staring out onto the road.

"We would have to travel all of Mirmina to build an army," Jin said, "but, I might have a solution."

"There are a lot of people in Lumina right now," Sara said.

"A lot of the enemy is still in Lumina too," Jin said. "I think it's wiser to bring them to us rather than the other way around. That way we can be ready for them."

"What should I do?" Sara asked.

Jin pointed to the sky. "People need to know you're back."

"A symbol?"

Jin nodded.

"But won't that draw Morica to us as well?" Sara asked.

"Like I said. If they come, we can be ready for them."

Sara wanted to tell Jin what she was truly worried about. But the way he reacted outside Tosia, she was afraid he would start to doubt her. He had said something on their way through D'arkadia, something that made Sara think he might trust her. He said something was watching them . . . like they were puppets. But he had gone through a bloody battle before he said that. He was still looking toward the Council. But a greater danger was brewing.

SARA stood with her eyes closed.

The fighters surrounded her with their weapons across their chests, but only the sound of the breeze passed her ears. There were no whispers. For a moment, Sara thought she might be alone.

Sara opened her eyes.

Benn was away from the crowd outside the circle of fighters. Had her eyes not lingered on him for more than a moment, she might have thought he was Bolton.

She looked to Jin.

He nodded to her.

"Okay." Sara held out her hands and closed her eyes.

The energy was rising to her fingertips. It left her in a rush, more energy than she had ever exhausted, and yet she was still standing.

She opened her eyes.

Water rained from the ground. The drops spread all the way to Lumina. They were hitting under her chin and rippling up her face.

The water gathered in the sky until it formed an upside-down triangle, the symbol for the Water Element. It wavered like a flag. More droplets were joining it.

She marveled at how effortless it was. She could maintain the symbol and at the same time raise the water from the ocean.

As the symbol developed in size, people were appearing from over the hill. At first, they were trickling in, but then they came in waves. They were coming from Lumina. A huge group of them were marching in the distance. They stopped and watched the emblem in the sky.

The sea of faces kept growing. Sara's chest was rising and falling. Even her tears were joining her symbol. The people flocked to her.

67

HOPE

"It might Surprise You that I am Not All-Knowing. Sometimes I get It Wrong."

THE smoke rose from Vella City, and the earth shook. Bolton stood on the cliff with Balin by his side.

"What's happening out there?" Balin asked.

"Come on," Bolton said. "We have to get deeper into the woods." Bolton led Balin into the trees. They careened around crystals until they were far from anything Bolton could recognize.

"Do you think they'll burn the forest down?" Balin asked.

"No. We'll stay here until the smoke clears. Then, we'll move on." Bolton leaned against a tree with his eyes closed.

Birds chirped from the trees. They reminded Bolton of

Orka. He would give anything to have that little, green monster snap at him right now.

He scratched his head. He hadn't noticed he drifted off. Balin was sitting on the ground with a stick in his hand. He was drawing figures in the dirt.

"What are you doing?" Bolton asked.

"Passing the time."

"How long was I out?"

"A while." Balin sighed.

Had the smoked cleared? Trees obscured Bolton's view. "I want you to stay here. I'm going back out there to check for soldiers. If it's clear, we'll move on."

Balin nodded and continued to play in the dirt.

Bolton walked through the forest, pushing aside the leaves and small branches in his way. He wouldn't be able to make his way back without a guide, so he marked the trees with a rock as he walked.

The smoke twirled in the air, and dissipated in the distance. *I need to get back to Sara without getting caught up in someone else's fight.* As he wandered through the trees, the sky turned amber.

Something barreled through. It let out a deep roar. Its breath warmed Bolton's back. A bear with grizzled black fur stood three feet taller than Bolton. Its teeth gleaned with its own saliva.

Bolton fell to the ground. The large creature towered over him. Its massive shadow covered Bolton in darkness.

He sent Lightning through the massive creature. The bolt hit it in the chest. The bear ambled towards him. But as the shadow grew deeper, someone yelled.

Balin was on top of the bear. He placed his hands on the sides of its face and sent a jolt to its brain. The bear shook

Balin off and ran into the woods.

Bolton scrambled to his hands and knees and rushed to Balin. The boy was sitting up now. "You've seen one of those before?"

"No," Bolton said, breathlessly. "That was a bear. It was probably running from the fire. You could have gotten yourself killed. Don't you ever do something like that again."

"It would have killed you."

"Then, let it kill me!"

Balin turned around. He slumped to the ground and crossed his arms over his knees.

Bolton shook his head. "I'm sorry. Hey." Bolton knelt next to him.

"You're just like my mother. What's the point of having power if I can't use it to help?"

"You're right," Bolton said. "Come on. Let's get out of here." He helped Balin to his feet.

They walked to D'arkadia and drank from the stream. Bolton washed his face and settled down next to the water.

"Do you think dad will like me?" Balin asked.

"He'll spend all his time trying to get you to like him."

"You think so."

"I know it."

"Am I like him?"

Bolton shook his head. "The way you handled that bear was one of the bravest things I've ever seen."

Balin smirked.

"But you shouldn't do stuff like that," Bolton said.

"You really do sound like my mom."

"Well, someone's got to take care of you. You're still a kid."

"I'm older than I look. I'm just small for my age."

"Sure," Bolton said.

"How far is it to Dustpath?"

"Miles still. We won't get there for days."

"I don't know if I want to see him," Balin said. "I mean, in my head, I built my dad up to be something great. And now, it sounds like everything I thought was a lie. I guess I just want to go on believing the lie rather than finding out my dad was some deadbeat."

Bolton sighed. "I know what you mean. I'm not going to lie to you and tell you he's better than you built him up to be or anything like that. But it did feel good to tell him what I thought, to get to say it to his face. I kind of found some peace."

"You think it will be that way for me?"

"I don't know. Just don't build it up to be something more than it is," Bolton said, "okay?"

"Sure," Balin said.

They walked through the entrance to Tosia. In the center of the city were small branches that had erupted from the ground to form a cage. The living bars had been breached, and the prisoners must have escaped through the large gap in the front.

"Cool." Balin gawked at the work. "What did this?"

"An Earth Elemental," Bolton said.

"Can I meet one?"

"When we get to Dustpath, there'll be lots of Earth Elementals, but I doubt many of them could have done this."

The branches grew up into the sky where the Great Tree was rotting away. Outside, the ground was charred. "I thought we could stay here for a night," Bolton said, "but it doesn't look like we'll be able to."

They moved on from the forest and walked until they

were tired. They were a mile from the Lake.

Bolton settled down and rested his head upon his bag.

Balin sat and drank from his canteen. He stared at the moon. "My mom had a story about the moon. Hundreds of years ago, there was a young girl whose father lived on the western coast of Mirmina. It got very cold there in the winters so he would send his wife and daughters to the Dark Lands where it was warmer.

"His oldest daughter was named Selena, and she fell in love with a boy who lived there. He was Endyein. Not much was known about him.

"One day Selena came back from the Dark Lands deathly sick. Her mother and father called the village doctor, but nothing could be done for her. It was a full moon that night, and as the doctor told her parents the bad news, a deep shadow covered the moon. The darkness did not lift until Selena had awakened.

"It was then that the villagers started believing Selena could control the moon. This thought inspired fear in them, so a few of the young men kidnapped her. No one ever saw her again.

"To this day, some people still believe Selena controls the moon, that when it goes down in the west, she is visiting Endyein and when it comes up in the east, she has returned to her father."

"That's a crazy story," Bolton said.

"She has lots of those." Balin folded his arm and rested his head under it.

BOLTON and Balin reached Wyvek. "It's not far now," Bolton assured his brother. They came upon the rock. It had been moved aside. A chill ran through Bolton. "Stand behind me," he ordered Balin. Balin walked behind him as he crept through the opening.

Hundreds of tents lay abandoned in the dust. The wind lifted the folds. Large craters sank into the ground.

"What happened here?" Balin asked.

Bolton ignored his question and ran to his and Sara's tent. He tore through the tent folds. The bed was unmade, and the kettle was overturned on the floor.

"What's wrong?" Balin asked. "Is this where Dad was?"

Bolton sat on the ground with his head in his hands. Balin knelt beside him and put his hand on his back. He didn't know what to say to his brother.

That night, they ate what the fighters had left behind. Bolton started a fire to cook the food. They ate in silence. Balin pushed the food around on his wooden plate.

BOLTON couldn't see. He tossed and turned all night, and that kept Balin awake too. In the morning, they packed to leave.

"Where are we going?" Balin asked.

Bolton shook his head. "Lumina, I guess."

"What's in Lumina?"

"I don't know."

"Maybe we should go back to the Insula?"

A raindrop hit under Bolton's chin. More raindrops erupted from the ground. The water ran along his raised arm and dripped up from his fingers.

Balin watched. "What is that?"

They looked up into the sky. A shape was forming in the distance.

Bolton threw on his bag, and ran to the entrance of Rebel Resistance Headquarters. Balin followed him in a rush.

"Wait, where are we going?"

Bolton raced down the road, not stopping to take a breath. People were gathering on the eastern hill. The fighters were gathered in a circle around her. She was smiling up at the sky.

"Sara!"

Her eyes met his. It was like his heart had started beating again. She tore through the circle of fighters and ran into his embrace.

68

ACROSS THE DESERT

"I have Built This World on the Blood of My Friends and Maintained It on the Blood of So Many Others."

RAI was sharpening her sword with a bit of leather. Vassal sat beside her. "It'll be dangerous for us to go by foot."

"We don't have a choice. I don't want to make a home of the desert, do you?"

"Guess not."

Rai didn't look at him. "It's bothering you."

"What?"

"That I helped you back there in the chapel."

Vassal looked at the sand. "Yeah, it is. Not that I'm not grateful. I just wish I knew why you did it."

"I told you why I did it. You just wish I'd done it for another reason."

Vassal smirked. "Yeah, I guess, that's it."

Thatch approached them. "Hey, we're about to eat if you two want to join us."

As they sat around the fire, Thatch had abandoned his food and was working on Stannum. Every now and then the large orange eye glowed only to go out again.

As they became tired, the group around the fire dissipated. Soon, it was only Rai, Atrus, Pentagon, and Vassal. Atrus yawned. "Well, I think I'm going to . . ."

Rai shook her head at him.

Vassal had his head down, but Pentagon noticed the gesture. Rai pointed to him and mouthed, "You, two. Stay."

"The weather's nice though," Atrus said. "I wouldn't want to miss out."

Pentagon punched him in the arm. Atrus made a mock show of rubbing his arm and saying "ugh" under his breath.

Vassal looked like he was about to fall asleep where he was sitting.

"Vas, are you alright?" Atrus asked.

"Yeah, tired a guess."

"Well, it's getting to be that time," Atrus said. "We're not as young as we once were."

Vassal chuckled. "You're the worst."

"Thanks," Atrus said with a look of confusion.

"I will call it a night." Vassal shuffled from his seat and settled down beside a wild bush so it could block the cool breeze.

"What is it?" Atrus asked in a harsh whisper.

"Why do you have to make things so damn obvious?" Rai asked.

"You haven't spoken to us since we got here."

"That isn't true."

"You only said enough to make it clear you weren't going to speak to us."

"Shut up, Atrus," Pentagon said.

Rai stared into the fire. Pentagon and Atrus grew quiet. "I think a lot about that night," she said. "It's starting to get kind of fuzzy, but there's something I need you guys to confirm."

"What is it?" Pentagon asked.

"When the guards caught Vassal, did you see anything strange?"

"Like what?" Atrus asked.

"Those things in the sanctums, did we bring them with us?"

"Why would you—"

"Because that's what I think I saw coming out of Vassal that night. Did you see them?"

Pentagon shook his head.

"No," Atrus said. "I didn't see that."

"You think those things got inside him?" Pentagon asked.

Rai laughed and looked away. "No, that's not what I think." She got up, leaving Atrus and Pentagon wondering. Rai stopped where Rodan lay. "I know you're not sleeping."

Rodan opened his eyes and looked up at her. "I'm afraid I might not wake up."

"Are you okay?"

"I'll be fine."

"Since you woke up, you've been different."

"Different?"

"You stopped asking me questions . . . you stopped prying."

"I'm sorry I bothered you." Rodan smiled.

Rai's eyes were on the ground, but she was smiling too. "I kind of liked you bothering me." She left him and settled down to sleep where the air was cooler.

"RAI, wake up!"

Rai touched her face. Her skin was wet, so were her clothes. Raindrops met her eyes. They were coming up from the ground.

Farah was shaking her.

Rai sat up. She looked around in bewilderment.

"Look at that!" Farah pointed towards the sky.

"What if it's a trick?" Rai asked.

"How can you fake that?" She pointed to the large upside down triangle wavering in the sky.

Spire cradled Canace in her arms.

"This is why she stopped us from leaving," Rai whispered.

"Come on." Farah led the way through the desert. "Hurry up!"

They saw Jin first.

"Dad." Rodan hugged his father, and Jin patted him on the back.

"Sara!" Farah ran up to her. She hugged her and Bolton.

Sara embraced Rodan. "You're okay?"

Vassal shuffled behind them, his face lost in the crowd. Rai approached Sara. Sara hugged Rai before she could say anything.

SARA dined in the tent at Resistance Headquarters. Her companions sat around the table in the center of the tent.

"So, Vella City is dust?" Farah asked.

"It's gone," Jin said. "What's left isn't safe to journey

through."

"Wow. And Morica didn't dare come here."

Jin took a sip of nectar and shook his head as he swallowed. "No, as far as we know. High Councilor Surnom and Romulus are alive in Lumina. High Councilor Jove is with us."

"So, what, we're going to march on Lumina with all these people?" Pentagon asked.

"That's not what the Commander said." Vassal put his cup down.

"You're the Commander," Jin said.

"I asked you to take it."

"I'm sorry. No disrespect Commander," Atrus said, "but didn't they give Sara this tent?"

"That's right." Jin looked to Sara. "From here on out, it is up to you. What's our next move?"

Sara put down her utensils. "I don't think the Council should be our main concern. There's something else going on here, and we all know it."

"Can we not talk war right now?" Atrus asked. "I say we enjoy this meal and live to plan battles another day."

"I can drink to that." Bolton was sitting across the table from the worn-out villains.

"It's good to see you again," Pentagon said.

"But it's too late. We've already found a new fourth." Atrus clapped Rodan on the back.

WHEN they left the tent, everyone had had their fill of food and wine. Rai walked back to her tent, Pentagon and Atrus joined her. Vassal followed them.

Rai didn't mind the company.

"Remember when the captain fell out drunk, and Pentagon had to steer the ship?" Atrus asked.

"It was clear no one else would have jumped to do it," Pentagon said, "and we had a ferryman's daughter aboard who had probably steered a thousand ships."

They laughed.

"She would have been much better at it too," Atrus said. "Pent nearly crashed us into port."

"I steered boats, not ships," Rai said. "Rowing a thousand boats doesn't prepare you to steer a ship."

"But apparently, it does prepare you to fly one," Atrus said. They laughed, drawing in closer to each other as they walked. "This is where we get off." He and Pentagon ambled off to their tents.

"Good night to you!" Vassal called after them.

"We'll be villains together and fools together. Forever!" Atrus yelled. He patted Pentagon on the back.

Rai shook her head. She and Vassal continued to their tents. When they made it to the next row of tents, Rai stopped. "Goodnight then," she said.

Vassal's eyes pinned her. It was like they were on that ship again, sailing to Lumina.

Vassal kissed her, too sudden for Rai to react.

"Sorry." Vassal looked at the ground.

Rai touched her lips. Her hand still gripped Vassal's arm. She let it drop.

69

POISON

"Power is Something We All can Understand. We may Not All covet It, But We can Understand It."

REBECCA packed up what was left of Jacopo's things: a cloak, two daggers, and a bit of twine. She placed them in a sack he could carry at his side.

A dark cat ran across as she worked. She hated that cat. Jacopo had it with him endlessly, and he loved the beast. She wanted to drown it. When she would try to pet it, it would hiss and bite at her. And, for no reason at all, when she would walk, it would nip and scratch at her heels.

"Let her be!" Jacopo commanded. He picked up the cat and placed it on his shoulders as he walked. It settled there, perfectly balanced.

That's how Jacopo made Rebecca feel.

Jacopo wasn't a bad man posing as a good man. He was a bad man, and he didn't try to hide that with a lot of promises.

Handling him, being with him was simple. His decisions and motivations were expected. Rebecca loved the lack of complexity and the feeling of being wanted. Jacopo had begged her to stay like a child would beg for his mother.

She stepped over a branch.

The sky was turning dull. Soon, they would have to walk by the light of the crystals alone.

The forest scarcely had animals roaming among the trees. It wasn't like the forest of Rebecca's village. It was picked clean of the living.

When she was a child, she was told that in the forests beyond, it was rare to find an animal. Hunters long ago had drove them into extinction in that part of Mirmina.

Rebecca loved the quiet of the forest, but here, it was too quiet. It was an unnatural quiet.

The branches covered the sky like the roof of a cabin open on all sides. It gave this false sense of security when she looked up.

Jacopo was asleep with the cat curled up against his stomach. His fingernails still had blood around the edges and underneath. She had never seen someone sleep so soundly and yet have so many troubles.

Growing up, Rebecca lived in a village far from the cities. The people called it Warren's Well because, in the center of the village, the first settlers had dug a large well. The leader went by the name of Warren. Without a well, the land would have been unlivable because the closest river was miles away near Tosia. Even the smallest lake was a day's journey by cart. Donkeys were expensive because there were so few. Horses were unheard of.

The well was bottomless, and the water smelled like eggs. As a child, Rebecca would stare down it, but the well was so deep and dark she never got much from it.

"What are you doing, child?" Her mother pulled her down from the well's edge. "If you lean in any farther, the young ones will be looking down on you."

"She's just curious," her father would say. "She's an adventurer."

The cabins faced the well, like thirsty hogs with wide faces. Grubby children ran into the mouths of the hogs only to be fussed at by their mothers who sent them out to the well to get cleaned up before dinner.

After dinner, Rebecca's father pulled the covers up to her chin.

"Dad, why don't you ever want to go on an adventure?"

Her father looked at her with eyes full of warmth. She could almost see the fire there. "Because, I have you, your mother, and your little brother to worry about. If I left, who would be around to tuck you in?"

"Mama would."

"Mama's afraid of the dark." Her mother always had an unnatural fear of the dark. She said there was too much loneliness in it.

"I could go with you."

"That's right." Her father tapped her on the nose. "I'll tell you what, I have a very important mission tomorrow. The doctor is sending me out to get something very special from Lake Marten. Do you want to go?"

Her father was the doctor's assistant. He was learning to be a doctor himself. One day, when the doctor died, her father would take his place.

"Of course," Rebecca shouted.

Her father put his finger to his lips and smiled. "I have to talk to Mama about it. Go to sleep now." He kissed her fore-head.

HER mother had a worried look on her face when they left. Her father had only gone to Lake Marten once before when she was younger. She couldn't remember the day, but her mother mentioned it twice before they left.

It was morning and the sun beamed down on them. Her father had a large sack of jars on his back. They clang together as he walked. That night in the forest, Rebecca lay awake for hours and listened to the sounds of insects and her father's snoring.

The next morning, they got up and ate the biscuits her mother had prepared. They were hard and crumbling. Rebecca wiped the loose crumbs from her lips with her sleeve.

"Your mother would die if she saw you doing that." Her father chided playfully.

Rebecca grinned.

Her father stood. "Ah, I can smell it from here."

"What?"

"That brackish water. Come on. It's not far now."

"What did the doctor send you here for?" Rebecca asked.

"Something very special. You'll see."

The water of the lake looked like the shadowy blackness of the well. It was a small, shallow lake compared to the neighboring ones, but it was the biggest mass of water Rebecca had ever seen.

Her father waded knee-deep in the reed banks. He had rolled up his pant legs.

"What are you doing?" she asked.

"Fishing!"

Rebecca didn't understand. She went to the bank, but her father put up his hand, signaling for her to stop. "Just wait."

Rebecca sat near the bank with her arms wrapped around her legs. After a while, her father walked back to the shore. Inch by inch his legs appeared from the water. Black things, an inch wide and two inches long, covered his legs.

"What are they?" Rebecca asked. Her thoughts were mingled with feelings of disgust and curiosity. She couldn't pull her eyes away.

"Leeches."

The village doctor believed leeches could suck the badness out of anybody. If you were sick or injured, the doctor would apply leeches to your body, and they would get to work sucking the illness out of you.

Every now and then, some of the leeches would curl up and die, and the doctor would need to send someone out to restock. This was usually his assistant.

Her father unscrewed the lid from one of the jars. He squeezed one of the leeches and plucked it from his leg. It left a nasty mark on his flesh, and blood dripped down his leg and from the mouth of the leech. He placed it in the jar.

The blood painted the clear glass. Rebecca looked through the bloody lens at the leech at the bottom of the jar.

Once all the leeches were off his skin, Rebecca watched her father wade into the lake for the second time and come back with more worms.

As her father was kneeing, pulling the leeches from his skin, Rebecca marveled at the creatures.

The water was still, black, and hypnotizing. She sat at the edge of the lake. Standing, she lifted her dress so it skirted the water as she walked into the brackish depths.

Her father turned his head. "Rebecca!"

The first leech sank its teeth into her skin. It felt like tiny needles. The stinging feeling hit her again and again until her legs were numb.

She tried to walk back to the shore, but she slipped on the mud and fell face first into the water. Her father pulled her back up and carrying her to shore. He plucked the leeches from her body.

She turned her head. One had latched onto her face. She pulled that one away herself.

Her father helped her to sit up. "Are you okay?"

She nodded. "I just thought I could help."

Her father laughed. "Of course you did." He wiped the blood off her face with an old rag. "Why don't you screw the rest of those lids onto the jars, and we'll get out of here?"

"Okay."

When they got home, her mother harped over the marks on her face and arms. As her father explained what happened, her mother fumed with her hands on her hips.

Rebecca went with her father to the doctor's house. Her father let her present the jars to the doctor. They all laughed after her father told the story of how she fell in the reedy banks.

The doctor gave her a salve for the marks. It was thick, pasty, and smelled like something rotten. Her mother made her apply it every night.

A man came to the village in the middle of the night. Someone spotted him drinking from the well. A young boy ran to get the doctor.

The man was pale and sick with some disease the doctor couldn't name. There were large boils all over his body, and he couldn't talk. The doctor said it was because his throat was on fire. Mothers pulled their children away from him in the street.

He was kept away in the doctor's house to be treated. Rebecca's mother begged her father not to go.

"Someone has to help the man," he said.

"That's what the doctor is for."

"One day I'll be the doctor, Laura."

"You won't be if you catch what that man has and bring it back to this family."

That was the last time Rebecca saw her father.

For two weeks, he was at the sick man's bedside. A day later, they heard the sick man died, but Rebecca's father didn't come back.

The doctor wouldn't let anyone see him. He said he had a fever, but Rebecca knew he had caught whatever the sick man had.

He died three weeks later.

On the same day he died, a baby was born to the only Elemental family in the village. They were Fire Elementals who used to perform for the children in the street. The couple had tried for many years to have a child.

The whole village was in celebration as if her father's death meant nothing to them. For years, he had healed their wounds and nursed them at their sick beds, and now he was being pushed aside.

Her mother wouldn't come out of her room.

Rebecca could hear her weeping behind the closed door.

She was still young enough to remarry, but she never did.

For much of Rebecca's life, she remembered that her mother kept mostly to her room. She would wake early to clean and cook. Rebecca used to sneak out of her room and watch her. It was one of the only times she got to see her mother.

She worked mechanically and without feeling. Her mother's presence reminded Rebecca that her father had died. It was like some invisible badness surrounding the house.

When she was sixteen, she stopped watching her mother.

On the road, she met a young man named Jin. She didn't know then that he was a soldier. He promised her a house and a life away from the woods.

Shortly after his banding ceremony, she was with child.

He wasn't there when her son was born.

JACOPO was snoring. His chest rose and fell with each breath. The cat that was once nestled against his stomach was now stretching with its paws out and back arched. It leapt off into the woods. It would be back.

Jacopo opened his eyes. Rebecca diverted her gaze, but she wasn't quick enough.

"How long have you been up?"

"Just now," she lied.

It was Jacopo's idea to follow the river. Rivers normally led to villages. They were running low on food. They wouldn't be able to travel the way they came on so little.

As they neared the coast, the trees became sparser. Cabins ran along the river. People collected fire wood from the forest and tended gardens behind the houses. Banners hung from the eaves.

Jacopo and Rebecca walked to the village. Some of the people stopped working and looked at them. A man exited his home. "Who are you?" he asked.

"Hungry travelers," Jacopo said. He looked to each of the men and to the banners bearing the Lightning Symbol. Rebecca caught his glance. He knew them.

"We're friends of Lady Sara," Jacopo lied.

The atmosphere lightened. The man extended his hand. "I'm Waviel, and we are the people of Wyvek."

JACOPO and Rebecca sat around the dinner table with Waviel, his three children, and his wife, Penelope. They ate dried fish and barley cakes. Jacopo ripped off a piece of fish with his teeth.

"Where are you headed?" Waviel asked.

Jacopo was still gnawing on the fish.

Uncomfortable with the silence, Rebecca opened her mouth to speak, but Jacopo put his hand on her leg from under the table. He finished chewing and answered, "We were going to Vella City to meet my cousin, but we got lost in the woods without much food."

"You don't know the way?"

"Afraid not. But I sure knew the way before we left home. Didn't I, sweetheart?" He looked at Rebecca as if prompting her to answer.

Rebecca smiled nervously and said, "You sure did."

Penelope wiped her lips on her napkin. "Oh, are you two married?"

Rebecca looked down at her lap. She wasn't old enough to be Jacopo's mother, but she was certainly older than him by quite a few years.

Jacopo nodded with his mouth full. "Yes," he said, still nodding. He took Rebecca's hand. "Almost five years now, and I still remember where we first met."

"Oh, where was that?" Penelope asked.

Rebecca felt like all eyes were on her, and she was not playing her part well enough. "At the pier," she blurted out.

"That's right the pier," Jacopo said. "The pier in . . ."

". . . in Lumina," she finished. That was where she had met Jin.

"That's right," Jacopo let go of her hand and continued eating. "So," he said, tearing through his food with a knife and fork. "Why did you leave Wyvek?"

Penelope looked down at the table.

"It was time for a change," Waviel said.

"The whole town?" Jacopo asked.

"There was something in that place," Penelope said.

"Penelope." Waviel grinned.

"We went through that way," Jacopo said. "The houses were boarded up."

"It didn't feel right just leaving," Waviel said.

Jacopo nodded, compliant in the lie.

After they dined, Waviel gave Jacopo and Rebecca a room in his home for the night. Once they were behind closed doors, Rebecca said, "There's only one bed."

Jacopo put on pretend shock. "My wife of nearly five years won't sleep in the same bed with me."

"They don't honestly think we're a couple."

"And why not?" Jacopo asked.

Rebecca sighed. "You drank too much wine. I'll sleep on the floor."

"But then they might think we were lying about being married, and that might lead them to wonder what else we're lying about."

"I wasn't the one who decided to lie about being married."

"In fact," Jacopo said, "we should make a lot of noise in here tonight. Appearances are everything."

"You're drunk."

"And you're cold," Jacopo said.

Rebecca pulled the covers from the bed and slept on the floor.

"REBECCA. Rebecca."

She opened her eyes. Jacopo was on the floor next to her. Rebecca closed her eyes. "It doesn't make much sense for both of us to be down here."

"I'm sorry for how I acted. I was drunk."

"Confession of the year."

"Why are you like that?" Jacopo asked. "I'm trying."

"To what?"

"To stop pretending I have anybody else."

"How do you know I don't have anybody?" Rebecca asked.

"You're not one of them. I knew that the moment I saw you. I don't know what you were doing with the people of Tosia, but I do know one thing. You're always with strangers when you don't have anybody."

"Always?" she asked.

"Well, not always," he said.

"So, you want to be my friend because there's nobody else," she said.

"No, I meant, there's nobody else I can trust."

"And you can trust me? You barely know me."

He laughed.

"See. I made a good point," she said.

"You know," he said, "I used to be in Hephaestus's army."

"Tell me something I don't know."

"I didn't want to be."

Rebecca opened her eyes.

"Yeah," he said. "A lot of people who know me don't

know that. I was thirteen when he came to my village. He wanted all the boys and men who were skilled in their element. He trusted Fire Elementals most. Before I left, my grandmother gave me this." Jacopo pulled the string from his neck. Out of his shirt came a vial of blue liquid.

"What is it?" Rebecca asked.

"My grandmother told me to pour it into the drink of my enemy. She didn't say who that enemy was. I kept this and brought it with me to Omega Ray.

"They trained us and roomed us together in stone houses. I still felt like a kid. I didn't have a dad. I think Hephaestus noticed because he asked for me one day. I was taken to the stone palace. He asked everyone else to leave. And he told me something I will never forget."

Rebecca waited for him to continue.

"He said men are not my enemy. That they are simply barriers to the true enemy that is their nature. And he asked me, 'and what made man who he is?' I shook my head. He said 'God.'"

"What did that mean to you?"

"Well, I thought he meant there would always be an enemy because you can't fight God. I took that as a challenge. I wanted to prove him wrong. I criticized everything he did, the way he led, the way he talked, the way he ate."

"But you never got the chance to poison him."

"I did, but didn't want to anymore. Because I couldn't show him how much better I was if he was dead."

FOR days, Jacopo and Rebecca lived among the people of Wyvek. Rebecca helped with the gardening. Jacopo helped the men carry firewood and building materials from the forest.

Waviel was a welcoming host, and Penelope hushed any talk of leaving around the dinner table.

Rebecca started to feel like she was home again, not the home she had built with Jin, but the home she would have had if she had stayed in her village.

It was becoming easier to pretend to be Jacopo's wife. She didn't question it when he cozied up to her in public. After all they were playing it off for the others. It was easy to justify sleeping in the same bed with him. Sleeping on the floor was uncomfortable, and they couldn't ask for separate beds because then they would be found out.

Not even the cat, which had found its way to the village, bothered her.

She was working in the garden one day, chatting with the women. Chatter and laugher filled the field. It rang into the air in gentle harmony.

But suddenly the harmony flat lined.

Everyone stared up.

Rebecca rose to her feet and looked up to the sky.

It was the perfect thing to ruin her harmony.

JACOPO packed, stuffing clothes and supplies into the bag.

"We're not really going to go?" Rebecca asked.

Jacopo paused only for a moment to turn his head to her. "Yes," hissed from his lips.

"But is this really a good idea?"

"We'll be surrounded by Wyvek soldiers. No one will notice us."

"But if they do?"

Jacopo shouldered his bag. He walked up to her and took her hands. "They won't." He sat on the bed to let the cat jump to his shoulders. He took Rebecca's hand and led her out of the room.

They joined the soldiers on the wharf where the ship was docked. Waviel looked happy they were joining them. He was leaving his wife and children behind. The ship sailed at noon, only two hours after the village had seen Sara's symbol in the sky.

EVENTUALLY, the symbol left the sky. They hadn't seen it disappear. It had hung there for days, which was the talk of the ship. Sara must have put all she had into maintaining that symbol.

But the ship's captain had marked where the symbol had appeared. If they continued north, they should reach her somewhere near Wyvek.

Rebecca looked at the water as she leaned over the railing.

"I thought you liked adventure?" Jacopo propped his elbows on the railing with his back to the sea.

"I didn't want to leave," she said.

"Why? Because you were happy playing my wife?"

"Right," Rebecca scoffed.

The cat walked along the railing without fear. "Why did you bring that thing here? It's unnatural to have a cat at sea."

"Everything's going to be fine," he said.

Rebecca turned to him. "No, it's not. You're going there to kill that girl, and all it's going to do—"

Jacopo took her arm. "Stop it!"

"All it's going to do is get you killed," she hissed.

"Do you trust me?"

Rebecca had never considered this, but the first word that came to her head was "Yes."

"Then listen to me. I'm not an idiot. This is going to be

quick. And when all's said and done, you're not going to miss that little village in the woods because I'm going to take you somewhere better."

"I've heard that before," she said.

"And that's the last time you'll hear it."

THEY arrived on the shores of Dustpath far from Lumina. After a long desert journey, they could see Sara's banners in the distance. They were golden banners with the Water Symbol on them. There were tents in wide circles around each other with a large one in the center. Above the large tent was the greatest banner of them all, wavering like water in the breeze.

Waviel was one of the first to step into her camp. There were soldiers everywhere in seconds, ready to strike.

"Who are you?" Rebecca recognized the bulky man. He was Yerish of Jin's army. He couldn't see her among the crowd.

"We are friends of Lady Sara. We saw the symbol in the sky, and we want to join her."

Sara emerged from the large tent. "It's alright. Let them pass." She hugged Waviel. "It's been a long time. Come on. It looks like you've had a long journey. Make yourselves at home."

They dined with Sara's army. There were thousands of people there. It was like a sea of life in the dry, abandoned desert.

"She's not trying to hide herself from her enemies," Rebecca said.

"She'll regret that," Jacopo whispered.

They were shown to their tents.

Jacopo was roomed in a tent with three other men, and

Rebecca slept with several female Resistance fighters who she didn't know.

The next morning, Jacopo found Rebecca at breakfast. He sat next to her and ate. He gulped down the food and said, "Meet me tonight outside your tent."

Rebecca nodded.

That night, she waited outside her tent. Jacopo had his head down as he approached. He sat next to her. "I need you to do something for me. It's very important." Jacopo ripped the string from around his neck and pulled the vial of poison from beneath his shirt.

"No," she whispered.

"Take it. If she sees me, she might recognize me. She'd suspect me right off." He forced the vial into her hands. "Slip it into her drink."

"But how am I supposed to do that?"

"I see servers going to her tent at dinnertime. Be one of them. Put it in the cup you serve her."

"But don't you want to show her how much better you are."

"Don't play games with me, Rebecca."

"You're sure this is what you want to do?"

"Yes," he hissed.

THERE was a tent where all the food was prepared. In front of the tent was a fire pit where everything was cooked. The food and drinks were then placed on platters inside the tent. They were served to the soldiers who sat at the long wooden tables.

The servers carried platters into the main tent to serve Sara and her company.

Without saying a word, Rebecca walked into the tent in

the hustle and bustle of the preparations. There was a serving platter with goblets full of honey mead. She looked around the tent.

The servers were focused on their tasks, getting food to the plates and platters, cutting vegetables, pouring mead. No one was looking at Rebecca.

She pulled the vial from her pocket and poured the poison into one of the goblets. She glanced around. She focused on the cup.

A knife rested on the table. She picked it up and pricked her finger. Using the blood, she marked the cup at its base. The blood pooled into a small engraving like the tiniest bit of spilled wine.

A procession of servers walked in line to serve the main tent. Rebecca grabbed the tray and joined them. Carrying their platters, they filed into the main tent.

Rebecca looked down. There was laughter and chattering. She strained her eyes upward, trying to keep her head down.

A large table sat in the center of the room. Some of Sara's companions were seated, talking and laughing like they had no enemies.

When Rebecca saw Jin, she looked away.

That's when she spotted her son.

Rodan had not sat yet. He approached Sara and hugged her. His smile was full of warmth, and when he opened his eyes, Rebecca saw something there she couldn't deny.

She was approaching the table. She tried to tip the tray just enough to knock the poisonous cup from it, but to no avail.

While the other servers were placing plates of food in front of the hungry guests, Rebecca put her platter at the end of the table. She kept her head low as she turned away from them. With her back turned, she knocked the deadly goblet from the platter and rushed from the tent.

70

REFRAIN

I was Engrossed in what the Creator was Telling Me. Power was not Even an Object to Him. He had It. He did not need to make Us Kneel. He did not need Us.

I wanted Him to Tell Me what the Gifts Do for us and Why. But I would Have to Be Patient.

SARA felt like she was walking through thick mud. All around her was nothingness, and it stretched for miles. She knew it did, just the way all people know things in dreams. What surprised her was that she knew it *was* a dream. She was becoming increasingly aware of her dreams. She was engrossed in it enough to feel the effect, but not so much that she was lost in it.

As she walked through the thick nothingness, she had the

distinct feeling she didn't want to be there, and although she knew none of it was real, that didn't make the feeling disappear.

"I know how you feel," said a small voice behind her.

Sara tried to turn around. It took her so long in the thick muck she thought the speaker would be long gone before she could set eyes on her.

It was the little girl with thick black hair tainted red by the sun. "I was watching you from the window."

"What window?" Sara asked.

But the girl ignored her question. "You look lost," the girl said.

"I don't know where I am."

"Just look around."

Sara looked up and around her. The nothingness was filled with buildings, streets, and lights. It was a city like none she had ever seen. The buzz of engines echoed in the distance. "Where are we?"

"Omega City."

"Omega Ray?"

"It wasn't always called that," the girl said.

"Are you from Omega City?"

The girl laughed. "Of course not."

"Why are you showing me this?"

The girl looked up. "All this is gone, hidden, but we don't miss it. We don't even know. We're so interested in preserving our lives as we know them, that we never think about what could be, if we just let go."

"Is that what I should do?" Sara asked.

"Have you ever thought about it?"

"Yes."

The girl's face was serious. Her features were so familiar.

She looked like Spire when she was mad.

SARA awoke suddenly.

Spire and Decca slept across from Sara's cot. Their partition wall was pushed aside. Canace's basket was in front of the blankets where they lay. There was a small hole in the basket where the weaving had become worn. The opening was big enough for Canace to put her fist through. Her head was turned towards Sara, but her eyes were closed.

"What's wrong?" Bolton asked, sitting up next to her.

"I had a bad dream. That's all."

"You've been having a lot of those lately."

"Yeah. It's the weirdest thing. It's like they're not dreams really, but conversations. A lot of things I learn from them come true."

"Conversations with who?" he asked.

"I don't know."

"You can't see the person?"

"No, I mean. I don't know who she is. It's a little girl. Maybe five years old. I don't know."

"You're under a lot of stress right now," Bolton said.

"I don't think it's that. I think these dreams are telling me something. But I don't know if I should listen. Something's happening. The Creator, he's preparing for something."

"For what?"

"It's going to be bad for all of us."

A long silence lingered between them.

Sara sighed. She gave Bolton a quick kiss and got out of bed.

"Wait. Where are you going?" he asked.

"You want to get out of here?"

Bolton chuckled and ran his hand through his hair. He

smiled down at the blanket and shook his head. He got out of bed and followed Sara.

They walked across the desert to a ruin partially buried in the sand. Sand was falling from the top of the building to the ground.

"What is this place?" he asked.

"Well, I don't know what it used to be, but I think it's an interesting place."

"Why do you say that?"

"You see the sand falling down," Sara said. "Well, it's falling because the building is leaning ever so slightly, and the sand that is kicked up by the wind lands on top of the building. On a breezy day, the sand on the ground is swept back into the streets. It's like a never-ending hour glass."

"Hmm . . . Wow."

"It wasn't always like this. At one time, this wasn't desert, but plains full of growth. The slight architectural mistake meant nothing for this building. It was just a flaw that no one could see. But now . . . it's beautiful."

"A lot of people had to die for it to be beautiful."

"You're right." Sara watched the sand fall to the ground. Without the wind to carry it away it pooled on the floor of the building.

SPIRE cradled Canace in her arms. Sara sat beside her at the table. "You look upset," Spire said.

"Do I?" Sara said. "I think I'm just forgetting to smile lately. I've been thinking a lot."

"About what?"

"All this."

"Your army?"

"*My* army." Sara laughed. "I don't think they're going to

like my next move."

"What move is that?"

"I was in Vella City during the battle. The only members of the Council left are in Lumina, and their soldiers are mostly gone. I don't think they're the real threat anymore."

"You say that like there's something worse we should be worrying about."

"There is," Sara said. "I felt something in Omega Ray that has never left me. I have these dreams. And I think that our real enemy is about to make a move. I don't want us to be exhausted from a petty battle with what's left of Morica."

"You plan to go up against the Creator, but that's sacrilege," Spire said.

"I don't think we have a choice. What happens might bring a paradise. I don't know, but even if it does, we could lose so much." Sara didn't want Spire to hate her decision. Spire had trained her. She had been there for her through battles and tears.

Spire closed her eyes. "You need to do what you think is best." She turned to Sara. "I have nothing left to teach you."

Sara held her hand out and let Canace grip her finger. "Yes, you do."

71

BLOODLINE

"For I Know the Plans I have for You. Plans You cannot be Privy to, but Plans to bring You Prophecy, Hope, and a Future."

SPIRE woke to whimpering. She rocked Canace until she calmed. Decca rolled over in his sleep. He had been startled by the slightest whimper, but Spire knew what it signaled.

She understood Canace like she could read her feelings in her eyes. Spire smiled. She was starting to feel like a mother.

The camp had newcomers from Wyvek and villages scattered across Mirmina. There were now thousands of soldiers both Elemental and non-Elemental. Some brought their families. They pooled their resources together to get food and weapons. Solace had emptied his wares and joined Sara. Others brought as much food and supplies as they could carry from their homes. The number of tents grew, and soldiers shared sleeping quarters.

Spire and her family were in the main tent with Sara and Bolton. Farah also slept there with Orka. Spire tried to help where she could, but taking care of Canace made things difficult. She was more restless lately, and if she got a mind to, she would have them all choking on dust and sand.

Spire cradled Canace and left the tent for some fresh air. Yerish stood guard outside. "Good morning," Spire said.

"Not quite morning yet," Yerish said.

"I couldn't stay in there another minute." The air was hot and thick, but it was worse in the tent. *How could the others sleep while they were baking?*

She walked between the rows of tents. Rai sat outside of her tent, sharpening the edge of her sword with a bit of flint.

"Can't sleep?" Spire asked.

"Trying to forget last night," Rai said, sending sparks against her blade.

"What happened?"

"Vassal kissed me. Not my proudest moment. I was drunk and stupid."

"Was *he*?" Spire asked. "Drunk?"

"Yeah." Rai laughed.

"He doesn't remember then."

"I remember," Rai said.

"But if *he* doesn't, you don't have to stay up about it anymore."

Canace started crying. "Shh," Spire cooed.

A man strolled between the rows of tents. He glowed as he walked. "Who is that?" Rai squinted.

"I don't know."

Spire rushed between the tents to the main tent. The man

was standing outside. He was old, but he stood upright, and his gait was strong.

Yerish pulled his sword from it sheath. "How did you get in here?"

"I'm here to see Sara."

Spire eyed the man. "I'll get her." She walked behind Yerish and into the tent.

Sara was sleeping next to Bolton behind the partition. Spire shook her arm. "Sara." She opened her eyes and blinked twice. She sat up, waking Bolton.

"What is it?" Sara asked.

"There's someone here to see you."

"Who?"

"A man. He has a strange scar on his face like a teardrop."

Sara pulled on her robe. She emerged from the tent with Spire, Bolton, and Decca.

"Destan," she breathed his name.

Yerish stepped aside, but he still had his weapon drawn.

Destan wasted no time with pleasantries. "Where is Lucerna?"

"Why?" Sara asked.

"We need her," Destan said.

"Who's we?"

"My brothers and sister."

Sara waited.

"The Creator is in Omega Ray," Destan said. "Lucerna is the only one who can help us."

"I don't know where she is."

"Dawn said you would."

"I don't," Sara said. "What is he doing in Omega Ray?"

"Gathering the darkness around him. He's going to expand the energy, then he's going to replace us. He's going to wipe the slate clean." Destan turned his head. At first, Spire thought he might be looking at her, but then she realized he was looking at her baby. "Where did it come from?" he asked.

Sara followed Destan's gaze.

"What are you talking about?" Decca shouted.

Bolton placed his hands on Sara's shoulders.

Destan pointed. His eyes were pinned on Canace. His pupils moved rapidly in fear. "Who?" he breathed, but that was all he could say.

"I think it's time for you to go now," Sara commanded.

Destan acted as if he had not heard her.

"Spire, go back inside." Decca ushered his wife and child back inside the tent.

"Go now," Sara repeated. There was fear in her voice.

"WHAT was he talking about?" Spire whispered though they were far out of earshot.

"I don't know," Decca said.

"He was looking at our baby . . . and he was scared." Spire had tears in her eyes. "Why was he scared?"

"He didn't know what he was talking about. Why don't you give me Canace and you lay down for a while?"

Spire nodded. She gave Decca the baby and lay down on the blanket.

Spire tossed and turned in her sleep. She saw a woman with long black hair holding Canace. "That's my baby," Spire said. "That's my baby!" she shouted. "That's my baby!"

"Spire! Spire!"

She opened her eyes. Decca stood over her. "Where's Canace?" She jolted up.

"She's with Farah." Decca put his hands on her shoulders and eased her back down onto the pillow. He placed one hand on her forehead. "You're burning up."

"It's hot in this tent," Spire said.

"You have a fever." Decca moved to get up.

Spire grabbed his arm. "Where are you going?"

"To see if I can find a doctor."

"I don't need a doctor." Spire shook her head.

"Yes, you do. You have a fever."

Spire watched Decca disappear behind the partition wall. She didn't remember drifting back to sleep. She was in a dark room. Two eyes glowed from the darkness. There was a growl. It had thick fur.

Canace was crying.

Spire opened her eyes, but only for a moment. A man stood over her, and Decca was looking at her over the man's shoulder. His eyes were full of worry.

Spire tried to keep her eyes open, but sleep had command over her. She drifted back to the dream.

The bear struggled on the ground. It shed its skin. Large lumps of fur covered the ground around it. Spire blinked, and in its place was a crying baby. She picked it up thinking it was Canace, but it wasn't.

Spire shot up in bed. Her hair, face, and chest were wet. The water was so cold. The man was standing over her with a bucket. Decca rushed to her side and stroked her wet hair. "It's okay. It's okay. The doctor had to get the fever down."

"I want my baby," she said.

Decca continued to stroke her hair. "Soon. You get better first."

SPIRE was in and out of sleep over the next few days. Finally, she managed to sleep through the entire night. The next morning, she got out of bed without feeling faint.

Spire walked out of the tent. Soldiers rushed back and forth, packing their bags with food and supplies. Tents went down all around her. They were rolled up and tied so they fit nicely on the backs of the fighters.

"Spire!" Decca was running to her. "How are you feeling?" he asked.

"I'm fine. What's going on here?"

"We're going to Omega Ray."

"What?"

"Sara commanded us to move out in the morning."

"We have no business getting in the way of the Creator," Spire said.

Decca looked at the ground.

"What?" she asked. "What aren't you telling me?"

"I don't want to worry you."

"Well, now I'm worried. Tell me."

"Sara said maybe that man was looking at Canace because he knows the Creator chose her to be a Keeper."

"No." Spire shook her head.

"Yeah."

"Then I don't want my child anywhere near him."

"We don't have a choice," Decca said. "I'm going to make sure he never lays his hands on her."

There were tears in Spire's eyes. "I knew it. I knew there was something wrong with her."

Decca put both hands on her arms and looked Spire in the eyes. "There's nothing wrong with Canace."

THE army moved toward the Lake. They moved together as one, taking rests along the way until they made it to the Crystal Forest. They slept in the forest. A few men kept watch.

Spire slept close to Decca. Canace was next to them in a

basket with blankets. Spire felt Decca's chest rise and fall. She listened to the sound of his heartbeat until she fell asleep.

She was startled by the sounds of twigs breaking. She looked out into the darkness. A pair of eyes glowed in the distance. Beneath Canace's basket was a murky darkness.

She jolted up and rushed over to Canace. She picked the baby up from its basket.

Canace cried.

Decca awoke.

Spire turned her back to the glowing eyes and chanted. "Not my baby. Not my baby." She was kissing Canace's head.

"Spire, let me have the baby." Decca held his hands out.

"Stop treating me like I'm crazy."

Decca stared at her, his hands still reaching out. "I know you're not. That's why I'm scared."

THEY set up camp in Jetty Verte, close to the forest. The other tents surrounded Sara's. Using stones and fallen branches, they built a barricade facing north.

"They want to meet with you beyond the barricade," Yerish said.

"The Keepers?" Sara whispered.

"Why do they want to meet?" Farah asked.

"They're being replaced," Sara said, "but not all of them know that. They're siding with the Creator."

Spire looked down at Canace. The baby was asleep in her arms. "Then we should tell them," Spire said. "We should show them." The look on Sara's face told her she didn't seem to like the idea. Had she stopped trusting her?

Decca took Spire's arm and led her out of the tent. Once they were away from the others, Decca's grip became tighter. His fingertips pressed into her arms. "You will not bring our baby out there," he hissed. "Give me Canace."

"No." Spire moved away from him.

Decca sat with her as Sara and fifty of her soldiers marched toward Omega Ray to meet with the Keepers. He watched Spire as she cradled Canace in her arms, but after a time, he allowed his gaze to wander.

"I'm thirsty," Spire said.

Decca leaned towards her and gripped her hand. "I'll get you something."

She watched Decca walk away. She stood and made for the barricade. Finding no way to climb over it while holding Canace, she found a small opening near the ground. "It's okay," she whispered and kissed her forehead. She placed Canace through the opening to the other side. She climbed over the barricade and dropped to the ground.

She ran to Canace. The baby wasn't crying. She was looking up at her mother as if to say, how did you know? Spire hugged her baby close to her chest and ran to where Sara's army had gathered.

She couldn't see the Keepers beyond the crowd. She pushed through them and breached the wall of soldiers like water through a dam.

A cracked voice was saying, "We are asking that you not march upon Omega Ray."

The Keepers stood before them, all but Destan. Sara was standing tall among the crowd. Though she had seen the power of the Keepers, she looked unafraid. "What the Creator plans to do, is not good for the balance," Sara spoke loud and clear. "And, for all our sakes, it is a risk we can't let him take."

"What do you think it will do?" Glaciem asked. Spire read the fear in his eyes, but then Fulgur interjected. "Our father knows what is best for us all. Even the ants that live among us masquerading as his children."

There was much talk among Sara's army. As she raised up her hand to silence them, Spire, holding Canace, emerged from the crowd.

The Keepers stared at the baby. Their faces twisted like they smelled something bad.

"You love the Creator," Spire said. "We all appreciate what he's done for us." She looked out into the crowd. We all do. But maybe he doesn't love you as much as you do him. "He's trying to replace you. Look!" She held up Canace. "He has new children now." She lowered the baby back into her arms.

Decca rushed through the crowd. He snatched the baby from Spire, and grabbed Spire's arm, pulling her away.

But Spire wrenched away from her husband. "That is what the father you love so much has done."

Glaciem, Vjetar, and Vuur opened their mouths in shock. Dawn was emotionless, but Fulgur's face was twisted in an anger that, once suppressed, rushed forward like an uncontrollable wave.

And slam.

The tide curled back and flashed toward the shore.

Lightning rocketed towards the innocent babe in her father's arms.

Spire watched in slow motion as the death blow came hurdling towards her baby. Canace's eyes lit, and a playful smile danced across her face. There was nothing wrong with her. She was perfect.

Spire ran in front, shielding her child. The bolt struck her, and she slumped to the floor.

72

CALLING

"Thieves come in the Night to Kill and Steal, But I come so You may Have Life."

SARA watched as her mentor, her adopted sister, slumped to the ground, hit by the errant bolt. The only sound was Decca's scream. He knelt to the body of his wife. Tears fell from his eyes as he clenched Canace in his arms. The baby wasn't looking at her mother. She was staring at the Keepers and reaching out her arms.

The other Keepers glanced at Fulgur, angered by his rash move, but then they fixed their stares on the enemy. Canace's eyes were still focused on the Keepers. Her small fingers still straining forward. As her father let out his tear-laden scream, Wind raced across the plain. It knocked the Keepers off their feet and pummeled them toward the mountain in one swift swoop. They were out of sight when Sara's army raised their weapons into the air, ready to charge. Metal chimed, swords flashed in the sun, and the elemental energy of the crowd surged through the seas.

"No!" Sara shouted before her army could advance. She rushed over to Spire, to where Decca was kneeling beside his wife. Spire's eyes were open but there was no life in them. Sara put her hand over the lids and closed them. She closed hers as well. After a moment, Sara rose.

The crowd, some with their heads bowed, waited. Sara sniffled and fought back the onslaught of tears. "Go back!" The soldiers retreated to their camps.

Yerish tried to lift Spire's body from the ground, but Decca placed his hand over her. Yerish turned and walked back with the others.

Bolton placed his hand on Sara's shoulder. She cried then.

Farah and Rodan tried to get Decca to get up, to let Farah take Canace, but he refused. "She'll get hungry, Decca," Farah said, trying to sound strong. He allowed Farah to take the baby.

Vassal, Pentagon, and Atrus walked away with the others. Rai bowed her head and joined them.

Sara looked toward the mountain where Canace had sent the Keepers. The mountain looked like a watercolor painting through the tears. She wondered how far Canace pummeled them. It wasn't possible what she did.

Farah looked down at Decca, her eyes full of concern and sadness. Rodan put his arm around her shoulders and walked with her back to the camp.

The sun was shining. It wasn't right. The clouds should be coming in. The night should be dawning. Everything should be dark and terrible.

The salty scent of the sea wafted in the air. The grass was soft beneath Sara's feet. And Spire looked like she was sleeping. And nothing in the world mattered. Sara wished she could believe that.

SARA waited. Decca didn't move. It had been over an hour. Bolton waited with her, but finally he said, "Sara, you have to eat something."

"I don't feel like eating," she said.

"Well, you have too. Decca, you too."

Decca didn't look up. He didn't move.

"Come on." Bolton put his arm around Sara's shoulder and led her away.

The camp was hectic. Soldiers trained. Dinner was prepared. But when Sara came back to the camp, everyone fell silent.

Sara retired to her tent. Decca didn't come back. After dinner, Sara walked out across the plain. He was kneeling beside the body.

Sara dropped to her knees. "Decca," she said, her voice barely above a whisper. "I'm sorry." Decca didn't turn to her. His eyes were dry and ached from the crying. Sara's ached too. "There's food for you back at the camp."

Silence.

Sara looked down at her hands. Tears were fighting their way back into her eyes. "They want to bury her." Her voice cracked. "We have to bury her." The soldiers had prepared a grave. Sara hated it. She hated that they were so ready to get rid of Spire. They couldn't send her out to sea as was the practice in Elementa so they had to put her in the ground. "Please," she said through the tears.

Tears fell onto the body as Decca bowed his head lower. But his hands eased themselves under Spire's back, and his powerful arms lifted her from the ground. Her head hung, and her long hair swept down to his knees and wavered like a surrendering flag as he walked back to camp. Sara followed behind him with her head bowed.

THEY buried Spire under the moonlight. Sara remembered when Spire asked her to call Water for the first time, and how surprised she was when Sara said she couldn't. It was only days ago that Spire said she had nothing more to teach Sara. Sara had assumed she meant she had no more to teach her about her element, but maybe she meant something more.

Farah was crying. Orka perched on her shoulder. Rodan folded his hands. Bolton had his arm across Sara's shoulders as she sobbed. But Decca was the most miserable. Shilo rubbed his shoulder, trying to comfort him. Decca couldn't cry anymore because all his tears had dried up. All he had left was the aching behind his eyes, but more distinct still was the twisting pain in his heart. Canace, too, was inconsolable. She cried all day. An older woman named Rebecca helped to care for her. Only Rebecca could quell her tears.

Sara stayed in her tent all day though it was getting hot beneath the thick folds. The soldiers and her companions went out to feel the chilled air from the mountain on their skin.

Sara screamed her silent screams alone.

Millions of times, she went over what she could have done differently. She should have spent more time with Spire in those critical moments. Spire was ill, and she hadn't visited her once. She was having feverish thoughts about Canace. Sara wished she had quelled those thoughts, that she had told

Spire the Keepers knew their fate and nothing could sway them. *But then why meet with them in the first place?*

With her head in her hands, she sat, contemplating how many more lives would be lost because she wanted to stop the Creator. Suddenly, a rough hand gripped her arm and pulled it away from her face.

Steel flashed.

A dagger was pointed at her chest.

Hate and anger coiled in his eyes. Jacopo from Hephaestus's army, a shadow of her past that had followed her into the present.

Sara's hands grabbed his arms as he tried to push the dagger home. Sara's own conscience wanted her dead, thinking that by her death, everyone would just go home. But what would be home? Would home be some cold place where all life would die? Would it be a place where time would run backwards, and they would all cease to exist? Or would it be a place commanded by a god with no freewill to speak of? These were the consequences of the Creator's three worlds. To let either one happen would mean to ignore the gift she was given.

Unbridled rage seared Jacopo's eyes. It would never stop. She had destroyed his happiness. She had to. His rage would have consumed nations.

Jacopo's body filled with water, so much he was drowning in it. Water issued forth from his mouth and pooled down onto Sara.

His arms slackened, and his eyes no longer held the same hate and anger. They held a look that read: Stop!

Hands grabbed Jacopo and forced him to the ground. It was Bolton. He rushed to Sara. His voice sounded far away. Yerish rushed in. Jacopo was still choking as Yerish dragged him from the tent.

73

BENN

"It is Not Something I have Discovered. It is Something I have Created."

"SO, what happened to the man?" Balin asked.

Bolton threw his apple core into the woods. "Yerish threw him in the dungeons of Jetty Verte below the ground. Rodan helped him secure one of the cells."

Benn approached. "Bolton, I need to talk to you." Bolton looked up at Benn with a look of quizzical disdain. Benn's gaze did not falter. He did not become stern or afraid. Bolton ruffled Balin's hair and followed his father among the tents.

"I'm telling Balin where he comes from," Benn said.

"Balin knows where he comes from."

"He doesn't know I raised him."

"Are you doing this for him or you?"

"For him."

"Liar," Bolton said. "You've barely spoken to him since you laid eyes on him."

"I'm trying."

"Try harder."

Bolton walked away from his father. He journeyed through the trees and sat among the crystals. Rodan sat beside his friend. "What's keeping you up at night?"

"This war. Spire's gone. So . . ."

Rodan had his head down. "That's not it."

"What?"

"You're still mad at your father."

"Yeah. I'm still mad at him," Bolton said.

Rodan put his arms on his raised knees. "But you're mad at him for a whole other list of reasons than you were before."

Bolton considered. "Well, it's not like I forgave him for the other reasons. I . . . my brother."

"You hate what your father did to him too."

"He lied to him. He was there all along, and he was too much of a coward to say anything."

"You're mad because he almost had what you could have had."

"Almost."

"Did you tell Balin about it?" Rodan asked.

"That his father was right there the whole time," Bolton said. "Hell no. That would just hurt him that his father lied to him. That he was playing dress up as some old man to hide himself from him."

"Because that would have hurt *you* if you knew the truth?"

"I hate that," Bolton said.

"What?"

"I hate when you talk that way. You were always good for

that. I missed when you were mad at me for stealing Sara. You weren't this damn sentimental then."

Rodan smirked and shook his head. Bolton wondered if that bothered him more than he was showing.

"I abandoned my mom, you know," Rodan said.

"What do you mean?"

"I left. First to Element then to the Resistance and now this."

"You didn't abandon her. You went to school. You got a . . . calling." The word tasted bad in his mouth.

"I'm sure she wouldn't see it that way," Rodan said. "When I was a kid, she used to say my dad abandoned us, and she begged me not to go when it was my turn. I still remember how white her hands were when I left. She hadn't eaten for days."

"That's not like what Benn did," Bolton said.

"I'm just saying everyone sees it the way they want to see it. It doesn't mean anyone's wrong." Rodan stood.

"You're going to leave me with that?" Bolton looked up at him.

"You'll figure it out." Rodan disappeared among the trees and headed back for camp.

After a few moments, Bolton sighed and walked back. He discovered Balin and Benn, talking and laughing in the distance. They sat side-by-side like they had never been apart. And truly they hadn't really, not for long.

THE next morning, the soldiers prepared to march on Omega Ray. The sky was black in the middle of the day. A dark cloud spread from the city. The snow on the mountain looked dark, and no stars shown through the clouds at night.

Bolton knew of Sara's fears. He didn't share them. He

had his own set of fears. He didn't know what was coming. The hardest thing to do was pretend everything was normal. It was easier the first time they journeyed to Omega Ray. At least he had a plan and a purpose. Now, how could he have a plan? He didn't know what they were up against.

Farah talked about energy, creating energy, and what that might do to Mirmina, but he didn't really comprehend any of it. Sara was having these dreams, but how she could know what they meant? *He* certainly didn't.

Benn stood next to him and watched the growing cloud. "There it is, I guess. The energy we're supposed to be afraid of."

"How can darkness create energy?"

"Sara told me that's all it was to begin with," Benn said. "We just can't see it."

"The darkness itself is some kind of expanding energy?"

"I think that's right."

Bolton smirked and shook his head.

"You don't believe that?" Benn asked.

"I don't know what I believe. I know what I want. I want this whole thing to be over. I want to go home with my wife, and raise a family. I thought I was done."

"Done?"

"Yeah," Bolton said. "When I woke up, I didn't know it had been three years. I thought we had just won the battle, and I was some kind of hero, and all of the bad stuff I did would be forgiven. I thought I'd just be with Sara. My biggest fear was Rodan duking it out with me again."

The cloud had only grown. It was mere feet from the sun.

"Did you tell Balin?" Bolton asked.

"Yeah. I never thanked you for bringing him back here. I wanted to do that."

"Did you think about it?"

"Yeah," Benn said, "I went over it again and again in my mind."

"You went through how you would epically thank me," Bolton said, "and that all the bad blood between us would just disappear?"

"It sounds like a fool's wish," Benn said.

The silence hung like lead.

"Did you love her? My mother?" Bolton gulped.

"Everyday. I still do. And I miss her so much. And every day I think about what I should have done."

"You should have gone back for her."

"Yeah." Benn choked back the tears.

"Am I supposed to forgive you now?"

"No," Benn said. "I can make any excuses I want, but I left your mother because I was scared. I did it for me."

Bolton gulped. He didn't feel the urge to lash out, to pummel Benn's face for his confession. Benn admitted it. He didn't dance around it with quiet words and circumspection. Bolton didn't want to pardon Benn either, but part of him was at peace.

When he turned to his father, it was like looking in a mirror twenty years later. He looked him in the eye, his expression even and calm. "I'll never forgive you for that . . . but I'm not going to get in the way of what you and Balin have." Bolton looked towards the cloud. It was growing and growing.

74

WHITE HILLS

"Life is Not Something to Be Confined to One Body. I have Lived for a Time this Way, and For a Time, I will Live Another."

THE sky was darkening as Rebecca looked toward the mountain. The cloud was darker than night, but she felt a certain sense of calm watching it. She hated that Jacopo brought her here. She would have happily stayed with him in the small village, but now everything was different. They locked him away in the dungeons below the ground.

Rebecca wasn't sad to see him go. It was as if she had already wept for him. Or maybe it was only because she had done enough weeping in her lifetime to cover the sadness for everyone she knew or would ever know.

Once they had arrived in Jetty Verte, Rebecca had

stopped hiding among the crowd and had revealed her presence to Rodan. She was glad for the reunion with her son. She didn't know him anymore, but she still loved him.

She rubbed her arms. They were covered in goosebumps. It shouldn't be this cold so far from the mountain with the forest at their backs. But frost covered the treetops. It happened overnight when everyone was asleep, and in the morning, the plain had grown cold, and it was getting colder.

Something rustled in the trees.

Rebecca turned around.

A man emerged from the shadows. He was wrapped in canvas and staggering into the open. His whole body shook in awful tremors. His fingertips and lips were blue almost purple. Light frost hung from his eyelashes. As he approached, he brought the cold with him.

Rebecca ran into the camp and alerted the fighters. She pointed to the man struggling near the forest. They brought him into the camp. Bolton knelt beside him. It was his element that made him suffer. Rebecca had never seen anything like it before: A Frost Elemental.

Bolton helped him calm the cold. Later, he was wrapped in blankets and his hands were wrapped around a hot cup of boiled nectar. His name was Tacitum. He was a painter and a friend of Sara. He didn't know where else to go.

While the others were busied with him, Rebecca snuck away to the dungeon. She climbed down. Along each side of the dungeon were rusty cells. A hand reached out to her.

"Rebecca!" It was Jacopo.

She took his hand. "Are you alright?" she asked.

"You have to get me out of here."

"I can't do that."

"What do you mean *can't*?"

Jacopo had worked on the bars, but his element wasn't strong enough to melt them in one sitting, not without adequate food and a comfortable place to rest. She was sure the rats were nibbling on him at night. There were tiny bite marks along his neck and arms.

"I can't do that," she said, "but I needed to see you."

"If you let me out of here. We can see much more of each other."

Rebecca shook her head.

Jacopo sighed. "Why?"

If she let him out, he would try to destroy Sara again, which might only get him thrown back down here or worse. He would never leave with her. They could never be anything.

Rebecca looked down. "I'm too old for you." She wrenched her hand from his and walked back towards the light.

Jacopo reached for her. His screams echoed through the dungeon as she shut the hatch.

75

A MESSAGE

"Although the Purpose in the Spheres was Not My Own, It was my Intention that the Gifts be Bestowed Upon You so You might Participate in what is to Come."

SARA looked out into the darkness. Through the mist and haze, five others approached her. They were beckoning her. They were not threatening. They were family. White worms glowed at their feet.

Who were they?

A warm hand clasped onto hers.

"Don't be afraid." The little girl looked on into the darkness with her.

"Do you know who they are?" Sara asked.

She nodded. "They are our brothers and sisters."

"Why are you showing me this?"

"He wants you to know who you are." The little girl disappeared.

The faces of the five came into view. Vassal first, then Tacitum. And Shashi, the little girl Bolton helped. Balin was among them. And one left in the shadows . . . *Canace?*

Sara jolted from bed.

They were the new Keepers.

THE sun blinded Sara as she emerged from her tent. She had been awake all night thinking about her dream. She needed to get everyone together, to find out if they were having the same dream.

Tacitum . . . his paintings.

"Yerish!"

Yerish was walking past her tent. He stopped when he heard Sara shout out to him.

"I need to call a meeting. I want to keep it quiet for now. Can you help me gather the attendants?"

SARA stood at the head of the long table inside the tent. She hadn't told any of them why she had gathered them here. Rai leaned against one of the posts with her arms folded. She didn't like how Vassal was glancing at her lately, but it had been her fault.

Sara spoke. "I brought you all here because I need answers. I believe some of you can provide those answers, and the others who I have asked to be here I trust with what I'm about to tell you." She reached under the table and pulled out several rolled canvases. She spread out each one and placed rocks at each corner of the canvases to secure them. As she unrolled them, she asked, "Have any of you seen any of these images?"

They were Tacitum's paintings. The others got closer to the table to look at them. Farah pointed to one of them. "Those are the white worms we saw in the sphere sanctums."

"This one," Vassal said with a shutter in his voice. He motioned to the one of the five shadowy figures elongated across the canvas.

"Where did you see them?" Sara asked.

Vassal kept his eyes on the painting. "I didn't see them here."

"Well, what is it?" Rai asked. "You either saw them or you didn't see them."

"I mean . . . I didn't see them in the real world. It was a nightmare I had. It happened on the night my element came back."

Balin looked at the paintings. "I've seen every one of these in dreams. I've seen the little girl. She told me about the people in the shadows."

"Who are they?" Benn asked.

Balin and Vassal shook their heads.

"I saw who they were last night," Sara said. "And I think I know why we are having the same dream."

"The three of you?" Pentagon asked.

"The four of us." Tacitum shivered. "I painted these from the dreams I was having."

"It's the Creator," Sara said. "He's putting these images in our heads because he's trying to get us to come together."

"Why?" Pentagon asked.

"We are his new children. His chosen ones."

"Keepers." The words came from Benn's lips like air out of his lungs. "Like what that monster did to me."

"Wait, wait," Atrus said. "You mean Keepers like Protectors of the Spheres? They're not *real*."

"Yes, they are," Sara said. "I met one. She told me what her father . . . what the Creator meant to do. His children sealed him in a tomb, and now he's angry, and he chose us to replace them."

"So, a Keeper for each sphere," Rodan said. "That would make Sara the Water Keeper, Tacitum would be the Frost Keeper, Vassal . . . Fire, Balin . . . Lightning."

"The Earth Keeper is Shashi," Sara said, "the little girl from Tosia who Bolton was helping with her element."

"Shashi?" Bolton recalled the young girl and her hopeful mother.

"But what about the Wind Keeper?" Thatch asked.

Farah looked up from the paintings.

"I believe it's Canace," Sara said. "The little girl in all the dreams . . . I think it's her."

"It can't be," Decca said. "Canace is an infant."

"The little girl in the dreams . . . she looks just like Spire," Sara said. Her eyes watered when she said it. "Somehow she has manipulated her appearance so she looks much older."

"No," Benn said. "He's not turning my son into one of them."

"That's not even on the table," Bolton said.

"What are we going to do about it?" Rai asked. "I doubt the Creator is the bargaining type. This isn't like battling Hephaestus. You knew his limitations. We don't know what the Creator is capable of."

"We don't," Bolton agreed. "But we do know he can be locked up."

"We're going to lock him up?" Rai asked.

"If that's what we must do," Sara said. "There's a dungeon. I know how to seal it."

"What if he gets out again?" Decca asked. "We should

have guards to make sure that doesn't happen."

"The Resistance would do it," Atrus. said

"That would be Plan B," Sara said.

"What's Plan A?" Pentagon asked.

"We're going to try to kill him."

"You can't kill him," Decca said. "He's the Creator. He's lived for thousands of years. If he could die, he would have done it by now."

"There might be a way," Sara said, "but we have to find Lucerna. She is the key."

76

WAVERING

"I did not come to Condemn the World. I came to Save It."

"WHAT were you thinking?" Dawn disparaged Fulgur for his behavior in Jetty Verte.

"I was saving us all."

"You were angry," she said. "And rash. If Father wants to replace us, he will. It doesn't matter how many babies you try to kill."

"That was no normal baby," Vjetar said. "I couldn't sense the Wind coming, and I could do nothing to stop it."

"I could sense something more," Vuur said. "I felt our Father when I looked at the child."

"Don't tell him," Dawn warned.

"Why?" Glaciem asked.

"Do you want him to favor her over you?"

Glaciem shook his head. The others stared at Dawn. "We'll go back now. We'll tell our Father Sara denied our request, and we'll say nothing more."

DAWN walked away. Fulgur followed her. Once they were well away from the others, Fulgur pressed her shoulders against one of the stone buildings. He knew it didn't hurt her, and he was sad about that not because he had wanted to hurt her, but because there was something tragic about not being able to feel pain. He shared that tragedy too.

"You're giving up," he sneered.

"I don't know what you mean," Dawn said.

"You want to sleep. That's why you're helping him. You're tired, and you want to sleep."

"I'm not afraid of death, and I am tired, but I have not given up."

"Then, why are you helping him?" Fulgur searched Dawn's sightless eyes. Her lips trembled. "Oh . . ." Realization dawned in his eyes. "Where's Destan?"

"Don't, Fulgur."

"You really think you'll fool Father? You don't want to die any more than I do."

"You don't know anything about that." Dawn shrugged away from his embrace.

Energy surged from the ground beneath them. Dawn searched the darkness as if her dead eyes could see.

"What is it?" Fulgur asked. Could she sense Lucerna's energy deep underground? It was faint, but it drifted on the air. Would Dawn discover what he had done?

"It's nothing." But her lips still trembled and not from the cold.

*   *   *

THE Keepers walked through the snow. In the valley, shadows fought with dark spears and swords. They flattened like true shadows, but without hosts. At any moment, they could rise from the ground and fight like men.

The Creator was down in the center of the city. His eyes were closed. He drew the energy from the spheres miles away to create the cloud. The cloud would soon enclose around Mirmina and block all light.

Vuur had kept the lamps lit in the city to see by and to strengthen the shadows.

They followed Dawn down to where their father was. He hadn't eaten in days. Beside him, Shashi clung to his cloak. Her dirty face was hidden beneath the folds.

"The Water Elemental won't listen to us," Dawn said.

Erebus opened his eyes.

No disapproval shone on his face. It was odd. He didn't look disappointed . . . like he wanted them to fail. But he must be disappointed. Not because he thought his shadow army was weak, but because like Destan, he had chosen Sara to carry the torch, and she had dropped it before his eyes.

His Water children disappointed him because their faith was like water, wavering.

Finally, their Father spoke: "She has sentenced her army to death. Let them come and taste it."

77

RODAN

"Fear is the Only Thing that will Unite You for what is to Come."

RODAN saw Bolton across the plain. He was looking up at the blackened sky looming overhead. Benn had walked away. He tussled Balin's hair, and the boy followed him in the direction where the sky was still bright and untainted. But Bolton couldn't keep his eyes off the gloom.

Bolton had asked Rodan to train with him. Rodan had a sword at his waist and one in his hand. "Hey, you alright?" Rodan asked.

"Hmm," Bolton let the air out of his nose. "I can't believe I'm standing here again. I thought Sara's face would be the first face I saw when I woke after the fall. Instead it was the face of that sightless, old woman. And when I did see Sara again, it was here where all my worst memories are mingled.

I wish someone would just tear it all down. All of it."

"Your brother's strong," Rodan said.

"Yeah, he's doing better now that he's with Benn."

"What was it like after all these years . . . the Insula?"

"I don't know. I didn't stay long."

"You didn't?"

"I know what you're thinking," Bolton said. "I tried so hard to get there, to get the glistenings. Betrayal. You . . . Sara. But when I got there, all I could think about was getting back to her. And then Balin's mother just poured glistenings into my hands like they were nothing."

"You're angry?"

"Aren't you?" Bolton asked. "I didn't want her to do any of this. I tried to stop her three years ago, and it wasn't just because I didn't want her to die. It was because if she lived, she would always have to play the hero. People would expect her to."

Rodan shook his head. "Sara isn't *playing* the hero. She *is* one. She's not doing this because people expect her to. Just like you're not here because people expect you to follow her. You're here because you want to help. Your choices didn't define you. You made this choice because it *is* you." Rodan threw him the sword.

"What's this?" Bolton asked.

"I thought you said you wanted to train."

"Yeah with our elements. I think it's a little too late for me to train with a weapon of steel."

Rodan drew his sword. "The Creator can find ways to manipulate your element. He has the Keepers. It's best to know more than one way to fight."

"And you think you can train me in a day?"

Rodan raised his sword against Bolton and brought it

down upon him. Steel clashed against steel as Bolton raised his sword to defend.

"See? You're learning already," Rodan said.

Bolton laughed. He parried his sword. As they battled, they forgot their worries. It was like they were on the training field of Element again. They were friends again when all that mattered was training and field tests and pride.

The two friends danced across the field. Bolton had gotten the hang of it rather quickly, but he was never trained, so many of his movements were foreign to Rodan. It was like playing chess against someone who didn't know how to play.

Bolton tried to buffet the flat of his sword against Rodan's head. When Rodan rose his arm to block, he felt a sharp ache. He dropped his sword and held his stomach. He lifted his shirt. Blood was seeping through the bandages.

"That doesn't look good," Bolton said.

Rodan put his shirt back down. "Don't tell anyone." He patted Bolton on the shoulder and staggered across the field toward the inn.

Rodan peeled the bandages off the wound himself. The infection had worsened despite it being tended to. He cleaned it up the best he could with water from his canteen. Watery blood dripped down his pants and onto the floor. He re-bandaged the wound. Then, he downed some meli for the pain. He had many more vials of meli in his tent.

THE soldiers were getting ready to march up the mountain. The snow was beneath Rodan's feet. But he was hot. The fever was getting worse. He didn't want Sara to know about it. He wanted to be with her through this.

Jin was instructing the fighters to unpack the tents. They were a few miles from the valley. Rodan didn't want to show his weakness, but he needed to rest or he would die on the slope of the mountain. Sara sat with him. The chilled wind numbed their faces.

Sara wrapped her shawl around her.

"How's Tacitum?" Rodan asked.

"Better," she said. "I can't imagine he's holding out too well in this cold." Sara clenched and unclenched her hands.

"Are you sure about this?" Rodan asked. "The Creator . . . he made us what we are. Why should we be afraid?"

Sara reached into her bag and withdrew her paper and charcoal. She drafted the creature she saw in the depths of Omega Ray. Then, she held the drawing up to Rodan's face. "This is the Creator. He's a monster."

Rodan took her hands and brought them down to her lap.

Sara clenched the drawing. "What he said to me . . . he only wanted power. We're like clay to him . . .we can be created, molded . . . destroyed. He can always make more."

"I remember the first time we climbed this mountain," Rodan said. "I knew what we were going to do. But you know what was odd? I didn't think I was going to die. I knew I wasn't going to die."

"I don't think anyone ever truly believes they're going to die," Sara said.

Rodan shook his head. A thin-lipped smile on his face.

"Rodan . . . I'm scared."

Rodan put his arm across her shoulders.

"I always do this. This is so much bigger than I am," she said.

"What do you mean?"

The snow was falling into her hair, turning it white. "I can't help but remember what happened last time. I was saved. If that Aether . . ."

"You don't really remember what happened that day?" Rodan looked Sara in the eyes.

"Yes," she said, "the Aether defeated him."

"No. Close your eyes. Go back to that day."

Sara closed her eyes. Hephaestus was pulled down into the muck. He had killed Talon. Bolton was his next target. Sara was angry and scared, and she wanted him to die.

Tears fell from her eyes.

"You defeated Hephaestus. Sara, it was always you."

She had willed the Aether with her emotions. Like her element, she had called upon it to do what she couldn't do with her own two hands.

She looked down at her hands, and tears fell into them. Rodan lifted her chin with his finger and touched the side of her face. "You're not that little girl on the water anymore. Look at everything you've done." Rodan's lips pressed against hers. He closed his eyes, and there was nothing else but the warmth of her mouth. Gently, Rodan pulled away from her.

"Rodan . . ."

Rodan searched Sara's eyes. There was no regret.

78

Omega City

"I do not Profess to Know All. But I do Know what is Coming. I have been Preparing for It for Thousands of Years."

SARA knew she was asleep.

There was darkness all around her, yet she could see. The darkness funneled to one perceptible scene: In front of her was a man. He was a strong man wearing a bearskin atop his head and across his shoulders. The bear's mouth was opened, showing off a set of sharp teeth. Its eyes were as black as its fur.

The little girl stood before the man. Her raven black hair was touched by blood. Suddenly, the man wasn't there anymore nor was the little girl. In his place, was the monster Sara met in the pit with his skin falling from his face. The Creator. And in his arms, was a baby without a blanket to keep it warm.

"Canace." The name escaped Sara's mouth like air. She knew it without needing to think about it.

Canace appeared in front of her. She was the little girl again. "He didn't choose me." The glowing worms were at Canace's feet.

"Did you do this?" Sara asked.

Canace nodded. "They're helping me like they helped my Father."

"Decca?"

Canace shook her head. "I mean my First Father, the Creator."

Spire stood in the distance. Her image was faded.

A flash of images assaulted Sara. The Creator, concentrating and cities falling, battered by every one of the elements, except darkness. He kept that one for himself. Hands grasping the spheres, the Creator making promises, reminding them of the devastation he blamed on nature. But it was him. It was him all along.

"Sara."

Canace and the Creator were gone.

Spire stood in front of her, and the darkness was receding. Sara hugged her. "I thought you were gone."

Spire pulled her back to look her in the eye. "I didn't die. Sara, everything in the world is energy: our bodies, our minds. Your spirit can fill all Mirmina and more." She smiled. Then, she looked around as if afraid someone would hear what she was about to say next. "You must find Lucerna. She is under Omega Ray. In the pit."

Spire's voice echoed in her head as she awoke to Canace's cries. She didn't comfort the baby. She shook Bolton awake. He turned toward her. "I'm rallying the men," she said.

"We're marching on Omega Ray tonight."

"Tonight?"

Sara tore the covers from her body. "I know where Lucerna is. We need to have enough men out there so the Creator can't sense my energy. If I go alone, he's sure to find me."

Bolton followed her out of the tent. "You're serious."

"Bolton, I need you with me."

Bolton nodded. "I'm always with you."

"Wake the others. I'm going to alert Jin and Yerish."

"I want to launch a surprise attack," Sara said.

"I don't think those things ever sleep," Yerish said.

"Even if they don't," Sara said, "they know we do. They won't be expecting us to come in the middle of the night." Sara shuttered to think they might have another enemy in their camp. She didn't know Canace's true intentions or why she appeared in her dreams as a little girl. She dared to think Canace might be appearing in the dreams of the Keepers too, and she wasn't sure whose side the powerful child was on. The more sudden their move, the better.

Jin and Yerish woke the soldiers. They prepared to march on Omega Ray.

Rai found Sara among the crowd. "Are you sure about this?"

"I want to send him back to that pit." Sara headed the crowd, and they marched together.

Bolton, Rodan, Farah, and Rai were beside her. Decca and Thatch were not far behind. They were armed with weapons of steel. Sara carried a sword. She was not well practiced. She remembered how she had tried to use a sword with Rodan, but it was only a precaution.

*   *   *

THEIR legs were tired from trudging through the snow of the mountain. The sky was benighted above them, and below, the city was like a cauldron filled with black bile. The shadows moved and twisted in the snow, fighting with their shadowy spears and lances.

From that distance, Sara could not see the Creator, but she could sense him there. The energy around him was strong. The cold wind ripped through the bodies of Sara's men to their very souls. They marched closer to the city, meeting it at its crumbling walls. If Sara sensed him, he must sense her. Yet, he had not made a move. Could it be his arrogance or something more?

"Stop!" Sara whispered to the men around her. The front line stopped, halting the rest of the men in their tracks. They stared beyond the wall at the shadows upon the snow, shadows without bodies.

The clink of metal ceased as did the sound of their heavy footsteps. Their breath was harsh in the cold air. Screams came from the back of the precession.

"Forward!" Sara raised her sword into the air and ran at the impending shadows.

The shadows rose from the ground and stood like men, their shadowy weapons raised. Their substance was not shadow. Their bodies were thick like tar, and it dripped from them.

Sara didn't doubt the blades were more than shadows, but she expected to hear the clash of steel. It wasn't there. She cut through the shadows in front of her only to have more shadows rise around her. Several of her men had fallen, blood issued from their wounds. They were battling the enemy under a sunless sky.

The heat of Fire and the battering of Wind was at Sara's

back. Slicing her blade through the enemy, she moved toward the crumbling castle. The sword swished through the air, but there was no sound of slicing through flesh nor the breaking and splintering of bones beneath their blades.

When Sara would cut an enemy down in front, he would appear behind her or to her side. She lost Bolton in the fray. Sara spun around, but didn't see him. She couldn't waste any more time. The closer she got to the castle, the less shadows she had to contend with. The castle was not well lit. Sara disappeared into the dungeons.

RAI slashed into a shadow with her fiery blade. Atrus fought next to her and out of the corner of her eye, she could see Pentagon.

Vassal was at her back. Energy pulsed from him ever since Rai discovered Vassal's power as a Fire Elemental. How hadn't she sensed it before? But she had. She remembered the warmth as he held her close. She had dismissed it as passion, but it was power.

Wind knocked down the shadow of a man at her side. Rai thanked Atrus.

Bullets popped in the air.

The sound was defeating.

As Rai swung her sword, she stepped over bodies and watched as the shadows with their blackened swords, axes, war hammers came down on the men she fought beside. Even in the heat of battle, she found her eyes searching. *Yes, they're okay*. Pentagon and Atrus had moved further away from her, but they were still fighting. The back of Pentagon's shirt was bloodied. The blood was red. It was likely his own.

Rai sliced through the shadows in front of her and to the

side. She spun around and her blade bit into the shadowy figure behind her. There was one more person she needed to be assured was still in this fight. She sensed his power before she saw him: *Vassal.*

His wooden leg dug into the snow. His left hand gripped his sword, and he assaulted the enemy. Vassal looked less exhausted than some of the more abled bodied men. She found no flaw in his fighting, no difference in his skill. He was just as impressive a fighter as he was in the old days.

Blood sprayed across Rai's face as one of the Rebel Resistance fighters was cut down in front of her. A massive shadow approached her. It couldn't be the shadow of a man. It was too big. A Maledixit.

But it wasn't a shadow.

Before she could attack. The Maledixit turned and accosted another Resistance fighter. Its nails dug into his flesh and it bit down on his shoulder. The man would fall sick and then he would turn. This Maledixit was breeding new monsters. Rai focused on the shadows around her, and by the time she had cut enough down to look back to where she saw the Maledixit, it was gone.

SARA felt along the wall of the dungeons. Something clamored along the ground. Sara reached down and picked it up. Talon's sword.

She felt the etchings on the stone wall. When she felt them, the wall glowed and opened to her. The pit was darker than the dungeons. She journeyed down into it. Her hands shook as they felt along the walls. "Lucerna!" she called at intervals as she journeyed deeper and deeper.

She tripped over something and fell. Her knees hurt when they fell on something hard. Sara remembered the pile of rat bones in the corner of the room. She rose to her feet, and made what she hoped was a wide circle around the pile.

"Lucerna!"

She passed into the tunnel branching from the room. She could touch the walls on both sides. Strangely, there was a glow where the tunnel curved to its end. At first, Sara thought her eyes were getting adjusted to the light, but when she saw the glow she ran to it. She fell and skinned her knee against the rocky floor. She stood back up, ignoring the pain, and moved towards the light. At the foot of the wall, was a small hole, big enough for her to crawl through. Light glowed from it.

Sara scrambled through the opening. Her breath caught in her throat.

It was a city. Possibly the largest city she had ever seen. Dead lamps hung over grey streets. Machines with wheels, like covered IMTs, lined the streets. Buildings stretched to the earthy sky, like a cave. And gathering at the ceiling of the cave were glowing Aethers. There were hundreds of thousands of them, trapped in this underground city. The light was coming from the Aethers as they floated along the ceiling.

"This is Omega City."

She turned around. It was Dawn. Her blue eyes looked up toward the Aethers, and Sara wondered if she could see them.

"I knew you would be able to find her," Dawn said. "With your new-found power, you can better sense Lucerna's element. We have always been able to find our brothers and sisters."

"I haven't found her yet."

"You will." Dawn moved out into the city, and Sara walked with her.

"What happened in Jetty Verte?" Sara asked. "Why did you let Canace do that to you?"

"We didn't," Dawn said without looking at Sara. "She is very powerful."

"But why?"

Dawn was silent for a moment.

"Why?" Fear edged Sara's voice.

"I don't know," Dawn said. "My brothers and I sensed something from the child."

"What?"

"She is his blood. She's a descendant of our Father. And she will do great and perhaps terrible things when she comes of age."

Sara remembered the little girl in her dreams, how knowing she was. The same knowing look tainted Canace's eyes.

RAI pushed forward. She soon lost Atrus and Pentagon in the fray, but Vassal was still close to her side. A few weeks ago, that would have given her no comfort. *Why does it comfort me now?* She so easily fell back into old times. The fight had brought it on. The dark skies, they reminded her of the dungeons, and with Vassal by her side, she would not be left here to die.

Without the thundering of Atrus and Pentagon's bullets, the sounds of the battles lighted once again to her ears. Fighters screamed and grunted. They were making sounds unheard outside of war. The unnatural sounds would haunt Rai's dreams. Some were the desperate sounds she heard in the dungeons, of men and women fighting, some others were the screams of their last hours, maybe minutes alive. Rai almost lost courage.

She stepped over a body as she sliced through another

shadow. She had only glanced at it, but her mind remembered it after. It was the body of Solace, the innkeeper. Beside him rested the large hammer he had wielded. He wasn't a warrior, but he had died one.

As the shadow in front of her slumped to the ground, splitting beneath her sword, Rai saw something glowing white in the distance. It was coming at them like a flood, and then she realized what it was.

Her voice wanted to scream *run!* But she couldn't. It was like she had forgotten the word. Instead, her arms hung to her side. *No.*

"Rai!" Vassal's voice was shouting. "Rai!" She heard it as if she was underwater. His hands grabbed her arms. His touch was even warmer than her own skin. He tossed her body away from the worms and the shadows. And then, he was consumed.

The worms trailed up his body and forced their way into his mouth. Rai was on the snowy ground. Feet trampled around her. Vassal's eyes glowed. It wasn't him anymore. Like it wasn't him outside the inn two years ago.

Rai got to her feet as Vassal's sword came down inches from where she had lay. The worms were controlling his body somehow, but they weren't as dexterous as Vassal was. His blows were no longer graceful and practiced, but he was lumbering towards her.

Rai sent a line of Fire between them. *I don't want to hurt you.* Vassal's face smiled, and he walked through the fire. Flames licked his wooden leg and the folds of his cloak. He made no move to put them out.

Rai raised her fiery sword in warning, but he continued to approach. Their swords clashed. Rai turned with her sword against his and the blades zinged, causing Vassal to drop his.

Parts of Vassal's lower body were still on fire. Rai slammed against him, forcing him to fall into the snow. The snow had extinguished the flames that assaulted Vassal's body, but Rai could still smell burnt wood, cloth, and skin.

Vassal got up and reclaimed his sword.

Rai stepped back. She was tired. Earlier she had been treating this battle like it was a marathon, but when she saw the Maledixit, the fear exhausted her. She hadn't expected one of her own to attack. *But* he's *not attacking me. Just like two years ago. I* was *wrong about him, but not in the way I thought.*

Their blades met again.

Vassal's body was less skillful, but he was still strong. He forced her down into the snow, sword raised above her.

Shadows were coming.

If Rai raised her sword to defeat him, the shadows would consume her. The dark cloud drew near. The walls were closing in on her, and there was no one to save her, not even Vassal.

But the sword did not come down on her.

Vassal had stopped and grimaced. It was like he was fighting with himself. "No!" he let out. He squeezed his eyes shut and backed away from Rai.

They dug inside Vassal's head, wiggling around in his mind. They were controlling him, moving his body like a puppet. But they didn't know his body. They didn't know how to make his movements fluid or to stop the fire from burning him. They didn't react as he would to the pain.

Still, no matter how much he screamed inside, they would not let him go.

As his sword was raised over Rai, he screamed, *No!* His voice echoed in his head, but did not make it out into the world until, he shouted again, "No!" He summoned enough control to stagger back. But they still had their hold on him.

He remembered when the possessed guards had hacked off his legs. He didn't want any harm to come to Rai. His feet moved towards her, unwilled by him. *No!*

He had to do something.

His grip tightened on his sword. He raised it up and pointed to his stomach ready to plunge it in. But then, his head was forced back in a sudden jerk.

The worms evacuated his body. They were coming out of his mouth, his eyes, his ears. Rushing out in a cacophony of unearthly, whistling screams.

Vassal knelt to the cold ground as the force of the worms' escape made his body weak. They were gone. He had control of his own body again, but it took him a second to realize it.

Shadows surrounded Rai. Her sword had fallen away from where she lay. Vassal would not be able to cut them all down in time to save her.

Vassal was afraid. He was so used to a sword, other weapons were foreign and untrusted, even one he was born with. But he couldn't be afraid now. He had learned that fighting Sphere Protectors. *You do what you had to do, and if you don't . . . well, you just died anyway.*

Fire erupted across the expanse. Rows and rows of it. The bodies of the shadows were melting as if they had been made of tar.

Vassal had extinguished the shadows surrounding Rai. She stood and took her sword. Vassal had swept the area in front of them clean, but the cloud was darkening. Vassal didn't think it was possible for it to become any blacker, but it did. And more shadows were rising.

GRASS grew from the cracks in the road. Sara had never seen buildings so high. Towering above her, everywhere they went, were the Aethers. They were banging at the earthen ceiling, like a man struggling against the ice after he had fallen into a frozen lake.

Dawn was right.

Sara hadn't felt it before, but when she concentrated, she could sense powerful bouts of energy. That was why her subconscious had her dream about finding Lucerna here, but she preferred to think Spire had come to her to show her things she couldn't see.

Instead of being led by her eyes, she allowed herself to be led by this feeling as it grew stronger. Curled up, in the darkest corner of the city, under piles of trash, was a girl with white hair. Sara could not see her with her eyes, but she could sense her there.

Sara pulled the trash away.

"No, please," Lucerna screamed. She shielded her eyes from the light.

"Let's get you out of here," Sara said.

"No." Lucerna begged. "I'm not going back into the pit."

"It's okay," Dawn said. "You have to come with us."

"Madam Dawn! I can't see you!"

"Come on." Sara put an arm around Lucerna's shoulders and led her away from the light. Once they were back in the darkness, Lucerna's hands fell away from her eyes. She hugged Dawn.

"I'm sorry," Dawn said, "but there's only one way for us to end this, and that's you, Lucerna." She reached beneath her cloak, and, in her outstretched hand was a glass sphere. "You must give your soul to the sphere."

"No." Sara gripped Dawn's wrist. "No more slaves to the

spheres."

Dawn turned to her with her unseeing eyes.

"You're not gods," Sara said, "you're slaves, and he made you that way."

"But to save us all," Dawn said, "Lucerna must be much more powerful, and the only way for her to be that is to sacrifice her soul to the sphere."

"There has to be another way," Sara said.

"There isn't."

79

THROUGH THE DARKNESS

"Just as the Rain comes down to Water the Earth, making it Flourish and Grow, when You Leave the Earth, Do Not Leave it Empty."

SARA and Lucerna emerged from the dungeons. Dawn could not go with them. She had to rejoin her brothers. Dawn pressed her forehead against Lucerna's. "Don't be afraid," Dawn whispered.

Tears fell down Lucerna's face.

Dawn approached Sara. "Protect her." The darkness was dotted by torches of fiery light as Dawn swept away across the rocky terrain.

Swords clashed against shadow blades. Blood filled the cracks of the abandoned city. Men were screaming their battle cries and grunts as they slashed the enemies. Feet slipped against the blood and the icy ground.

Darkness spread at Sara and Lucerna's feet. The shadows surrounded them. Sara looked to the torches and the clusters of shadows beneath them. "It's the fire," she said under her breath. Sara blasted the nearby torches with Water, and the shadows disappeared.

The fighters looked around in awe. Sara walked onto the battlefield, and doused the flames to a watery death. Fire Elementals were trying to fight the shadows with fire, increasing their numbers. Sara extinguished the flames. "They're casted by the light," she said. "He must be drawing energy from the fire so he can focus on his cloud."

But soon the torches were relit. Fire was sent from across the field. It was one of the Keepers. They were pushing them back, trying to keep them away from their father.

As the shadows rose again so did the swords. Sara tried to use Water to douse the flames, but each time she did, they were relit. The shadows surrounded them. Dousing the flames rid the shades from the ground, but it did not rid them of the beings that came from the shadows, the murky monsters dripping with tar.

Sara put her sword out in front of her and held onto Lucerna's wrist.

There were forty, maybe fifty, of them.

Sara didn't know what to do. Maybe she could drown them out?

As they got closer, she waved her sword in front of them.

One of them leapt, and bright light blinded Sara. She shielded her eyes with one hand, keeping her sword raised in the other.

The dark figures disappeared. Their shadows were no longer casted by the light. They were just gone, like they never existed.

"Lucerna?"

Lucerna stood shaking. She had the Light Sphere in her hands. "How do I do it?"

Dawn's voice echoed in Sara's head. But behind it, a whisper, growing louder, told her to look beyond what was in front of her to the essence. It was Spire, and soon Spire's voice crowded out all others. *Don't just focus on the object. Focus on the essence. That was it. The essence . . . the energy . . . that's all anything was.*

She looked at Lucerna. "Not now."

Sara didn't have time to explain. She assaulted the torches with Water, and she kept it up until soon the only torches still lit were the ones in the distance, far away from Sara's army.

The men pulled back and gathered their wounded, bringing them beyond the wall. Sara's army retreated to the far side of the mountain beyond the valley. The wind was biting.

Rodan neared the stone wall. He was hacking away at the wooden torches. As Sara and Lucerna headed from the valley, he stopped and made his way toward them. "Where'd you find her?"

"In the pit. We have to get her somewhere where she can build her strength."

Rodan put his arm around Lucerna's slim shoulders.

"Rodan," Sara said. "There's so many of them . . . Aethers. All under the city. Maybe hundreds of thousands. They were beautiful."

Rodan grimaced. He looked like he was going to be sick. "Are you alright?"

He nodded. "Yeah. Let's get out of the cold."

Sara pushed back the flaps of the tent where they were keeping the wounded. The soldiers lay in rows. Some wrapped in bandages, others groaning on their blankets. Blood soaked the blankets. The ice was just beneath them, and not even the warm wool could keep it out.

Rebecca was cradling Canace, protecting her from the cold. Jove was getting bandages ready for wounded warriors.

Farah and Rai sat with Vassal, Pentagon and Atrus. Thatch was wrapping his arm, which was sliced in the fray.

Decca took Canace from Rebecca's arms and embraced the child. He was indebted to Rebecca, who cared for Canace since she was left motherless.

Bolton was trying to help Tacitum, who was so cold, his fingertips had turned blue. But he wasn't frozen because of the biting winds and frost. He couldn't master his element. It had come upon him in such a short time, and he knew no way of controlling the energy. He blew on his hands. One of his toes had blackened. Rebecca covered him with blankets to combat the unwinnable.

When Sara and Lucerna entered the tent, Bolton looked up. Lucerna clung to Rodan's arm, but when she saw Tacitum, she walked to Bolton's side. "He can't control it," she whispered.

Bolton shook his head. "We haven't made much progress, but Benn . . . he's good at these things. He's with Balin right now, but he'll be here soon."

Lucerna knelt at Tacitum's side. "Can I try?"

Bolton moved aside.

Lucerna took Tacitum's hands. They were chilled to the touch, like cupping handfuls of fallen snow. She closed her eyes and sensed Tacitum's energy. She focused on it. It receded until there was none.

She opened her eyes.

Tacitum no longer shivered. His blue fingertips had

turned pink. The chattering of his teeth had ceased.

Bolton caught Lucerna before she slumped to the floor in exhaustion.

Sara and Rodan looked on. Sara turned to Rodan. "Spire taught me to focus on the essence. With swords, we're only fighting the physical. We can't stop the Creator with swords. The Aethers are beneath the ground. There are thousands of them, possibly more. That's why the Creator chose Omega Ray. The Aethers possess all the elements, all that energy. His power is energy itself. He's using it and us to power his cloud. What Lucerna has . . . she eradicates energy. That's what Destan created. She can stop him, but not like this. Lucerna has to give her soul to the sphere."

Rodan searched Sara's eyes. "Why are you telling me this?"

Sara looked out into the distance. Her eyes were full of worry. "Because I want you to tell me all the reasons it's wrong."

Rodan took her by the shoulders, and she faced him. "What's your plan?"

"We need to get there before she becomes a Keeper. Right now, her element is weak, and it will be difficult for the Creator to sense. We could get her there under the guise of coming to him. All his new . . . *children*. We could shield her from him until we get close enough to eradicate his energy. We just need to get to him."

SARA'S army retreated along the snowy trail of the mountain where they had set up camp. Benn and Balin joined Sara and the others in the large tent. Sara had explained her plan to them.

"That would mean sending you all to him without an

army," Jin said.

"If we push forward with an army," Sara said, "he'll never let us through, but if we go alone, he'll suspect less. He'll want his children with him."

"This is insane," Decca said. "How do you know what he wants? He might kill you all before you can get close enough to shout to him."

"Because I've held the sphere," Sara said. "I've held it long enough to give myself over to it. I've felt the longing and the certainty he wanted me to feel. He wouldn't have chosen us if he didn't think he could convince us to side with him."

Benn shook his head and put his hand on Balin's shoulder. "Balin can't control his element. I can't let him go with you."

Sara turned to him. "I've seen you overcome fear despite what you've done in the past. I know now it wasn't my place to judge you for that. But this isn't your fight to run from."

Balin did not look for his father's approval. "I want to go." He looked up at Benn. "When I go back home to my mother, I want to be able to say I'm not a monster . . . that I did things I'm proud of."

Decca watched as Canace reached up to Rebecca's face as she was cradled in her arms. "She's just a baby."

"She's also the Wind Keeper," Sara said. She worried her tone was unfeeling.

Silence hung in the air as Sara eyed Decca. He was going to break her resolve. She couldn't take Spire's baby into battle.

"She's not the Wind Keeper." Farah stepped from behind Vassal.

Sara gave her a puzzled look.

"I know she's not," Farah said, "because . . ." She gulped.

"Because I've been having the dreams too."

Sara approached her. "Why didn't you say something sooner?"

"Because I didn't want it," Farah said. "I've been running away from one thing all my life that made me important. Why would I want to add something else? I didn't believe in the Creator. I thought he was some myth people made up to explain something they couldn't. I figured I didn't have to say anything. I didn't see how it would make a difference. That's the only reason I'm saying something now."

"You wouldn't be saying it just to keep a baby out of battle?" Atrus asked from behind her. "That would be noble of you."

"She's telling the truth." Destan walked in. The red light pulsed from his hand. The frost on his skin did not melt. But he felt nothing.

"You!" Decca lunged for him, but Shilo held him back. "He's one of them. They killed my wife."

Destan didn't flinch. "That child is not what you think she is."

"What do you mean?" Sara asked.

"She's not a Wind Elemental."

"Of course, she's a Wind Elemental," Decca said with distain. "We've seen it."

"You don't know what you saw. She's imitating Wind because her mother was a Wind Elemental. She's manipulating the energy around her," Destan said.

"So, she is an Elemental," Sara said.

"Yes," Destan said. "A Dark Elemental."

Decca shook his head.

"Not even the Creator can do that," Jove whispered.

Sara turned to Jove. *What did the old man mean?*

"No, Father can't," Destan said. "That's why we were so afraid. We could sense the dark energy, but she was manifesting Wind. Do you know what this might mean?"

"I've heard of it before," Jove said. "Transmutation—changing energy. It's believed to be impossible."

Destan looked to the child, like he was staring into a frightful void. "You need to carry her away from here so my father doesn't find her. If he senses her element, he will rip her away from you." Destan lifted the folds of the tent. "Whatever you plan to do, you should do it quickly. The Creator is weaving something that could destroy this place. He only cares about his elements, not the children upon whom he bestowed them."

THE sea of shadows teemed below them like hungry birds searching for their next meal. The torches had been relit, and the shadows thrived on them with enough darkness to exist and light to cast their shades. The sky above them had turned blacker, and Sara had no doubt that it had spread to Lumina.

Her army gripped the cold steel hilts of their swords as the wind battered their faces. Sara gave the signal, and their feet thundered upon the icy ground, moving towards their enemy, swords raised.

Blood and black bile sprayed across the dark skies.

Decca wrapped Canace in a warm cloak. He kissed her forehead as she was cradled in Rebecca's arms. "Take her away from the mountain and don't come back until the cloud clears."

Rebecca covered the baby's face against the wind. "What if it never clears?"

"Then you must get her as far away as you possibly can."

The war raged at their feet.

Bolton caught Sara by the arm. "I want to come with you."

Sara shook her head. "You can't. Your element is strong. He'll sense you coming and think we have come to ambush him. We'll have Decca with us." Sara put her face against his cheek. "Don't worry. If I die, I might pop up again in three years."

Bolton laughed behind glassy eyes. He took Sara's hand and held it to his lips.

RODAN watched as Sara and the others fought through the shadows. They were headed towards him, the Creator. The dark cloud was thick and looming over head. It didn't seem ethereal like a cloud, more like a thick blanket covering the sky.

Bolton was at his side. He had a sword, but Rodan doubted it would be much use to him. If he used his element, the Creator could leech energy from it to fuel his cloud.

At first, Rodan wondered why the Creator didn't care more for them, his creations. What were they doing that was so wrong?

Then, Rodan thought about what he must do. *The Creator thinks he's doing it for the greater good.* That was the only way Rodan could understand it. But Rodan couldn't let his friends suffer. That was how his human heart felt.

The Creator had the heart of a god. He had seen people come and go. He might have cared about them as a whole, but not individually.

Rodan sliced through the first shadow. He thought he recognized it. A person he might have known? But it happened too fast. Not long enough to pinpoint who he thought it was.

Rai was not far away fighting beside Atrus and Pentagon. Rodan thought about her like he thought about the girls he was interested in when he was younger. He had gotten over them all. Not that he didn't think of them fondly, he just didn't think of them. They were distant memories that didn't matter to him anymore. He had something greater to do. She didn't need to be part of it.

Bolton fought beside him like they did years ago. He clumsily struck a shadow with his sword. It was difficult to fight without their elements. They fought more naturally with them. They wouldn't be able to fight without them for long. What did it really matter anyway? The cloud was unnaturally large now and the larger it got, the more attention the Creator might pay to it.

Jin and Yerish joined them.

Newer recruits, ones Rodan had just met, Taryn and Dema, commanded their own small militia. He hadn't seen Jin enlist them, but it was a good thing he did. They were young and taking down shadows quickly, even without their elements.

Jin cut off the head of one of the shadowy figures. He was better with a sword than Rodan was. That was probably because Rodan was better with his element. Even Jin admitted he took up the sword because his element was weaker and less of an asset to him in battle. So, this was the perfect battle for him, one where his element was irrelevant.

Rodan cut down another shadow. He winced, holding his side. The bandages were still intact, but he imagined his wound was gushing. He reached into his pocket and took out a small vial. He downed the vial of meli and hoped the pain would fade soon.

An unnatural howl called through the night. Black bile

sprayed across Rodan's face. He wiped it away. A creature was lumbering through the fight. *What is it?* The massive creature was among them.

A scream assaulted Rodan's ears. But he had already turned around. It was as if he knew before it happened.

The creature bit down into the flesh of Jin's shoulder, his sword arm. Jin dropped his sword and knelt to the ground. The beast turned to Rodan.

"Rodan!" Bolton shouted. Lightning struck the ground between Rodan and the beast.

He's trying to conserve his element. He knows using too much might strengthen the Creator. But Rodan was trying to conserve his element too. Of course, it was for a different purpose.

Rodan raised his sword as the creature approached. It rushed him. Rodan side-stepped it just in time. He dug his blade into its back. The beast turned on him. It smelled like rotting bodies. From its teeth hung large drops of venomous drool.

It clawed at him. He jumped out of the way just making it. Rodan raised his sword again and the pain shot up his side. Nearly dropping his weapon, Rodan realized he could conserve his element no longer.

He focused on where Bolton had sent the Lightning. Beneath the snow down to the once-frozen dirt, the heat of the bolts created grainy glass. Rodan ripped it from the ground. It hurtled toward the beast.

The glass accosted its face and chest. It howled. In seconds, Bolton was on its back. He hacked at its neck with his sword. Rodan would have never been able to get up there with his bulk and his wound, but it had been no problem for Bolton. However, the hacking was a problem. Either the beast's flesh was too thick or Bolton wasn't strong enough.

The most practiced swordsman would have trouble hacking through the neck of a man, much less a beast.

Bolton continued his attempt to hack off the beast's head. But eventually he swore and dropped his sword. He placed his hands on either side of the beast's head. From his hands, shoots of lightning zapped, invading the beast's brain.

It slumped to the ground with Bolton still perched atop its shoulders. Rodan sauntered over to Bolton. "Is that enough to kill it?"

"I don't know." Bolton had done a decent job at hacking at its head.

Rodan raised his heavy sword and finished the job. He looked to where his father had fallen. Yerish was fighting the shadows surrounding his commander.

Yerish was a big man, and his greater mass made him slow. Before Rodan and Bolton could help, a shadow stabbed Yerish. Others piled in to stab him like careless butchers. It was as if they had personal vendettas against him. They must have, for after Yerish's bloodied body settled to the ground, the shadows dissipated, having no interest in Jin.

Jin, still holding his shoulder, reached a hand out to Yerish's body. Several of Jin's other fighters rested on the ground around him. Rodan approached his father. He didn't like that look in Jin's eyes . . . like he had failed.

"Dad . . ."

"Rodan, he's been bit," Bolton said. "It was a Maledixit. That means he'll either die or turn."

Jin reached for Rodan's sword arm. "I have served Mirmina. Not in the way I wanted, but in the best way I could have. It's okay, son."

No, I can't kill him.

"I'm sorry, Rodan," Bolton said. "Do you want me to do

it?"

"No." Rodan knelt in front of his father. "Dad, I'm going to see you again, soon." He closed his eyes and plunged his sword into Jin's chest.

SARA and the others marched onto the city. Decca was at the head of the group. Tacitum, Lucerna, and Balin were in the center while Sara, Vassal, and Farah defended. Vassal had his sword drawn, and Farah had her daggers ready. Sara, who had not yet mastered the sword, was focused on her element should she need it to defend.

The murky shadows were around them. Vassal sliced through one of them. His blade went in like a knife through something doughy and dense. His sword was covered in the black ooze from which the creature was made.

Farah fended off the shadows from behind. Focusing Wind to rail against them, and halting their approach.

As they got further into the city, the number of shadows lessened until the torches casted no shade.

Sara's heart hammered in her chest. With every stride, she could sense they were getting closer and closer to the center of the darkness. She couldn't help but to think of Veil. She hadn't thought of him much since she cried over him in Tosia, but she remembered the void that raged across Lumina and the same hopeless feeling engulfed her now.

Veil had not learned to live with his element. Now Canace was plagued with it as well. Sara couldn't see any good in the darkness. She didn't understand how it could ever be anything good.

Suddenly, her eagerness sank like a heavy stone in a bottomless ocean.

Shadows were surrounding them in great number. Their

gloomy feet left black muck in the snow as they approached.

Vassal cut a few of them down.

Farah slashed another.

All that could be heard was the sloshing of feet and grunts of the warriors. But something else was growing even louder—Sara's heartbeat.

A flood of water sprung at her feet and swept away the shadows in front of her. It was a quick reaction, without thought. Decca was at the front of the group, but they weren't a group anymore. Fighting the shadows had drawn them apart from each other. Tacitum and Balin were exposed to the shades.

Balin would be afraid to use his element. Instead, he had the dagger Benn had given him out and ready. But the way his hand trembled made Sara nervous. She wasn't sure if Tacitum's element had returned since Lucerna had taken it from him. Sara could not sense his energy.

Lucerna closed her eyes. If she used her element, she would become exhausted, and they would have to carry her the rest of the way. What's more, she might not wake by the time they found the Creator.

Sara rushed to them and sent a rush of swirling water around herself, Lucerna, Tacitum, and Balin. The approaching shadows were swept away as soon as they hit the powerful jet stream.

Decca swung his mace against the shadows. He hacked at them with laborious skill until, suddenly, he stopped. A shadow was approaching him. Sara tore down the swirling water in time to see the figure. *Spire*. Before Sara could do anything, before she could think, the darkness reached inside Decca's chest.

It's not her!

Shock rang upon his visage as he watched the murky shadow of his wife reach inside his chest and blacken his heart. Decca's face was going red and his body was kneeling.

Sara ran to him.

The shadows were fading, and others were retreating. The only evidence they had been there was the black footprints littering the snow.

Sara knelt beside Decca. Her tears were for him, but they were for Spire too. In that moment, Sara forgot Spire was dead.

Decca's hand clenched his chest. He gasped. He grabbed Sara's arm. His eyes were urgent. Sara brought her ear down to his lips. His breath was raspy and hollow. "Protect Canace no matter *what* she is."

80

RESISTANCE FIGHTER

*"I am Not Afraid to Die for I Know I cannot. But what I Know of
This Life May Die. And for That I Need You."*

THE sun fought through the dark cloud above, casting
dim light down on the fighters below. The cold winds
whirled across the valley touching the ocean. They
drifted towards the far reaches to lands unknown.

The winds bit against Rodan's face as he stood back to
back with Bolton. They were ripping through the shadows
with their blades. Rodan treated his sword like an extension
of his arm, but Bolton swung inexpertly into the darkness. Pe-
riodically, Bolton would flash lightning down to aid him, but
the shadows were increasing, and he didn't want to exhaust
his element.

Their swords were black with the dark ooze of which the

shadowy figures were made. It dripped down the blades over the hilts and onto their hands. It was sticky and thick like warm tar.

There was seemingly no end, and the shadows were becoming harder to see as the sky darkened. The hacking had become almost mechanical.

Rodan pulled his sword from the shadow in which he had plunged it, and the mass sank to the ground in a gooey heap. He could feel Bolton's back to his and was acutely aware of his presence as they fought. They had both touched death, and yet Rodan had not mentioned it to Bolton. Back at Element, Rodan shared everything with Bolton, especially anything of importance. Bolton had kept secrets but Rodan hadn't. Of course, what was important to him then seemed frivolous now.

"What was dying like?" Rodan asked. Black muck strayed across his face.

"You mean when I fell from the cliff? I didn't die." Bolton's breathing was labored from the effort of wielding the heavy steel. "Everything just went black . . . like passing out, but without dreaming. I always thought when I died the first person I would see was my mother, but it wasn't like that at all. It was like a light just went out . . . I didn't sense it . . . it just . . . happened."

Rodan paused for a moment. "I need you to do something for me."

"Now?"

THATCH was unused to battle. Members of the Rebel Resistance had tried to teach him to use a sword, but it was more unfamiliar than the gun Rai handed to him in Breeze. He didn't want to enter this battle with the latter. He stayed close to those who knew how to fight. Which meant he was very near Rai, Pentagon, and Atrus. Sev or, Shilo, Decca's brother, was fighting with them as well. He was very practiced with a sword.

I'll die out here, and Uncle Tag thought I would be fit to run his city.

A shadow struck out at Thatch. He had taken too long to reload. He shot just in time, and then let out some even less confident shots into the group of shadows floating a short distance in front of him.

They looked like humans . . . sort of. Their faces were obscured, but Thatch thought if he looked close enough he might be able to recognize them.

Why are you trying to recognize them? Won't that make it harder to kill them? But, was he *killing* them? Could shadows, wait . . . pure energy, be *killed*?

We're just trying to provide a distraction, long enough for Sara and the others to reach the Creator.

The Creator. Thatch was never a religious man. He was a man of science. Not that the thought of religion never came to his mind. There was only the Creator, and what did he have to pray to him for. He wasn't an Elemental. Now, weren't they going against the Creator himself? It all seemed odd to Thatch. He didn't understand Sara's dreams. He wasn't religious, but he did understand that dark cloud was menacing. He also understood that the world had finite energy. Creating more of it couldn't possibly be a good thing, could it? And then there was what Stannum said about the three possibilities. It was surreal and scary.

Fighting Hephaestus made more sense. He was a direct threat. What he was doing was killing people. But in the three possibilities, wasn't there one where they all would live?

Rai and Pentagon were fighting the shadows a distance away from him. Atrus was beside him. "Getting the hang of it, ha?"

"I would have rather stayed with the ship," Thatch said. He shot an approaching shadow.

"It's always better to have multiple skills," Atrus said. "You'll be better at some than others, but having them makes you more valuable. Being more valuable keeps you alive."

"And what skill are you better at," Thatch asked, "building, shooting, or stealing?"

"Depends on who you're talking to."

Shilo swung his sword at the shadows. He was offset from the others, but not in much danger. He lacked his brother's bulk, but he made up for in it in speed and endurance. *How long had they been fighting?* And Shilo was still swinging vigorously as if he had just started the fight.

There was a roar.

I know that sound.

Chariots approached from the cliff. They looked pretty busted up, but they were flying. It couldn't be Morica. Jin's army wiped out the High Council at the battle in Vella City. Without the High Council, Morica was disbanded. They had retreated to lick their wounds. But if it wasn't Morica . . . *Shift!*

"I need you to go to Sara," Rodan said.

"She told me the Creator would sense my energy," Bolton said.

"She's not going to do it, Bolton. You know that. She won't sacrifice someone else."

"I know."

"You have to go."

"I can't leave you here."

"I'm a trained Resistance fighter and a powerful Elemental," Rodan said. "She needs you." Rodan waited for Bolton's answer. He couldn't have Bolton stop him from doing what he needed to do. They used to be close, but they had grown apart. It was the one last thing Rodan could do for his friend.

"Watch your back," Bolton said.

Rodan felt Bolton leave him. He turned around to slash the shadows behind him and watched Bolton's disappearing form until the darkness swallowed him.

After slashing a few shadows within swords reach, Rodan knelt to the ground. Sara's words echoed in his head. *There are so many of them . . . Aethers. All under the city. Maybe hundreds of thousands. They were so beautiful.*

Rodan placed his hands on the ground, and the earth shook.

THE ships . . . the ones Thatch had been working on before he fled Breeze, Shift must have found a way to repair them. He wasn't as knowledgeable about machines as Thatch, but Shift *was* Tag's son. He would have needed the help of the city, and it looks like he got it.

Shift's vessels blasted the shadows from above, thinning them out. The cliff was almost clear of shadows. Thatch imagined Shift, like his father, yelling orders over the communicators in each vessel.

Thatch knelt to the floor. He felt the earth shake. *What was that?* Transparent masses were moving towards them. They were leviathans. And they were coming their way. *Sphere Protectors!*

BOLTON cut through the city. The earth trembled beneath

him, but he ignored it, ambling toward where he knew Sara was confronting the Creator. *Rodan is right. Sara would never sacrifice Lucerna to stop him.*

Cracks swept across the ground.

Bolton raised his sword as murky figures rose from the snow. The Creator was growing stronger. The energy from all the Elementals who had gathered here to fight was powering him. *This is what he wanted. That's why the dreams . . .he wanted them all here to fuel him.*

Bolton's sword sank into the tar body of one of the shadows. There were too many. As he fought, he was being pushed further and further toward the edge of the city, closer and closer to the cliff.

81

THE CREATOR

"To My Son, Destan,
"Forgive me for Leading You Astray. For making You hate Me. It was
Necessary.
"Only a descendant of the Mother can Advance Me. For Only She has
Authority over Aethers."

DESTAN saw his brothers and sister. He sensed their energy from the vast distance between them. Destan had wandered the snowy peaks of Regret Mountain for years. The cold didn't torment him. He was numb already. His father had done that to him. Not his real father, *that* man he had forgotten long ago. He couldn't remember the consequences that led him to become a Keeper of the Sphere. He remembered a flood and a woman, a woman he loved. But he couldn't remember her name, and he couldn't long for her.

He couldn't remember what it was like to feel cold or warmth, to know that the sun was on his skin. He had been tricked into this life by omission.

And so were they.

Destan emerged from the darkness.

"What are you doing here, Traitor?" Vuur asked.

Dawn stood straight-backed, her sightless eyes wanting to turn to him. "Destan?"

Fulgur was at her side. *Why does she let that man get so close to her?* Vjetar and Glaciem were standing together not far from Vuur. The Keepers barely moved. They were like statues in the cold.

"She's coming," Destan said.

"The ant that seeks to challenge giants," Fulgur said.

"You should go, Destan," Vuur said. "She'll never get here without a Keeper on her side."

"She *is* a Keeper," Dawn said.

"Then why is he still here?" Vjetar asked.

"She didn't give her soul entirely to the sphere," Destan said. "I stopped her, or rather, I allowed someone else to."

"You should have let her finish," Vuur said. Fire rose around Destan. Dawn glared at Vuur with her blind eyes. The flames leapt into the air.

A ring of Water crashed down to drench them. "Stop playing games," Destan said.

"Why?" Fulgur asked. "I love games." He sent bolts of Lightning dashing towards Destan. The bolts blasted from Fulgur's hands, his glowing palms out and open. Destan was enmeshed in the bolts. They caused him no pain, but they did make his face twist into an involuntary grimace of despair.

Dawn ran thick vines under the ground and pinned Fulgur's arms to his sides.

"You think I'm a Child of the Sphere?" Fulgur asked. "Such things do not stop me." The bolts continued to assault Destan, this time coming from the sky.

Harsh Wind swept Fulgur off his feet and the Lightning bolts ceased. "My brother may be a traitor," Vjetar said, "but it is not up to us to deal out his punishment."

Fire accosted Vjetar's flesh. Vjetar spun around with the speed and grace of a younger man and slammed Vuur to the ground.

Glaciem frosted Vuur's body into the snow, pinning him there. Spikes of ice jetted up from the ground racing towards Fulgur.

Vuur melted the ice easily and was up again.

Fulgur dodged the ice spikes. Sparks of Lightning materialized between his hands.

The ground trembled. A large fissure ran through the cliff where they stood. "Stop fighting," Dawn said. "Or you all can drag yourself up from the gorge."

The Keepers stopped. They weren't even breathing heavy. They weren't breathing at all.

"We have to do this," Vjetar said. "He is our father."

"This?" Destan asked. "To turn these people into slaves again?"

"What do you care for ants, Destan?" Vuur asked.

"So, this is it?" Destan raised a typhoon against them, threatening to wash them into the gorge as Dawn had. The cyclone of water went straight into the air, but it was wavering on either side.

THE Wind pushed Sara's army back. Fire erupted behind her. Her fingers were turning blue as the Frost assaulted them. The Keepers were using their powers to turn the tide, but they couldn't use all their energy because the Creator was drawing off that too.

She found them before she saw them. She sensed their energy.

Destan raised a typhoon. She wasn't sure where he was about to send it, but it was wavering towards her army. Sara focused on the cyclone and sent it crashing down.

"Stop this!" She blasted a wall of Water toward them, knocking them off their feet.

The Keepers rose, unhurt from the fall.

Energy was building in Fulgur, but Dawn put her hand on Fulgur's arm to stop him. "She's our sister now."

"I know what he did to you," Sara said. "To all of you. What he said to you was a lie. It wasn't nature you were battling, it was him. Before you, the elements were all he had. They were draining his power. He knew he could only focus on one. That's why he gave you your power. But he lied to get your trust. Nature didn't ruin your homes and kill your families. It was him. He did it to show you how cruel nature could be, that we need to control it. But he lied."

"No." Fulgur shook his head.

"He did," Dawn said.

Glaciem, Vuur, and Vjetar had equal looks of doubt on their faces.

"He doesn't love us," Destan said.

"It's not much hearing it from you, Traitor," Vuur said.

"We were pawns to him," Destan said.

"He gave us the world," Vjetar said. "He gave us power."

"He gave us death," Destan said.

Fulgur with his hand raised, thundered toward Destan. Dawn put her hands on his shoulders, and Fulgur relaxed his arm. "No," she said. "He took your soul, Fulgur. And now he's using it to destroy this world like he did to the lands beyond."

"That's not what he's trying to do," Vuur said.

Dawn turned to him. "But that's what he *will* do. He's using all our souls for energy, and then, he's going to replace us with new Keepers. Ones he hopes will follow him to the death. He's not our Father. He never was. And now, he's doing something that could destroy us all. If we were ever their gods, we need to help these people."

BENN fought among a group of Resistance fighters. Massive vessels flew. *Chariots. Morica?* No, Sara told him Morica wasn't a threat anymore, that they were mostly dead.

That boy, Thatch, the one who knew so much about machines, must be the one behind this.

Benn hated using a sword. As the Old Scholar, he learned incredible control over his element. If there was one thing touching that sphere did for him, it gave him a greater understanding of his element. He wasn't ruled by it, and he understood why.

He marveled at how Balin have forgiven him. The boy wanted a father so badly, he would take a broken one. Bolton would never feel that way. But Benn thought perhaps he hated him less.

Benn swung his sword at the shadow in front of him. He had been staying close to the other fighters, letting them take most of the kills. It wasn't running. *I'm staying to fight. Maybe Bolton will see that and forgive me after all.*

Benn looked around. *Where were the other fighters?* Had he strayed from them? Or maybe they had spread out without him noticing? Or maybe they died?

Benn searched the ground for corpses. There were certainly many dead. But there had been more living. Hadn't there?

Benn dropped his sword.

Ana!

PENTAGON fought beside Rai. As he watched her laboring strokes, he couldn't help but compare it to the ease at which he wielded his weapon.

I'm even better than Atrus now.

He shot down three approaching shadows. There were still many, but the chariots had managed to knock out a large majority near the cliff. It was hopeful to know, at least, that their numbers were starting to dwindle.

Then, the earth shook.

The Protectors were approaching.

Pentagon doubted his gun would be any use.

When he, Atrus, Rai and Pentagon fought Protectors, the trick was to distract them with your weapons long enough to pull the sphere. Despite their screams, he doubted the weapons ever did any real damage, but without a sphere to pull, how could they defeat Protectors?

Pentagon started shooting.

REBECCA watched from the mountain as the cloud became thicker and darker. She cradled the baby against the cold. Canace no longer cried. She seemed content.

Why cry now . . . when it will all end soon? That was what she was watching: the end of the world.

She had spent so much time alone—being angry at her husband—being angry at her son. Now, she wouldn't speak to them. Rodan didn't have the chance to hug his mother. He might die, and she didn't show him she cared. All that time . . . wasted.

Rebecca stared out beyond the cloud. Surely it did not touch everything . . . yet. She had heard of lands beyond Mirmina . . . quieter lands. Perhaps land where the darkness couldn't touch.

She wrapped Canace in the blanket and fought against the wind. She journeyed down the mountain. Her feet sank into the snow as she walked. She wasn't dressed for such weather, and her body had become accustomed to living in the hot climate of Dustpath.

She wondered what Dustpath looked like now. Perhaps just an empty desert with a dark cloud overhead. Just when she was getting used to being part of a family again, that was taken away from her. But she couldn't blame Jacopo. He couldn't control his army, but his heart was good. She could see it beyond the fire in his eyes. There was something almost childlike behind the damage and rough-earned wisdom.

With every step, her numb feet somehow got number. She felt the urge to look down to see if they were still beneath her. She felt the mountain tremble, and some of the snow was shaken off the uppermost peaks.

Yet, Canace did not cry.

Rebecca uncovered her face.

The baby looked up at Rebecca. Her eyes were old like she had lived a hundred years over. She knew when tears would earn her something . . . but she also knew when that didn't matter anymore. And there was something else . . . something that in part, amazed, and in part, frightened Rebecca. Despite the wisdom already grown there, there was space for something more . . . something greater perhaps.

Rebecca shielded the baby's face and continued her

trudge down the mountain until she reached its base. As she descended the mountain, it shuttered several times more.

Once upon flatter ground, Rebecca could run. Her feet were starting to warm up, sending shoots of pin-needles up her legs. Ignoring the discomfort, she ran as far as she could as the ground rippled beneath her.

As she ran past the cave, her breathing exhilarated beyond any pace it had before. As a child, this discomfort would have signaled her to stop, but she couldn't stop. She kept going, past the point of her lungs burning, clenching Canace in her arms, praying she wouldn't fall as the ground trembled.

The cracks of Jetty Verte were widening. The earth was opening.

Something roared in the distance.

Snow cascaded down from the top of the mountain. Had she stayed, she and the baby would have been enveloped in a snowy tomb.

Rebecca ran far across the plain. She searched as she ran. *Where is it?*

There!

With Canace in one arm, Rebecca lifted the grating with the other. She sunk down into the dungeons. She still had the key . . . the key she had managed to get from Yerish after a drunken night of banter.

She fit it into the lock.

Jacopo was weak from lack of food. They had forced him to exhaust his element. But despite all this, he rushed into Rebecca's arms with what must have been the last bit of his strength.

There was still something between them.

Rebecca lifted the blanket. Canace's eyes stared up into Jacopo's.

PENTAGON rushed forward. Atrus now at his side.

"Fighting Protectors again," Atrus said. "I wouldn't have guessed we'd see the day."

"I never thought I would be fighting Protectors with bullets," Pentagon said. "I hope they're more effective than swords."

The Dark Sphere Protector reared its head. The Beast of D'arkadia. Pentagon and Atrus loaded bullets into its body. It screamed but didn't stagger.

Rai, Shilo, and Thatch were fighting the Water Sphere Protector. Pentagon hated that one. In their journey, they didn't come across Scylla because the Water Sphere was broken, missing. There was no point to go into the cave. But Pentagon had recently crossed paths with the Water Sphere Protector, and it had been particularly unpleasant.

Rebel Resistance fighters were attacking the Earth Sphere Protector.

How did they all get here? At least one of them doesn't have legs. The Fire Sphere Protector certainly couldn't have flown here? How did it get off the island?

The chariots turned around and continued their assault. This time on the Protectors.

Pentagon had enough to handle with the Dark Sphere Protector, but he wanted to have an idea of where the other Protectors were in case he would have to deal with them.

The Fire Sphere Protector was breathing flames at the chariots as they sailed through the sky, blasting him with their missiles. The Lightning Sphere Protector held up its hooves against the Resistance fighters. Bolts of Lightning rose in the air.

That can't be good. They must be fueling the Creator's energy too.

Pentagon wasn't sure, but Sara had warned the Elementals against using their elements unless they were in dire need. *I would think any of this counts as dire need.*

The air got colder. The fingers of Pentagon's hand gripping the gun grew numb.

Something towered over the Beast. It was crystalline, like ice. But Pentagon was only looking at a portion of it. His eyes went up.

Above the massive feet like the sides of a mountain made of ice, were claws like sharp icicles, a translucent glacier-like chest, and a head with pointed icy teeth. Its breath puffed out into the icy air, making it icier.

Atrus pumped bullets into it. Some of the bullets embedded in the ice. It didn't even scream. *Frost Sphere Protector*. Pentagon had never seen it. Didn't know it existed. And there it was. Atrus continued to load bullets into it. Pentagon joined suit unloading on the monster.

Suddenly, a click rang out. At first, Pentagon thought it was his gun, but it wasn't. "Atrus!"

The Protector swept his massive ice clawed hand down. Pentagon flew to Atrus and knocked him out of the way. The claws raked across Pentagon's body. He was tossed into the snow.

Pentagon hadn't meant for it to happen that way. He thought he could clear it. He thought wrong.

But Pentagon didn't lose consciousness. He did close his eyes, and when he opened them, Atrus was kneeling next to him.

You're just using me as an excuse to leave the fight. Pentagon thought he said those words, but Atrus would have responded to them with one of his backhand comments.

The ice from the snow had sealed the blood in his wound.

"How bad is it?" Pentagon hoped he had actually said that one.

"It's bad," Atrus said. "What were you thinking, Pent? I know I think my life's worth more than yours, but you don't have to go thinking that."

"I didn't. I thought I was going to get out of it."

Atrus laughed. "You're becoming as arrogant as me. There's no way I'm getting you back to camp, you know that, right?"

"You're going to let me die in the snow," Pentagon said.

"I'm going to give you meli," Atrus said, "and you're going to stay low until we finish this battle."

Pentagon shook his head. "I'm going to die." *Is my voice fading?*

"At least let me give you meli."

"It will be wasted on me," Pentagon said. "I can't feel anything."

Atrus cradled Pentagon's head in his hands and leaned in, pressing his lips to his forehead. "I'm coming back for you." Pentagon watched through blurred vision as Atrus ran back towards the battle. And then, everything went black.

THE new Keepers pushed through the battle. Sara doused the flames in their wake, extinguishing the shadows with them. "Stay with me!" Sara shouted to the others.

Erebus was in the center of the city where the darkness was the thickest. But Sara could sense him. His strength was growing. She wondered if his plan just might be working, if he was creating energy.

There he was.

His skin was rotten. His nose was gone, leaving a gaping hole in his face.

Not far from him Shashi peered from around a crumbling building. Her face was dirty and bleeding. Sara ran to her. "Shashi, do you remember me?" Sara reached her hand out to the little girl. "Do you remember Bolton? I'm Sara, his wife."

Shashi turned to Sara and looked at her hand.

"It's okay," Sara said.

Shashi took her hand.

"Child of Water!" Erebus shouted. "Have you come to thank your Father?"

His voice boomed against her back as if the sound had weight. She didn't let it deter her. "Yes!" Sara shouted back. "We all have."

Sara and the others approached Erebus. Sara was holding Shashi's hand. They stood in a circle around the Creator.

"Then you have come to lend me your strength."

"Yes," Sara said.

Erebus closed his eyes.

Their heads were jerked up to the sky as the Creator drew from their energy. Sara's energy pulled from her into the cloud. It was not just her elemental energy, but her bodily energy. She was being rung out like a dish rag.

Suddenly, their heads could relax back. Erebus looked to each of his children.

Destan, Dawn, Fulgur, Vuur, Vjetar, and Glaciem emerged from the darkness. Each stood behind their younger brother or sister.

Then Lucerna came out from among the gloom. Her white hair was like a beacon of light. She carried the sphere clenched in her two hands.

The Creator's eyes rested on Lucerna. "I didn't choose her."

"We often don't choose our children," Sara said.

"ANA!"

She was so close to him, Benn could have leaned in to kiss her.

She was a shadow, black muck dripping in a pool. These shadows, they were their demons. And his time was done. That's why she was here, to take his life with her. But she didn't move to strike him nor did she have a weapon. She stood there waiting.

"Benn."

He touched her face. Something was strange. He started to wipe the tar from her face. It wiped clean. Her skin was still soft. He could see her eyes. He ran his fingers through her muck-covered hair and pulled her close to him.

"Ana!" He kissed her.

She didn't feel dead.

This is what he wanted. Balin. Bolton. Their forgiveness. That hole he was trying to fill. It was for her.

Benn found himself weeping. His face was becoming blackened by the inkiness of her hair.

"Swim away, Benn."

"What?" He pulled back to face her.

"Swim away," she whispered.

Lightning crashed in the distance. Tears were still in Benn's eyes. He backed away from her. His emotions . . . he had started a lightning storm without realizing it, and that storm was being sucked into the clouds.

And it was a *storm*.

Lightning radiated across the valley. All his power, all his control. Gone.

He's using me.

The cloud grew larger, spreading across the sky. There was no light. And the storm grew. And Ana laughed.

A big rock rested in the snow. The shadows were moving in, and they would kill him. *But it's the best thing I can do. I can't be a coward. It's the only thing that will keep him from using me.* Benn slammed the rock into his head, as hard as he could, and passed out in the snow.

THATCH had run out of bullets. He scanned the area for Atrus, but he couldn't find the man.

I should have taken a sword.

The chariots helped slow down the Protectors, but they weren't enough.

I just must stay alive long enough for Sara to defeat him. He picked up a bloodied sword.

The Earth Sphere Protector whipped its thorny appendages towards Thatch. It lashed his shoulder. Thatch's hand flew up to cover the wound. Blood seeped over his fingers. He dropped his sword.

The Earth Sphere Protector's enormous mouth gaped open, and two thorny appendages reached out for Thatch.

This is it. No element. No weapon. This is what building machines and training large birds has got me.

Suddenly, a caw sounded through the air. The great bird, Thermal, sailed through the sky. His massive talons plucked the Earth Sphere Protector from the ground and tossed him several yards away.

As Thermal cawed again, brilliant flames issued forth from his mouth. The tips of his wings sizzled with Lightning. Yet, those things did not harm the great bird.

Wind blasted the Protectors away from the fight, closing them in at the cliff. The darkness seemed to gather around

Thermal. Some of the shadows were pulled towards him.

As Thermal sent the elements, it was blinding. Flashes of Fire, trails of Wind, blasts of Water, Frost, Darkness, Lightning, Earth. All together in blinding brilliance. Thermal was sending wave after wave at the Protectors.

It was like a universal scream. Not of despair. More like . . . *triumph.*

The Protectors broke down into tiny glowing worms. They weren't invading Thermal's body. He was taking them in as if harboring them from a storm.

Their souls were part of him now.

SARA'S eyes were glued upon the Creator. "This is what this is. Energy. You knew before anyone else. We are all that ever was and all that will be. We all are. Together."

"Your faith is wavering like Water. You don't understand what you're doing." His bulging eye stared at Sara. "Did you think this was the right thing to do? Poor child." His voice was solemn and genuine. He no longer looked to the cloud looming above him but into her eyes. "History has made me into a monster, but I was cruel to be kind. I wanted them to value life, to respect their gifts. To know what I had given them."

He looked to the darkness spreading across the sky. "You don't know what this is, do you? It's an energy cloak, wide enough to encase the world. It's not to be feared, but cherished. You're afraid because you don't know what it brings. The bit of humanity left in me can understand that."

Sara watched the old man. Her eyes burned as he spoke.

"I know I'm asking a great deal from you. I'm asking you to turn away from the destruction and not to look back. I'm telling you that you are one of the chosen ones and must live. I'm asking you to suffer the worst for the promise of something better, something greater for all. To have blind faith.

"You don't know who you are.

"You've already defeated the darkness. You think I chose you because you're the last Water Elemental? I could have given anyone that power. I chose you because you're strong, and you'll always do what is right even if it means risking your own life. You are good and pure, and your soul is not wasted away. You watched Hephaestus drown into the darkness. I know you saw then my eyes peering back at you from the abyss."

"If you wanted something good, why did you kill your own people?" she asked. "Why did you force them to consume themselves?"

"Compassion to a man is different than compassion is to a god. I wanted to save them from who they might become. If they feared punishment, they wouldn't misuse their gifts and destroy themselves. I remember what you said about greed and power down in the pit. I didn't want that either. This disease—it makes me a beast, and I know that. But we want the same thing. Let me show you."

Erebus reached out to her.

Sara broke the chain. Her hand was shaking as she inched towards him and clasped his hand.

FOUNTEN and Erebus were alone in the snow, the wind biting their faces.

"Why are you so eager to go against the gods?" Founten asked. "There must be a reason for all this? Even I am starting to believe in them. The hunt has never been so difficult before."

"Because they are the wrong gods," Erebus said.

"How could you say that? We will die on this mountain."

"If you believe so much in the cruelty of your gods then we are already dead," Erebus said. There was ire in his voice.

"What are you saying?"

"Athanati . . . her belly has not yet fully grown, but she is with child."

"How would you know that?" Founten asked. His regal form was hunched against the wind.

"The child is mine," Erebus roared against the onslaught of rushing wind. "Where are your gods now?"

Founten's face changed. It was like everything that was keeping him a man was broken and a beast emerged. He raised his axe against Erebus, and before the Bear could defend, he brought it down on him, cutting into his shoulder. Blood spread upon snow as Erebus knelt. His eyes rolled back as a roar sounded in the distance.

Founten look frightened by what he had done. He ran off, back in the direction of camp, and left Erebus there in the cold.

A bright, white light glowed. She saw Erebus kneeling in the snow. His bear skin cloak and headdress rested beside him. His face was untouched by decay. He looked young and scared and cold. He looked human. His tears were frozen on his cheeks as the wind whipped his face.

Suddenly, his eyes went white and his hands clenched the snow around him. And Sara could see what he saw. There was a woman. She was old with beaded clothing.

"Mother," he whispered.

She was the Mother of his village. A woman born on the thousandth full moon.

She spoke to him.

"They will die," she said. "Nature will take them to their graves, but it has more in store for you. You mustn't let them suffer. Go to the place where the earth yields to its fiery core and you'll know what to do. There will be many gods, but centuries will pass, and they will be forgotten. The world will be sinful and careless. And the people will bring about their own destruction. They will create machines to replace them. They will pollute the earth and desecrate the holy forest. But you can put a stop to that. You can save them." The old woman's voice was fading. "There is a beast coming. Bow to it. Right now, the only way you can survive is to become what it is."

The color returned to Erebus's eyes.

Something black approached from within the flurry.

Erebus bowed his head into the snow and gave himself up to the Maledixit.

He traveled, blood dripping onto the white snow until he made it back to camp. He could see his companions through the flurry. His eyes were enhanced by the curse of the Maledixit. Founten was rushing to him. The others couldn't see, but Founten withdrew his dagger as he approached Erebus. He wanted to finish him off before the others found out about his wife's disgrace. Erebus could understand this. He loved Athanati too. But there were greater things at stake. Before Founten could assault his broken body, Erebus ripped into Founten's shoulder.

Frost was on the lips of his companions. He had mercy on them. He would not let the cold take them. But he couldn't kill her. He looked into her eyes. He knew she carried his child.

Years had passed before the fire lighted on his skin. He crawled from the volcanic ash with a sphere clenched in his hands.

* * *

SARA ripped her hand away from Erebus.

Everything he had done . . . he had done for the good of all.

Sara's eyes darted to Lucerna. Sara snatched the sphere from her. Holding the sphere between her hands, she sent energy into it until it cracked. She continued to overwhelm the sphere until it crumbled to shards of glass.

Erebus's lips curled into a smile.

Sara felt hands around her neck. She didn't see whose they were, but they were bony and cold.

"Fulgur!" Dawn's voice carried like an echo in Sara's ears, but her eyes were still focused on the Creator.

"I didn't do it for you!" Sara's voice was raspy as she forced the sound from her obstructed airway.

"No, you did it for you . . . because you can't live with that decision. Gods must make decisions where others can't. They have to live with their sacrifices."

Someone pulled Fulgur off her. His shouts sounded like they were coming from the end of an empty hallway.

The Creator was here in front of her, not in books, not in legends. He was a man. He was a greedy man. Or was he more?

Maybe he was . . . necessary.

Water rose above the cliff.

Suddenly, the heads of the old Keepers were thrust back. Lightning, Wind, Fire, Earth, Frost, and Water darted into the sky as they were being pulled from the old Keepers.

The new Keepers could only gaze up in alarm.

Across from Sara, Farah's eyes glowed from the light of the elements, being ripped from the bodies of the old Keepers so forcefully, the energy looked like huge pillars in the sky.

The ground shuttered. It ripped. The energy was coming from far away across the mountainous expanse. Aethers floated from the fissures. The Aethers hung in the air above them, casting a glow on Sara's face.

They caught themselves as the ground shuttered again. Erebus released his Children. A wave hung over them, but casted no shadow as the plain was already darkened.

Dawn's hands wrapped around Sara's shoulders. "You must do it!"

Erebus stood still, looking up to the sky. Words whispered from his lips that Sara couldn't hear. It was like he was praying to the Aethers above.

What was he doing? Hadn't he just tried to convince her to save him? Did he really think it would be that easy? He was right . . . about Lucerna. Sara didn't want to make that decision . . . not even for the greater good.

An image appeared like a ghost, but more solid. It was . . . the Mother. She clasped hands with the Creator.

Sara didn't know if the others could see her.

Your spirit is beyond this world . . . beyond thoughts . . . beyond its human tomb . . .

Then the Mother looked at her. "Child of the Right Moon. Have you ever wondered why you can control such spirits . . . Aethers? Why Founten was drawn to you? Why you have fallen right into our hands?"

"I don't think . . ." Sara wasn't speaking to the Mother. But it was too late. Her heart had already whispered to the Aethers what it wanted.

Erebus looked up at the Aethers filling the sky. The Aethers glowed with a brighter light. They migrated toward Erebus and began to fill him. As the Aethers filled his body, Erebus did not scream. He did not cry out to his children for help. He looked to the sky. His countenance was peaceful and calm among the rotting tissue.

Sara thought maybe, he had a smile on his face.

Light was emitting from him, like the sun through a cracked window until the whole valley erupted with Light so bright Lucerna was the only one who could see.

Sara couldn't see, but she felt it. Across Mirmina, the spheres shattered on their pedestals, and the pedestals crumbled from their foundations.

THE wave hung over the city, but Sara was too distracted to control it. She watched the place where the Creator had stood. There was nothing left to show he was there. She wondered if she had dreamt it. She wondered when Bolton would shake her awake.

Sara stared into the gaping hole that had formed to allow the Aethers to escape. Below, Sara could see the hidden city nestled in a deeper valley of the mountain.

Someone shouted, "Run!"

The ground continued to quake and fragment. Sara looked out toward the wave. Destan stood in front of it. Sara ran to him. "I can't control it. You have to run."

Destan did not face her, but continued to gaze at the hovering water. "I cannot die."

"The Creator is gone. You don't know that anymore."

Destan turned his head so Sara could see only the mournful profile of his face. She could have sworn he looked like a much younger man. "Then I would welcome death. If it comes."

Sara turned and ran. She dodged the many fissures and cracks that littered the ground as the quakes continued. She couldn't see where the others had gone. The darkness was only starting to dissipate. Sara had thought the darkness would be eradicated along with the Creator, but it lingered in a way that frightened her.

She was afraid to look back.

The ground shook, and Sara tripped. Her chin hit the exposed ground where the snow had been shaken away. Her vision blurred. She pushed herself up from the ground as her vision slowly returned.

Out of the corner of her eye, she saw Bolton struggling to get up over the cliff. He had managed to get onto his elbows when another shock trembled.

Sara reached out and grabbed his arm before he lost his bearings. "I'm not losing you again."

"I was trying to get to you." Bolton managed to get his elbows back over the cliff. "There was a light in the sky and the wave . . . are you doing that?"

Sara's hands were clinging to him. "The wave? I can't control it. He said things to me . . . I don't know if I . . ."

"Sara . . . look at me." Bolton looked into her eyes. Hers were darting, but his were still and constant. "You did the right thing."

Something drew her to him. Without thought, she pressed her lips against his with more force than ever before. The wave crashed down, biting only the edge of the southern cliff and shrinking back into the sea.

Sara pulled her lips away from Bolton's and pressed her forehead against his. They stayed this way for a long moment, not speaking, not listening to the sounds around them. The tremors had ceased, and the ground was quiet. The sky was becoming increasingly bright as the Aethers floated overhead.

Bolton got his footing against the side of the cliff, and Sara helped to pull him up.

THEY walked along the fissured ground careful not to trip

upon the deeper ridges and wider gaps. The ground was patterned like Jetty Verte.

In the distance, someone was slumped upon the ground. No one had come to aid this man as he was miles away, on the outer reaches of the city.

Sara and Bolton ran toward the fallen soldier. He was face down on the icy ground, a pool of blood beneath his body.

Bolton turned him over.

Sara's breath caught in her throat. It was Rodan. She rested his head in her lap and wiped the dirt from his face. Tears fell onto his face, and she wiped those away too. She felt warmth all around her, pushing away the coldness of the mountain air.

Bolton pressed his fingers into Rodan's lifeless arm. He pressed his ear to Rodan's chest.

"What are you doing?" Sara tried not to let her tears swallow her words.

"Get away from him."

Sara looked at Bolton.

"Put his head down!" Bolton said.

Sara moved away from Rodan. "What are you doing?"

Bolton pressed his hands over Rodan's chest. He pressed down, sending energy into Rodan's body.

Sara looked on with tears in her eyes. "Stop it," she whispered.

Bolton continued to press down on Rodan's chest, sending bursts of electricity through his body. Bolton forced his hands down with more pressure.

"Stop it!" Sara said. "He's gone. He's bleeding . . . let him go."

Bolton pressed down again.

Rodan's head jolted up, and he gasped.

Bolton smiled and patted his friend on the shoulder. "You didn't think you were going anywhere, did you?"

Rodan didn't say anything. He looked down at the blood that had pooled beneath him.

Bolton helped him to sit up. "Lucky for you, the frost looks like it helped slow the blood. That's an ugly wound you got."

Bolton put Rodan's arm across his shoulders and helped him stand. Sara took Rodan's free arm and shouldered the rest of the burden. His bloody side pressed against her, reddening her clothes. Sara felt guilty that she had accepted his death so readily. When Rodan had kissed her on the mountain, she felt like she was back at the lake in Element, with the whole world ahead of her.

EPILOGUE: NEVER LOST

When He was Done, I set Down My Pen. Somehow, I was Sustained Despite that I had been There for Months, without Sleep or Sustenance, Chronicling His, no Our, Past, Present and Future. What He told Me filled Many Volumes. Some of Which I have Hidden because They were Not for Mortal Eyes.

I must go Away Now.

He Touched Me. I felt Energy Surge through Me, and I Knew I would Live Forever.

THE spheres were gone as were their pedestals. The Protectors' souls had been absorbed by Thermal.

Thatch petted Thermal. "I'm going to miss you," he said to the great bird. Thermal could be a caged bird no longer. The great bird took flight and sailed across the sky until he was no more.

Canace was missing. They had searched the valley, the mountain, and all Jetty Verte. They could only hope Rebecca had kept her safe and she would return with her once the dark cloud had dissipated.

Lucerna couldn't stay, she needed to go somewhere new. Somewhere, perhaps, where her element wasn't as oppressive. She wanted to travel to the Dark Lands beyond Mirmina. She hoped that there, she could perhaps find something to relieve her of her element. Not in all the books written by the Builders had anything been revealed that could relieve her of it. Even after Sara had broken the sphere, Lucerna's element still lingered long after the battle. The others had lost their elements now that the spheres had been crushed, but not Lucerna. But after what she had done for Tacitum, she knew it was possible. So little was known of the Dark Lands. There might be answers there.

Glaciem moved the ice for Lucerna's boat to sail across the cold waters.

The Keepers stood beside their own vessel. Except for Destan. He had not returned. The wave had swept the outer edges of the cliff, and they could only assume he was tossed to the sea.

Sara and her companions had gathered to watch them leave.

Farah waved to Lucerna in the distance, her small boat making it for the Dark Lands.

Sara lifted the Water Sphere. It was cracked. "Now that the spheres and pedestals are gone, so are our elements."

Dawn turned her eyes up to the Aethers that lit up the sky. "The spheres and pedestals were simply a vehicle to deliver the energy. Now that they are destroyed, that energy lives in you. The Aethers will allow you to repair the sphere so your elements will be returned."

"But what about after us?" Sara asked.

Dawn shook her head. "Only the Builders can repair the pedestals, and they are gone."

"So, that's it," Sara said. "Now, there'll be no more Elementals."

Dawn touched Sara's belly and smiled. "She will be the last for she was conceived before the pedestals fell."

Sara frowned at Dawn.

Dawn only smiled. "You didn't think it was you who created that wave?"

SARA watched the sails flap in the wind. The ship was docked in Elementa. Farah hugged her. "I'm going to miss you."

"You can come," Sara said. "You'd love the Insula. There'd be so much for you to explore. And I could use some help with him." Sara touched her pregnant belly.

"Do you think it will be a boy?"

"I don't know. Are you sure you can't hop on board?"

"I can't," Farah said. "I need to help Shift rebuild the city. My father would have wanted that."

Sara nodded. "We'll come back. I promise."

Shilo was helping the sailors to undo the ropes holding the ship to the dock. He walked over to Sara. "Have a safe trip."

"What will you do?"

"Keep looking," Shilo said. "I can't stop until I find my niece."

"Shilo, I . . ."

"I understand," Shilo said. "You loved her too. You once said Spire was like a sister to you. We searched for months. A pregnant woman shouldn't be on her feet for so long. You need to look to your own family now."

"She is my family," Sara said.

"Then, so am I," Shilo said. "You can trust me. I won't stop looking, and once I've found her, I will write to you. It's what Decca would have wanted."

Bolton embraced Farah. He laughed.

"What?"

"It's not going to be the same without you"

Orka chirped.

"And Orka," he added.

"I can't believe Rodan didn't come," Farah said.

Sara looked in her direction when she mentioned Rodan.

"Well, he's still recovering," Bolton said. "Plus, if I were on that much meli, I'd forget my shoes in the snow. He knows we'll be back. So, goodbye isn't really goodbye anyway."

Sara hugged Shilo.

She and Bolton boarded. They waved as the ship left the dock.

SARA sat on the deck of the ship, her hands blackened by the charcoal sketching. Bolton settled down beside her. His eyes rested on the drawing. "You have to stop drawing him, Sara."

She looked down, seeing past the paper.

"What's wrong?" Bolton asked.

"I'm just thinking. It all happened so fast, but it's been months since then and I still feel like I haven't had enough time to process everything."

"What's there to process?" He put his arm around her shoulders.

"I heard something, like someone whispered it in my ear . . . a woman's voice. She was saying something about the spirit being beyond its human body."

Bolton's hand squeezed her shoulder.

"Do you think . . . it was a trick?" she asked. "That he never intended on replacing his children . . . that he wanted us to replace *him*? Energy doesn't mean living eternally in one body. He wanted us to release him from that body. He wanted to cure his disease."

"Sara . . ."

"He knew about me, Bolton. He saw what I did to Hephaestus. Maybe he knew I could control Aethers. That was the only way to release him from his earthly body."

"You're over thinking this. Sara, he's gone, just like Hephaestus. You did that. You've saved this world twice." He rubbed her shoulder. "You deserve to rest. Your body is so used to fighting that your mind just doesn't know that yet."

SARA turned in her sleep as if she could feel the thundering of massive feet across the waters. But she wasn't with Lucerna. She had no body, but she could see all Mirmina as if she were a bird flying across the land.

Her focus turned to Omega Ray past the crumbling walls and worn citadel to the center of the city. Something dark rose from the muck and blackness. The head of a bear, but beneath that was the face of a man. His powerful fingers sank into the ground, and he was pulling himself up out of the darkness.

Your spirit is beyond this world . . . beyond thoughts . . . beyond its human tomb . . .

Upon a cliff sat a figure with a massive fur headdress. The figure turned its head. The headdress was the pelt of a bear and inside its lifeless maw was a face. A face that Sara knew . . . *Canace!*

Sara closed her eyes. When she opened them, she was on a pier looking out over the sea. She reached down to her pregnant belly. The seas were rising to the skies, great waves leaping in the bottom of the ocean.

She wasn't doing it.

Sara looked down to her growing belly. Beside her was the little girl with dark hair. She had her hand on Sara's stomach.

"Canace," Sara said.

"Aren't you afraid of what she'll become?"

Sara looked away from the sea. Beside her was Spire. She couldn't see her, but her energy surrounded Sara.

Sara opened her palm. In it was a white flower streaked with gold.

"No," Sara said, "I'm not."

The sea touched the sun, the fire of the sky as Sara watched, one hand feeling the energy emitting from the unborn child inside her and the other cradling the flower. For once, the heat and the smoke had cleared.

Talon's calloused hand gripped hers, drawing her through the sea of faces. The water was cool beneath her feet. She might have never danced on water. She might have lived and died without question like so many do. She might never have seen the darkness from which she came or felt the urgency of her own soul rushing to escape the solid tomb it is confined in. She might have never faced her own demons. She might have stayed in Elementa and lived a quiet life. But she was glad she hadn't.

The boat was freed from the wharf. It trembled on the cool waters and sailed into the ocean beyond.

ABOUT THE AUTHOR

L. M. PERALTA graduated from the University of New Orleans with a degree in English and holds a law degree from Tulane University. She lives in Louisiana with her husband. She is the author of The Elementals trilogy (*The Elementals, The Council,* and *The Creator*), The Arcadian Steel Sequence (*The Wings of Heaven and Hell, The Seven Archangels of Heaven,* and *The Seven Princes of Hell*), and *United Trace*. She was a finalist for *The Elementals* in the Dante Rossetti Awards 2013 for Young Adult Novels.

Follow L. M. Peralta on Facebook
www.facebook.com/authorlmperalta

Follow L. M. Peralta on Twitter
www.twitter.com/l_m_peralta

For free content, updates, and
behind the scenes information,
visit www.lmperalta.com